A DYING NOTE
The Sixth Silver Rush Mystery

2019—Macavity/Sue Feder Memorial Award for Best Historical Mystery Finalist

2019—Killer Nashville Silver Falchion Award Finalist, Mystery

2019—Will Rogers Medallion Award (Western Maverick) Finalist

2019—"Lefty" Left Coast Crime Award Finalist, Best Historical Novel

2019—NCIBA Golden Poppy Award Finalist, Suspense/Mystery

2019—Best of the West—1st Place Winner in Mystery, Best Fiction by *True West Magazine*

2018—*Foreword Reviews* Indie Award Finalist, Mystery

2018—CIPA EVVY Winner, Mystery

2018—CIPA EVVY Awards 2nd Place Winner, Historical Fiction

"Set in 1881, Parker's exuberant sixth Silver Rush mystery brims with fascinating period details, flamboyant characters, and surprising plot twists."

—*Publishers Weekly*

"Parker, whose grandparents lived in Leadville, has a real knack for making us feel as though we have been transported to another time and place, and her characters breathe life into the vividly evoked landscape. A fine entry in a series that deserves more attention."

—*Booklist*

WHAT GOLD BUYS
The Fifth Silver Rush Mystery

"Parker wraps up the mystery deftly but leaves Inez's future sufficiently unresolved so that readers will eagerly await the next installment."

—*Publishers Weekly*, Starred Review

"Once again, the fifth from Parker is much better history than mystery, drawing the reader into the stunning beauty and harsh realities of life in 1880s Colorado."

—*Kirkus Reviews*

"Parker expertly captures the roughness of a mining town where saloon owners and brothel madams seek to separate prospectors from their money."

—Historical Novel Society

MERCURY'S RISE
The Fourth Silver Rush Mystery

2012—Macavity/Sue Feder Historical Mystery Award Finalist
2012—Bruce Alexander Historical Mystery Award Winner
2012—Colorado Book Award Finalist
2012—WILLA Literary Award Finalist
2011—Agatha Best Historical Mystery Award Finalist
2011—"Recommended Read" of 2011: *Colorado Country Life Magazine*
2011—"Favorite Read" in Western Mysteries: *True West Magazine*

"A dazzling amount of historical detail is woven in yet never overpowers this story of deceit and greed. Laden with intrigue, this will also appeal to readers of historical Westerns. Parker's depth of knowledge coupled with an all-too-human cast leaves us eager to see what Inez will do next. Encore!"

—*Library Journal*

"Parker smoothly mixes the personal dramas and the detection in an installment that's an easy jumping-on point for newcomers. Fans of independent female sleuths like Rhys Bowen's Molly Murphy and Laurie King's Mary Russell will be satisfied."

—*Publishers Weekly*

"Featuring new characters and an intriguing variation in setting, this is an excellent addition to a steadily improving series."

—*Booklist*

"Parker remains worth reading for the historical detail and the descriptions of a stunning area of Colorado."

—*Kirkus Reviews*

LEADEN SKIES
The Third Silver Rush Mystery

2010—Colorado Book Award Finalist

"Parker is proficient in showing the crossroads between civilization and the frontier, including emerging new roles for women. A cliff-hanger ending sets a promising stage for the next installment."

—*Publishers Weekly*

"Parker has created a lively historical tale with a strong female protagonist. The intricate plot, lively characters, and vividly realized historical landscape will appeal to those interested in the Old West as well as to historical-mystery fans."

—*Booklist*

"Parker's deft evocation of a lost era in Western American history—the life of the mining boom town—and her complex characterization make *Leaden Skies* an absorbing read. Her final, cliff-hanging sentence will make every reader desperate for the next installment in Inez Stannert's epic tale. A riveting historical mystery."

— Stephanie Barron, national bestselling author

IRON TIES
The Second Silver Rush Mystery

2007—Winner of the Colorado Book Award for Best Genre Fiction
2007—Arizona Book Award Honorable Mention for Best Mystery/ Suspense Novel

"Plenty of convincing action bodes well for a long and successful series."

— *Publishers Weekly*, Starred Review

"The characters have depth, their motivations are subtle, and their pain very human. Add carefully researched and fascinating period detail, and one has a well-crafted novel that will appeal to readers of mysteries, historical fiction, and genre westerns."

— *Booklist*

"Full of sharply etched characters set firmly in history and pulled along by a narrative engine as powerful as any of the locomotives getting ready in 1880 to connect Leadville to the outside world."

— *Chicago Tribune*

SILVER LIES
The First Silver Rush Mystery

2004—Winner of the WILLA Literary Award for Historical Fiction
2003—"Best Mysteries of 2003"—Pick by *Publishers Weekly* and
the *Chicago Tribune*
2003—Spur Award Finalist
2003—Bruce Alexander Award Finalist for Best Historical Mystery
2002—Colorado Gold Award for Best Mystery

"*Silver Lies* is a tale of greed, lust, and deception set in Leadville
in its heyday, when men—and not a few women—stopped at
nothing, not even murder, to strike it rich. Ann Parker gets it just
right, and the result is a terrific debut novel."
—Margaret Coel, *New York Times* bestselling author

"Drawing on historic facts and figures of 1870s Colorado, Parker
tells a gripping tale of love, greed, and murder in the Old West,
with a cast of convincing, larger-than-life characters, including a
brief appearance from Bat Masterson himself."
—*Publishers Weekly*, Starred Review

"Like the wonderful black-and-white photograph of historic
Leadville on its cover, her first novel, which won a regional writing contest last year, combines a kind of gritty grandeur with a
knowing wisdom about the way the present shapes our perceptions of the past.
—*Chicago Tribune*

Also by Ann Parker

The Silver Rush Mysteries

Silver Lies
Iron Ties
Leaden Skies
Mercury's Rise
What Gold Buys
A Dying Note

MORTAL MUSIC

MORTAL MUSIC

A *Silver Rush* **Mystery**

ANN PARKER

Poisoned Pen
PRESS

Copyright © 2020 by Ann Parker
Cover and internal design © 2020 by Sourcebooks
Cover design by The BookDesigners
Cover images © rzarek/Shutterstock, mashuk/Getty Images

Published by Poisoned Pen Press, an imprint of Sourcebooks
P.O. Box 4410, Naperville, Illinois 60567-4410
(630) 961-3900
sourcebooks.com

Library of Congress Cataloging-in-Publication Data:
Names: Parker, Ann
Title: Mortal music / Ann Parker.
Description: Naperville, Illinois : Poisoned Pen Press, [2019] |
Identifiers: LCCN 2019031438 | (hardcover)
Subjects: GSAFD: Mystery fiction.
Classification: LCC PS3616.A744 M67 2019 | DDC 813/.6--dc23
LC record available at https://lccn.loc.gov/2019031438

Printed and bound in the United States of America.
SB 10 9 8 7 6 5 4 3 2 1

Dedicated to the Parker and McConachie clans—
Artists, adventurers, scientists, musicians

"It is always fatal to have music or poetry interrupted."

—GEORGE ELIOT

ACKNOWLEDGMENTS

Special thanks to Colleen Casey for sharing her knowledge and love of San Francisco and its history, to Steve Parker and Sue Stephenson for musical assistance, Wm. Sean Casey for supplying firearms expertise, Wendy McConachie for bird suggestions, the San Francisco Public Library's History Center and its librarians for their help and advice, and the San Francisco Palace Hotel staff for an amazing tour and their patience in answering my questions. All errors, omissions, and slips into alternate realities are mine.

I'm very grateful to my family—Bill, Ian, and Devyn, as well as the wider McConachie and Parker clans—for their love and support. Thanks are also due to critique partners and beta readers who offered suggestions and support: Bill McConachie, Camille Minichino, Carole Price, Colleen Casey, Dani Greer, Devyn McConachie, Janet Finsilver, Mary-Lynne Pierce Bernald, Nannette Carroll, Penny Warner, and Staci McLaughlin. Here's a tip of the hat to Maddee James and the gang at xuni.com for designing my website and keeping it spiffy and up-to-date. Additionally, I'd like to give a shout-out of appreciation to my agent, Anne Hawkins of John Hawkins and Associates.

Lastly, special thanks to Barbara Peters, Robert Rosenwald, and the staff at Poisoned Pen Press for all the guidance and support these many years. It's been quite the journey.

Chapter One

There had been occasions in the past when Inez Stannert had looked a man—and even, once, a woman—straight in the eye and felt justified in pulling the trigger. And she suspected there might be times in the future when she would have to do so again.

But she would never harm a child.

Never.

However, there were times that sorely tried her soul.

This was one of them.

Face contorted in agony, twelve-year-old Antonia Gizzi clapped her hands to her ears and implored Inez. "I can't stand it! Please! No more!"

Inez frowned at her young ward and tried to stem her growing irritation. At least Antonia had staged her protest in a whisper, loud though it was. And at least they were seated in a mezzanine box of the Grand Opera House, not in the balcony or orchestra where Antonia's groans and grumbles would disturb others. Inez snapped her silk fan closed, set the silver guard sticks against Antonia's arm, and pressed down. "This is the encore. The performance is almost over."

Inez had intended the evening to be an early Christmas gift to the girl—an elevating experience, but also a partial apology for sending her away from San Francisco for the upcoming holiday. However, Antonia seemed to view being subjected to the recital by a highly acclaimed prima donna as punishment heaped upon punishment, reacting as if knives were being plunged into her ears.

The beautiful strains of *"Dove sono i bei momenti"* soared through the air, touching the frescoes, flying off the light-blue drapery, stilling the scattered murmurs and shufflings of the two thousand or so viewers. The singer below shifted her stance, raising one languid arm as her voice climbed the scale. Her gloves and dress—a glittering affair of gold and silver—captured the illumination from the footlights, shimmering like her voice. The piano accompanist, a gentleman with dark, silver-streaked hair that had its own metallic sheen, leaned into the keyboard with intensity. A little too much intensity, Inez thought. In her estimation, he should have gone with a lighter touch so the instrument was not warring with the singer for dominance.

At a particularly fulsome trill, Antonia rolled her eyes skyward, looking for all the world as if she were about to have a fit and fall from her chair. Luckily, for Inez's patience and Antonia's ears, the aria ended and the audience erupted into applause and enthusiastic plebeian whistles, punctuated by "Brava!" or "Again!" depending on the admirer's familiarity with opera and Romance languages. Antonia jumped up from her chair. "Now do we get to go backstage and see all the scenery and ropes and rigging and interesting stuff?"

As an additional treat, Inez had used her connections as co-owner of the D & S House of Music and Curiosities to persuade Mr. Thackery, the assistant manager of the opera house, to give them a peek behind the proscenium arch and a personal introduction to the visiting diva. At this point, Inez was tempted to quash the tour as retribution for Antonia's boorish behavior during the recital. But looking down at the girl's expectant face—her plaits of dark hair coming undone, even though she had done little besides sit and squirm for the past three hours—Inez didn't have the heart to do so.

Besides, she was just as curious as her ward to see what lay beyond the footlights.

"We are to wait here for Mr. Thackery to arrive and escort us," said Inez.

No sooner had the words been said than the curtain to the box swept aside, revealing the assistant manager. A toothsome smile came out of hiding below his walrus mustache. That smile, the mustache, his slightly bulging blue eyes, and thinning reddish hair made Inez think of him as an over-eager squirrel—all he lacked was a mouthful of acorns. "Mrs. Stannert and little Antonia. I hope you both enjoyed the performance."

Antonia glowered. Inez, who suspected the girl was about to blurt out her real opinion of the singing, gave Antonia's arm a light pinch as a warning.

Thackery didn't seem to notice, possibly because Antonia's glare was muted underneath her bonnet. Or it could have been because his perpetually pop-eyed gaze was so firmly fixed on Inez.

The scowl disappeared from Antonia's face, replaced by a too-wide smile. "Oh, yes, Mr. Thackery," she piped up with what Inez knew was patently false earnestness. "The seats were excellent and the performances most exquisite."

"Glad to hear," he said.

"It was wonderful, and we are ever so grateful for your consideration," added Inez.

He beamed, then said, "This way, ladies, this way, if you please." He started to take Inez by the arm.

She avoided what she deemed a familiarity by deploying her fan with a twist of the wrist while turning to Antonia and saying, "Be on your best behavior, Antonia. It is a great honor to see behind the scenes of the Grand Opera House and to meet Mrs. Carrington Drake. She has come all the way from Philadelphia to sing here in San Francisco."

"That's right," enthused Thackery, who bowed them out of the box and led them to an elegant curved staircase. "The Golden Songbird has returned to the city where her voice first took flight and charmed the masses. Not here at the Grand, of course, as we only opened seven years ago, in seventy-four. I recall seeing her ten or more years ago, at the Melpomene Theater. The Melpomene was well known in its time, but it was never as grand as the Grand is now."

A gentleman, who had been mounting the stairs against the tide of operagoers surging down, stopped before them. Blocking their path, he boomed, "Mr. Thackery!" He ripped the bowler hat from his head, but Inez doubted it was a gesture of respect.

Inez retreated a step, dragging Antonia with her. The man's wild gaze was alarming, and Inez was glad it was not directed at them. All his attention focused on the assistant manager.

Thackery, to his credit, stayed put, and even bristled. "Mr. Teague. It is not necessary to raise your voice."

Two burly ushers at the bottom of the staircase glanced up at the fracas. One started up the staircase, but the other stopped him. They stayed where they were, watching closely.

"Well, if it's the only way I can get someone's attention around here, then I guess it *is* necessary." Teague ran an ink-stained hand over his longer-than-fashionable unruly hair, which was the same dark-red hue as the beard that threatened to engulf his bow tie.

He pointed at Thackery. "Where's Graham Drake? He must be here. After all, his wife was your star attraction."

"He is not available," huffed Thackery. "If you wish to speak with Mr. Drake, you shall have to do so elsewhere."

"You don't think I've tried that? He's avoiding me. Every place I track him, he's been and gone. Or, he's 'not available.' Thackery, I bought one of your high-priced tickets for tonight's performance and I'm here on legitimate business."

"You are not a theater critic, Mr. Teague. You came as a member of the audience."

Thackery must have made some secret signal, because the two ushers were in motion, making their determined way upward.

Thackery continued, "The performance is over. It's time for you to leave."

The ushers grabbed Teague's arms and roughly hauled him backward. Stumbling, he was half dragged, half hauled down the stairs. In a voice that would have carried easily from the Grand's stage to the back seats, Teague shouted, "You tell Graham Drake he can't hide from me forever. I know who he is, and what he is, and I take it as my professional duty and honor as a member of the fourth estate to tell the world."

As he was thus escorted across the elegant lobby, the departing patrons paused, watching this unexpected epilogue to their evening's entertainment. The women pulled their long elegant skirts aside as if his passing might contaminate their new winter ensembles. The men murmured to each other and eyed Teague with calculation, as if weighing his words upon the scales of rumor and truth. Upon reaching the exit, the ushers unceremoniously thrust him outdoors, and his shouting ceased.

Thackery turned to Inez and Antonia on the steps above. "Well. That sort of excitement was common twenty, thirty years ago in the city, not so much these days."

Inez could see that Antonia was burning with questions. She took the girl's shoulder, a silent admonition, yet couldn't help but ask one question herself. "So, this Mr. Teague. Is he a local newspaperman?"

Thackery looked about, perhaps hoping the question was addressed to someone else. With no likely suspects nearby, he finally said, "Yes, yes, he is. Or perhaps, was? It seems I heard some story or other, but since I cannot say for certain, it is best I not say at all. I can assure you he is not a theater critic, nor a reporter of musical news nor high society. So, let's continue, shall we? To more pleasant things."

He guided them down the stairs to the entrance hall, bright

with crystal chandeliers, past the fountain in the center of the lobby. Inez inhaled the fragrance of lavender cologne water as it plashed softly from innumerable needle jets. Scent and sound died as Thackery guided them across the floor to a set of side doors.

They proceeded through a corridor, heading back in the direction of the stage, with Thackery chattering all the while. "We are honored, Mrs. Stannert, that you and Miss Antonia take such a strong interest in the arts, particularly the theater. The Grand, with her architecture and amenities, proudly surpasses any of the other theatrical venues the West has to offer."

Inez murmured politely, distracted by his Adam's apple—large, prominent, bobbling with excitement. It paired oddly with his enormous, drooping mustache, and she found herself wondering, not for the first time, why he hadn't grown a beard to conceal his throat.

He continued, "We have an art gallery over the entrance hall. Perhaps you'd like to return and see it during the day when you can fully appreciate the skylight, which is a work of art in itself. There are numerous offices all along the gallery, designed as artists' studios. We have corridors that connect to the theater, featuring paintings by local artists as well as select pieces by European masters. It is a most excellent area for promenading, and I shall be delighted to be your guide, next time you grace us with your presence."

He stopped and bent down, bringing his face to Antonia's level. "Ah, but I know what you came to see, little Miss."

Antonia took a quick step back. Inez hoped Antonia's small but deadly pocketknife was at home and not tucked in her coat pocket. The *salvavirgo*, sharp but innocuous in appearance when its blade was folded away, had belonged to Antonia's deceased mother. The girl had a bad habit of carrying it everywhere and pulling it out whenever she felt threatened.

"The stage, eh?" He winked at her. "Would you like to stand on center stage? See what it's like to look out over the auditorium?"

Antonia's posture relaxed. "Oh, yes, sir!"

Inez was glad to see she had remembered her manners enough to add the "sir."

Antonia added, "I'm wondering if it's like the Grand Central Theater in Leadville. Leadville's where we used to live."

A deep furrow joined his eyebrows in puzzlement. "Lead... what?"

Inez interrupted hastily, hoping Thackery was ignorant of the notoriety of that particular Grand theater, which stood hip-deep and proud in the red-light district of Colorado's premiere silver-mining boomtown. "This is a different class of theater, Antonia. This is a proper opera house. Famous actors and actresses and singers of the first order come from all over the world to perform here."

The girl tipped up her head to view Inez from under her bonnet brim. "But Mrs. S, they have actresses and singers at the Leadville Grand too."

Inez cleared her throat, thinking that the honky-tonk singers and so-called actresses of the Leadville Grand, who doubled as prostitutes to augment their pay, would probably go cross-eyed and mute should they be shoved onto the stage of the San Francisco Grand. She squeezed Antonia's shoulder lightly in warning before locking her gaze on the assistant manager. Summoning a smile with just a hint of demureness, she said, "Mr. Thackery, we would be most thrilled to see your stage and honored to stand upon it."

With the clucking eagerness of a hen herding its chicks, he led them through the backstage area, providing a nonstop commentary on the opera house's merits. He interrupted his own monologue to occasionally squawk warnings at the stagehands as they hauled on ropes, lifting scenery to the top of the building or lowering it through openings in the stage into the basement.

"The stage is eighty-seven feet deep and one hundred and six feet wide." He halted as an enormous canvas flat, painted to show stately columns and a rolling countryside, was being hauled aloft with ropes by a clutch of stagehands. It was ascending in fits and starts at a dangerously crooked angle with much clattering and ratcheting.

Thackery strode forward and barked, "You there, you men with the backdrop. Carefully now."

"Are they going to drop it?" Antonia whispered to Inez, almost as if she hoped they would.

Thackery waited while the men grumbled and tussled with the ropes. Once the backdrop righted, Thackery returned to Inez and Antonia and continued his verbal annotations in a normal tone. "The flats are twenty-four feet high, the highest of any in the world. They can be lifted to the top of the building or lowered into the basement until needed."

They walked out onto the stage, their hard-soled tread upon the boards echoing into the upper reaches of the building and out into the vast space of the auditorium. Antonia, who had been gawking at the rigging and machinery, stepped to the edge of the stage and peered over the footlights powered, according to Thackery, by electricity.

"Electricity?" Inez exclaimed.

He preened. "The Grand is exceedingly modern and employs the latest in technology."

Antonia commented, "There are sure a lot of chairs out there."

"We can seat three thousand souls," said Thackery. "Only two theaters in the United States have larger auditoriums."

The stage itself was mostly empty, save for the grand piano, right of center. The ghostly notes from the arias recently played seemed to swirl around it, calling to Inez. Her fingers tingled in her gloves, longing to recreate what she had just heard. Unable to resist, she headed toward the piano.

"A magnificent instrument," said Thackery, pacing her. "We are so grateful your music store had a Broadwood in stock. We usually use Steinway, but Mrs. Drake, she, ah..."

Inez spared a glance his way as his chatty stream of words dried up. He was visibly uncomfortable, seeming to be seeking a way forward. He finally finished with "Mrs. Drake preferred a Broadwood."

"They are certainly well suited to such surroundings," Inez replied, as much to ease his discomfort as to reassure him that Mrs. Drake's preference was completely understandable. Inez smoothed a gloved hand over the curve of the open lid, marveling at the silky sheen. She had another Broadwood that took "center stage" in the music store, but here in the opera house, the instrument was in its element. Unconfined by pressing walls nor dulled by carpets on the floor, open to the vastness of the auditorium, it stood upon the stage as aristocratic as any diva.

More than anything, she wanted to touch the keys, hear the notes pour out from her fingers to the keys and hammers, out over the orchestra pit, and experience what it was like to send music over the now-empty seats. "Mr. Thackery, may I?"

The toothy smile broke through again. "Of course, Mrs. Stannert. It does have a lovely tone, as I'm certain you know."

Inez settled onto the bench, taking care she wasn't sitting on the tassels of the mauve satin sash decorating her overskirt and that the long, knife-pleat underskirt stayed untangled from her satin shoes. She removed her gloves, lifted the fallboard to reveal the keyboard, and set her fingertips upon the smooth, cool ivory keys. She pondered. What to play? What would be a proper offering for such a musically sacred setting?

A short reflection, and the choice was obvious. Simplicity, and a nod to the amazing purity of Mrs. Drake's voice.

Inclining her head over the keyboard, Inez half closed her eyes, pulling up from memory "Ave Maria."

The flowing melodic line wrapped around her. Antonia, Mr. Thackery, the stage, everything else disappeared, becoming mist to the music.

The last notes had not yet died when a touch on her shoulder startled her.

"Perfectly and impeccably exquisite."

Inez twisted around at the euphonious female voice. The prima donna, Theia Carrington Drake, stood close behind her.

Chapter Two

Mrs. Drake was still dressed in the shimmering gold-and-silver gown from her performance, a smile gracing her heart-shaped face. A small gold bird with black markings on its head, wings, and tail perched on a gloved finger, raised up and to the side. The opera star's feathered companion cocked its head as if listening to an echo of the final chords. A delicate gold chain linked one tiny leg to an intricate, finely braided bracelet encircling the singer's wrist. The slender tether glittered and swayed as she extended her free hand in greeting. Light glinted off her gloves, white kid with the backs richly worked with seed pearls and silver and gold beads.

Inez rose. "Madame Drake. Thank you for your kind words. I did not know you were listening. It's an honor to meet you." She took the diva's hand, feeling awkward without her own gloves.

The footlights behind them cast a halo about the diva's upswept light-brown hair. "And you are Mrs. Inez Stannert? Or so Mr. Thackery told me. You do this wonderful instrument justice. Would you consider playing 'Ave Maria' again? For me, this time?" Theia turned to Antonia, still frozen near the footlights. "Come here, child. What is your name? Do you like birds? This is my pet, Aria. Would you hold him while I sing?"

Inez held her breath, praying that Antonia would hold fast to her manners and not burst out with something rude or outré, such as "Those high notes almost made my ears bleed."

Antonia mumbled her name, adding a stilted "If you please, ma'am, I would very much enjoy holding your bird."

Inez exhaled with relief.

Theia smiled. "Antonia. Lovely name. Do you know, there is an Antonia, a young girl, in a new opera by Monsieur Jacques Offenbach, *Les Contes d'Hoffmann—The Tales of Hoffmann*. Mr. Drake and I were fortunate to see it at the Opéra-Comique in Paris. Now, extend your arm and hand, so."

Antonia copied Theia's raised arm and pointing finger. Theia unclasped her bracelet, which glinted as if made of rust-red wire, and wrapped it around Antonia's wrist. She refastened the intricate gold clasp before encouraging the little bird onto the girl's finger. After some flapping about, Aria regained his equilibrium. "There!" exclaimed Theia. "Now, all you must do is stay just like that, as still as can be, until I am done."

A delighted smile spread across Antonia's face as Aria began preening. Other than the curving of her lips, the girl remained motionless.

Theia turned to Inez. "Begin when ready."

Inez lowered herself onto the bench, her stomach clenched as tightly as at her first recital in her parents' New York City salon more than two decades ago. She took as deep a breath as her corseted lungs would allow, let it out slowly, and positioned her hands on the keyboard. Then she looked up into Theia's expectant face, nodded once, and moved into the first chord.

The introductory notes opened the door to Mrs. Drake's soaring soprano. Inez eased her touch, allowing the singer's voice to take precedence. Like the movement of the tide, piano and vocals flowed back and forth, passing from one to the other in a circling dance of sound. As the last notes faded away, Inez heard Antonia exhale a breathy "Wow."

Inez pushed back the bench and rose, lightheaded. Applause erupted from the nearby wing and she saw Thackery and Mrs. Drake's accompanist. A soft swish of cloth against wood and Mrs. Drake pirouetted to face them, hands pressed prayerfully to her breast, and offered a modest bow. She turned and gestured to Inez to come stand beside her. As Inez approached, she realized she stood nearly eye to eye with the singer—an unusual sensation since she was accustomed to towering over women and even many men.

"*Bravissima,* Madame Drake," said the pianist. "Extraordinary, as usual."

"Thank you, Señor Rubio," she replied, the melody from music carrying over to her speaking voice. She then turned to Inez and grasped her hands. The color of the diva's pale-brown, almost amber-colored eyes, tinged with gold, reminded Inez of weak tea. "However, the applause belongs to Mrs. Stannert."

Those eyes—anything but weak in character—bore into her in a way Inez found uncomfortably intimate.

Mrs. Drake gave her hands a squeeze. Inez gasped a little, surprised at the strength in the grip, and gently extracted herself. "Thank you, Mrs. Drake."

One gloved hand flew to her lips. "Forgive me. A pianist's hands are like a singer's voice and must be treated with great care and reverence, yes?"

Thackery and Rubio approached, with Thackery saying, "Mrs. Drake, I didn't mention, we rented the Broadwood from Mrs. Stannert's store, the D & S House of Music and Curiosities. Over on Pine and Kearney."

Theia seemed to brighten even more, if that were possible. "Then, I owe you a debt of gratitude, Mrs. Stannert, for I could not sing without a proper instrument to accompany me."

"I am glad we could help," said Inez.

"The *D* is for Donato," interjected Rubio. "A most distinguished violinist in the city. It is his store, as I recall." He offered a short bow to Inez, adding, "Please tell him, Señor Luis Rubio offers his salutations and will come by the store and provide them in person, when time permits."

Inez caught her breath at this and said quickly, "Mr. Donato is no longer part of the business. His sister, Miss Donato, has taken his place."

"Is that so." Mrs. Drake's response was indifferent, as if the change in conversation were a speck of lint to be brushed from her sparkling skirt.

It was definitely so.

In counterpoint to the diva's disinterest, Rubio's dark-eyed gaze narrowed. Inez fancied she saw his nose twitch. In that moment, he reminded her uncomfortably of one of those sleek, dangerous panthers she'd seen in majestic paintings of California's mountain wildernesses.

She decided it was best to change the subject. "Mrs. Drake, I must give credit where credit is due. The prompt and timely delivery of the Broadwood is all due to the diligence of my store manager, Mr. Thomas Welles. Mr. Welles is also a pianist of considerable talent."

"Welles," muttered Rubio under his breath. Inez thought she detected a disdainful sniff.

"He certainly can be no more talented than you, Mrs. Stannert," said Mrs. Drake. "Please call me Theia, and I shall call you Inez. I believe we shall come to know each other better in the coming days." Theia seized Inez's hands again, but gently. "You see, Inez, I have decided. I am scheduled for a number of very important appearances, and you will be my accompanist. You will be compensated accordingly."

Startled by the request—which had the tenor of a command—Inez tore her attention away from the diva as she debated how to respond.

Her gaze landed on Rubio. He stood behind Theia, a murderous look on his face.

A shiver chilled Inez as she registered that his ire was directed not at Theia, but at her.

Inez lifted her chin a little higher and stared back, not to be cowed. Rubio's jaw tightened. Theia pivoted to follow Inez's gaze. The anger fled Rubio's face, and a smooth mask descended.

"Madame." He smiled ingratiatingly at Theia. "Perhaps you are unaware. Your husband contracted with me to be your accompanist throughout your stay. You have been so focused on preparing for your performances, he probably did not want to distract you with details."

Another feminine voice floated in from offstage. "Is something amiss, Madame?"

Inez startled. Then she chided herself: *I have become complacent. In the past, I would have known who was present and where.*

A young woman emerged onto the stage, smiling her question, hands clasped before her. Her fashionable, but modest, dark-blue outfit didn't hide a youthful, blooming figure. Inez realized there were physical similarities between the young woman and Theia, in coloring and height. However, the younger woman glowed in a way that made Theia, even in her glittering outfit, pale by comparison. Seeing the two women side-by-side, Inez realized that Theia must be older than she had first assumed. Forty, perhaps? Even older? But undeniably a handsome woman whose force of personality was such that Inez imagined age didn't stop Theia from charming anyone she wished.

Inez wondered if the young woman and Theia were mother and daughter, or perhaps older and younger sisters. Before she could ask, a man stepped out from the dark, behind the woman in blue. Dressed in the uniform of the Palace Hotel staff and holding an empty, cupola-shaped birdcage, he stopped a respectful distance away from them all. His dignified ebony face betrayed no emotion whatsoever.

Theia beckoned the young woman over. "Here is my understudy and protégée, Miss Julia Green. Miss Green, this is Mrs.

Inez Stannert. I have just arranged for Inez to be my accompanist for upcoming performances."

Inez wondered if this was how Theia approached the world: I speak, and thus shall it be. She opened her mouth to protest that her employment was not a done deal, not by a long shot, but reconsidered. Now was not the time. Best to watch and wait, get a better measure of the actors before entering the scene.

Shock flooded Miss Green's face. "But I thought—"

Inez saw her eyes flicker toward Rubio.

Theia must have seen it as well, because she remarked irritably, "Well. It seems everyone knew about that arrangement but me! I shall have to discuss this with Mr. Drake. Did he fashion this agreement? He must have. But he did not consult me. Julia, your business is your own, of course. You are free to continue with Mr. Rubio's services for your lessons and practice sessions, should you desire."

Julia retreated, her clasped hands rising in silent plea. Or perhaps in defense.

Was there a note of threat behind Theia's pointedly neutral words? Inez scrutinized the diva's furious expression. Her barely contained anger seemed out of proportion with the situation. At least, on the surface.

Perhaps realizing this herself, Theia continued in a more measured, regal tone. "Mr. Rubio, I am certain Mr. Drake will arrange compensation for your unfortunate assumption." Theia turned her back on him—a deliberate snub, it seemed to Inez—and addressed the man holding the cage. "Jacob, Aria needs to return to the hotel."

The man from the Palace Hotel set the birdcage on the piano seat and opened the wire door. Theia beckoned to Antonia. "Come, child. You did well. Aria uttered not a peep and did not try to fly off. You must have a natural affinity for birds." After coaxing the bird onto her own finger, Theia delivered it to the cage and unfastened its little shackle.

Antonia flexed her fingers. "Is Aria a canary?"

"No, child. Aria is a yellow warbler. He stays this pretty color year-round, while a canary turns drab and dull in winter. Aria was a gift from an admirer. He said Aria was the perfect pet for me. Always beautiful, always singing, no matter the season." She hooked the cage door shut.

Staring at the cage, Antonia asked, "Is that real gold?"

"Bronze. A cage of gold would be worth a fortune and would be a treasure nearly as dear to me as my little Aria." Theia made little kissing noises at the bird, now safe behind bars. Aria responded with a tuneful trill. Theia fluttered a languid hand at the Palace Hotel porter. "Away. It grows late. Where is Mr. Drake, do you know, Mr. Thackery?"

The assistant manager stepped forward from the sidelines where he'd been hovering. "Examining the night's receipts, Madame. It was a sold-out show, as you probably know."

"I leave the business to Mr. Drake. I focus on my art," said Theia. She sighed. "I am tired now. Would you take me to him, Mr. Thackery? Julia and I must return to our rooms in the presidential suite at the Palace Hotel. Oh, Inez, please have another Broadwood delivered tomorrow morning to the suite's music room. The piano the hotel provided will not do."

"Another Broadwood?" Inez thought of the masterpiece sitting in their showroom. "Very well. I have one more available for loan. I shall have to set up the delivery and it is now late."

"Yes, yes." Theia's tone made it clear that the details were not of interest. As she moved away, she threw over her shoulder, "As early as possible, then. I am not one of those prima donnas who lies abed and breaks fast at noon. I shall expect the piano no later than nine o'clock. Earlier, if possible. And you and I have a lot of work to do to prepare for my next appearance. We should convene in the morning as well, so I can go over the program with you."

Rubio, who might as well have been a ghost for all the attention she gave him, tried again. "Madame Drake, wait. Please." That single word rasped out, as if seldom used. "Surely, this is all just a misunderstanding. We should talk."

"I have nothing to discuss with you, Señor Rubio," said Theia. "We are done. *Fini.*"

She began to walk offstage, leaving Rubio standing with his mouth agape like a fish. Julia Green, with a last helpless glance at Rubio, followed Theia.

Without warning, Rubio walked over to the piano and slammed the fallboard down. Inez gasped as the piano jangled a dissonant protest. "Sir, that was quite unnecessary! If the instrument is damaged or requires retuning, you shall pay."

He stalked past Inez, saying under his breath, "Rest assured, we are not done."

"Are you addressing me?" Inez demanded.

He walked off into the wings without answering.

Inez suspected there was more to this quarrel than she was privy to. Becoming the rope in a cryptic tug-of-war between Theia and her now-fired accompanist was not a position to which she aspired.

"Mrs. Drake, a word." Inez hastened to catch up with her.

The diva dramatically placed the back of her gloved hand against her forehead as she turned to Inez. "As I said, call me Theia. What is it? I feel a headache coming on. Please, be brief. We can talk in the morning."

"This being the holidays, the store requires all my focus and attention," said Inez. She didn't add that business had fallen off since the departure of Mr. Donato, creating a worrisome situation that threatened to consume her in her efforts to bring back much-needed customers. "Much as I am flattered that you would ask me to be your musical accompanist, I must regretfully decline the honor."

"Decline?" Theia's eyes narrowed in the shadow beneath her upraised hand.

Inez thought for a moment that she might actually try to slap her with that elegantly gloved palm.

The singer rolled her shoulders and tipped her head up. "Oh, I cannot talk about this now. I must rest. Tomorrow morning, when you deliver the piano and Mr. Drake is with us to work out the particulars to your satisfaction, we shall address this anew. Good night, Inez."

Shock at being so cavalierly dismissed stunned Inez into uncharacteristic silence.

Theia turned away slowly. The footlights, still glowing, played over her gown like twinkling stars in a night sky as she left the stage on Thackery's attentive arm, Julia at her side. The trail of Theia's gown hissed along the boards with a sound like an icy winter wind whispering through the evergreens in the high Rocky Mountains.

Chapter Three

"Theia Carrington Drake asked *you* to be her accompanist?" D & S manager Thomas Welles repeated his question to Inez with the same astonishment.

Inez took his proffered hand, stepping down from the carriage into the grand court of the Palace Hotel. "Is that truly so unbelievable? As I already told you, yes. She did."

They walked over the marble floor of the vast entrance chamber to the hotel, the scent of evergreen and the profusion of wreaths and red ribbons a reminder that Christmas was nearly upon them.

Welles persisted. "And you *declined*?"

Inez sighed and looked skyward. The opaque glass of the hotel's lofty domed roof cast morning light down upon the pine-garlanded galleries circling each of the seven floors and onto the plants, statuary, and fountains crowding the central court—all without warming her face.

The repetitive nature of their conversation nettled Inez.

Not that she was feeling patient to begin with.

She had said goodbye to Antonia and Carmella Donato, titular half owner of the D & S House of Music and Curiosities, at the ferry station at dawn. Even though Carmella was dressed in mourning for her brother, Inez noticed several young men directing admiring glances at Miss Donato as they hurried past to board. Carmella didn't seem aware of their appreciation, apparently focused on reassuring Inez about Antonia and the upcoming trip. "Do not worry, Inez. When we get to Los Angeles, my uncle will meet us. He has a chicken ranch, and they also have horses and orange trees… Can you imagine? All that fresh air will do Antonia a world of good. And there are other young ones to keep her company so she does not have to spend all her time with me."

"I'm not a young one," Antonia grumbled to Inez. "I'm twelve years old. Nearly thirteen."

"You are not acting like it," said Inez in an equally low voice. She planted a quick kiss on Antonia's forehead and murmured, "Remember, you are doing this for Carmella's sake. This trip is exactly what she needs right now, to leave the city for a while, particularly for the holidays. And she wants your company. It's the least we can do for all her kindnesses."

Antonia seized Inez's hand, whispering, "But I want to stay here. It's Christmas! You'll be all alone."

"Do not worry about me. And you and I will have many more Christmases together." The ferry horn sounded a warning. "Come. It's time to go. You two have a train to catch in Oakland."

"Can I have a bird when I get back?" Antonia asked as Inez guided her to the ramp. "Maybe one like Mrs. Drake's? All yellow?"

"We'll see." Inez was not going to be maneuvered into a last-minute guilty promise by her precocious, manipulative ward.

Carmella, preparing to pull her veil down over her face, paused, brightening at Antonia's query. "A pet bird? I had a parrot once. We had to give it away. Perhaps you would like a parrot? They are so colorful. And you can teach them to talk."

"Oh yes!"

Over Antonia's head, Inez caught Carmella's eye and emphatically shook her head. *No.*

Thinking back on the scene, Inez shook her head again. *I'll not be surprised to have them return with a squawking companion. If so, it goes home with Carmella.*

"So you are not going to be Mrs. Drake's accompanist?" asked Welles. "Why not? It would be excellent advertising for the store. You could hang on Mrs. Drake's coattails, or whatever the female equivalent is, and garner new customers and students as well."

"Hmm." She was loath to admit it, but there was wisdom in his words.

When they reached the hotel's reception area, a clerk directed them to the second floor. "The piano was delivered to the main parlor attached to the Drakes' set of suites," he said, his expression as stiff and somber as his waxed mustache and starched collar.

Welles thanked him and told Inez, "I sent a standard lease agreement along with the instrument and included the usual additional charge for a rush delivery."

"We should have charged them more," Inez muttered. "They can surely afford it."

As they moved toward the hydraulic elevators beyond the receiving office area, Inez returned to their discussion. "But it is the holidays—and a terribly inconvenient time for me to be away from the store. You and I, we need to direct all our energies to drumming up business. And now we'll need to acquire a piano for the showroom. A short-term lease, I imagine."

"I can handle the store, find a piano to lease, and call in extra help if need be. On the cheap," he added quickly. "Off the top of my head, I can think of a percussionist and a cellist, both responsible chaps, who wouldn't mind helping out to earn a little extra."

"More expenses," Inez grumbled.

As they waited for the elevators, he added, "Consider, the Drakes have a suite on the second floor here at the Palace. I'll bet they can pay top dollar for your time and talent. I should mention, I don't think it's wise to turn down Mrs. Carrington Drake. I remember her a little from her early days here in the city, when she was Miss Carrington. Even then, the Golden Songbird had a reputation. She doesn't hesitate to retaliate when she doesn't get her way."

The elevator operator whisked open the latticed elevator gate and they stepped into the compartment. "Second floor," Inez said to the operator, then turned to Welles. "I'll think about it."

Welles settled onto a seat and caught Inez's gaze in one of the mirrors gracing the interior walls. His square face was creased in a frown, his brown eyes concerned. "Think quick, then, Mrs. Stannert, because I guarantee *Madame* will assume you have acquiesced to her wishes unless you speak up and say otherwise. If you say yes, she'll probably be happy to send people our way. If you say no…" He shifted on the maroon leather bench, and his fingers drummed on his trousers, the absentminded action of a keyboardist with other things on his mind. "Did she have an accompanist last night?"

"Yes, another pianist, Señor Luis Rubio."

Welles looked shocked. "Rubio? He's back in town?"

"Apparently so, but now without a position."

"Rubio is good," said Welles. "He'll find something. If he can stay sober."

"He seemed to know you when I mentioned your name."

His eyes shifted away. "I'll bet when my name came up, he looked like he'd bit on a lemon. Rubio never thought much of me. He made that clear enough. Did you know, he's a native *Californio*? Family had a huge land grant around here before the Gold Rush. He trots out his pedigree as if it places him a cut above the rest of us. He and I crossed paths more than once, competing for the same jobs. He always took it personally when I bested him. Huh. Rubio and Madame Carrington Drake. I can't see the two of them getting along."

They certainly were not getting along last night. Inez almost said the words out loud, but then glanced at the elevator operator. For all the expression on his face, he could have been deaf to their conversation. *Still, best not to talk too freely here. Word gets around the staff, and from there, who knows?*

The elevator clanked and rocked, and the wrought iron hand on the dial above the door moved incrementally to the brass "2." With a shudder and groan, the elevator halted. The operator announced, rather unnecessarily, Inez thought, "Second Floor."

He opened the ornate cage door and Inez and Welles exited.

"Did the clerk say the room numbers?" Inez asked, surveying the doors lining the gallery promenade.

Welles gestured behind her. "That way, I suspect."

Inez turned to see the piano tuner they had hired to test the Broadwood walking toward them with his bag of tools. He stopped when he reached them, lifted his cap and said, "Mrs. Stannert, Mr. Welles. She survived the journey and sounds good."

"Excellent. But do not leave until we've had a chance to hear for ourselves," said Inez.

Obligingly, the tuner turned around and walked with them.

"Was Mrs. Drake there?" Inez queried.

"Nope. Just the mister. And the help. Everyone buzzing every which way. Made it a mite difficult to get the tuning done proper."

He paused in front of a set of double doors and backed up, letting Welles step forward and knock on the door. A cacophony of voices stilled, and the door opened. One of the Palace's chambermaids, a girl with wide black eyes and rosy brown skin looked out at them, one hand clutching a dustpan that held bits of white, broken porcelain.

"Who is it?" called a male voice from inside.

"Mrs. Stannert and Mr. Welles, from the music store." Inez nodded at the chambermaid, who opened the door wide. Inez entered, loosening the clasp of her cloak. "We are here to make sure the piano meets Mrs. Drake's requirements, to obtain the signed lease for the piano, and—"

The man, clearly a gentleman, straightened up from his inspection of the piano and smiled at them. "Excellent. I am no musician.

I was hoping someone would test it out before my wife makes her morning entrance." He approached. "Graham Drake, at your service."

Inez's first thought: *So this is the husband.*

Her second thought: *But he is so* young.

She chided herself. After all, what mattered if he was? Many an attractive older woman—especially those cloaked with fame, fortune, or charm—found no difficulty in bringing younger men into their orbit. Still.

His blond hair showed not a single strand of silver. His complexion—pocked most likely from a long-ago brush with the pox—was bracketed by a neatly groomed set of sideburns that matched a mustache as delicate as a lady's eyebrow. A fan of crow's feet at the corners of his eyes added to his charm, and only the faintest of lines creased his brow. After greeting Inez and Welles, he gestured to the piano. "She's all yours."

As they moved toward the instrument in the center of the room, Inez took the opportunity to glance around. The parlor had clearly been converted into Theia's domain. An army of dress forms lined the walls, many of them holding outfits that Inez could have sworn heralded from the House of Worth or other houses of high fashion. Morning dresses, walking dresses, visiting dresses, tea gowns, evening dresses, traveling clothes, daytime party dresses…the only thing missing, Inez decided, was an outfit for playing croquet. Wool, silks, satin, and velvet brocades in stripes, checks, and plaids bedazzled the eyes. The palette ranged through the rainbow, including cream, ivory, rose, canary yellow, emerald green, and royal blue. Three armoires took up strategic posts along one wall.

A covered birdcage, which Inez assumed held Theia's pet, Aria, stood off to one side. Staff and servants rushed this way and that through connecting doors that must have led to other rooms of the suite. Inez spotted several hotel chambermaids, all clad in simple, long gray skirts, light-colored shirtwaists, and spotless white, hem-length aprons. They moved purposefully about the large room, busy with feather dusters and brooms or carrying piles of linens. One exited the suite, allowing a porter to enter with a silver tray holding a coffee set. A sturdy older woman, pale of skin and hair, directed the activity. Given the woman's air of quiet authority, Inez guessed she belonged to the Drakes' entourage,

Mr. Drake chuckled as Inez took in the sight. "We arrived with fifty trunks, thirty hatboxes, and any number of valises, only a small number of which were mine. But I deny my dear wife nothing. What she desires, is hers. Which reminds me—" He seized some papers from a nearby occasional table and held them out to Welles. "The lease agreement for the piano."

"Thank you," said Inez, intercepting the contract. She glanced over it to be sure all was in order, then tucked it into her valise. "And now, to our other item of business."

Drake looked quizzical. "Other item?"

She cleared her throat. "Mrs. Drake indicated she wanted me to act as her accompanist for her upcoming events. She said you handle the business details." Inez decided to play her cards close about her availability. Since the master handled the money end of negotiations and not the mistress, Inez reasoned, she might be able to angle for a better rate if she demurred, just a little. "I should warn you, I am not certain this is a task I have time to perform."

As she spoke, she watched his mobile face move quickly through a spectrum of emotions nearly as varied as Theia's on-display fashions, starting with surprise and confusion, moving on to a flash of anger and annoyance, and finally settling on a dawning comprehension. He held up a hand. "Whoa, hold on, Mrs. Stannert. Are you saying my wife *hired* you?"

"Last night she asked me to replace Señor Rubio." Inez returned his stare. "You are aware she relieved him of his duties as accompanist?"

"Oh, I'm all too well aware of that." His brows drew together. "But your proposed employment is news to me."

At this, Welles turned away and pointedly moved to the piano, out of earshot. The piano tuner drifted with him. Welles sat on the bench, lifted the fallboard, and began a run of scales while the tuner listened and nodded along to the rise and fall of notes.

Inez saw no choice but to continue on her chosen course of action. "As I explained to your wife, Mr. Drake, I have obligations of my own. To the store and so on. Her proposal came out of the blue. So, she did not discuss this with you?"

He put his hands behind his back, gazing at Inez thoughtfully. She could almost see the wheels turning. "She did not. However, that is not unusual. Still, if she wants to engage you, then my job"—a small, humorless smile escaped—"is to make that happen. As quickly as possible, and on terms satisfactory to both you and her."

As I thought. Inez quelled a stab of relief.

"That is very kind of you, sir." She injected notes of concern and apology into her voice, adding, "However, to be fair, I should point out my available time is very circumscribed. I have many responsibilities and, much as I consider it a true honor to be asked to provide musical accompaniment to such an accomplished, acclaimed vocalist as Mrs. Drake, I am not at all certain I could be available to the degree she would require for—"

"I am certain we can come to an understanding." He talked over her, as smoothly as the racing water in a river rushes over a worn stone in its path, with barely an additional ripple. "It is only until the end of the year, you know."

"I did not know. She did not discuss the length of time nor any other details."

"Her last appearance is New Year's Eve. After that, done!" His hands, which he had thrust into his pockets, now appeared in the open and swept up grandly out from his sides.

Inez wondered if "done" meant leaving town or perhaps meant the end of the tour.

Before she could ask for clarification, he continued, "I am

familiar with the going rates these days for accompanists. After all, we have employed four in rapid succession since we left Philadelphia. Mr. Rubio was with us the longest, from Denver until now. I must say, I didn't see any signs that she was tiring of him, but then…" He shrugged.

Inez thought he talked very dismissively about a man his wife had humiliated and fired.

"In any case," he said, "I would be happy to go far, far above that rate, provided you will promise to stay with us through New Year's Eve. What with all that is going on, I do not want to be scrambling for another pianist between now and then. That said, I will speak with Mrs. Drake and have my business manager draw up a draft contract. I'll bring it to your store later today, where we can discuss it in a less frenzied setting."

One of the connecting doors flew open. "Good morning, Inez," Theia sang out as she entered, perfectly coifed, attired in an elegant morning dress, and with no sign of the previous night's exhaustion.

Drake turned to her. "My dear, did you engage Mrs. Stannert in Mr. Rubio's stead?"

She looked at him as if he were dense. "But of course! Didn't I tell you?"

A knock on the exterior door stopped his answer.

"Oh good," she said as a chambermaid hurried to answer. "I called for Jacob, that must be him. My poor little Aria must be starved."

It was indeed the stone-faced porter, bearing a tray with a small china dish of birdseed.

Theia took the dish with a flourish and said, "Yvonne, would you uncover the cage?"

The private maid did as she was told.

Inez blinked, wondering if her mind was playing tricks on her. Theia gasped.

The cage was empty.

Theia whirled around, the china dish clutched in one trembling hand. "Find him. Find him now!"

If the room had seemed abuzz before, it now positively exploded.

Chambermaids checked behind dress forms and peered under skirts. The two hotel porters—Jacob and the one who had brought the coffee service—looked under the tables, settees, and a scattering of chairs and behind the fireplace screen. The tuner, Welles, and Inez clustered by the piano, trying to stay out of the way.

Mr. Drake moved quickly to his wife and took her in his arms, seemingly oblivious to the fact that they were not alone. "We'll find Aria," he said in a soothing voice. "He must be here. No windows were open. He could not fly away."

Theia's trembling increased and she wailed, "How did he get out? How? I myself put him back in the cage after my performance at the Grand." Her frantic gaze turned to Jacob, pinning him to the wall. "*You* did this. What have you done with my Aria?"

The porter spoke—fear and indignation in equal measure. "Ma'am, I did nothing! I brought him back, just as you asked, put the cage there, just like you always said I should. I didn't look under the cover, I heard him a-stirring around. I give you my word, he was in there."

She tore herself out of her husband's arms and threw the china dish at the porter, shrieking, "You lie!"

He ducked, too late, and the dish hit him in the forehead, scattering birdseed over his dark uniform and the carpet. Blood seeped from a gash above one eye. He pulled a handkerchief from his pocket and pressed it to the wound, backing slowly toward the door.

A loud gasp caused everyone to freeze in place. Theia's maid was standing before one of the large wardrobes, its doors partly ajar. Hands to her throat, as if to choke back any further outburst, she backed away slowly from the closet.

Inez, despite her better judgment, went to see what was hidden in its shadowed depths. Theia rushed past Inez, reaching the wardrobe first and flinging open the two doors. Light from the bay windows bathed the contents. Inez spotted a pile of glittering gold-and-silver fabric crumpled on the floor of the wardrobe: Theia's dress from the previous night.

Theia picked up one corner of the shimmering cloth. The dress was slashed into tatters.

As she drew up the long length of material, something small tumbled out of its folds.

The broken, crushed body of Theia's pet songbird landed on the rug at Theia's exquisitely shod feet amid a tiny flurry of feathers.

Theia screamed—a perfect-pitch B-flat over high C—and swooned.

Chapter Four

Once the ink was dry, private investigator Wolter Roeland de Bruijn folded his invoice into precise thirds, placed it in the envelope, already addressed, and applied a seal. He leaned back in his leather chair in his parlor office at the Palace Hotel with a suppressed sigh.

Another case closed.

This time it had been a local capitalist's wife, frantic that she could not find the diamond necklace her husband had given her on their fifteenth wedding anniversary. She had come to de Bruijn and poured out her woes. "If he finds out the necklace is missing, it matters not that I have nothing to do with its disappearance. He has a vicious temper and I fear that he…he…." She stuttered to a stop. After applying a lacy handkerchief to her eyes, she added, "I confided in my sister, who gave me this."

She pulled out one of de Bruijn's business cards and pushed the small pasteboard across his desk toward him with a silk-gloved fingertip. There, in simple script, it stated:

W. R. de Bruijn.
Private detective. Inquiry agent.
Finder of the lost.

She continued, "You helped my sister recently. She assured me you are trustworthy and discreet. Will you, sir, please find my necklace? My husband expects me to wear it to the gala we are attending Saturday. There is not much time. I will pay any fee you ask if you can find it before then."

A woman in distress. Pleading for his help.

Of course he said yes.

It had been a simple case, quickly solved. He retrieved the necklace from the wife's light-fingered nephew, who had impulsively lifted it to pay off a substantial gambling debt. De Bruijn had taken pains to ensure that the nephew would not attempt such a feat again. Yesterday, after he had handed the missing piece of jewelry to the wife, she'd clasped his hand in relief. He was used to such occasional demonstrative impulses from female clients and had extracted himself with well-practiced tact so she would feel neither embarrassed nor rejected.

She had asked that he send the bill to her sister. Between the two women, they had devised some scheme of payment so the husband was none the wiser.

De Bruijn rose from his desk, crossed the parlor room that served as his office, and pushed the electric call button to summon a porter. He could have gone down the hall and used the third floor "tubular conductor" that carried outgoing mail directly to a central box in the Palace Hotel office. However, he did not trust the mechanism, having heard stories of mail stuck in the delivery system and lost forever, or extracted in a mangled state. He preferred to use a trusted source to deliver his reports and billings, particularly when extra precautions were required.

While waiting, he wandered to the bay window overlooking narrow Annie Street at the back of the hotel and the buildings beyond. He spared another troubled thought on the wife. De Bruijn had learned more of her husband in his investigation, enough to verify that her fear of violence was justified. If such a man would respond in such a manner over the loss of a bauble—valuable, yes, but for a man of means, nothing that could not be replaced—it did not bode well for the wife in the future. Too, there was the husband's mistress, tucked away in a pied-à-terre in the Palace Hotel, just a few floors above de Bruijn's office. The investigator had pondered whether he should broach the subject of the mistress but had discarded the notion. He had learned through experience—that painful but thorough taskmistress— that stepping uninvited into the affairs between man and wife never ended satisfactorily. Spouses, wives in particular, usually knew at some level of their partners' infidelities and peccadilloes.

In the end, she had not asked, so he had not offered.

A three-part knock at the room door brought him out of his reverie. He straightened his tie and smoothed down his gray waistcoat as he crossed the floor, his steps silent on the carpet, then opened the door. "Jacob," he said by way of greeting, and paused at the sight of the sticking plaster on the porter's forehead. However, all he did was hand the porter the envelope and a handsome tip, and say, "Please have this delivered by noon. It should be handed directly to the lady of the house at the address on the envelope."

Jacob Freeman nodded. "Yes, sir. Thank you, Mr. Brown."

De Bruijn had long ago become accustomed to answering to "Brown," "de Brooojin," "da Bron," and other attempts that only vaguely approached the proper pronunciation of his surname. But something in Jacob's demeanor made the detective think the porter had more to say. So he waited, not closing the door quite yet.

Jacob hovered on the threshold, lips pulled in, uncertain. He finally said, "Mr. Brown, may I talk with you? It will not take long. It is business, sir."

"Of course."

De Bruijn led him inside to the desk. He gestured to the chairs, but Jacob shook his head and remained standing. His gaze darted left and right, as if taking in the parlor for the first time.

He began, "There is a gentleman guest who is probably coming to see you. He's got a problem. I told him about you, how you help folks and such. I expect he won't listen to me. But he'll probably be talking to management, and they might send him your way."

"And the problem involves...?"

Jacob brushed a nervous hand over his forehead, touching the bandage. "I think it best he tells you."

"Very well, Jacob. I appreciate your discretion."

"I just want you to know"—his agitation became more pronounced—"I've got nothing to do with the trouble. Nothing. No matter what you hear. You know me. I need this job. I got a family. I don't drink. I don't do any of that. I'd not take chances on losing my position here."

"Of course." De Bruijn was curious, but he could tell by the set of Jacob's mouth that it was no use questioning the distressed porter. He supposed he would learn what the "problem" was, in good time.

As it turned out, it didn't take much time at all.

Less than an hour later, another knock at the door yielded a gentleman of means. It required no great powers of observation to come to this decision, although the bespoke frock coat, gold signet ring, and expensive shoes did provide clues. He wore neither hat nor gloves, and his highly polished footwear showed no signs of dust or the street, all of which convinced de Bruijn that he most likely came from within the hotel rather than from outside. That, and the card he held out as if it would provide passage.

"Mr. de Bruijn?" He tried, but like most, defaulted to *Brown*. "I am Mr. Drake. The Palace manager, Mr. Leland, thought you could assist me with a situation. He praised your expertise, and vouched for your caution and circumspection. He emphasized he has always been most pleased with the results of the services you have on occasion provided to the hotel guests."

De Bruijn thought "pleased" was a mild word for the hotel manager's response when de Bruijn had first approached him about providing services, as needed, to the hotel and its guests.

In a hotel the size of the Palace, with over seven hundred rooms and often more than a thousand guests and residents, there were always incidents that the hotel, or the guests themselves, preferred to address away from the eyes of the local police.

It helped, too, that de Bruijn knew Warren Leland from before. De Bruijn had lingered in San Francisco twice in the past. The first time was briefly in 1870, before the Palace Hotel was even a gleam in the eye of its creator, silver baron and financier William C. Ralston. The second time, in the mid-70s, de Bruijn had resided at the Palace while plying his particular trade. The hotel had been new then, with exterior stone walls of blinding white stone not yet besmirched by the smoke and soot from the low-grade coal that powered the city.

But those were the early days, when the hotel and de Bruijn were still relatively unmarked by time's passage.

Returning to the present, the detective took the card from Drake's well-manicured hand. A glance assured him that the card, which included his room number, was of the style he had had printed specifically for Leland, his assistant managers, and the head clerk to give to hotel guests.

Drake added, "I apologize for not making an appointment, but this matter requires immediate attention."

De Bruijn opened the door wider. "Please, come in, Mr. Drake." Ushering him inside, he added, "May I offer you coffee? I could call down. It would take but a moment."

"No, thank you. I expect we shall be able to conduct this business in short order." Without a glance to left or right, Drake took the leather seat directly in front of the desk.

Ah. No time to waste. No dilettante or gentleman of leisure. A businessman of some sort, most likely.

De Bruijn circled the desk and lowered himself into his chair. When he had had the room set up as his business office, he had asked the hotel to provide two leather club chairs and two floral-patterned, befringed chairs. After all, women clients were no less frequent than men, and he was always conscious of giving his clients choices that would put them at ease.

"So." He clasped his hands on the leather desk blotter. "How may I be of assistance?"

Drake appeared to gather himself, tugging on his black waistcoat and adjusting his heavy gold watch fob chain before sitting straighter in the chair. He directed a steady gaze at de Bruijn. "I need you to find the person who perpetrated a crime against my wife."

De Bruijn unclasped his hands. "Sir, if this is a crime of law, you should go to the police. I can give you the names of local police detectives who are circumspect and trustworthy."

Drake shook his head. "As I explained to the chief clerk and to Mr. Leland, we do not wish to involve the police and suffer the attendant publicity. My wife is of a delicate nature and prone to hysteria. Besides, the crime is not of the sort that the local law would address with the seriousness it deserves."

He leaned forward, placing his large hands flat on the desktop. "I need you to find whoever destroyed one of my wife's valuable evening gowns and killed her pet bird last night. Whatever your usual rate, I shall pay double."

De Bruijn blinked. He couldn't help it, and he was certain Drake caught the disbelief on his face. He tried to reassemble his expression into one of sympathy. "Mr. Drake, I understand why your wife would be distressed by such events. But this is not the kind of case I handle."

Those outsized hands balled into fists; the signet ring glinted. "Mr. Leland *guaranteed* me that you were the man for the job. He said you have a successful track record in finding lost objects and lost people, as well as tracking down the perpetrators— pickpockets and confidence-men, rogues and tricksters, the demimonde, gilt-dubber, picker-up, and occasional panel-thief— who look to prey upon the guests. Mr. Leland is anxious to keep this incident under wraps. As am I."

De Bruijn's eyes narrowed. That such a well-dressed gentleman should be acquainted with the lexicon of rogues and artful dodgers was, in his experience, unusual. Added to that, in the heat of the moment, Drake had not slipped into any appreciable accent that would identify him as being a longtime resident of one part of the country or another, or from abroad.

He sat back, the better to regard Graham Drake and take his measure more thoroughly. Drake was of indeterminate age. He could have been anywhere between twenty-five and forty-five. His angry, flushed face showed a brush with smallpox—the pitted scars appeared pale in the otherwise heightened coloration of his skin. A head of dense, gold-colored hair, no beard, a straightforward, light-blond mustache that was almost invisible. Broad shouldered. Sturdy. Not running to paunch, as men of means often did. But clearly a man who was used to having his requests honored without question. Additionally, a man whose immediate posture across the desk suggested he had no qualms in settling matters with his fists, should it come to that.

Perhaps realizing he had overplayed his hand, Drake leaned back in the chair and rubbed his face. "My apologies, Mr. de Bruijn. I did not mean to speak so harshly. I sit before you, a desperate man and concerned husband. You see, my wife is a leading lady of the stage, well known in Europe—Bavaria, France, all the better-known opera houses. She has several performances scheduled between now and the end of the year. This incident threatens to unnerve her, putting those appearances at risk. She cherished the bird, and the dress was her favorite. Not that she doesn't have a dozen others from Paris. She said that this attack upon the things dearest to her felt as if someone stabbed her through the heart. You can, perhaps, appreciate my situation."

"Apology accepted. And there is no need to pay twice my fee."

If Mr. Leland saw fit to direct this Mr. Drake to me, then obviously he is a man of some purport. De Bruijn was not entirely convinced that all was as it seemed—niggling doubts wiggled inside him like snakes—but he resigned himself to taking the case. For Mr. Leland, if nothing else.

Drake looked relieved. "So, you shall help us?"

"I will." De Bruijn pulled out two copies of his standard contract and took up a pen. "A few preliminary questions, and I can take up the rest with your wife. With your permission, of course."

Drake waved a hand. De Bruijn took that for agreement.

"I need a description of the bird and the dress, and the approximate value of each. Also, where the incident took place."

After entering the information provided by Drake on both copies, de Bruijn entered his signature and the date at the bottom of both and slid them to Drake. Handing Drake another pen and gesturing to the ink bottle, he added, "I assume you wish me to take direction from you and your wife on this matter? If so, place your full name and hers on the first line of the copy you leave with me. If there are others you want involved, please note them as well."

"Only us two," Drake said, as he penned in names on the indicated line.

"Who else is traveling with you?"

"We have a small retinue. My personal secretary. Business manager. Valet. A general errand boy. Mrs. Drake's understudy, Miss Green. Mrs. Drake's personal maid, who also acts as chaperone to Miss Green, although Miss Green is one of those independent-minded modern young women. My wife's accompanist, Mr. Luis Rubio. Oh, actually, he was dismissed last night, so he is no longer with us."

De Bruijn raised his eyebrows. The surname Rubio belonged to a well-to-do family with deep local roots. If this pianist was one of them, he would need to be cautious. "Is he residing at the hotel?"

"Not anymore," said Drake ominously.

"Do you know where he is staying?"

"No."

That meant he would have to uncover Rubio's current whereabouts. Perhaps, thought de Bruijn, the hotel manager would know. "Are there others who have ready access to the room where the bird and dress were kept?"

"They are—were—kept in my wife's music room. It was one of the grand parlor rooms, but we had it refurnished for her personal use. So, that means chambermaids. Porters. On the recommendation of the Palace's head clerk, we hired one of the hotel's porters to take charge of the bird and carry the cage when Mrs. Drake was out and about. That bird goes—went—everywhere with her."

"The porter's name?"

"I do not recall. He is a Negro." Drake tossed that off, as if it were an excuse for his not recalling a thing about the man.

De Bruijn thought of Jacob's visit earlier that day and recalled his words: *There is a gentleman guest who is probably coming to see you. He's got a problem.* De Bruijn made a mental note to talk to Jacob and whichever chambermaids minded the suite. "Anyone else?"

"During the day, my wife gets an assortment of visitors. Theater agents. Society women. Society reporters. A veritable circus of people come and go, during visiting hours and whatnot. You would have to ask Mrs. Drake."

"Is Mrs. Drake touring with a company? What about her manager?"

"No company. She fired her manager in Denver, so I have taken on those duties as well." He shook his head. "She can be… difficult. High-strung. Demanding. A perfectionist. Have you ever had dealings with those in the arts?"

"I have."

"Well then, you have probably encountered the feminine artistic temperament, so you understand."

De Bruijn nodded. His thoughts veered to his first sojourn in the city, more than a decade ago. Before the Palace was built, before the streets were paved, when the Barbary Coast was the black, beating heart of the city. Back when he was new to the country. New to the investigation business, still finding his way. Which meant, of course, losing his way on occasion. A memory, as seductive as a woman's whisper in his ear, tugged at him.

He pushed it away.

Drake's shoulders eased beneath his well-cut jacket. "Then I need say no more. Except to add that this is her 'farewell tour.'" He glanced at the contract and frowned, suddenly appearing older. "Leaving the stage is not easy for her, but it is necessary."

"And why is that?"

Drake looked up, almost as if he'd forgotten that de Bruijn was there. "My investments and businesses have become increasingly diverse. We spent years abroad, while she trained and toured. Then there was New York, Chicago, Philadelphia. But now we are settling here in San Francisco." He stood, contract still in hand. "I recently bought *The San Francisco Times*. Directing it will take much of my attention and time. Eventually, I intend to enter into politics."

A publisher with political aspirations. De Bruijn was surprised. Not by Drake's ambitions, but by the route he had chosen to attain his goal. De Bruijn would have wagered that Drake was an industrialist or capitalist. Someone who came by his fortune in the silver fields. He seemed more the sort to swing a pick than ply the pen.

But no matter.

What *did* matter was that Drake had evaded answering the question directly. De Bruijn wondered why.

Drake handed him the completed contract, adding, "I must be going. Much to do today. Thank you for your assistance, Mr. de Bruijn. I look forward to a speedy resolution to this incident." His tone darkened. " I do have an additional request."

De Bruijn realized that whatever he was about to say was not going to be a request, but a requirement.

"Once you find the miscreant who has caused such pain to

my wife, I want you to deliver his name to me personally. I shall handle it from there."

De Bruijn elected not to respond. Once he found the perpetrator, and he expected to do so quickly—*After all, how many people would have access to both the bird and the dress at a time when no one else was around*—he would decide how to proceed. He scanned the contract to make certain it was complete and that he had the necessary preliminary information.

There was the husband's name: Graham Alonzo Drake.

And there was the wife's: Theia Carrington Drake.

Theia.

His breath stopped in his throat.

He could have sworn his heart stopped as well.

No. It cannot be.

He set the completed agreement on the blotter, willing his hand not to shake nor his voice to falter as he handed Drake the client copy. "Your wife is, or was, Theia Carrington?"

Drake nodded, took the proffered contact, folded it, and slid it into his jacket pocket. "You know of her?"

De Bruijn grasped for the simplest truthful explanation. "When I was first in the city, twelve years ago, a Miss Carrington sang here."

Drake smiled. "Yes, that would be about right. That was before we married and went to Europe, where the Golden Songbird learned to soar." He stood. "I'll have a check prepared covering the requisite advance for your services by day's end."

"That will be fine." He was surprised to find his voice sounded entirely normal.

The two men shook hands. The detective then ushered Drake to the door and took a breath. He had to ask. "Does Mrs. Drake know you have hired a private investigator?"

"Not yet," Drake said, one hand on the doorknob. "As soon as I spoke with Mr. Leland, I came straightaway to you. No sense in wasting time."

"Ah." The whole situation was taking on the character of some convoluted Italian opera. De Bruijn dreaded the moment he would be called from the wings to face her and play his part. What would he say? What would she?

"I will give her this before I leave the hotel" Drake held up the detective's business card between two fingers—"and let her know to expect you later today."

"Of course." De Bruijn wondered how she would react when Drake handed her the card. The past and all its current ramifications suddenly loomed large in his mind.

Drake added, "I assume you'll want to examine the scene of the crime, so to speak."

De Bruijn forced himself to focus on the matter at hand. "Yes. About that. Was the room cleared and left as it was found, once the discovery was made?"

"Hardly. We had a handful of people and visitors milling about at the time. Quite the audience. My wife fainted. I immediately called for the house physician. Frankly, it didn't occur to me to have the room cleared and the door locked. I assume people have been coming and going, even as we spoke here."

De Bruijn mentally groaned. "Was there at least an attempt to keep them away from the scene?"

"I'm afraid not." He didn't sound at all contrite. "The chambermaid and my wife's personal maid did their best to clean things up. Others helped. I wasn't really paying attention. I was more concerned with Mrs. Drake's physical and mental state."

"So, were the remains of the bird and the dress disposed of?"

Drake seemed surprised at that. "I could hardly allow my wife's pet to be discarded so callously. The…corpse, I suppose you'd call it, was put back in the cage. The dress, or what's left of it, will be set aside for a dressmaker. Mrs. Drake wants a similar gown made for her final appearance on New Year's Eve. Not much time, all around."

"Of course," de Bruijn repeated. Really, what else could he say?

Drake departed, taking the room's oxygen with him. De Bruijn retreated to the bay window. He unlatched one of the double-hung panes, opened the sash to its full extent, and inhaled a lungful of salt-and-smoke-tinged air.

He clasped his hands behind him and stared out over the tops of nearby buildings, their multiple brick chimneys spitting out soot. Overhead, a seagull circled, screeching its ugly cry.

After Theia had left the city, eleven, almost twelve years ago, he had moved on as well. He had returned to San Francisco later, after a handful of years had softened and blurred the memories of his previous stay.

Much had happened since they had parted ways. To both of them, it seemed. Strange that they should meet again, under such circumstances.

Would she remember him, after all this time?

De Bruijn didn't know if he hoped she would, or prayed she wouldn't.

Chapter Five

Arms crossed, Inez stood in the middle of the showroom of the D & S House of Music and Curiosities, surveying the large space. In general, all was as it should be. The neat racks of sheet music, lined up like soldiers on parade. A collection of instruments beckoned: woodwinds, brass, strings, for the discerning professional or amateur musician. The amateurs were usually ladies of leisure or their daughters and the children of striving middle-class parents. They played on Sundays, holidays, and for each other in their private parlors or music rooms. The workaday musicians counted on their instruments to pay for their room and board. These professionals could be found in the many theaters, gardens, dance halls, and, when times got tough, the establishments along the Barbary Coast that needed a little musical background to temper the less savory goings-on.

The glass display cases, lining both sides of the store, were dusted and cleaned of fingerprints and smudges. Many held small objects from the Orient—delicate vases, statuary, and paintings—fulfilling the promise of "curiosities" indicated by the store's name.

Pale sunlight filtered through the large display window at the front of the store, creeping inward, touching on the potted plants and festive holiday arrangements of pine boughs, ferns, holly, and boxwood. The window, trimmed with wreaths, exhibited several fans of Christmas sheet music along with flutes, drums, and other instruments that might entice parents of the younger set to purchase musical gifts to place under the trees for their offspring.

Outside, a stream of pedestrians and horse-drawn vehicles moved briskly up and down Kearney, swift-moving shapes against the gray buildings under a blue, cloudless winter sky.

All of this—the festive decorations, the life pulsing through the city under an indifferent sky—only made the space on the Persian rug normally occupied by the showcase Broadwood grand piano seem larger, emptier. Inez stood in the center of the carpet, digging a boot heel into an imprint left from one of the piano's clawed feet, while Welles paced the rug's perimeter.

"The Steinway will be fine," he assured her. "It's a superior instrument with a great tone. Mark my words, Steinway is becoming a major name in the business. It won't hurt to hitch our wagon to their star. In fact, you ought to go to their store sometime, introduce yourself."

"I'll leave the niceties to you, since you know the family," said Inez. "I just hope the piano shows up soon. We need one here, through the holidays, to lure customers in. In any case, the Drakes will return the Broadwood after New Year's, once they leave town."

Welles stopped pacing and rocked on his heels, staring at the Christmas tree they had erected by the entrance. Its pressed tin stars and paper streamers twisted slightly in an invisible breeze. "Rumor has it they aren't leaving. That they are here to stay, in San Francisco."

"Really?" Inez was intrigued. "Are you certain? Where did you hear that? Mr. Drake indicated his wife would only need an accompanist through the end of the year, so I just assumed... We *did* specify an end-date for the rental of the Broadwood, did we not? I left the lease to you and did not read the fine print." She gave the rug at her feet a little kick, thinking of the store's accounts and how the income was barely breaking even with the expenditures.

Welles turned a somber aspect her way—but then, he always looked somber, unless he looked downright grumpy—and said, "Don't worry about the lease. I set it up and I'll handle any problems that arise. If the Drakes decide they want to buy the Broadwood, I'll make sure they pay a pretty penny for it. Also, I meant to tell you. On my way to the store this morning, before our trip to the hotel, I ran into Rubio coming out of the Barbary Coast. He's obviously been on a serious bender. I think he's still smarting from getting the sack by the Drakes."

"I hope he doesn't blame me. You should have seen the look he gave me last night when Theia sprang her decision on him, and on me. You urged me to take the position, remember?"

"Because it's good for the store and for you," said Welles. "I only counseled you to do what I or any pianist in the city would have done. If the Drakes had asked me, I'd have jumped at the chance without a second thought. The musician's lot is a tough one, Mrs. Stannert. Especially here in San Francisco. We may pal around, be friends, go drinking together, play cards, and whatnot. But when it comes to work…" He stopped.

Inez nodded. He didn't have to explain. She'd seen the desperate lengths musicians went to just to obtain steady work. It was a cutthroat business, and many of the operators thought nothing of pitting one player against the other to get away with paying as little as possible.

"Anyway," he continued, "appearing with Theia Drake will put a feather in your cap. You'll soon have more offers and requests to appear than you can shake a stick at."

"Well, that's not what I want. I have my hands full with the store, the lessons, and, of course, Antonia," said Inez, thinking that two years ago in Leadville, Colorado, she'd have jumped at the chance to be at the fore. In Leadville she'd made a name for herself, not for her talent at the keyboard, but for her finesse at poker, her business savvy in turning the Silver Queen saloon into a money-making bonanza, and her charm and skill behind the bar.

But in this city, in this new life she was building for herself and for Antonia, she preferred the shadows. As a woman, it was easier to build a fortune and connections by staying out of the limelight. Yet, here she was, about to be thrust onstage with a diva who was not shy about claiming center stage. *As she did this morning.*

Inez shook her head. "It all happened so fast, the to-do at the hotel."

"A nasty business," agreed Welles.

Inez replayed the scene in her mind. No sooner had Theia Drake screamed and fainted amongst the crumpled gold-and-silver fabric and small yellow feathers than people had seemed to pour out of the woodwork. One of the chambermaids had screamed as well. Theia's maid had dashed into a side room for smelling salts. Graham Drake, cradling his wife's head, had said, "Quick, get a doctor!" At that, a well-dressed older man, possibly Mr. Drake's valet, had nearly shoved Inez and Welles out the door, suggesting they return later.

"Who would do such a thing, kill a little bird. And destroy a dress." Inez had a sudden thought. "You don't think Rubio…?"

"I don't think anything of the sort," said Welles.

One of the many top-hatted figures going past the display window slowed, turned, and opened the door. The small bell above the entry clanked to announce their visitor: Graham Drake.

Welles mustered a rare smile—Inez suspected he was relieved to escape the conversation—and moved toward Drake, saying, "Good day, sir. I hope your appearance here means your wife is recovering from the morning's events?"

Drake said, "She is resting and doing as well as can be expected under the circumstances." He tipped his hat to Inez. "Mrs. Stannert."

She nodded back. "Mr. Drake."

He looked around at the store, smoothing his glistening bronze-colored hair back from his high forehead. It had to be an absentminded gesture, Inez thought, because not a hair was out of place. He said, "Oriental novelties and antiques, as well as sheet music and instruments. Unusual combination, but charming. And I happen to have a penchant for the Orient and its arts."

He turned to Inez with an engaging smile that overshadowed his subdued mustache. The mustache was trying its best, but between its light color and constrained size—it went the length of his lips, and no further—it would forever play second fiddle to the smile, which was accompanied by deep dimples. Inez had not noticed the dimples before. But then, Mr. Drake hadn't had much occasion for smiling that morning.

His expression sobered and the dimples disappeared. "I apologize for the confusion this morning. First, my ignorance of my wife's offer, and then all the business that followed. Shocking. But it's being taken care of, I assure you. I hope the goings-on do not affect your opinion of her, or us."

Without giving Inez a chance to respond, he continued, "I am here to finalize our agreement so that you and she can proceed." He unbuttoned the top buttons of his frock coat and extracted a folded set of papers from an inside pocket. "Her next engagement is for a private event at the Cliff House on Christmas Eve, a mere three days hence." He glanced around. "Is there somewhere we can discuss the contract?"

Welles jumped in. "You go ahead to the office, Mrs. Stannert. I'll mind the store."

"Very well. Mr. Drake, if you please, follow me."

As they walked toward the office in the rear of the building, a curtain drew back from a hidden alcove and John Hee, the store's assistant, stepped out, cradling a large red vase in his arms. "Mrs. Stannert. You want this in front?"

"Yes, thank you, Mr. Hee. That will look perfect in the display window."

"Wait." Drake put out an arm to stop Hee and moved closer to examine the vase. "I have been looking for objects my wife might like for her music room. This, the color, it would be perfect." He looked at Inez. "Can you give me the particulars? Is it unusual? How much?"

Inez's mouth tweaked. *Expensive, rare, and the right color are the requirements, apparently.*

She replied, "Mr. Hee is our resident expert when it comes to the Oriental pieces in our store." She nodded to Hee, encouraging him to speak.

A small, sturdy man of indeterminate age, Hee cleared his throat and twisted his head, as if his starched white collar and black string tie were tightening around his neck.

Inez knew he was not comfortable being called out as "the expert," nor coming out onto the floor when customers were about, but she had insisted he lend her a hand with the antiques. Once the elder Donato was gone, along with his expertise on the store's Oriental pieces and curios, Hee was the only one in the store with the acumen to buy and sell the advertised "curiosities."

Inez suspected that Hee, as a Chinese man working outside San Francisco's Chinatown, preferred to stay anonymous and unseen. With his long, braided queue tucked out of sight beneath his jacket and his large brimmed hat shadowing his face, he would arrive at the store early each morning and disappear into his curtained alcove to repair instruments. At other times, he would go to the docks or Chinatown to haggle with the antiquities importers. But there were occasions, and this was one, when he had no choice but to show his face and share his knowledge.

He cleared his throat again. "This"—he set the elegant vase carefully upon the nearest glass-topped display case—"is *Langyao hong*—some say oxblood." He pronounced the *el* in "blood" with special care. "Qing dynasty."

"How much?" Drake persisted.

Hee shot Inez a nervous glance. "Must discuss with Mrs. Stannert."

Drake reached out, stroked the curve of the vase, its brilliant red glaze aflame, then waved his hand. "Name your price, Mrs. Stannert."

She moved closer to John Hee and murmured, "Write a fair price on a piece of paper and give it to Welles, please." Then she addressed Drake. "Why don't we deal with the business at hand, and come back to the vase?"

Once in the store's back room, Inez wished she'd had advance notice that a person of Drake's stature was coming to call. The area, which ran the width of the building, was divided into thirds: behind a door at one end, her private office with its desk; in the middle, a space with a large, round mahogany table for visitors; and at the other end, a glassed-in area with an upright piano, where she conducted music lessons. Inez removed a stack of invoices from the table, along with a half-empty cup of coffee, stacking them by the parlor stove.

She indicated one of the chairs. "Please, if you would, Mr. Drake. I'll just fetch pen and ink." She went into her office while he settled into the chair.

She thought briefly on the various types of people who usually sat at that table. Vendors and buyers, there on store business. Parents, looking to set up music lessons for musically-inclined daughters or sons. The loose group of musicians, friends, and colleagues of Welles who gathered Monday evenings (when theaters and other musical venues were "dark") to play a friendly game of cards and gossip. Local businesswomen, searching for financial backing to start new ventures or to extend their small enterprises—women with whom she formed partnerships or to whom she extended loans: laundresses, milliners, bakers, printers, dressmakers. One by one, sometimes in pairs, they found their way, mostly by word of mouth, to her back office.

As she sat down across from Drake and set the writing supplies between them, it occurred to her that his obviously expensive and hand-tailored suit, silk top hat, fine kid gloves, and altogether upper-class appearance virtually shouted *Money!* to anyone with half a wit to observe. He looked like the kind of mark that she would have, in her previous life, been tempted to lure to her poker table—if only to test his mettle and discern whether he was the greenhorn his open demeanor implied or if a cold-eyed manipulator lurked beneath that blue-eyed gaze.

He smiled again.

She reminded herself to be on guard against that smile.

And those dimples.

He began, "My wife seems much taken with you, Mrs. Stannert. She told me that when you played at the Grand, it was as if the heavens had called to her." He separated one paper from the rest he carried and set his fingertips ever so lightly on top of it. The motion reminded Inez of the gesture of a pianist preparing to play, or a cardsharp testing the deck and the attention of his opponents.

"My Golden Songbird can be a trifle melodramatic," he continued, "but that is simply her nature. I know the difficulties that can arise in working with someone of her temperament. When she told me she offered to hire you and you hesitated, I understood. No accompanist worth his salt would accept without knowing the conditions. What she doesn't understand is that you are not some itinerant pianist or amateur, nor a professional musician, but a businesswoman. I am a businessman myself, you see. I handle the finances, hiring, and contracts for her appearances. I knew your reluctance came from the suspicion that, in taking up a side venture such as this, you would be taking time from your store, and during a particularly busy season at that."

Inez kept her face neutral, even though the word *busy* stung. She wondered if, when he had walked into the store and looked around, he had noticed the paucity of customers.

The paper inched its way toward her. He released it and pointed at a line with a penciled-in figure. "This is what I propose as total compensation, assuming you spend half a day, each day through the holidays, excepting Christmas Day, in practice and rehearsal, and most likely a full day for each of the three performances she has between now and the end of the year."

"Hmm." Inez pulled the paper toward herself and scrutinized the language and the proposed payment. She worked hard to keep her mouth from falling open upon seeing the number 2,000 carelessly scribbled after the dollar sign. *If Rubio was anticipating anywhere near this amount, no wonder he was so angry at being fired.* "What if Madame Drake decides she needs more of my time? Or another performance is added to the list you have here?"

"I shall pay you for the additional hours and event, of course."

Inez looked up, arranging a serious expression on her face. "I am certain you understand that unexpected demands on my time would cause complications. If I must spend hours aside from those you have enumerated here, I shall have to rearrange my own schedule and that of my students and ask my manager to work extra hours or find someone who can. In such cases, I would insist the compensation rate be twice what you have here." She slid the agreement back toward him. "Such additional requests upon my time should, of course, be based on real need and not whimsy or caprice."

His eyebrows drew together. The furrow in his forehead disappeared as he smiled again. "Of course, Mrs. Stannert."

She curved her lips in a returning smile. "And, if Madame Drake—or you or whomever you designate—should cancel any performances or practices listed here, or if you decide my services are no longer required, as happened to Señor Rubio, I expect to be paid in full." She tapped the contract with a finger. "Once those changes are made, I shall be delighted to sign."

"I'll have the contract redrafted and prepared for your signature." He tucked the papers into an inner pocket. "Would it be possible for you to come to the hotel later today and meet with Mrs. Drake? She is determined to proceed, despite the morning's events."

"Certainly." Inez stood. He followed suit. She held out her hand

and they shook. Inez added, "Now, let's find out the disposition of that vase you were interested in."

They returned to the showroom. Welles handed Inez a slip of paper on which was printed $100. John Hee was nowhere to be seen. Inez slipped the piece of paper in her pocket and turned to Drake, who was admiring the vase. "We would normally sell it for one-hundred-and-fifty dollars. However, in light of our soon-to-be-sealed agreement, I shall ask only one-hundred-and-twenty."

"Done. No need to have it delivered. Just wrap it and I shall take it myself."

Inez glanced at Welles, eyebrows raised. He raised his in turn, but picked up the vase and carried it to John Hee's vacant alcove to parcel it up with brown paper and string.

Drake said, "Please open a store account for us and add the vase to it." He looked around. "Your Chinaman. Where is he?"

Inez refrained from retorting that John Hee was not "her Chinaman" but a highly valued associate. Instead she said, "I expect *Mr.* Hee is making a delivery or perhaps meeting someone. When merchants arrive from the Orient, he is often among the first to greet them."

"I'd hoped to talk more with him," said Drake. He settled his top hat. "Another time."

Welles emerged with the bundled vase and handed it to the diva's husband. Inez walked Drake to the door, saying, "Please let Madame Drake know I'll be by soon. I can sign the revised contract then. If Mrs. Drake would prefer to wait until tomorrow, I can be reached here by telephone." She smiled at his surprise. "Yes, a telephone in a music store. Unusual, I know, but the previous owner had it installed and it has proved its worth." She handed Drake a trade card of heavy, ivory-colored stock. One side sported a bluebird perched on an Oriental-style vase holding roses, ferns, and other greenery. A wave of musical notes emanated from the bird's open beak and wrapped around a scroll. At the top was "Donato & Stannert House of Music and Curiosities."

The address and telephone exchange number appeared at the bottom.

"Thank you. I have a boy, Toby, who runs letters and dispatches for me. With him, I know if messages are received, or not." Drake saluted her with the card and departed.

Welles leaned on a display case. "The vase. Twenty percent added to the price for…?"

"For difficulties, as yet unknown, that I am certain will arise," said Inez. She looked down at her gray-and-black, no-nonsense business ensemble. "I leave the store in your capable hands, and John Hee's, once he returns from wherever he has vanished."

"You're leaving now?"

Inez glanced up at the ceiling, thinking of her flat above. "Soon. Since I am to meet Madame Drake on her turf and terms, I must be attired so that it is clear I am not a hireling she can order about as she wishes. Besides, no proper lady wears her morning outfit all day."

In addition, there was another bit of business she had to conduct at the hotel before she met with the diva—a meeting Inez was not looking forward to, but which she could not put off.

Chapter Six

De Bruijn was still in his office, having determined to set remaining tasks quickly to rights—and to give Theia Carrington Drake a chance to receive his business card. If this had been a normal case, de Bruijn would have gone directly to the suites after his meeting with Mr. Drake. Normally, he would ask to view the scene of the so-called crime and to interview Mrs. Drake and any of the Drakes' entourage or hotel staff who had access to the room.

But this was not a normal case.

One of the most important steps, that of gathering physical evidence of the crime before the scene had been disturbed, would probably be futile. Still, he would do his best. And de Bruijn wondered if he would be able to get a complete picture of everyone's comings and goings beforehand. In this case, he suspected that determining motive would be essential. Which meant that, more than usual, he would need to have his wits about him. *If only it weren't Theia.*

De Bruijn was not given to hashing over old history or regretting his actions, but a few dark spots in his past still had power to give him pause. Theia Carrington was one of them.

However, the sooner I begin, the sooner I will be done.

He was buttoning up his sack coat when a quick, determined knock sounded on his door.

De Bruijn frowned. He wasn't expecting anyone. There had been no messages from the main desk to alert him that someone was asking for him. Perhaps it was Jacob, with additional information. But it did not sound like Jacob's knock.

The tapping began again as he crossed to the door. He grabbed his hat from the hat stand, his gloves from the ivory tabletop. The items in hand would make it clear he was heading out. He would tell whoever it was to make an appointment for later.

He opened the door. Before he could say anything, his visitor, Mrs. Stannert, exclaimed, "Well. It's about time. Do you always keep the ladies waiting, Mr. de Bruijn?" She gave him a small smile, as if to reassure him that she was in jest. However, he knew her well enough from their past business doings to intuit the smile was strained.

She was wearing a dark green hat, almost a miniature version of a man's derby, with a feather curled around the crown. A complementary green skirt peeped out at hem level beneath her usual black cloak, the fabric folded in knife-sharp pleats. Even her walking boots appeared to be of dark green leather. All quite a departure from her usual daytime ensembles, which tended toward dark and somber shades. He wondered momentarily what had caused such a fashion transformation, before recalling his manners and bowing. "Mrs. Stannert. Had I known you were coming, I would have been at the door, awaiting your arrival."

His surprise at seeing her went beyond her general appearance. For one, he did not recall telling her the whereabouts of his new office at the Palace. Their previous meetings had always taken place in public venues, such as the hotel's dining room or her music store. Well, there was that one time she ambushed him in his previous rooms, out of concern for his health. On that occasion he had been recovering from a serious concussion and was barely able to stagger, properly attired, from his bedchamber.

Finally, aside from their first encounter, which had gotten their acquaintance off to a rocky start, their meetings had always been arranged in advance. Such convenings either involved business, such as the investigation during which their paths had initially crossed, or Antonia.

The firm set of Mrs. Stannert's mouth and the unwavering gaze of her hazel eyes made de Bruijn suspect that this was not a business call.

So it must be Antonia.

He stepped aside. "Please, come in."

She entered, her eyes traveling to the hat and gloves in his hand. "You were leaving?"

"I can spare a few minutes."

"Good. I have business elsewhere as well, and I promise this will not take long."

They moved to the desk. He stood, waiting for her to take a seat first.

She took a moment to examine the room, adding, "You appear to have moved up in the world, Mr. de Bruijn. Or, should I say, in the hotel. This is far superior to your previous accommodations."

He smiled, to set her at ease as much as anything else. "Since I am staying in San Francisco for now, it behooves me to have a proper office for receiving clients."

Her scrutiny took in the paintings; the furniture; his desk, neat and bare; and finally the seating arrangements—feminine chintz-styled chairs to one side, masculine leather club chairs to the other. She raised an eyebrow at him, almost as if to say, "I know exactly what you are up to." She sat in the club chair and tossed her closed umbrella—green, of course—onto the vacant, flowery cushioned seat. Crossing her lower limbs in a most unladylike fashion, she leaned back in the chair. One boot-shod foot began to swing. It was an immodest display, one he suspected she took up deliberately, to throw him off his guard.

Whatever she has to say, it cannot be good.

He pulled his gaze up to her face, with the firm intention to keep it directed away from the metronome of buttoned-up green leather ticktocking back and forth just above the rug. "Is this about Antonia?"

She nodded, once.

His heart sank a little. When he had returned to San Francisco this last time, one intent had been to find Antonia Gizzi. Two years ago, he had made a promise to Antonia's mother to protect and take care of her and her daughter. He had failed. As a result, Antonia's mother had died and left Antonia an orphan. Mrs. Stannert had saved the girl, protected her, and pulled her from a perilous life into one that offered safety and stability. He was thankful for that.

De Bruijn knew Antonia would probably always view him askance. Although she had come to accept him and his explanations of what had happened back then, she remained wary and reserved. All in all, he supposed her hard-edged view of the world—sad to see, in one so young—was for the best. When Antonia grew into a young woman, she would be less naïve than most, which would help her stay strong unto herself.

All that aside, when he had completed the investigation that had brought him back to San Francisco and into Mrs. Stannert's and Antonia's orbit, he had decided to stay—because of Antonia. Mrs. Stannert seemed perfectly capable of taking care of the girl, but de Bruijn felt a duty to Antonia's mother, a duty to keep watch over the child and be ready to offer help, should the time come when it was needed. He wondered if that time was now.

Mrs. Stannert began. "I wanted to talk to you about this sooner, but you were unavailable." Her hands tightened on the armrests of the chair. The foot stopped swinging. "Carmella Donato asked if Antonia could accompany her to Southern California to visit relatives for the holidays and I consented."

De Bruijn raised his eyebrows. "For Christmas?"

"Yes. As you know, Carmella is part-owner of the store now.

Furthermore, she is a friend and is dealing with great sorrow, having lost her brother. It was the least Antonia and I could do for her. But Carmella's request is not the only reason I sent Antonia away. I also need some time to make a decision." Her mouth tightened. "Antonia is in trouble at school. Again."

He shook his head. "I thought she was doing well. May I ask what happened?"

One of her gloved hands began tapping the chair arm. "Things *were* going well. But it didn't last. The principal called me in. It turns out, notes had been given to Antonia to convey to me, none of which I received. The principal actually called me on the telephone, of all things. Antonia"—she took a breath—"had invented a 'game' that involved spitting out the second-story window. The number of points rewarded depended on the, shall we say, target. Certain fellow pupils garnered one point. Teachers, more. And if one succeeded in attaining the ultimate goal, which was the principal..." She cleared her throat.

De Bruijn shut his eyes, then opened them again. "A game. So she was not the only one involved?"

"No." Her cloak whispered softly as she shifted in her chair. "She had recruited a confederate, a girl from her class. Katie Lynch."

"Lynch." He made the connection. "Police detective Lynch's daughter?"

"One of his several daughters, yes." She bristled a bit. "I was glad enough to see Antonia making friends in her class. You know I was concerned about the Lynch boy, Michael. He's a little old for her, and he seemed a little too inclined to go along with Antonia's wilder schemes. But Katie is her age and seemed more...proper, I suppose. I was glad to see she and Katie were getting along. Katie even invited her to join the Lynches for Friday dinners."

De Bruijn sighed. First, the San Francisco detective's son. Then, one of the daughters. Antonia seemed to be infiltrating the family as a whole.

"Of course, the girls were punished," said Mrs. Stannert. "But I knew nothing about all this until the principal reached me. And now, I must decide."

"Decide what?"

"Antonia is on a knife-edge at that school, close to being expelled." She exhaled, hard. "If she were a boy, it would be a ruler slap on the wrist and a 'boys will be boys' scolding. But since she's a girl—"

"You say she is 'close to being expelled,' so no decision has yet been made?"

"Not yet. We are going to see if this break may help. When she returns, she and I will have a serious discussion. The principal suggested that I consider taking her out of public school and sending her to boarding school or engaging a private tutor."

"No boarding school." The words were out before de Bruijn even knew he had said them.

"I agree. It would destroy her. She needs to be here. With me. Not thrown in with the inevitable pack of she-wolves at a boarding school."

De Bruijn wondered what experiences Inez had had in a boarding school environment. Apparently enough to realize such a situation would be a disaster for Antonia.

"A private tutor is possible." The foot began swinging again. "But I feel it would be a step backward. I do not like the idea of closeting her away from the world, away from others her age. I wager she'd make her tutor's life a living h—" She checked herself and substituted "unbearable."

De Bruijn nodded. He knew he had no voice in Antonia's upbringing. The girl was not his ward. He was glad he and Mrs. Stannert were seeing eye to eye. On this, at least.

Mrs. Stannert nodded as well, her attention directed above his head, perhaps at the landscape painting of Yosemite Valley and its waterfall. "Thank you. I did want to let you know the situation and my thoughts. There is no one else I can talk to about the girl.

I shall ponder the situation while Antonia is away. Perhaps have another conversation with the principal. It is possible we can come to a meeting of the minds before she returns."

"If there is anything I can do to help—"

Those hazel eyes snapped to him. "She is, ultimately, my responsibility. I shall let you know my decision, once I have made one." Mrs. Stannert glanced at the clock on the fireplace mantel. "I should be going. I have a business engagement and have taken enough of your time."

She stood. He did as well. Retrieving her umbrella, she continued, "As I recall, Mr. de Bruijn, when I came a-knocking at your door, you appeared to be on your way out as well."

"Indeed." As they walked to the door, he added, "Allow me to accompany you to the elevator."

She waved a hand. "If you like. It is hardly necessary. My appointment is in the hotel."

He was tempted to ask who her appointment was with but decided she would probably consider the question intrusive. He had already observed signs of her backing off, after she had revealed her troubles with Antonia. Being overly interested in her affairs would most likely elicit one of two responses—retreat and evade, or bristle and snap. So, instead he said, "I am curious. How did you get my room number? I only divulge it to prospective clients."

Mrs. Stannert gave out a mysterious little half smile—a Mona Lisa expression, if ever he saw one. "I spoke with a front-office clerk. Told him I had engaged you for business in the past and showed him one of your cards, while fluttering my eyelashes and handkerchief. I said I had an appointment with you but, alas, had forgotten the room number of your office. Easy enough."

They were at the elevator. De Bruijn reached over and pushed the button. A buzz sounded from beyond the grill, into the shaft. "May I ask his name, this clerk?"

"You may, but I shan't tell you. I may need his help again

sometime and I'd like to stay in his good graces." Her glance slid sideways to him. The grinding and clanking of the descending elevator grew louder. "I'm certain you understand, Mr. de Bruijn."

He did.

The elevator arrived, and the operator slid open the iron gridded gate. Another couple waited inside, dressed for going out on the town. Inez entered first, announcing, "Second floor, if you please."

De Bruijn stepped inside the mahogany "lifting room" and, suddenly uneasy, studied Inez anew: Her uncharacteristic *à la mode* outfit. A determined tilt of the chin. A subtle change in intonation. An undefinable air of…refinement, was it?…had descended over her like a fur-lined cloak as soon as she entered the elevator.

The operator closed the grate and the apparatus lurched into noisy descent.

De Bruijn didn't believe in coincidences. But that didn't mean they didn't happen. Only, in his experience, they seldom happened for the best.

The carriage lurched to a stop. "Second floor," announced the operator.

The grate slid open and Inez stepped out.

So did de Bruijn.

She looked at him, curious. He simply said, "I also have business on this floor."

They turned in the same direction. Proceeded to the same door. Halted at the same time.

De Bruijn heard singing inside—a voice so pure it sent a small shiver through him.

Mrs. Stannert looked as alarmed as he felt. "You have business with the Drakes?"

Nothing would be gained by prevaricating. And de Bruijn disliked lying, unless there was no choice. As a rule, falsehoods had a way of spinning around and attacking their creators.

"I do. I am investigating a small matter for them."

She now seemed torn between amusement and disbelief. "Would this be the matter of the bird and gown? Doesn't seem like your caliber of crime, Mr. de Bruijn."

Nettled, because that was exactly what he had thought when Graham Drake had come to him, he said, "How did you hear of it? Through your hotel informer? And what is *your* business here, Mrs. Stannert?"

That air of refinement returned and she turned to face the door, giving him her profile. "I have been retained as Madame Drake's accompanist through the holidays." Her gaze slid sideways toward him. "I was there, you know. Or rather, here. When the discovery was made."

De Bruijn stared, nonplussed.

At that moment the door flew open, and liquid sound poured out, nightingale sweet. The door also disgorged a hotel chambermaid, moving swiftly, her head bent, not looking where she was going. She ran full tilt into Inez, who grabbed de Bruijn's sleeve to keep from falling.

"Ma'am, I'm so sorry." The maid, who seemed not much older than Antonia, retreated into the room, clutching a laundry bundle. Dark brown eyes, wide and frightened in a brown face sprinkled with freckles, switched back and forth between the two on the threshold.

The singing choked off, and a voice de Bruijn had not heard in over a decade said, "Sing from a *forward position*, Miss Green. I want to hear nasal resonance, not from the back of the throat. You must *project* the sound, find the right balance of light and dark. *Chiaroscuro*."

The maid seemed uncertain whether to come or go. She called inward, "Excuse me, ma'am. Visitors." Then she sidled into the hallway and headed to the servant's staircase.

A scurry of sound—the silky swirling of feminine materials, the flat sound of slippers on polished floor—and Theia appeared at the door.

His mouth dried. He couldn't have said a word right then if he had to.

At the same time, his treacherous heart accelerated, the blood pounding through his veins with the ferocity of a feeling he had thought long dead.

She was, in some ways, exactly as he remembered. The light-brown hair, soft and curling about her face. The amber eyes, as familiar to him as if they had parted yesterday. A mouth made to smile or pout or purse at will. But she was different as well. Singular strands of gray threaded that magnificent hair. Her figure—always the epitome of womanhood—was now fuller, more curved. In addition, he detected a redness and puffiness to her eyes. From lamenting the recent death of her pet, perhaps? She had lines around her eyes and mouth that had been absent all those years ago. Lines of sorrow, he thought. Or, they could be signs of displeasure, because she was also frowning.

Not at him, but at Mrs. Stannert.

"Inez. I was expecting you earlier."

Mrs. Stannert released de Bruijn's arm—he'd been unaware she still clutched it—and responded calmly. "Is that so? Mr. Drake did not indicate when I should arrive. He merely asked that I come see you this afternoon."

De Bruijn could imagine Theia saying the same words, in the same tone.

Theia sniffed, and some of her displeasure dissipated. "I had hoped you would be in time to supply the appropriate musical accompaniment for Miss Green. However, we are finished."

Her gaze flicked to de Bruijn, eyelids half-lowered, as if she were shielding her reaction and thoughts from him.

The tension was unbearable. So he broke it, removing his hat and saying, "Madame Drake. At your service."

She blinked. Perhaps it was his voice, but he saw her mask waver and he knew she remembered him, just as he remembered her. It was all over in a moment, and she said with a note of haughtiness, "You must be Mr. de Bruijn, the private investigator. My husband told me you would come by this afternoon."

Her gaze shifted between him and Mrs. Stannert. "Do you know each other?"

Ah. Here is the rub. For a number of reasons he had no time to tease apart, he was reluctant to disclose his relationship with Mrs. Stannert. A platonic relationship based on mutual respect and concern for Antonia, but still…

As de Bruijn pondered how to reply, Inez said, "We just happened to arrive at your door at the same time." She brushed her skirt, remarking, "That clumsy girl. She nearly knocked me over."

Mrs. Stannert's intonation, attitude, and very gesture were a precise imitation of the Theia he remembered—a woman who was sometimes dismissive, and occasionally almost vicious, toward those she considered beneath her. De Bruijn felt certain that the echo of mannerisms was deliberate and covered Mrs. Stannert's true inclinations. She was nothing if not champion of the underdog.

Inez's response seemed to mollify the diva. She said, "Oh gracious, my manners. Please, come in." She opened the door wide and ushered them inside, adding, "It's just, this morning…"

Theia pulled a lace handkerchief from her sleeve and dabbed her eyes. "I tried to rest as the doctor advised. But my sorrow over the suffering of my poor little pet, who was all innocence and song, would not abate. The only remedy was to proceed with the day. Although as you see—" she indicated her fashionable but subdued lilac gown—"I mourn my little Aria's passing within these four walls, where none dare mock my grief."

De Bruijn's initial assessment of the parlor-*cum*-practice room was that it was clearly a feminine dominion, one firmly under Theia's authority. She led them toward the grand piano in the center of the room, where a young woman stood, waiting. She was so like Theia in coloring and height he would not have been surprised to find the two related. Mrs. Stannert addressed the young woman with "Hello, Miss Green. I dare not say 'good day,' given what happened earlier."

So, Mrs. Stannert has already met some of the principals in the case. He wondered who else she had interacted with, and where and when. He was glad that, as part of the investigation, it would be natural to include her in the interview process. He knew from their past interactions she was a sharply observant woman. Given that she had been there at the discovery of the "crime," she might have insights that could hasten the discovery of the culprit.

Realizing that Miss Green had turned toward him, he introduced himself. The singer's clasped hands were trembling and her eyes red, as if from weeping. She gave the impression of holding herself together with the thinnest reserves of self-control.

He had barely uttered his name when Theia interrupted, saying, "This is the private investigator Mr. Drake hired to find out who killed my sweet Aria and destroyed my dress."

Miss Green's hands twisted tighter together. "Pleased to meet you," she murmured.

Theia sighed dramatically. "Miss Green, if you cannot project your voice in everyday conversation, how do expect to do so on a stage the size of the Grand?"

A shadow passed over the understudy's face, but all she said was, "Madame, I will endeavor to do better next time. Since you say we are finished for the day, with your leave, I shall take care of a small errand I must do." She brushed past de Bruijn and Inez, went to a nearby coat stand, and gathered a crimson cloak and a similarly-hued bonnet.

De Bruijn said hastily, "Miss Green, at your convenience, I would like to speak to you about the recent unfortunate events."

She was already at the door, her back to him, the bonnet dangling by its strings from her fingers. He saw her shoulders rise, almost imperceptibly. After a moment, she nodded. "I should be gone for only an hour or so," she said, still facing away. "If that is not convenient, please leave your card and we can arrange another time." Without looking around, she departed.

Theia waved him to a clutch of chairs by the fireplace. "Make yourself comfortable, Mr. de Bruijn, while I take care of some business with Mrs. Stannert."

"If it is all the same, Madame, I would like to see where the destroyed gown and your pet bird were discovered. And view the remains themselves, if I may. Mr. Drake said the bird was still here."

She placed a hand over her heart, as if his words pained her anew. "If you must. Aria is in his little cage. The dress is in one of the clothespresses. It was my favorite for performing on stage. Custom-made for me in Paris. The lines were timeless, the fabric exquisite." Her face hardened. "I fear it cannot be repaired." Theia turned into the depths of the room, calling out, "Yvonne!"

Another maid, who was busy brushing one of the many lavish costumes that de Bruijn guessed comprised some of the diva's professional attire, turned around. When he saw her, past and present collided, yet again, in a most unexpected manner.

All his brain could muster upon seeing her was: *My god, she's THAT Yvonne.*

Before he could process this development further, Theia continued, "Yvonne, would you please show the tragedy that is my poor Aria to this detective, Mr. de Bruijn, and the dress in the wardrobe as well. Answer any questions he may have."

Theia turned to Mrs. Stannert, almost purring. "Please, come with me to my private parlor and we'll discuss what I need from you."

De Bruijn tore his gaze from the maid in time to see Mrs. Stannert's mouth quirk. Could she be looking forward to the interaction?

She replied, "As Mr. de Bruijn so aptly put it, I am at your service, Madame."

De Bruijn watched the two imposing women walk to a curtain suspended on a side wall. Theia pulled aside the heavy fabric to reveal a door, which she opened with a key hanging from a nearby hook. While Theia was busy, Mrs. Stannert glanced at de Bruijn. He thought she actually looked triumphant. The two women entered the room beyond, and the door closed with a click.

Into the lion's den.

Yet de Bruijn had the feeling that if Theia should decide to snarl and unsheathe her claws, Mrs. Stannert would not hesitate to unfurl and snap the whip.

Salvaging his equilibrium, he returned his attention to Yvonne and pondered what to say.

She stared back at him, her cool gray eyes unreadable. Waiting.

He finally said, "So, Miss Marchal, we meet again. Would you be so kind as to show me what is left of Mrs. Drake's pet?"

Chapter Seven

Inez wondered if she had imagined it, or if there might indeed be something between de Bruijn and Mrs. Drake—or rather, Theia, as she had insisted on being called. Inez wasn't positive, but she thought she'd sensed an unspoken connection, revealed through a shared glance, quickly broken. A sudden catch in de Bruijn's breath on Theia's first appearance at the door, an inhalation that Inez felt more than heard while she had been clutching his arm.

Although Inez had known de Bruijn for nearly two months, during which they had been entrapped together in a perilous situation or two, he remained an enigma. He was the absolute epitome of equanimity. So much so, Inez often found herself itching to get a rise from him. He reminded her of a grizzly bear in the zoological displays at Woodward's Gardens, locked behind bars, looking out at the world through hooded eyes. He seemed caged by his steel grip on propriety. She longed to poke him with a stick and see if she could make him roar.

As she perched on the settee indicated by Theia, she gave the room a quick glance. Theia's private parlor was a riot of roses and songbirds embroidered on cushions and painted on wallpaper, small Louis XV-style tables, and endless chintz and folderol. Inez returned her attention to the diva with renewed interest. She could not fathom what connection the very flamboyant prima donna might have with the so-very-private private investigator. If a connection or relationship existed, why were they pretending otherwise? In Inez's experience, there was only one type of "relationship" that a married woman and a gentleman not her husband would both be anxious to conceal.

Inez pushed aside those notions, intriguing and titillating though they were. She was about to have her own tête-à-tête with Theia, and if she didn't want to be pegged as one of the diva's browbeaten minions, she would need all her wits about her.

Theia advanced from her secretary desk, holding a sheaf of papers. "Señor Rubio still has the sheet music for my upcoming performances." She said his name with as much distaste as if he were a bit of horse dung that clung to her lavender kid-leather slip-on shoes. "So, I am afraid we shall have to share my copies. At least we have the Broadwood here. You can come and practice as often as you'd like."

Inez was about to retort that as owner of a music store, of course she would have replacement sheet music. However, it occurred to her that it might not be such a bad thing to have ready access to the room where the "crime" had taken place and to the people therein. De Bruijn said he had been tasked to investigate the goings-on. So if she, Inez, were to uncover something that helped him solve the mystery…

Having de Bruijn beholden to me could be useful.

There was a good chance that some of the help, and even Theia and Miss Green, might let slip a remark they would not necessarily say in the presence of the detective. Inez knew how to make herself invisible. If that served the purpose, well then, she would put her fashionable outfits aside and return to her dark gowns. Blend into the woodwork, as it were. It might be better, tactically, to forgo challenging Theia and instead take on an agreeable aspect. At least, for now. As Inez paged through the various musical offerings, she became convinced it might be better, all around, to acquiesce whenever possible, so as to gain a longer-term advantage.

She looked up. "Of course, Madame Drake. But I will need you or Mr. Drake to alert the front desk so I am permitted the key to the room, assuming it's kept locked. Now, could we go over the dates of your performances and the venues? And do you have a set program for each?"

"But of course." Theia shifted in her chair, the fine silk rustling softly against the velvet seat. "Thank goodness the programs have been determined already, except for the one at the Melpomene, which I am working on. The first date is a few evenings out—a private gathering at the Cliff House on Christmas Eve."

"An evening event?" Inez was a little surprised. The Cliff House, although a perfectly respectable dining and drinking tourist establishment during the day, suffered from a somewhat tarnished after-dark reputation.

Theia shrugged. "I gather my husband knows the gentleman who recently bought it. Mr. Drake wants to fete business associates and decided to do so there. As part of the festivities, I am to sing for them." She sounded slightly offended, as if she suspected her spouse of putting her onstage to perform like a dancing bear.

She continued, "Graham recently became owner and publisher of *The San Francisco Times*. What he knows about running a newspaper you could fit into a thimble. However, he sees it as key to forging a future in politics. Once he makes up his mind about something, that is that. Besides, I gather expertise in the publishing field is not a prerequisite to owning a newspaper. One only needs the lucre and the intelligence to hire the experts. Here." She handed Inez several additional papers, each with a venue and time at the top and a list of musical entrées beneath. "This should give you what you need."

Inez reviewed the program even as she mentally sat back, wondering why Theia spoke so freely—and dismissively—of her husband. From what Inez had observed when Graham Drake came to the music store, the man doted upon his wife. It did not appear that the wife returned the sentiment. Why would that be? Once again, her musings flitted to de Bruijn. Once again, she pushed them aside; the singer might simply be in ill humor from the loss of her bird and dress. *Understandably so.*

Inez moved on to the next page. "After the Cliff House, you are to appear at the Melpomene Theater on December thirtieth." The Melpomene, too, didn't seem like quite the venue for someone of Theia's professional stature.

As if she could read Inez's mind, Theia sighed, a dramatic heaving of her ample bosom. "That is an obligation, for old time's sake. It is where I got my start, here in the city." She touched the carefully styled curls tangled in her pearl-drop earrings. "I owe the owner a debt for his kindness to me in those early days."

There it was again, a touch of discontent in the voice.

Theia pointed to the final sheet. "I return to the Grand on New Year's Eve."

Inez mentally marked the musical selections she knew well and weighed them against the unfamiliar ones. "Is this everything?"

"Well, everything for me," said Theia, as if that were all that mattered. She added, "You might speak with Miss Green. She may need your assistance. Unless she decides to employ Señor Rubio. I have tried to discourage her from such a move, given his choleric temperament."

Inez folded the papers into her purse. "Do you foresee any changes to the programs, aside from that for the Melpomene, which you say is still being developed? Additional appearances, however tentative, which might require my attendance? If so, please do mention them."

Theia placed one finger on the point of her chin, as if pondering, then held the finger aloft. "Of course! How could I forget? A small, informal concert, here at the Palace, for some of the ladies. How glad I am that I remembered. The day after tomorrow,

December twenty-third. In the afternoon, entertainment for a low tea. I will need you there. I have not even thought about what to sing yet. Probably Christmas carols and other tunes appropriate to the season, nothing difficult. I shall decide so we can rehearse tomorrow morning."

Inez ground her teeth into a smile. *Exactly what I thought might happen. Events not listed in the contract. I wonder if Mr. Drake knows about this "informal" concert?* "Very well. I shall look forward to tomorrow, then." She started to rise.

Theia said plaintively, "Also, I must engage a dressmaker and schedule fittings to replace the gown that was destroyed. It will have to be ready in time for my New Year's Eve appearance. Goodness, I will hardly have a moment to breathe between now and then."

"Do you have a dressmaker in mind?" Inez thought of several she had backed financially since her arrival in San Francisco. But on such short notice, would any of them be available? It was the holiday season, after all. Still, it would be a major accomplishment—and money in the bank account—of any seamstress who could perform such a feat.

"There was one I employed occasionally when I was last here. A very skilled seamstress. Quick, with clever fingers. I found her name in the city directory and have sent an urgent message to her. I hope she is available"—Theia's brows contracted—"and she has not lost her touch in pattern-making nor with a needle. After all, it *was* a long time ago."

"May I inquire as to her name?"

"Clarisse Robineau. Might you know of her?"

"What a happy coincidence! I do indeed!" exclaimed Inez, pleased. "I commissioned a walking suit from her, in gray wool, earlier this year. She is, as you say, skillful and clever, and I found her to be very prompt."

"So, you recommend her?"

"Unreservedly. She is a wonder. A true professional in her trade."

What Inez *didn't* say was that she had first met Mrs. Robineau the previous summer, when the dressmaker had approached her, looking for a modest infusion of capital to refresh and advertise her small business. Robineau was repaying the loan, little by little. Inez suspected, although Robineau did not say so, that business was still slow. Hearing Clarisse's name fall from Theia's lips, Inez seized the opportunity to steer the obviously wealthy woman the dressmaker's way.

"Excellent. I will not look any further."

It seemed the diva was willing to accept Inez's recommendation as the final word. Inez hoped her endorsement would not twist about like a serpent caught by the tail and bite her.

Theia stood, a clear signal that they were done. "I suppose I must meet with the investigator and answer any questions he might have."

Inez rose as well. "Such a terrible situation. Who on earth would do such awful things?"

Theia drew herself up. "I can't help but recall Señor Rubio's terrible rage last night." She shivered, then seemed to collect herself.

"Does he have a key to the music room?"

"He does. The hotel had several, so we let him keep one. Unfortunately, he stormed off before we could retrieve it. Graham spoke with hotel management this morning and reassured me Señor Rubio will be persona non grata, should he return. I am so glad that is over."

So, he has a key to the practice room, where the bird and gown were kept. Inez thought about the hotel: its enormous size, its many entrances and staircases. Then she thought of the destruction wreaked upon Theia's belongings—her pet bird and her exquisite dress, the very dress she had been wearing when she summarily fired Rubio—and wondered if things were truly as "over" as the diva seemed to believe.

Theia led Inez out of the private parlor, taking care to lock it behind her. In the practice room, de Bruijn was listening intently to Theia's personal maid. The maid broke off and hurried to open the door before Inez could reach it.

Theia called to Inez, "Tomorrow morning. Nine o'clock."

Inez bowed her head. "Very well." She glanced at de Bruijn and caught his flitting expression of astonishment.

Theia said in a musically sweet voice, " Mr. de Bruijn, I am at your service."

Inez rode down the elevator, questions and musical phrases running through her mind. As she exited the hotel, the outside world intruded, pushing her ruminations aside. A melee was underway, with hotel porters and watchmen surrounding a loud, incoherent drunk. Curious passersby stopped to watch, blocking her view of whoever was raising such a fuss. The voice sounded vaguely familiar, but she was not about to join the throng.

She hadn't called for a hack and had no desire to linger and flag one down. Turning her back on the tussle, she walked up New Montgomery toward Market. It was but a short walk to the store by way of Kearney. The stroll would help clear her head, help her focus on the tasks ahead. Luckily, the store was not far. She was forever grateful it was not located farther up Pine, on say, Stockton, requiring a steep uphill trudge. Her green boots were adequate to the task, provided she stepped lively across Market's cobbled street. The thoroughfare was slick with horse dung and urine, plus the other ordinary city filth.

She gripped the handle of her umbrella, glancing toward the heavens. The skies remained an innocent blue. The air, although cool, was hardly the take-your-breath-away iciness of Colorado or the Eastern Seaboard.

She sauntered along Market, past substantial stone buildings that stood as architectural assertions of commerce, civilization, and society. The multistory structures stretched skyward, as if trying to match the grandeur of the Palace Hotel now receding behind her. The holly wrapped around the lampposts and the decorations in the windows and on the doors of high-end mercantile establishments reminded Inez of the season.

San Francisco. The Paris of the West. The city of gold.

Yet, as with almost every shining dreamscape, one need only peer into the shadows to see darkness. The Barbary Coast, Chinatown, and Channel Street had areas one dare not go after nightfall. Even wandering just a block or two from the Palace onto nearby Mason Street, one caught signs of the frontier town San Francisco had once been. Damp and muddy streets instead of cobblestones, half-rotting planks instead of stylish boardwalks, tumbledown shacks instead of stately stone buildings or elaborate mansions. In humble neighborhoods, "corner groceries" sold liquor and took in bets, making more with those activities than they made selling milk and cheese. In more dank and dangerous locations lurked opium dens, houses of ill repute, and alleys where drunks and addicts hid and hooligans waited for the unwary.

It was all there, should anyone care to look.

However, most who came to the city with stars in their eyes and hope in their hearts turned their heads aside. This suited those in power who strove to present San Francisco as the premier city of the West, which it certainly was, in many respects. These same men also preferred that the dark side of the metropolis stay hidden. Thus the city herself seemed to resolutely turn her back on the destitute and desperate, shaking her skirts as if to dislodge them like so much dirt and mud clinging to her hems.

Inez reflected that she had once been one of those who felt the tug of San Francisco's siren song calling her for many years, calling her westward. And not just her, but her now-former-husband, Mark Stannert, and their business partner, Abe Jackson. The three of them had wandered westward after Mark and Inez's whirlwind courtship more than a decade ago in New York. Gamblers and occasional confidence men, Mark and Abe had not shielded her from their lifestyle, but had welcomed her into their peripatetic existence, seeing an advantage in having a "proper lady" in their ranks.

But truth be told, they had not had to twist her arm nor batter her conscience. She had been willing, even enthusiastic, to set foot upon the free-and-easy and sometimes dangerous road they had chosen to base their livelihood upon. That road, which eventually lost its luster, ended in the silver mining boomtown of Leadville, Colorado. They had planned to make their way to San Francisco, but instead they settled in Leadville to "mine the miners," the investors, the capitalists, the mine owners—any who came to the Silver Queen saloon for a drink or a game of cards. Still, Inez had yearned westward.

And now she was here, having shed her cheating husband and acquired Antonia. Like so many others in the city by the bay, she hoped to bury her past—or at least bury it deep enough so as not to taint their chances for a decent life. She was glad she had not allowed herself to be bought out of her share of the Silver Queen in the divorce agreement. After all, had she not poured her heart and soul into the saloon, making it a success, while her absent rogue of a husband was nowhere to be found?

Inez's share of the saloon's profits as an absentee co-owner was the engine that powered her ability to provide loans to local female entrepreneurs. However, should the music store fail, she would need that income for other endeavors. For one, without the music store, Carmella Donato would have no means of support—a situation Inez had promised herself and Carmella's deceased brother she would not allow to happen. In that case, she would have to use the saloon's proceeds to support herself, Antonia, and probably Carmella. Any remaining monies from that and other investments would be held hostage as collateral for a bank loan to start her own small business elsewhere, should she decide to do so.

Not a pleasant prospect.

Now that she'd had the chance to think it through, she realized her manager, Thomas Welles, was right. Being hired by the wealthy Drakes could well be the bonanza that she and the store needed.

Mulling all this over, Inez approached the busy, three-way crossing of Third, Market, and Kearney and stopped a respectable distance behind a huddle of businessmen. They all waited for the policeman directing traffic to indicate they could cross. Across Market at the little island formed by the junction of the three thoroughfares, Lotta's Fountain thrust skyward, a cast-iron symbol of actress Lotta Crabtree's love for the city that gave her a start. Inez wondered idly if the Drakes might erect a similar homage to "the Golden Songbird."

A rough hand came out of nowhere and clamped on her left arm.

Inez yelped in surprise.

"You!" roared a voice in her ear, nearly deafening her with its volume. The word was carried on a blast of sour, alcohol-laden breath.

She twisted around, umbrella already rising to smack her attacker. Señor Rubio glared at her with the bloodshot eyes of the damned.

He pulled her closer. "I saw you come out of that den of snakes."

The man who faced her bore little resemblance to the suave, debonair musician she had met the previous night at the Grand Opera House. He still wore the same evening wear, *sans* hat, but his fine tailcoat was a wrinkled, dusty mess and the small, tidy white bow tie was no longer tidy nor white. His black waistcoat was unbuttoned, and the once-starched, spotless shirtfront was stained and streaked with sweat. He reeked of cheap liquor.

She raised her voice. "Unhand me, sir!"

The nearby gentlemen turned. A policeman advanced toward her. Yet, they all seemed to move much too slowly, while Rubio's hand—strong from his vocation—twisted mercilessly.

Her muscles began to scream.

"I *know* what you are," he snarled at her, his breath foul. "I know *what* you are, and *what* you have done."

Adrenaline, electric, surged through her. Her umbrella,

sweeping up high, reversed direction. Rubio raised his own arm to block it from descending on his head, but Inez stepped into him, pushing him with her captured arm and forcing him off balance. She quickly stepped back. With an energy and vigor to match his own, she slammed the side of his face with the umbrella shaft.

He screamed, and let go.

Then, they were all upon him. The well-dressed businessmen, the policeman, even a couple of street urchins. Inez suspected the urchins had piled on, not out of noble intentions but rather to seize the opportunity to pick a few well-lined pockets.

The policeman grabbed the soused and angry musician by the collar, restraining him. The gentlemen, thus relieved of their duty, turned their attention to Inez. "Madam, are you all right? Did the ruffian hurt you?" asked one earnest older fellow, his gray burnsides aquiver on his ample jowls.

The pain in her arm had raced up to her shoulder. She shivered, not with cold or fear, but rage. "I shall be," she glared at Rubio, "once this fellow is behind bars."

"She's a monster," Rubio yelled, still struggling. "*Diablesa Loca!*"

The hovering gentlemen closed ranks protectively around her.

"Enough!" hollered the policeman. His hat had fallen off in the scuffle and his red hair was in disarray. "Off to the calaboose with you, now. Drunk and disorderly, and attacking this fine lady."

He looked around, perhaps hoping for some of his brethren to appear and help out, but none did. So, instead, he waved down an empty passing carriage. He then turned to Inez, keeping Rubio's collar twisted tight in his fist. "D'ye wish to press charges, ma'am?"

"I'll consider it." Inez nursed her arm, silently thanking the gods that it was not broken. Her other arm had just recently healed, and now, with Theia's many appearances in short order, Inez didn't want to think what would happen if she injured her arm badly enough that she had to break the contract. "May I have your name, officer, in case I decide to come to the station?"

"Officer Lynch, ma'am."

Inez's heart sank. *Oh damn. Another Lynch.*

Inez was aware the Lynches, as a family, proliferated in the police force. Additionally, a non-officer-Lynch ran a transport service she used frequently. And there was Antonia's school "situation" with the younger Lynch daughter.

Perhaps sensitive to the number of Lynches, the officer amended his introduction to: "Officer Daniel Lynch, ma'am. For the record, may I ask your name?"

Rubio, fighting for breath, managed to bark, "She's the whore of the devil."

Her patience and prudence evaporated.

Inez pushed through her circle of protectors, who were harrumphing and murmuring indignantly on her behalf, and stepped close to Rubio. "Bastard. Should you be so unwise as to attack me again, Señor Rubio, I swear I'll kill you!"

A sudden stiffening of the lawman's posture told her, too late, she had gone too far. *Better I had swooned and fainted.*

Rubio spat back, *"Vete al infierno."*

Officer Lynch addressed her. "So, you know this man."

She took a deep breath and clutched her sore arm, willing her pounding heart to decelerate. "We are acquainted. I own and manage the D & S music store. This *man*, I cannot call him a gentleman after what he has just done and said, is Mr. Luis Rubio, a local musician."

Something shifted behind the policeman's light-blue gaze. "Your name, ma'am?" His tone was a little less deferential.

There was no prevaricating now. She lifted her chin. "Mrs. Inez Stannert."

She could almost see the gears in his mind turning and then clicking into place. "Faith and... You are little Miss Antonia Gizzi's aunt?"

Inez nodded grimly. Aunt and niece. Such was the fiction

they had spun, to make their relationship less complicated for the school and in general.

Officer Lynch shook his head and then dragged his prisoner to the waiting carriage. "Well, Mr. Rubio, sir, you're off to spend one night, at the city's expense, in our least commodious and most odious accommodations. If Mrs. Stannert wishes to extend your stay, she is within her rights."

The gentlemen, as if on cue, tipped their hats to Inez. One of them added, "Sorry business. Glad you were not harmed. What happened here, in this part of town, during broad daylight, is an aberration. Although, granted, in other sections of the city—" He stopped, and exchanged glances with his colleagues. "Well, as you are a lady, I expect you would have no reason to frequent dangerous areas nor wander about on your own after dark. Therefore you have nothing to fear, aside from the occasional pickpocket at the public gardens, that is." He smiled, apparently trying to soften his admonition by passing it off as a jest.

Inez knew his warning was no joke. And she knew, from personal experience, how dangerous some of the less-desirable areas of the city were, once the sun's light was extinguished in the Pacific and night descended.

Inez thought of her Smoot pocket revolver, which had been her constant companion in Leadville and even before. It had proved its worth many times in the past. Since arriving in San Francisco, she had fallen out of the habit of securing it in pocket or purse. She determined right then and there to clean it that very evening and return it to its proper place in the hidden pockets of her skirts.

She turned to her concerned saviors and said, "Thank you, gentlemen, for your assistance and the encouraging words, which I shall turn to for reassurance."

And, if all else fails, I shall turn to my revolver.

Chapter Eight

De Bruijn watched Yvonne as she approached the birdcage. *She has changed since I last saw her. Of course, that was more than ten years ago.*

He had spoken with her only once, early in that past investigation. Yvonne Marchal had been a dancer at the Melpomene while Theia had graced the stage as a singer and actress. Soon after he had been hired to find the missing Theia Carrington, he had learned the two were confidantes. Thus it had been natural for him to approach Yvonne and ask if she knew Theia's whereabouts.

Upon meeting the dancer, de Bruijn had adjudged Yvonne, a slender wisp of a woman with white-blonde hair, to be in desperate straits. Not only had her dearest friend vanished, but she was unable to dance, having injured her ankle. He remembered visiting her in her threadbare boardinghouse room. When he entered, she had pushed the half-empty laudanum bottle beneath a shabby cushion as if afraid he might snatch it away.

When he had told her, without going into detail, of his quest to find Theia, the dull apprehension in her eyes had sparked into hope. After that, she had been anxious to tell him anything that would lead to her missing friend. "I fear some misfortune has befallen her," she'd confided. "She would not leave without telling me otherwise." Her answers to his questions, along with information he had gathered elsewhere, helped him break the case.

He recalled the shape of those events as he watched Yvonne, no longer slender and young, but solid and middle-aged, remove the birdcage cover and unlatch the cage door. He felt certain Theia had prepared her for his visit, for she had shown not the least surprise in seeing him again. Nor had she responded to his acknowledgement of their shared history.

Yvonne said, "Poor little thing. It's not as if it did anything other than sing for the pure joy of being alive." She slid her hands into her apron pockets. "In there." She couldn't have made her reluctance to handle what was inside the cage any clearer if she had shouted.

De Bruijn peered into the cage. On the bottom was a small lump, swaddled in a linen handkerchief. He removed and pocketed his gloves, picked up the bundle, and lifted the little shroud. The dead songbird, a flattened, broken mess of bloody yellow feathers, lay on its side, tiny claws curled, eyes dull and dry. It looked to de Bruijn as if the bird's head had been wrenched around and its body crushed.

Surely, the bird would have made some sound. No living creature, however small, would endure such treatment without a fight, given half a chance.

He rewrapped the body, noticing the initials *TCD* embroidered in white in one corner of the handkerchief. *Theia's.* He put the bird back in the cage before addressing Yvonne, who lingered nearby.

"So, the bird was found not in the cage, but in a wardrobe?"

She nodded and covered the cage. "I was the one who opened the armoire door and found the gown. I did not know the bird was there as well."

She walked over to one of several large wardrobes, opened the double doors, and stood aside. He examined the polished floorboards as he approached the cupboard. No sign of where the bird met its demise. Of course, Graham had said that they cleaned up.

Inside the hanging cupboard, a pile of gold-and-silver fabric lay crumpled on the floor.

Yvonne murmured, "*C'est très terrible, non?* Who would do such things?"

De Bruijn leaned over to peer closer at the gown. He found himself more reluctant to handle the dress than the murdered bird. He glanced at Yvonne. "I would like to see the dress as a whole, to better assess the damage. Would you please straighten it out on the floor?"

She hesitated, then gingerly picked through the folds before drawing out the shoulders of the garment. Backing up, she pulled out the length of it.

The gown took shape: small sleeves, a low décolletage, lace down the front.

He could imagine how Theia looked onstage, draped in such finery. And how, when she sang, the material would have reflected the richness and brilliance of her voice. *She would bring strong men to their knees.*

He shook his head. He had to focus, not allow his judgment and perceptions to be clouded by past emotions and memories.

Yvonne finished arranging the dress and stood back. One sleeve was almost ripped free, hanging by a few threads. The lace on the torn bodice had a few spots of blood and a distinct smudge over the heart. He guessed that might be where the crushed body of the bird had been placed. The skirts showed some tiny reddish-brown speckles as well.

"Would you please turn the dress over?" he asked.

Yvonne wrinkled her nose but complied.

The reverse had a lace-trimmed train and was embellished with the various draperies and flounceries which fashion seemed to have decreed were feminine necessities. His gaze traveled down a line of tiny silver-gold buttons holding the back seam closed. *Women and their clothes; the fastenings are so complicated. I don't know how they get in and out of them without help.*

The buttons glimmered and winked at him with a metallic sheen. He imagined how they would catch the light as Theia moved, directing the viewer's gaze from the nape of her elegant neck, down the arch of her back to—

He cut off that train of thought through sheer force of will and continued his inspection of the dress. The material here had also been slashed, but not as badly as the front. The lace at the bottom of the train was torn. There were no bloodstains, except for a small smear high on the skirts.

He looked closer.

It almost appeared as if someone had wiped their hands on the fabric.

A small sound caused him to look up. Yvonne stared down at the gown, the fingers of one hand spread wide over her heart.

"Miss Marchal? Is something wrong?"

Her hand abandoned its protective post to dig in an apron pocket, eventually pulling out a handkerchief. "Pardon, Monsieur de Bruijn. This is the first time the dress is out and I see it all. I don't understand how..." She pressed the handkerchief to her lips and finally finished with "Madame's favorite gown. Her beloved pet."

Right then, her aspect reminded him of the Melpomene dancer he had first met years ago: alone, bewildered by events she did not understand.

"That is why Mr. Drake hired me, Miss Marchal," he said gently. "I am here to find out who did these terrible things, and how and why."

She nodded and focused on her handkerchief, folding it into halves and then quarters before depositing it back in her apron pocket.

Not wanting to distress her further, he himself turned the

dress over again to the more damaged side. He bent down to examine the shredded material, curious as to the instrument of destruction. He guessed a knife was used, or perhaps shears, with one blade used in a knife-like fashion. There were places where the metallic threads had caught and snagged. The sleeve had separated where it joined the dress, as if the attacker had tried to rip it off. De Bruijn wondered if the attacker was envisioning Theia in the dress as he—or she—destroyed it.

He straightened up and surveyed the room, trying to place the location of the wardrobe and cage in perspective. Both were on the far side, away from the hall door and closer to the bank of bay windows. They were not adjacent to the interior doors which led to other rooms in the suite.

Aware that time was slipping away, he turned to Yvonne. "I have a few questions for you now. I may have others later."

"Of course, Monsieur de Bruijn." She hesitated, then blurted out, "When we talked all those years ago, you had many questions then too."

"So you remember me."

"Remember you? And the Melpomene? But of course." She lowered her voice. "It was long ago, Monsieur. Much has changed. We do not speak of those times. Ever. To anyone."

He nodded and wondered how much she remembered. How much she knew. And if she knew what had transpired between him and Theia back then. "Were you here last night?"

"Of course." She had reverted to being polite and distant, as if they spoke of nothing more consequential than the weather. He realized the momentary breach in the wall around her emotions had been repaired.

"I understand the bird accompanied Mrs. Drake to the theater and was brought back here separately. Were you here when the birdcage was delivered?"

She raised pale, nearly invisible eyebrows. "I was at the theater with Madame Drake. I always go with her when she is to sing—to do her hair, make her tea, help her prepare. So, no. I was not here. I only saw the cage, covered, when we came back."

"Did anyone check the bird upon returning?"

"Not that I know." She looked toward the cage. "As I said, the cage was covered. No one is allowed to touch the cage when it is covered. Madame's orders. She does not like her pet to be disturbed when it is resting."

"What about the dress, then. Did you place it in the wardrobe?"

"That is where the dress is stored."

"Did you put it there last night?" he persisted.

She hesitated. "I . . . was dismissed. Before her evening toilette was complete."

"Who dismissed you?"

"Monsieur Drake."

"Why?"

A longer pause. "It is not my place to say. You should ask Madame and Monsieur."

The tightness around her mouth told him he would get no further information in that direction. So he went in another. "How is the suite arranged? Where do the doors lead?"

The tension in her face ebbed. She gestured to the door Theia and Mrs. Stannert had taken, hidden behind the curtain. "Madame's parlor is beyond that door. Beyond that is her boudoir, and then Monsieur's rooms. Each private parlor has a door to the corridor, of course."

She did not specify Graham Drake's rooms—how many or what kind—but de Bruijn decided he could ask Graham directly. His gaze traveled down the length of the practice room, past the three bay windows facing San Francisco's busy Market Street, to the door on the far side. "Does that door connect to the suite as well?"

"It leads to my room." Her voice turned frosty, almost as if she were afraid he would ask to go inside.

That arrangement was expected. The personal maids, valets,

and other staff of guests usually stayed in nearby rooms. "Did you hear anything last night, after you retired?"

"No."

The word was abrupt and dismissive, just short of insolent. Perhaps realizing how she sounded, she continued in a softened tone. "Madame and Monsieur were still here when I was dismissed. As was Miss Green and"—she cleared her throat—"Monsieur Rubio. He is…was…Madame's accompanist. The conversation became loud. I was released from my evening duties."

She hurried on, as if to head off further questions. "As for the conversation, ask Madame or Monsieur. From my room, I heard voices but did not hear words. Nor did I wish to."

The door to Theia's private quarters opened and Mrs. Stannert and Theia emerged. Mrs. Stannert wore a polite, bland expression that nonetheless had a cat-that-ate-the-canary cast to it. De Bruijn was curious whether she had picked up anything useful during the meeting. Theia would no doubt be more at ease with the woman, whom she now employed. He wondered how the singer would receive him and his questions, whether she would be less forthcoming with him.

He addressed Yvonne. "Thank you. You have been most helpful."

The maid winced, but all she said was "*Certainement*, Monsieur de Bruijn. Please, excuse me." She went to open the hallway door for Mrs. Stannert.

Theia stopped partway across the room and called after Inez, "Tomorrow morning. Nine o'clock."

"Very well." Mrs. Stannert inclined her head as if she were no better than a chambermaid.

So soon? He supposed he shouldn't be surprised that Mrs. Stannert was jumping into her role so quickly and obediently, but he was. Then again, she could dissemble with the best when she deemed it necessary.

Theia faced him and said, "I am at your service, Mr. de Bruijn, should you have any questions for me."

"Indeed I do, Mrs. Drake." He looked about the voluminous but cluttered room at the various clusters of chairs and settees, trying to decide where it would be best to talk with her. Someplace away from Yvonne, who hovered nearby, and the two chambermaids—one who had, all this time, been assiduously dusting the many surfaces and objects overwhelming the tables and the other who stayed busy applying a carpet sweeper to the Oriental rugs spread throughout. He searched in vain for some nook that would be private but still public.

"Well then." Theia swept toward her private parlor. Yvonne followed like a pale shadow.

"Madame, wouldn't you prefer…?" He indicated two chairs by the fireplace.

"We shall be more comfortable in my parlor."

There was nothing to do but comply. Yvonne opened the door for them and made as if to enter, but Theia stopped her. "I know you have duties to perform. And Miss Green will return shortly. Please let her in, when she does. I imagine Mr. de Bruijn will want to speak with her."

Yvonne, reluctance in every word, said, "As you wish, Madame," and closed the door, leaving the two women alone.

Theia took a chair and pointed to another facing hers. "If you would."

He settled himself, feeling anything but. His unease spiked when, without warning, she slid from her chair to her knees on the floor and grasped his hands in hers.

"Wolter, can you ever forgive me, for the past? For what I did to you?"

"Madame Drake," was all he could manage to say.

"I know I treated you abominably. Used you. But I was desperate. Any woman would be, in my situation. I hope you can forgive me and we can agree to let bygones be bygones."

The warmth of her bare hands seemed to sear his flesh. He could no longer push away the memories. Not with her extraordinary eyes gazing up at him, her voice winding around him, her beautiful face, imploring.

As if it were yesterday, he remembered: The owner of San Francisco's Melpomene Theater, sweating from fear of financial ruin and discovery by his wife, had hired de Bruijn to track down his stolen funds, along with the variety hall singer-actress who had enchanted so many—including the owner. Unfortunately, this singer had also magicked the previous month's sizable revenues from his office safe and disappeared.

Yes, the Golden Songbird had flown, her pockets and carpet-bags well-lined with ill-gotten gains. Armed with what Yvonne and others had told him, de Bruijn had headed east toward the Sierras and caught up with Theia Carrington, as she was then, in a Sacramento opera house. He'd seen her sing onstage and, for one of the few times in his life, had lost his heart.

But not his wits.

At least, not entirely.

He had returned to the city with Theia and the stolen funds. On the way back, she had begged, pleaded, and employed the usual feminine weapons, not realizing there was little more she could do to wound him. He was already smitten, but he was also bound by duty. However, all his determination to "do the right thing" had been for naught. For, once the gold was back in the hands of the Melpomene's owner, the man had no desire to press charges against Theia. "If the missus finds out," he'd lamented, "I'll be good as dead anyway. Let her go."

It wasn't right.

He should have handed Theia over to the police.

But even if he had, the client would not have pressed charges and would have denied anything had been stolen.

What possible good could have come of it? Theia had sworn, up and down, she had not planned the theft. She had merely yielded to a momentary temptation, the open invitation of a safe door, carelessly left ajar. She would never do it again, she said. She had learned her lesson.

So, against his better judgment, he'd told her she was free to go.

But Theia had not left. Not immediately.

After her freedom had been handed to her, there had been one night. And then, she and Yvonne had vanished. From San Francisco. From his life.

Until now.

De Bruijn stood to help her back into her chair. "Mrs. Drake, the circumstances of which you speak were long ago."

She didn't stand or release his hands, but hope colored the desperation in her voice when she said, "Yes! Yes! Long ago. And I must tell you, my husband knows nothing of what transpired, of my fatal moral weakness. Yvonne and I, we agreed to never speak of it. That the Melpomene gave me my start, I cannot deny. But my transgressions, the pain I caused you—"

"I see no reason to mention the past to your husband or anyone else," de Bruijn interrupted, growing increasingly uncomfortable with her protestations and apologies, and above all with the sensation of her fingers on his. "As you say, let us agree to let bygones be bygones, and focus on the present situation."

Theia sighed with relief and said, "Thank you, Wolter. Or rather, Mr. de Bruijn." She allowed him to guide her into her chair, where she relinquished her clasp.

He sought to steer the conversation to safer ground. "As you know, I have been hired by your husband to find the person who destroyed your pet bird and your gown. So, perhaps we can start with the events of last evening." He sat down, preparing to listen.

Theia folded her hands in her lap. "What is there to say? I performed at the Grand Opera House last night. Once the performance was over, I sent Aria in his cage back with the servant we hired from the Palace. I returned from the theater sometime later with my husband, Miss Green, and Yvonne. We were all in the music room while Mr. Drake went over the results of the performance with me. There was a pounding at the door, and Mr. Rubio just walked in! It all became very horrible at that point. He accused me and threatened me. Graham ordered him out. And when he wouldn't go, Graham threw him bodily out of the room." She shuddered. "My husband can be so…physical, sometimes. It's frightening."

"What then?"

"Well, I was very upset. I had my tea with honey and a sleeping draught waiting for me, so I drank it and retired."

"What about Yvonne? And Miss Green?"

"They were very upset too. Yvonne was dismissed at the first sign of trouble. Miss Green stayed with us until we were certain Mr. Rubio was gone. Oh, it was awful! Graham escorted her to her room, just to be sure she would be safe."

"Where is Miss Green's room?" He realized he did not know.

"Just beyond Yvonne's room. There is a connecting door. That way, if Julia needs help, Yvonne is right there."

Unless she is attending you, de Bruijn thought. Still, modern young women could be quite independent, so having a room to herself would not be an issue. Especially with the speaking tubes available, in case of distress.

"Did you check your bird before you retired?"

"No, the cage was covered, and I…I didn't want to wake dear Aria." Her voice became tearful. Her eyes filled. "My poor little songbird. I should have looked." The tears spilled out, and she pulled a lace handkerchief from her sleeve.

Waiting for the sobs to subside, de Bruijn observed that her dainty linen square was not up to the task, so offered his own more substantial handkerchief. He never understood how people became so attached to animals, but who was he to judge the depths of her sorrow? Although those sobs had a distinctly theatrical air. He chided himself for being cold, and said, "I am sorry for your loss. And now, forgive me, but I must ask. Your dress. Did Yvonne put it in the wardrobe?"

She shook her head. "I did not call Yvonne back after the uproar. I took care of it myself."

"You put it away, then?"

"No. I draped it over a chair for Yvonne to handle in the morning."

De Bruijn tried to call up the room with all the scattered chairs and seating arrangements. "Do you mean the chair against the wall, close to the wardrobe?"

She looked at him as if he were a simpleton. "Of course."

That meant whoever came in didn't need to know where the gown was stored. It would have been lying where anyone could see it, provided there was light to see it in.

Another question: "Were the drapes open?"

"They were when I came in here."

"Did you hear anything last night after you left the music room?"

"Nothing. I drank my tea, went to sleep, and didn't wake until morning." She broke down again. "Who wishes to destroy me? That dress is, was, my signature gown. I cannot return to the Grand without a replacement. My final appearance is scheduled there New Year's Eve. Now, I shall have to have another made, in no time at all. And poor Aria. I wish I had lifted the cover and taken him out when I came back to the room." She stopped, and her eyes widened. "Maybe he was already dead by then. Murdered!"

"If so, by whose hand?"

"The Palace porter who was in charge of him. The man we hired. Maybe he killed him."

Jacob, thought de Bruijn. "But why? Has he some reason to wish you ill? And do you think someone else came into the room during the night and destroyed your gown?"

"You are the investigator," she retorted. "Isn't this what you've been hired to do? Find out who did these things, or if it was more than one person? It could be. And it could have been him. You should see the way he looks at me sometimes." She shuddered.

"Where was Mr. Drake during all this time?"

She sighed, as if tired by his questions. "He accompanied Miss Green to her room. I suppose he then went down and told the hotel manager that Mr. Rubio is dangerous and should not be allowed to enter the hotel again."

"Did he return after that?"

"I don't know. If he did, he went to his rooms. Or perhaps he went the hotel bar. I have no doubt he would have wanted a drink by that time."

De Bruijn wondered briefly at the sensibilities of a man who would not return to comfort his wife after such an incident. "What did Mr. Rubio say to you?"

She waved a tired hand. "Ask my husband. I was so terrified, I cannot recall."

He stood. "I have taken enough of your time, Mrs. Drake. If I have other questions, I shall let you know."

"Thank you, Mr. de Bruijn." She offered him her hand. After some hesitation, he took it and pressed it briefly. Once released, that hand floated up to her forehead. "I need to rest now. Miss Green might be here. You should talk with her as well."

At the door, he turned. "One more question. Did you lock the music room door to the hallway?"

She looked at him oddly. "No. I did not. I assume Mr. Drake did, when he left with Miss Green. Or perhaps Yvonne came back after everyone left and locked it herself."

More questions without answers. Such was the way of investigations always went, at first.

De Bruijn let himself into the music room. Yvonne, waiting close by, pounced. "Madame must rest," she announced, almost as if she'd been listening outside the panel.

He scanned the empty room. "Miss Green isn't back?"

Her fingers already wrapped around the doorknob to Theia's private chambers, Yvonne paused. "Not yet. You could leave your card for her."

De Bruijn pulled out one of his hotel business cards and looked around for a card tray.

"It is probably best if you leave it for her at the front desk," said Yvonne primly.

He tucked the card into his jacket pocket. "I have one more question, Miss Marchal. A quick one. Did you lock the hallway door last night? Perhaps after everyone left?"

"No. As I said earlier, I was dismissed. I took a draught and slept until morning." She looked down at the doorknob. "Shall I show you out, Monsieur?"

"I can find my way," de Bruijn assured her.

Without a further word, Yvonne went to join Theia.

De Bruijn walked through the large parlor one more time, looking for anything out of the ordinary, out of place. Anything that might catch his eye.

When nothing did, he left the room, shutting the door behind him. He stood outside in the open hallway, staring past the colonnades at the open promenade across the airy space that housed the central court and circular driveway below and the leaded glass skylight above. The winter light was waning, casting the covered walkways into gloom.

I wonder...

He faced the room again, twisted the doorknob and, just as a test, pushed the door. The panel swung open without a sound onto the empty room.

In the dead of night, with an unlocked door, anyone could have done the same, gained easy entry, and walked silently across the carpeted floors, doing whatever he—or she—pleased.

Chapter Nine

The next morning at the Palace Hotel, Inez hesitated outside the door of Theia's practice room. She checked her modest pocket watch, which read five minutes to nine. Behind the door, she heard the murmur of women conversing, Theia's distinctive musical timbre guiding the flow.

Theia had said to arrive at nine o'clock for their session. Inez wondered: would arriving early be viewed with approval, as a sign of her being punctual and serious about her role as accompanist? Or viewed with suspicion as being presumptive, perhaps even intrusive?

Inez hated bowing and scraping while someone else called the shots. It was yet another reason she was happy to share ownership of the store with Miss Donato, who was content to let Inez run the show.

In this case, the show was not hers to run, but Theia's.

And Inez realized she had good reasons to settle meekly into the role of second fiddle. First, there was the money. If she could swallow her pride for a week plus a few days and do Theia's bidding, she would earn a substantial sum—far more than the store would earn over several months. Second, there was the prestige.

She would be accompanying the singer in front of many of the city's most influential, wealthy citizens. Finally, if there was any information she could gather that would help de Bruijn with his investigation…well, that was all to the best.

Beyond that, she was determined to stand apart—as much as possible—from the histrionic ups and downs of the Drakes and their entourage. *I shall keep my ears and eyes open. But I shall not let their dramas intrude on my private life nor my business.*

It was now nine o'clock. Inez tucked her pocket watch into the waistband of her plainest black outfit and tapped on the door.

One of the hotel's chambermaids cracked the door open. "Good morning, Mistress. May I tell Madame who is here?"

Theia's voice floated out. "Mrs. Stannert, is that you? Come in."

Inez entered to find Theia posed atop a dressmaker's platform, her back to the front door. She was dressed in little, aside from her unmentionables, which included a stunning corset of gold silk topped with gold lace and ribbons. Inez wondered what the response would have been if someone other than herself—say, a porter or de Bruijn—had knocked at the door.

Theia's private maid, Yvonne, was in a focused, fluid Gallic conversation with a tiny, dark-haired woman, who alternately nodded and shook her head with a *"Oui"* and then a *"Non"* and a *"Mais oui."*

Inez knew who that woman was, even though she faced away. *So, Theia brought in Clarisse Robineau after all.* Inez cleared her throat. "Madame Drake? Am I too early?"

Heads swiveled toward Inez. Clarisse stared at Inez with the despairing expression of a rabbit cornered by hounds. Yvonne's expression was unreadable, but her hands, which had been gesturing along with her speech, immediately grabbed handfuls of her apron and twisted, almost as if she were strangling something. Or someone.

Theia, her back to Inez, snapped her fingers. "My dressing gown."

Yvonne barked at the quaking chambermaid still standing by the door. "You heard Madame. Her gown. On the chair."

The chambermaid, who seemed to be assisting Yvonne as a subordinate lady's maid, scurried over to where a dove-gray shimmer of silk crepe flowed over the back of a chair. She hurried it to Theia, depositing the long length into her impatient hand.

After covering herself in its elegance, Theia tied the sash around her waist and turned to face Inez. Sinuous branches and leaves created out of pink and silver silk thread wrapped around her voluptuous figure. Silver leaves encircled the lower section of the kimono, accentuating her lower limbs, while the pink-toned, silk-embroidered bamboo foliage at shoulder level enhanced the pink flush in her cheeks and sparkle in her light eyes. Up on the pedestal, above them all, Theia dazzled. Inez could well imagine her on a stage in Europe, her feet covered with flowers thrown by enthralled throngs. A goddess in her own right.

"On time!" she exclaimed. "Excellent! I cannot abide those who say they will be here-and-there at such-and-such a time and then do not have the courtesy to honor their promises."

Inez forbore to point out it was not her who set the time of arrival, but Theia.

Yvonne helped her mistress descend from the pedestal. Theia turned to the dressmaker. "Mrs. Robineau, you have the measurements you need. You have the fabric from the original gown. A like material, gold-and-silver and of equal quality, should do. I look forward to the muslin fitting and to viewing fabric samples the day after tomorrow. Only the softest fabrics. My skin cannot handle the rougher, cheap materials. I *must* have the dress for New Year's Eve."

Clarisse bobbed her head in time to Theia's words.

Theia continued, "I remember you were a clever seamstress all those years ago. And Mrs. Stannert here vouches for your excellence in the present. I pray I made the right decision and you do not disappoint. You may go. We are done."

Inez bristled. She did not hold with treating tradesmen or tradeswomen with contempt. Was Theia always like this? If so, Inez knew she would have trouble keeping her peace.

The trapped-rabbit aura emanating from Clarisse intensified. "*Oui*, Madame," she murmured. "The *toile*, ah, the muslin fitting, as you say, and the gown, they will be ready." The dressmaker unwound the measuring tape draped around her neck and tossed a desperate glance at Inez as she retracted the tape into its sterling case. Tape measure, work apron, and a worn leather notebook went helter-skelter into a large valise.

Inez felt a pang of pity and wondered if she would regret pointing Theia in Clarisse's direction.

Yvonne glided forward, holding a well-made but well-worn black dolman and a large carpetbag, which Inez presumed held the ruined dress. The personal maid looked at Theia. "Madame, shall I accompany Mrs. Robineau to her studio? I could look at the materials she has on hand and see if any might be suitable."

"Excellent idea, Yvonne," said Theia. "It will save much tiresome to-ing and fro-ing if you identify some fabrics I might choose from. Something modish. You know my tastes."

Inez winced at the diva's tone.

While Yvonne fetched her own hat and coat, Inez glanced around, hoping to draw Theia's attention before she disparaged Clarisse any further. In the profusion of furniture, fashion, and objets d'art, Inez's gaze fell upon a familiar item perched on a pedestal beside the fireplace. "The *Langyao hong* vase!" she exclaimed, pleased to see it prominently displayed and overflowing with botanical bounty. "Mr. Drake acquired it from my store just yesterday. He picked wisely from our collection. It presents well by the hearth. And such lovely flowers."

Theia sailed toward the red vase, the loose folds of her silk kimono floating in her wake. Clarisse took that moment to escape with tiny, rapid steps and hunched shoulders. Yvonne, toting the carpetbag, kept pace with a languid stride. The chambermaid followed them, exiting and closing the door behind her, leaving Inez and Theia alone.

Theia stopped before the vase and cocked her head to one side, reminding Inez of the now-defunct pet bird. "Yes, it's extraordinary." The ceramic seemed to glow with a light all its own. The diva passed one hand over its length, a caress. She touched the petal of one vibrant rose. "Beautiful, and like the flowers within it, eternal."

Inez blinked. "They are artificial?"

"Some are wax, some are silk. I love silk." Theia allowed her fingers to drift through the dense arrangement of flowers and greenery. "Their beauty will never fade." She smiled at Inez. "Mr. Drake has promised he will give me another vase, just like this one." An identical pedestal, empty and waiting, sat on the other side of the hearth.

Inez wondered if, at that very moment, Graham Drake was perhaps at the music store, tapping at the "Closed" sign, preparing to demand that John Hee find him a twin to the rare oxblood-colored antiquity.

Theia continued, "I must have balance, you see. Harmony. It is what I strive for, in my music and my domestic life."

Inez thought this a strange comment, given how much havoc Theia seemed to create for those around her. *Perhaps that is where she finds comfort, in setting all out of balance. A strange definition of harmony.*

"Now." Theia clasped her hands together like a child, holding them under her chin and beaming at Inez. "We can begin, you and I, to create our own balance and harmony. But first"—she cast an appraising eye over Inez, head to toe—"I want to say, what you are wearing is *perfect* for our performances. With your olive complexion, dark hair, and lovely eyes…Are they green? Brown?"

"Hazel," said Inez.

"Black is a color that suits you extraordinarily well. Perhaps you might add a pair of silver earrings for our more formal appearances. Alas, I look like a ghost in black."

Inez smiled. "I have several gowns, appropriate for evening or day wear, so I will have them ready accordingly." Next to Theia, she would end up fading into the background shadows, which was, Inez suspected, exactly what the diva wanted.

"Our first performance will be easy," said Theia. "The afternoon tea here, tomorrow afternoon." She glided to the piano. Inez followed.

Theia handed her a sheaf of sheet music that was lying on the closed lid of the grand. "These are the pieces. Since most are popular Christmas carols, accomplished pianist that you are, I am certain you will have no problem following along. The pièce de résistance will, of course, be 'Ave Maria,' which you already play exquisitely. If you have suggestions for one or two additional tunes, I am willing to consider them."

Inez glanced through the music. Truthfully, she hadn't given a thought to the program but had spent the previous evening cleaning and tending to her pocket revolver. The small weapon now nestled deep in a pocket concealed in her overskirt. She considered the revolver "insurance" should Rubio suddenly appear out of nowhere in a violent temper as he had the day before.

"I have not thought on it, since I was waiting to see what you decided," said Inez sweetly. "At a glance, I agree that this musical itinerary should not present any difficulties. By the by, am I to also accompany Miss Green? Has that issue been settled, one way or another?"

Theia's mouth twisted in distaste. "She has decided to continue with Mr. Rubio. Unwise, but what is one to do? She does not listen to me nor heed my counsel. One of these modern young women who ignores advice from those who are wiser, more experienced in the ways of the world. She will find San Francisco can be a dangerous place for a headstrong woman. And to take up with Señor Rubio…"

She shook her head. The disgust settled about her, and it was as if a cloud blanked out the sun. Inez thought she detected some sorrow as well in the darkness. "I would send her away for her own good, but to where? She has nowhere to go."

Surprised to hear the soft-spoken understudy described in such a manner, Inez asked, "No family?"

"None. I took her in, encouraged her talent, treated her as if she were my own daughter. Look how she repays me." Theia turned away from Inez and moved to take her place by the piano. "We have much to do, you and I. First, we shall warm up. After that, 'Silent Night.' And then we shall revisit 'Ave Maria.' Shall we begin?"

Chapter Ten

DECEMBER 22

The winter sun was low in the sky when Inez left the Palace Hotel, arms and hands aching, head spinning. She flexed her gloved fingers, wondering how they would feel come tomorrow's event. As expected, Theia had been a stern taskmaster, going over each piece again and again until satisfied with the tempo, the tone, the legato, the phrasing.

Inez had a hard time controlling her irritation as Theia took on the tone of a teacher addressing a slow student. "Listen to the story," she urged over and over. "Not simply the notes, but the *words*." Their session had lasted seven hours, with only a short break for a small meal. Now, stomach growling, forearms complaining, and head stuffed with Theia's voice, Inez wondered how she would survive the next week and a half. She would have to guard her temper. Losing it could lead to a summary dismissal, *à la* Rubio.

When she had begun her trudge up Kearney, the sky was a wash of soft gray, the clouds a spill of pale yellow like curdled milk. By the time she reached the music store, the gray had advanced and darkened and the sun was hidden behind the forest of buildings and hills that was San Francisco. Light still shone out the display window. Glancing through the glass, Inez prayed to find the store thronged with customers. However, all she saw was Welles, behind one of the counters, conferring with a lone gentleman who faced away from her. She wondered if he was one of the penny-poor musicians who frequented their store or perhaps someone new with a comfortable bank account, looking to buy an expensive instrument for a Christmas gift.

She shook her hands to bring feeling to the fingertips, which felt simultaneously numb and tingly, then pushed the door open. The shopkeeper's bell, which really needed to be replaced, gave a sad and solitary *clunk*. As she entered, her nose was assaulted by noxious cigar fumes and a familiar, gravelly voice said, "Evening, Mrs. Stannert. Keeping late hours?"

Inez mustered a smile. "Mr. Haskell, I could ask the same of you. What brings you to our store on a non-Monday evening?"

Roger Haskell, fortyish, was publisher of *The Workingman's Voice*, a small, passionately pro-labor San Francisco newspaper. He grinned at her around his cigar and tipped his dented, ash-dusted bowler hat.

Haskell, who had a special kinship to the city's musical scene, attended the penny-ante poker games Inez hosted for a tight-knit group of musicians on Monday nights, when most theaters and musical venues were dark. During those gatherings, Inez encouraged Haskell's natural inclination to expound, as he often imparted useful bits of gossip and news about the city's arts, politics, and business scenes, especially when his pile of pennies and nickels was waxing instead of waning.

Haskell turned to Welles, and said, "And you. I was surprised to find you here so late in the day. Mrs. Stannert keeping you on the hop and from hearth and home? The missus can't be too happy about that."

Welles, who had arranged a collection of flutes on top of a glass case, responded, "The missus is more than soothed by the steady paycheck Mrs. Stannert provides. Being manager of the store pays for the groceries and rent whereas being a pianist wandering about town, hat in hand, was not nearly so satisfying to the pocketbook."

Inez walked toward the two men, eyeing the display of woodwinds. "So, Mr. Haskell, are you renouncing your exhortations to the workers of our fair city to unionize and joining the ever-growing legion of musical artists instead?"

Haskell scratched one iron-gray sideburn as he surveyed the instruments. "A nephew of mine, a lad of thirteen, is taking up the flute. Who knows where he got the notion. His father works for the government at the mint. None of the family shows a whit of interest in music. But since I'm the indulgent uncle, I thought I'd humor him. Mr. Ash is giving him lessons and suggested I get the boy an instrument for Christmas."

"Which Mr. Ash?" Inez asked. The Ash brothers—William and Walter—were flautists and reed musicians and regulars at her Monday evening gatherings.

"William." Haskell returned to his perusal of woodwinds. "He mentioned a few different ones. Which was it that he particularly pointed out?"

Welles picked up one of the slender instruments. "This. An eight-key wooden flute. Handsome piece, but older, so the price is right. The maker was George Catlin, prominent back in the day. Based on the 'simple flute' system. Good for the serious beginner, and it will put your nephew through his paces."

Turning to Inez, Welles added, "William came by earlier today with his recommendations. I'm not up to scratch on woodwinds yet." In the time since he had accepted the position as store manager, he had been diligently expanding his knowledge of other instruments, an effort that endeared him to Inez all the more.

"Sold," said Haskell. Glancing at Inez, he shifted the cigar from one side of his mouth to the other. "Besides, if the little hooligan changes his mind, I can always bring it back, right?"

"Within reason," said Inez.

"I always knew you were a reasonable woman," said Haskell.

"I have reason to question my own sanity at the moment."

Haskell raised his eyebrows, and Welles explained. "Mrs. Stannert agreed to be keyboard accompanist to a classical singer, Mrs. Theia Carrington Drake, for the holidays. I'm guessing she's finding the position more taxing than expected."

"It's certainly turning out to require more of my time than I had anticipated," Inez said dryly.

"Hmm." Haskell rocked on his heels, thoughtful. "Theia Carrington Drake, you say. The Golden Songbird? Married to Graham Drake?"

"Indeed she is."

"I'd like to hear her perform sometime."

"Well, if you want to hear her, she has two upcoming public appearances. The Melpomene on the thirtieth and the Grand on the thirty-first."

"The Melpomene. Hmm. I heard her there once when she was just Theia Carrington. A fresh, new face, with the voice of an angel and a flair for the stage. Had to be ten or more years ago. Look at her now. Quite a step up in the world."

"If you want to see her perform again, get tickets soon," Inez warned. "I understand she will be retiring at the end of the year. At least, that is what her husband said."

Haskell looked bemused. "In her salad days, Theia Carrington didn't impress me as the kind of woman to bow to the yoke of domesticity. But times change, and people with them. Maybe Drake has the magic touch—tamed and caged her, all in one."

His expression sobered. "I heard Graham Drake was in town to stay. Word is that he's busy shaking things up at *The San Francisco Times*. Sounds like he's not going to be a hands-off owner. Has his own ideas as to how a newspaper should be run and thinks he'll make a profit while turning it into a city powerhouse. Never an easy proposition, even when you know the business. And from what I understand, he doesn't know the business, nor the city."

Inez had a sudden thought. "Mr. Haskell, do you know an inkslinger named John Teague?"

"Ho!" The exclamation was expelled with a particularly nasty cloud of smoke. He pulled the cigar out of his mouth and looked at Inez curiously. "Teague doesn't exactly move in your kind of circles, Mrs. Stannert. At least, I don't think he does."

"So you do know him." Inez crossed her arms. "What's his connection to Graham Drake?"

"Where did Teague's name come up? Surely not at the opera house."

"As a matter of fact, exactly at the opera house. He was there, looking for Mr. Drake. He was, let's say, choleric. Most insistent."

"Huh. That's Teague." Haskell's attention shifted to the cigar in his hand, which he seemed to be examining intently. "It's a bit of a story, and I don't have all the details." He reinserted the cigar and pulled out his pocket watch. "I should get going. How about I tell you what I know another time? And hey, Welles, could you wrap up the flute for me? Put a bow on the case or something. I'll pick it up tomorrow afternoon."

Haskell nodded to Inez and started toward the door. Not willing to let him off so easily, Inez followed him. "One more question, Mr. Haskell. You know the undercurrents of the local music business, in some ways better than many musicians do. And you say you knew of Mrs. Drake when she was first in the city. Can you think of anyone who might wish her ill?"

He paused, one hand on the doorknob, the other straightening his lapels. "No, can't say that I do. But I can think of more than a few who wouldn't mind seeing Graham Drake take a fall." He winked at her and pulled the door open.

She grabbed the edge of the door to hold it shut until he told her more, but he slipped out and was gone.

Inez grumbled to herself. She would be at the tea tomorrow

afternoon with Theia, so would not be able to corner Haskell when he returned for the flute. Then she would be preparing for the Cliff House event. No time to go to Haskell's office and query him further. Besides, she hated to interrupt him at work. She resolved to pry information from Haskell on Monday evening, either before, after, or during the weekly card game.

Welles started to turn off the overhead gaslights in the show-room. "I can take care of closing up here. Unless you plan on spending some time in the back."

"Not tonight. I need to rest my hands, prepare for tomorrow."

Welles set aside the long-poled valve-key for extinguishing the chandelier lamps. "I meant to ask, have you done much work as an accompanist?"

Aside from the small music recitals of her youth, most of her public performances had been at the saloon. The latter usually involved taking a seat at the old upright to accompany those customers who wanted to warble mournful songs from "the Old Country" or bawdy ballads. "Very little," she said. "And nothing of this magnitude."

Welles nodded. "Okay. Here's a few tips for aching hands. Make a fist and wrap your thumb around your other fingers. Squeeze, but just to the point of tightness, not pain. Then release and stretch your fingers out and wide. Another one: hold one hand, palm down. Place your other hand beneath the fingers, then gently pull them back. Do the same for the other hand. And don't let Mrs. Drake keep you at it nonstop. Take breaks. Say you need a glass of tea, or to freshen up, or whatever ladies do."

Inez thanked him. He added, "I'll think of some more exercises tonight and let you know what I come up with."

"You've done a fair bit of this kind of work, then?"

"Oh, sure. Over the years. Not so much recently. But the issues that arise between singers and their accompanists don't vary much."

Inez said good night and stepped out onto the dark city

sidewalk. She was grateful her living quarters were above the music store and that the door to her rooms was just a few steps past the display window. Walking past the window, head bent, Inez experimented with the finger lift exercise. She was so focused on her hands that a light touch on her elbow made her yelp.

A small, hooded figure recoiled with a hop, apparently shocked in turn.

Inez's right hand slid into her pocket to clasp the grip of her pocket revolver. She stepped toward the heavily cloaked person, who retreated.

"What do you want?" Inez demanded in a threatening tone.

"M-Madame Stannert," squeaked a terrified voice.

Clarisse.

Inez withdrew her empty hand from her pocket and grabbed the tiny dressmaker's shoulder to keep the woman from falling off the boardwalk and into the gutter. "Mrs. Robineau, what is it?"

The little woman pulled her hood back. Her wide, panicked eyes looked like deep black pools under the nearby streetlamp. "Madame Stannert, I must talk with you. Now. It is *très* important. It has to do with…" Clarisse peered about, as if she were afraid someone would hear them. She then leaned forward and spoke so low that Inez had to bend over to hear her words. "…Madame Carrington Drake."

Chapter Eleven

Inez surveyed the streets. Thursday evening, not yet six o'clock but already dark. The gas streetlamp on the corner of Pine and Kearney hissed, casting yellow light over the busy intersection. Vehicular and equine traffic crowded the roads. Pedestrians hurried by, detouring from sidewalks into the gutters when those in their paths moved too slowly.

The last light inside the music store went out. The display window went dark. Welles would be exiting at any moment.

Her decision made, Inez said, "Come, we'll talk upstairs in my apartment."

Once inside the stairwell, Inez lit an oil lamp, hung her serviceable black coat on an empty peg by the door, and turned to help the dressmaker with her cloak. Clarisse shook her head, clutching the dark wool folds close around her neck.

Inez held the light high to illuminate the staircase leading to the second floor. "Upstairs then. No one will disturb us. We will have complete privacy, and you can tell me"—she almost said "what the problem is" but decided to take a more neutral approach; after all, if trouble wasn't knocking at the door, why invite it in?—"about Mrs. Drake."

Once they were inside the apartment, Inez escorted Clarisse to the small kitchen area. Right then, Inez regretted not having a parlor room to receive visitors. But after all, how many visitors had she and Antonia entertained in the seven or so months that they had lived here? None. Still, Inez registered the dressmaker's shocked expression as she surveyed the spare kitchen, devoid of any personal touches that would make the space a home.

"You *live* here, Madame Stannert?" Clarisse ventured, taking one of the two straight-backed wooden chairs at the modest-sized dining table. Inez busied herself with turning on the gaslights and coaxing a fire in the small stove so they could both have tea.

"It is convenient," said Inez, thinking the only good thing about a small stove was that it heated quickly. Luckily, there was a kettle of water on the top and tea leaves in the tin.

Clarisse seemed bewildered. "But it is so, so—" She was saved from whatever she was going to say by the earsplitting ring of church bells, calling the devout to vespers.

However, it wasn't just one house of worship sending out the call, but a veritable flock of them, all of diverse denominations. Every day, at six in the morning, noon, and six at night, they vied with each other to see which could send out the loudest, brassiest, most resonant peals. By Inez's estimation, more than a dozen churches were within ten blocks of the store. Clarisse clapped her hands over her ears, almost dislodging her small black hat.

Inez paused in the act of spooning tea into the blue spongewear teapot. "They will finish soon," she assured Clarisse.

She brought over the sugar bowl, glad to see it wasn't empty as Antonia was wont to sneak the sugar cubes. Teaspoons, napkins, teacups, and saucers followed in short order. With the final dying knell, she set the teapot on the table and settled in the opposite chair, saying, "I apologize that I cannot offer you anything to eat, but I was not expecting company."

Clarisse lowered her hands to the teacup, her fingertips dancing nervously over the exterior. "Madame Stannert. *I* apologize for interrupting your evening. But I must talk with you."

Inez poured the tea. It was somewhat weak, but she judged that Clarisse needed something to sip, something to warm her hands in those fingerless gloves. "And now, we shall talk. What is this about Mrs. Drake?"

She took a deep breath. "I must ask for another loan. An advance, so I can complete the dress for Madame Drake in time for her recital on the eve of the new year."

Inez took a sip of tea to cover her frown as she thought of her own fiscal situation: the anemic finances of the music store; her own advance from Mr. Drake, forthcoming, but not yet arrived. "Surely you are getting an advance on your work? Partial payment?"

"Oh, *oui*, yes. But it is not enough. You see," she squirmed. "I must hire another seamstress to help me with the sewing."

Inez's eyebrows shot up. "Really?" She then backtracked. "So, are you saying you have no reserve set aside for expenses? I thought your business was improving. More customers, more recommendations, and so on."

Clarisse looked embarrassed. "I made a sizable purchase of new fabrics and trimmings recently, expecting much demand in the new year, for the new styles and materials. I haven't what I need for this project." The warm tea seemed to add heat to her urgency. "Yvonne, ah, Miss Marchal, she looked at the fabrics I have now. I had hoped that the gold faille and satin cream silk might meet with approval, but Miss Marchal, she said *non*. She is certain Madame Drake will want a different fabric—both gold and silver. I have but a small sample of the one Miss Marchal approved. If Madame Drake chooses it, then I must buy it, which will mean additional outlay."

She paused. "And there is more." She twisted the cup with nervous fingers. "I meant to ask Madame Drake if she would need gloves to go with the outfit, but there was no opportunity.

Yvonne didn't know, so if I must also have a *gantière* design and make the gloves, *bon sang! Excusez-moi,* yes, business is good, but to meet Madame Drake's requirements on time, I cannot without a loan!" The tiny woman burst into tears.

Confounded, Inez handed her a cloth napkin to stem the flood. Clarisse grabbed the cloth without so much as a *merci* and dabbed at her eyes. "Why did you give her my name?" she wailed.

Inez grabbed the sugar tongs and added two sugars to her own tea. She could tell there would be no dinner tonight. It would shortly be too late to go to the boardinghouse where she had secured board for herself and Antonia, so tea and sugar would have to do.

"Clarisse, Mrs. Drake mentioned *you* to *me*. She had already sent you the note inquiring about hiring you. She told me she was a past customer of yours, from her early days in San Francisco. She asked if I knew you. Of course I said yes! She asked for my opinion of your work. I told her I found you an extraordinary seamstress and very responsive to customers."

That only brought on another freshet of tears. "She will ruin me!"

"Is it that complicated, what she wants?"

"The new dress, she wants it much as the original dress, which, although torn, I can use as a pattern. Princess style, which must be precisely fitted. There is little room for error in the measurements and fits. And in so few days! And she wants the lace from the previous gown, whatever can be reused, so I must gather new lace that will complement it. And then, perhaps gloves." Her brows drew together and her eyes narrowed. "This is why I am here. Please, I must have another loan or my reputation, my business, all will be ruined!"

Inez took a breath. "I have expenses as well right now, Clarisse." She hated to reveal even that much of her own situation to the dressmaker. Indeed, to anyone. "Can you buy the goods on credit? Promise payment to whomever you hire, once the project is done?"

Clarisse shook her head, looking guilty. "I have not told you all of my situation."

A hollow feeling grew in Inez's nearly empty stomach. She picked up her spoon and stirred her tea vigorously. "If what you have *not* told me pertains to the business at hand, then you had best tell me now. And do not leave out anything."

The dressmaker squeezed her eyes shut, as if to blot out Inez's expression. "Years ago, I was married. He, my husband, destroyed my business with his gambling and drinking. Do you know of the Dun report, Madame Stannert?"

"Of course." The R. G. Dun & Company credit reports were used widely to determine the worthiness of applicants.

She opened her eyes. "My husband ruined my record. He left me, but his debts are with me still and we are still married, although only in name. One of the wholesalers, when he refused me credit, took pity and told me what the report said about me and my business. It said I have a dissipated husband who hinders my progress and spends a great deal of my money. And then, the report said that I am a 'slow pay.' I was mortified! That is why I must pay in cash, always." She looked down at her cup of tea and said, in barely a whisper, "Why do you think I came to you, Madame Stannert, instead of a bank, to borrow? No bank would give me a loan."

And I might have not, had I known. Inez pushed the thought away.

One question remained unasked, so Inez asked it. "Given your travails and your current lack of capital and inability to gain credit, why did you accept the commission? I assume Mrs. Drake, when she was Miss Carrington, was just as exacting then as she is now. Surely you knew, or suspected, this would be a problematic venture."

Clarisse took a gulp of tea, then said, "I could not say no to her." Color flamed in her pale cheeks. Inez sensed another secret lay beneath that flush.

"Clarisse, you must tell me," she said grimly, "since it seems we are in this muddle together. Does she hold something over you?"

"You will think less of me than you do now." The tears began to well up again.

Inez put her palms on the table, as if to push herself to a stand. "Did you kill someone?"

The blunt accusation had the desired result, stopping the tears and releasing an angry protest. "You cannot believe what you say!"

"When you quaver and prevaricate, I suspect the worst. And that is the worst I can imagine. So, if you want to borrow anything from me ever again, even a penny more, you must tell me the rest." Inez did not, of course, add that she had intimate knowledge of the scars and dark wounds that resulted from the taking of human life. Such was cheap in Leadville, where a murderer was safer than a horse thief. There and elsewhere, Inez had seen how little value life had when not accompanied by wealth and power or, in the case of women, beauty and virtue.

"I will tell you." Defeat clouded her voice. "When I first met Madame Drake, who was then Mademoiselle Carrington, I was a seamstress for the dancers and singers at the Melpomene Theater. And I did work for others."

"What others?"

"Well, you see, at that time, it was different. The women who set the fashion in the city, who wanted to look like the plates in *La Mode Illustrée* and *Townsend's Monthly*. They were, they were women who..." The words seemed stuck in her throat.

And Inez saw. Or thought she did. "They were," she hesitated, searching for more delicate term than *soiled doves*, "the demimonde?"

Clarisse lifted one hand to a flushed cheek. "Back then, it was acceptable. All the women in society watched to see what they would wear. A proper woman would see them stroll through the gardens and look away, but not before noting the fabrics, the lines. They would then come to us dressmakers saying, 'Make me a dress with such-and-such and so-and-so,' and we would know which of the demimondaines she had admired. Many of us accepted them as customers. But now, if anyone were to know that I had anything to do with those women…"

Inez reflected on some of her own unsavory business dealings in Leadville. One of her fears was those arrangements would be revealed in the light of day, and the San Francisco connections and status she was slowly building in the city would vanish like fog in sunlight.

So she understood Clarisse's concerns.

"Does Mrs. Drake know of this aspect of your past?" Inez asked.

Clarisse nodded.

Inez thought of Theia's extensive wardrobe, her love of luxurious clothes and beautiful things. Then she thought of how, from her observations, the line between entertaining on the stage and entertaining in the boudoir was thin, at best.

She cleared her throat. "So. Was Miss Carrington one of those women?"

Clarisse shook her head, but Inez saw the minute hesitation.

Inez continued, "I imagine that as her dressmaker you had her confidence. She is a beautiful woman and no doubt had many admirers—admirers who indulged her fancies with the latest fashions."

"She is married now," said Clarisse, "and to a very powerful and wealthy man. She need only whisper of my past to others and I am done. What they think of her," Clarisse lifted a shoulder in resignation, "what does it matter? She is the Golden Songbird, loved by all. Anything I could say about her and those days long ago, it is just a small pebble tossed in a pond. It makes a small splash, then vanishes from sight. Whatever words fall from her lips would be heard and heeded by many. If I make this dress she desires and she finds it to her liking, she will wear it on the stage before thousands and speak favorably of me. Then the women who are wives of men like Monsieur Drake will come to me. If she does not approve, or if I fail…" She pushed away the saucer and barely touched tea. "I do not know what she will say about me then. That is why I ask for another loan."

Inez sighed inwardly. Leadville with its mineral riches and silver kings. San Francisco with its banks, stock exchange, and railroad barons. The two worlds were not that far apart. Money moved with money. Power whispered to power. Those who had both were the people who could act with impunity. Woe betide any beneath them who tried to make their fortunes in areas outside their place in the social order.

"How much do you need?"

"Two hundred dollars would be enough."

"Two hundred," said Inez bleakly, thinking of what she had in the store safe and what sat in her private bank account, the account which held the monies that flowed in and out from her personal business dealings with women such as Clarisse.

"When?" Inez asked.

"Tomorrow? I am to show the fabrics to Madame Drake the day after tomorrow, before noon, for her to decide. I must then be quick to get the materials. It is almost Christmas."

"Very well." Inez stood. Clarisse did likewise. Inez said, "Tomorrow morning, I shall be in the store office by eight o'clock. Come to the back door and we shall finalize the paperwork and the loan." Inez calculated she could provide the dressmaker with the cash from the safe, go to the bank when it opened, pull replacement funds from her private account, and return before Thomas Welles arrived to open the store.

Clarisse clasped her hands together, prayerlike. "*Merci*, Madame Stannert. I am in your debt."

Inez picked up the lamp to guide Clarisse downstairs, thinking, *Yes, you are. I truly hope you can repay me and Theia does not bring us both to ruin.*

Chapter Twelve

DECEMBER 23

The dark brought little sleep for de Bruijn. Through the small hours after midnight and on into the dawn, he roamed the enormous hotel. He spoke first with the various night managers. He moved on to interview the yawning attachés who manned the front desk; the watchmen who regularly patrolled the building, its hallways, staircases, and public places; and the porters and chambermaids who worked from dusk to daybreak. He asked them to search their memories of two nights previous, looking for any details that might shed light on the comings and goings on the second floor in the vicinity of the Drakes' suite of rooms.

In addition, he inquired if any had seen the porter Jacob Freeman during the time he had delivered the cage and later that night. Aside from the front desk, who had given him the key, none had.

De Bruijn was also curious as to who had participated in Rubio's "removal" from the Drakes' suite and if any of the night staff had, perhaps, seen him return to the premises later. Those who had been summoned to escort Rubio out of the hotel recalled that Mr. Drake and the pianist had nearly come to blows in the hallway. "We took Mr. Rubio down the rear staircase. Didn't want to disturb the guests, and he was putting up quite a fight," explained one watchman. Another added, "And he's a Rubio. So we had to be careful."

The more de Bruijn talked with the employees, the more he came to realize that Rubio was no stranger to the hotel. "He has lived here on and off, sometimes for months at a time," said Adams, one of the night managers. "He resided at the hotel early this year and left over the summer, as I recall. I heard that he'd been east. In Denver, mostly. We didn't see him again until he checked in with the Drake party." His straightforward gaze wavered. "He's never been much of a problem."

"Not *much* of a problem? So, there were times when...?" de Bruijn let the question hang.

The manager compressed his lips and his waxed mustache twitched.

"I am conducting an investigation with the blessing of your superior, Mr. Leland," said de Bruijn. "If you have doubts about confiding in me, I can ask him to speak to you personally."

"No, no," said Adams hastily. "I understand. It is just, well, you know he comes from a prominent local family. And we are bred for discretion, particularly when it comes to the hotel's guests." He used his forefinger and thumb to smooth the wings of his mustache, as if the perturbation of his mind had disarranged its linear precision.

"So, as to Señor Luis Rubio," prodded de Bruijn.

Adams glanced at his closed office door. De Bruijn thought it the unconscious gesture of someone who wanted to be sure of privacy. He then sighed and nodded.

De Bruijn nodded back, encouraging.

Adams began, "Our staff in the bar and grille know Señor Rubio's temper can get the best of him when he is drinking. They have developed techniques for stopping violence before it starts."

De Bruijn was a little surprised at the direct statement, but he decided Adams just wanted to get the unpleasantness over and done with, quickly.

"He, Señor Rubio, that is, also, on occasion..." Adams faltered, then rallied. "He has a certain allure younger women find attractive. Daughters of important guests." He shifted uncomfortably in his chair, not meeting de Bruijn's eyes. "This is also a situation we work to manage when he is a resident here. Since he has family in the city, that makes things easier in some respects, more difficult in others."

"More difficult in that...?"

"Well, they do not like to hear of his transgressions. To have his transgressions made public, even less so. So if stories start to circulate, they look for someone to blame. Someone other than one of their own, that is."

"I understand. And easier in that...?"

"His bills are always paid promptly. There is no quibbling over charges due to damages." He fiddled with a cuff link. "His relatives support his lifestyle. Indulge him. He is a musician who picks and chooses his appearances to feed his hubris." He looked up, disconcerted, as if the words had slipped out without his permission. "My opinion only. I should not have said that. It was incredibly rude and petty."

"No apology necessary," de Bruijn assured him. "Whatever you say to me is confidential. I appreciate your straightforwardness. You have had opportunity to observe him. I have yet to meet or even see him. Do you know where he is now?"

Adams shook his head. "When we had to escort him out last night, we offered to pack his rooms and forward his luggage, but he refused to tell us where he was going."

The night manager's interview proved to be the most illuminating of the many de Bruijn conducted that night.

Some of the lower-level staff provided physical descriptions matching the one given by Adams. But no one admitted to having seen Rubio after he had been loaded into a late-night hack at a back entrance. And no one claimed to know where he might have gone after leaving the hotel. His luggage had been stored for him, should he call for it.

Once the day shift arrived, de Bruijn convened with the hotel manager, Warren Leland, in the manager's office. Over cups of coffee, de Bruijn asked Leland what he knew about the incident and about Rubio himself.

Leland explained, "Mr. Adams supervised Mr. Rubio's departure after the fracas. Mr. Drake spoke to me the next morning and said in no uncertain terms that we should bar Mr. Rubio from returning to the hotel." Leland looked uncomfortable at that. "Certainly, we will honor the request while the Drakes are our guests. But Mr. Rubio has been a guest—you might say a resident—of the hotel in the past. Too, the Rubios have ties to the area that date to the days of Alta California. They still wield a certain clout today. So we must tread carefully."

"Is it possible," said de Bruijn, treading carefully himself, "that Mr. Rubio could have reentered the hotel later that night, say before daybreak?"

"It is possible," said Leland. "It was only after I arrived at the hotel that morning that I heard about the incident from Mr. Adams and Mr. Drake. I made certain that word of his status went out to the watchmen, the attachés in reception, and the other staff. When he tried to enter the hotel later that day, obviously inebriated, we stopped him. It became a public spectacle. A nasty business. It's never good when squabbles like this become public."

De Bruijn nodded, grim. *He could have returned through a different entrance, and few would have thought anything of it.*

Leland cleared his throat. "Have you spoken to the porter Jacob Freeman?"

"Not yet."

"You should, and soon. Impress upon him the gravity of his situation. I shall have to let him go if he is unable to prove his innocence. And the proof has to be ironclad. I might have to dismiss him in any case. The Drakes are convinced of his guilt and are becoming very insistent."

"I'll be sure he understands."

"Good." A knock on the door had Leland setting down his coffee and pulling out his pocket watch. "My next meeting is here. Thank you, Mr. de Bruijn, for tackling this problem. I know of no one better able to handle such delicate matters with the discretion that the hotel and its guests require. I am certain I do not need to say the sooner you can wrap up this unfortunate incident, the better it will be for all of us."

For all of us with the possible exception of Jacob Freeman. De Bruijn did not share his thought, realizing it would do no good. He nodded, put down the coffee cup, picked up his hat, and left to go in search of Freeman.

He found the porter, now relegated to the luggage rooms, where he and a host of broad-shouldered, sweating hotel workers were checking tags and moving trunks and other baggage.

They found some comparative privacy in a corner behind a wall of luggage. Freeman faced de Bruijn, arms crossed protectively. No matter what questions de Bruijn put to him, Freeman stayed adamant in his innocence. "I didn't do nothing wrong. I swear on the Good Book. On whatever you want. That bird was alive when I left him in the room."

"Was anyone in the carriage with you when you came back to the hotel with the cage?"

"No, sir."

"You took the elevator to the second floor?"

"No, sir. Took the staff stairs."

De Bruijn was afraid of that.

"Did you see anyone on the stairs?"

"No, sir."

"Did you stop and talk to anyone on your way to the room? Another porter? Another member of the staff? A guest?" *Someone, anyone, who might have heard the bird chirp or move around in the cage.*

"No, sir."

"Was anyone in the room where you left the cage?"

"No, sir."

"Did anyone see you go in or out?"

"No, sir."

De Bruijn tried a different tack. "Did you have a key to the door? Was it locked when you went to put the bird away?"

"Yes, sir. It was locked. I had a key from the office. I put the cage inside, left directly, locked the door, and returned the key."

De Bruijn made a mental note to talk to whomever was in the office that night, to see if they could tell him when the key was provided and when it was returned.

"So, you didn't look in the cage? Lift the cover?"

"No, sir."

"Did you hear the bird inside?"

"Like I told you before. I heard him move around a little. But Mrs. Drake, she was very particular about her pet. No one pulls off the cover or peeks inside but her. When I'm told to do or not do something, I follow directions."

"Can anyone vouch for your whereabouts later that night?"

He dropped his defensive pose. "What you saying? They think I did this? That I came sneaking in, while folks were sleeping, and killed the poor little mite, one of God's innocent creatures, then tore up Mrs. Drake's fancy dress? Why would I do that?"

De Bruijn lowered his voice. "I am trying to establish where everyone was that night. Whatever you can tell me about where you were from the time you took the cage at the theater to the next morning will help. If others can support what you say, all the better."

Jacob's face sagged. "After work, I went home. Just like I always do, every night. I was home sleeping until morning. My wife will tell you that."

What your wife says would be but a feather against the tonnage of Graham Drake's word, backed as it is by wealth and privilege.

Jacob's expression told de Bruijn that he might as well have said the words out loud as thought them.

"So, that's how it is? Am I going to lose my job here?"

"I am doing what I can to resolve this matter quickly," said de Bruijn, trying to inject a note of reassurance.

Freeman shook his head. "I can't believe this. I knew I should've turned the job down. When my supervisor took me to meet Mr. Drake, Mr. Drake said to him, 'Don't you have a white man who can do this?' I should've found a way out of it right then. But I thought about Christmas, how the extra money would come in handy for the family."

"Freeman!" The supervisor's voice rose above the mountains of luggage. "The time you spend jawing'll come out of your meal break!"

"I got to get back to work." Freeman took a worn, folded cap from his pocket and settled it as carefully on his head as if it were a silk top hat. "Please, you *got* to make Mr. Leland and Mr. and Mrs. Drake understand: I didn't do nothing wrong."

"I'll do my best. What's needed is proof of your innocence." De Bruijn tried to smile encouragingly, all the time thinking the odds of convincing Mr. Drake of Jacob's innocence loomed higher than the walls of trunks hemming him in.

Chapter Thirteen

Inez paused before the practice room door and gave herself a quick inspection before knocking. Hat straight. Hatpin anchored. Hair tidy, no strands loose from its knot at her nape. The cream-colored lace piecrust frill at her neck, correct and very modest. Theia had said to wear all black. If she complained, Inez was prepared to point out that the singer would not want others to think she'd hired a widow, still in weeds. Such speculation would draw attention away from the diva and to her. She was certain Theia would concur that Inez's invisibility was much preferred. Inez smoothed the fabric on her right hip. Her revolver was well-concealed in its pocket, hidden under the hip-length gathers of her overskirt. She heard murmurings inside, but none of the voices sounded like the musical overtones of the diva. Inez raised one kid-gloved hand and rapped on the door.

It opened to reveal a Palace waiter holding a bouquet of silverware in his white-gloved hand. "Madam, I do apologize, the tea is not set to begin for another hour yet."

"I am Mrs. Drake's musical accompanist." She nudged the door. "She is expecting me."

"Of course." He moved back to let her in.

Inez stepped into the room and stopped, thinking she must have made a mistake.

When Theia had told her to come to the practice room ahead of time, Inez had assumed they would rehearse a number or two, perhaps the strangely troublesome "Silent Night," and then proceed to one of the other large parlor rooms on that floor.

But no.

Instead, the entire practice room had been transformed into a grand parlor, set for an afternoon of tea and entertainment. Theia's trunks, artwork, wardrobes, dress forms, the comfortable little scattered chairs, settees, and occasional tables—all gone. The space was now occupied by a multitude of round tables, currently being carded and set by a small troupe of waiters. The grand piano remained. However, to Inez's horror, it had been relocated to one end of the room.

"Who moved the piano?" she demanded sharply.

The waiter looked about. "The staff that cleared the room earlier, I believe."

Inez cursed under her breath as she approached the instrument. She followed the curse with a prayer that whatever treatment the piano had endured had not jostled it enough that it was noticeably out of tune. Inez sat and ran through a few scales, a short passage from "Ave Maria," a handful of chords. All seemed well. She sighed with relief and rose.

Behind her a door clicked open and the diva's irritated voice floated through. "Well, where are they? I need those gloves!"

Inez turned to see the curtain covering the door jerk aside. Theia emerged from her private chambers in an elegant dove-gray gown.

Yvonne followed close behind with a pair of small scissors. "Theia, please, let me get the loose thread."

Inez glimpsed the simmering anger on the singer's face as she stopped short of the piano and turned to Yvonne, silk and satin swirling. "Where are my gloves? You must have put them away. Think!"

Yvonne glanced first at Inez, and then at the floor, embarrassed.

Theia, eyes still on Yvonne, said, "Inez. You are early."

Inez curbed her temper and her tongue. "Theia. Good afternoon. You asked me to come an hour before the reception to rehearse."

Theia flipped a bare hand dismissively. "No time. We shall manage when the time comes. Yvonne, where did you see them last?"

"The night of the Grand, Madame. You had them on here. In this room, afterwards."

Theia raised a hand to her lips, then lowered it to her throat. "But I left them with the dress on the chair. I am certain. Surely you or one of the chambermaids put them away the next morning. They must be in one of my wardrobes. Or maybe in one of my glove boxes."

All three women looked around the transformed room as Theia's words sunk in. Theia slumped onto the piano seat vacated by Inez. "They must have been put away."

"I did not see them at all, Madame. Certainly not while I was having the room readied for you, nor after we found your dress in ruins and, and…"

Theia looked up at her in horror. "Are you saying that whoever killed Aria and destroyed my gown, took my gloves? More likely they were stolen by one of the hotel chambermaids."

Yvonne hurried on. "None of the maids brought them to me and I watch them very closely when they are cleaning. As for anyone else, I cannot say. Only that I was in the room early, and I did not see them anywhere. I assumed you or perhaps Monsieur Drake had put them aside or in your private chambers."

"It is not your place to assume anything, Yvonne," snapped Theia. Then, apparently realizing Inez was still standing nearby, the diva looked over, pinning her to the wallpaper with those strange brown eyes, now blazing. "You may go. Come back at the reception hour."

It was as cold a dismissal as Inez could recall having received in a long time. However, she had no desire to be audience to Theia's outburst.

As she turned to go, she heard Yvonne say, "Perhaps the pale-gray suede, with silver thread embroidery and seed pearls?"

"Perfect!" Theia's voice noticeably brightened. "They are here? Not packed away?"

"In my rooms. I had them out, to fix a loose button."

"Yvonne, you are an angel. Bring them to my chambers and we can finish my toilette."

Back out in the hallway, Inez shook her head, thinking of Theia's volatility. She wondered how much of it was natural and whether any of it was feigned for onlookers or to gain an advantage.

There was only a short while before she had to return. On impulse, she decided to see if de Bruijn had made any progress. Besides, she wanted to tell him about her interactions with Rubio and with Clarisse.

She knocked on his door without result. Planning to leave him a message at the reception desk, she started toward the elevators. Not half a dozen steps later, de Bruijn's voice floated from behind her. "Mrs. Stannert?"

She turned. He was coming from the direction of the back staircase.

"Are you looking for me?" he asked.

"Yes. I was hoping to speak with you. I have a little time before I must be at one of Mrs. Drake's functions, a tea and recital."

"Please, come in, then."

Once they were inside and seated, she scrutinized him. His face was drawn, and he looked tired. "A busy day?" she asked.

"Much to do." He clasped his hands on the desk blotter. "You have something to tell me?"

"It's about Theia's dressmaker. And Señor Rubio." She noticed he sat up straighter at the second name.

His hands unclenched and flattened out on the blotter. "I'm listening."

Inez described her troubled conversation with Clarisse Robineau, finishing with, "It seems Mrs. Drake is not above blackmail."

He frowned. "Did Mrs. Robineau say this?"

"No, but she said Theia knew of her past, and she implied—"

"Implications are not facts. It is possible that Mrs. Robineau reads too much into Mrs. Drake's requests. Understandable, since Mrs. Robineau appears to harbor some feelings of guilt."

"And now who is reading into others' motives?" Inez saw from his expression that she had gone too far. "It's possible, of course, that you are right." She sighed. "As it is, I felt I had no choice. I could not turn her away. I gave Clarisse the additional funds she needed for Theia's dress."

He nodded. "And Mr. Rubio. You said you had some interactions with him. More than one?"

"Yes. And nothing pleasant, I assure you."

"Perhaps you could start with your first meeting. Tell me everything you can remember—words, gestures, facial expressions, actions—as well as your impressions."

"You want me to 'read into' what happened?" Inez couldn't help but be amused.

De Bruijn must have seen the humor of his request as well, for he allowed a smile to slip out. "You are an astute woman, Mrs. Stannert. I value your observations and, yes, your 'read' on what might be going on below the surface of the events."

Gratified by his interest, she rehashed the scene in the Grand Opera House when Theia had fired Rubio. Once she finished describing his attack on her outside the hotel, de Bruijn was frowning again. All he said was, "Mr. Rubio has taken a dislike to you."

"An understatement, I believe," she said dryly.

"You must be careful."

"He was arrested."

"And most likely released today. Do you know where he is now?"

"I have no idea."

The concern in his face deepened. "I have yet to meet Mr. Rubio, a task I will now make a top priority. Since I was not there to witness either event, I would like your objective opinion. Do you think he is dangerous?"

"Not to me." Inez pulled out her pocket revolver and set it carefully on the desk. "If he persists in stalking me, I am ready."

His gaze shifted to the gun. "Do you think it necessary to carry a weapon?"

"I would rather be safe than sorry."

"Do you think he is a danger to Mrs. Drake?"

"I only saw Theia interact with him that one time," Inez said. "Keep in mind, she fired him. Very unexpectedly and in public. She can be rather cruel."

"I suspect she had reason."

Inez studied him and weighed his words. *He defends her. Not once, but twice.*

"Perhaps," she said, adding, "You ask if he is dangerous. He obviously has a temper. I hazard it is worse when he drinks. That is my opinion, formed from years of observing the effects of alcohol on a variety of men."

"Leadville," he said.

"In Leadville, of course. And elsewhere. Consider, too, Mr. Drake must believe he is a threat, since he had Mr. Rubio banned from the hotel." She changed the subject. "And you? Have you made any progress?"

He dragged one hand over his face as if to erase the lines of exhaustion etched in it. "I spent the early part of the day—some of it very early—speaking with the hotel guards who were patrolling that night, and then with various hotel staff and management."

"And?"

He spread his hands, the universal gesture of futility.

"What about the porter who was taking care of the bird?"

"His name is Jacob Freeman. I spoke with him. I know him well, having worked with him in the past. I doubt he had anything to do with this. He has too much to lose by engaging in such rash actions. Besides, he is accustomed to dealing with demanding guests."

"Well, he certainly has had to put up with plenty of abuse from Theia," said Inez. "Goodness, she threw a dish at him. And it hit him in the head!"

De Bruijn glanced at the mantel clock. "When do you have to be at the tea?"

Startled, Inez looked at the time. "I'd best be going." A little disgruntled that she had not been able to worm more information from him, she stood.

He did likewise and escorted her to the door, saying, "While this case is underway, it might prove advantageous if we continue the fiction that we do not know each other."

"I agree. If we are spotted together, or someone sees me coming here, or you talking to me there, we can always put forth the explanation that you are interviewing me. It makes perfect sense, since I was there when the damage was discovered and am now employed by the Drakes in Rubio's stead." She shook her head. "All this over a bird and a dress," she mused. Then she added, "Besides, it is true, you know."

"What is?"

She lifted an eyebrow. "We don't really know each other, do we, Mr. de Bruijn?"

Chapter Fourteen

DECEMBER 23

After Mrs. Stannert departed, de Bruijn returned to his desk to pull his thoughts and notes together. He reflected that her unexpected visits often provided useful information—although they also could be disruptive to his plans and sometimes to his disposition. The quirk of eyebrow and the teasing smile that had accompanied her final comment: Had he been imagining things or had she been toying with him, like a cat with a mouse?

He dismissed the notion as entirely irrelevant and probably a fiction of his tired mind, focusing instead on what she had said about Luis Rubio. The revelation that Rubio had gone so far as to physically lay hands upon her was troubling. More than troubling. He wished fervently he had been there and that he knew where Rubio was.

De Bruijn closed his eyes to better review his conversations from earlier that day. Clearing Jacob of the crime would be difficult. He would have to have solid evidence to back up his conclusions. Particularly if the perpetrator was someone such as Rubio. Someone with connections. Someone with a champion or two waiting in the wings to push back on whatever proof was presented. Or someone with enough influence and authority to simply brush the evidence away, make it disappear, as if it never existed.

Rubio was not the only suspect populating his mental list. There was Yvonne Marchal, for instance. He had witnessed Theia's imperious treatment of the woman who was once a friend and now a servant. Was it possible that Theia had said or done something that caused Yvonne to strike back? She had access. Possibly motive.

And there was the husband, Graham Drake.

Nothing concrete pointed to him, nonetheless de Bruijn questioned Graham Drake's part in the drama. His wife did not want to quit the theater. In private she no doubt had had words with her husband about her displeasure with his mandate. Graham had let slip some of the frustration he felt toward his wife. Her demands far exceeded his very public generosity. Her impulsive nature could cause serious damage to his political ambitions. Had Theia pushed him too far?

However, Drake had hired him to investigate. Why would he do that if he was the perpetrator?

No sooner did he ask himself the question than de Bruijn answered it: if he was very clever, that is exactly what he would do. As the client, he could easily send de Bruijn hither and yon, chasing down various possible suspects, and none the wiser.

At the bottom of his list was the person everyone but de Bruijn seemed to want burdened with the crime: Jacob Freeman. There was some discord, clearly, between the porter and the Drakes, but Jacob by all accounts had behaved professionally, letting none of his ire show. That he was angry over his treatment in the affair, de Bruijn was certain. However, de Bruijn believed he knew the man well enough to determine whether he was lying. And by all he had observed, Jacob was not lying.

Finally, there were the unknowns: a stray porter or chambermaid, who perhaps saw a chance to get even with some slight or other. Graham Drake's secretary and his valet, who appeared to keep themselves scarce and far removed from Theia's orbit, focusing on serving the master only. Theater critics, hopeful impresarios—the possibilities became quixotic. One could cast a wide net and come up with all kinds of implausible suspects and scenarios.

And what of Miss Green, with whom he had yet to speak? She was one more relative unknown, but close enough to the diva to perhaps harbor resentment. Add to that, she had an ongoing connection to Rubio, since she apparently was continuing to use him as an accompanist against Mrs. Drake's wishes...

A knock on the door jolted him awake. De Bruijn realized he had dozed off in his chair. "One moment," he called out as he ran his hands over his face, seeking to scrub the sleep from his mind. He pulled a comb from the top drawer of his desk and quickly tidied his hair, beard, and mustache, then stood wearily, feeling every one of his thirty-plus years.

He was half-expecting Mr. Drake, demanding to know what progress had been made. Or perhaps Mr. Leland, wanting to know if he had spoken with Jacob. Instead, it was Miss Green, in a crimson-red wrap, holding his business card in one gloved hand and a closed, red-and-black umbrella in the other. Her hat, a towering, complicated affair of red roses, feathers, lace, and fringe, made her even taller than her natural height, so he felt a bit below her. Which might, he thought, have been the desired result.

"Hello, Mr. de..." She glanced down at the card. "Broon? I understand you wish to speak to me about the mess with the bird and the dress. I was not there when the discovery was made, so I'm not certain how much help I can be."

"Good day, Miss Green. Your pronunciation of my name is fine," de Bruijn assured her. "I am more interested at this point in events the night before, at the Grand and afterward."

"Ah! Well, I will tell you what I know." She glanced around the hallway. "Could we talk elsewhere? Perhaps we might go to the top floor and stroll around the conservatory. It's a wonderful place to walk, and I feel the need to move about. I have spent most of the day so far hiding in my rooms while Theia had everyone scurrying in circles, preparing for her special tea." She snapped the last word with scorn.

"We may speak wherever you prefer, Miss Green," he said. "So, you are not attending the event?"

Julia Green tossed her head. "Certainly not!"

De Bruijn marveled that her hatpins must be legion to keep her hat from tumbling off.

She continued, "Theia would never tolerate having me in the same room where I might steal the limelight from her."

With some difficulty, he kept his expression neutral. *This will be an interesting conversation.*

He put on his jacket, gathered his hat and gloves, and together they strolled to the elevators. In the rising room, Miss Green paced the length of the large compartment, her fingers moving restlessly from the collar of her wrap to the wide lace ties of her bonnet, to the buttons of her gloves. De Bruijn let her be. If she preferred silence in the elevator, so did he. Besides, it gave him the chance to arrange his thoughts.

Once they arrived at the top floor, Miss Green burst from the elevator, hardly giving the operator time to pull the iron gate completely open. She began to march along the carpeted arcade of the conservatory floor. De Bruijn hurried to catch up with her.

He was glad that the open halls were mostly deserted, giving them a modicum of privacy. He began, "The night in question, you were at the Grand, I understand."

"Of course. As Theia's student and understudy, I'm required to attend her performances, to help her prepare and to stand by in case she cannot continue and I must step in. However, I have come to realize that my main responsibility is to add my voice to the masses who sing the Golden Songbird's praises. Pah! I am sick of bowing and scraping to her."

De Bruijn was curious about the relationship between the

two singers—and what drove Miss Green's scorn. However, he thought it best to wait to question her on this after he had a better grasp of the events and had established a rapport with the ingénue.

Miss Green stopped her mad rush down the open hallway, placed her hands on the railing, and looked up at the roof-sized translucent skylight arcing overhead. "How sad the glass here lets in only a diffused light. I would love to look up and see the sky."

De Bruijn leaned on the railing beside her and commented, "At least we have the view below, with its constant parade of humanity." Seven floors down, two carriages had entered from New Montgomery Street and were coming along the circular interior driveway, the clip-clop of shod hooves and squeaks of wheels and springs drifting up small and tinny, like so many children's windup toys. People walking along the circular marble-tiled promenade toward the lobby entrance were small and anonymous, insignificant in the vastness of the interior space.

The ingénue glanced at the scene, shuddered, and stepped back.

De Bruijn looked at her quizzically. "Are you afraid of heights, Miss Green?"

"Of heights? Never. I love the heights, to look ever upward. However, I am afraid of depths, looking down." She hugged herself and moved to the center of the wide hall. "So, what do you want to know, Mr. de Bruijn?"

"To begin with, I am curious about Mrs. Drake's dismissal of Señor Rubio."

"She is impossible!" exploded Miss Green. "Just like the rest of them!" An elderly gentleman snoozing in a nearby rocker opened rheumy eyes, blinked at de Bruijn, and gave the furious Miss Green an admiring once-over before shutting them again.

"Perhaps we should move to the other side of the promenade, where we can speak without being overheard," said de Bruijn, thinking that Miss Green was certainly worthy of admiration. Especially now, with the color high on her cheeks, her eyes flashing, and a proud, defiant tilt to her head. Her appearance, her bearing, and even the pitch of her voice reminded him of Theia when he had first met her more than ten years ago. Theia had been thirty then. Julia Green couldn't be more than a few years past twenty.

Miss Green tossed her head again. "I don't care who hears me!" However, she walked to the other side willingly enough. She continued, "After all, how did they expect he would react to being publicly humiliated, much less here, in his home city, where he is well known and his reputation is at stake!"

"And so sudden a dismissal as well," said de Bruijn.

"There was no indication, none, that Theia found fault with him before she gave him the boot. It was a complete surprise."

"He reacted violently?"

"He reacted as any man would, who found himself unjustly replaced by a woman!"

Now that surprised him. Miss Green had been held up as a model of the modern young woman, so he hadn't expected she would bristle at having an accomplished woman such as Mrs. Stannert asked to take Rubio's place. There was something more behind Julia's indignation on Rubio's behalf, de Bruijn was certain.

"Did you return to the hotel on your own?" he asked.

"I went back in the carriage with the Drakes and Yvonne."

"How was the journey?" He was curious as to how circumspect the Drakes were with their discussions in front of Miss Green and Yvonne.

"Oh, it was vastly uncomfortable. Theia went on and on about how the audience loved her, how wonderful it was to be so appreciated, how she could be the prima donna of San Francisco." Miss Green rolled her eyes. "Since Mr. Drake announced he would enter politics and she would have to give up the stage, she has not stopped trying to change his mind."

"Hmm," he said encouragingly. "But to no avail, I gather."

"None whatsoever. At least as far as I know," she added hastily.

"Did he say much, on the ride back?"

"No. But I could tell from his face there would be trouble behind closed doors later."

De Bruijn made note of that. "You said Yvonne was in the carriage as well?"

"She was." Julia quick-stepped around a corner and proceeded along the second wall of the square promenade. Marble statues of gods and goddesses in classical poses stared solemnly down as she paraded by.

"And where did you go once you arrived at the hotel?"

"We all repaired to the music room. Usually, we go over the performance. Theia likes to hear how much the receipts pulled in, and we are all supposed to fawn over her while we drink cups of tea with honey. Good for the throat, you know. Only this time, things went awry."

"In what way?"

"Well, she had to tell Mr. Drake why Señor Rubio was not present, didn't she? He said 'Not again!' and she started talking about what a terrible accompanist Señor Rubio was, always playing too loud, upstaging her so she had to sing fortissimo, and how that would ruin her vocal cords. Then Mr. Drake said, what did it matter, she wouldn't be singing on the stage much longer, and oh! That was the wrong thing for him to say!"

Miss Green came to a full stop so abruptly that de Bruijn had to back up a few paces to stay at her side.

"What happened then?" he asked.

She took a deep breath. "Señor Rubio burst into the room. Without knocking. At that point, things definitely went fortissimo. He told Mr. Drake they had a written contract and Theia couldn't dismiss him, just like that. Theia started yelling at him, saying, oh yes, she could. Yvonne and I just stood there."

"It must have been very unpleasant," said de Bruijn.

"Extremely. Mr. Drake told Yvonne to go to her rooms, immediately."

"What did you do?"

"I—" She covered her mouth, shook her head, and dropped her hand. "I said Theia was being very unfair and cruel."

"You said that?"

She nodded. "I was angry. Theia turned on me. It was frightening. But then Mr. Drake grabbed Señor Rubio and dragged him out into the hall. The door was still open, all this time, by the way. They began to scuffle. I'm not sure if Señor Rubio tried to punch Mr. Drake. Señor Rubio is a pianist, so I don't think he would jeopardize his hands that way. But there was a lot of shouting and cursing. Theia rushed out into the hall, screaming that she would see him blacklisted forever. A couple of the hotel night watchmen rushed up and pulled Mr. Drake and Señor Rubio apart. Mr. Drake ordered Theia back into the music room and slammed the door on us."

They had made their way all around the promenade and were now standing by the elevator again. "I understand this is probably difficult for you to talk about," said de Bruijn.

"Nonsense," snapped Miss Green. "I am no shrinking violet. It is probably a good thing that Mr. Drake came back into the room, because I was ready to scratch Theia's eyes out, given what she had said to Señor Rubio. She wanted to destroy him, completely!"

"So Mr. Drake came back inside…" prompted de Bruijn.

"…And he sat Theia down in a chair. He told her he would see to it that Señor Rubio was banned from the hotel and would not bother her again. Then he walked me to my quarters." Her rapid-fire delivery of events slackened on the final sentence. She started walking again, more slowly.

"A distressing evening," de Bruijn observed. He took note of her expression, which had taken on a troubled cast, and added, "You have been very patient with me, Miss Green, and very complete in your description of events. I have just a couple more questions."

"Very well."

"Do you have any idea where Mr. Drake went after he escorted you to your rooms?"

There was a bit of silence, then she said, "Once he left, I remembered I had left my cloak in the music room. I waited a bit, then went back to fetch it. I could hear the pair of them inside, so I hesitated to knock. I didn't want to disturb them."

"Disturb who?"

She looked at him oddly. "Mr. and Mrs. Drake, of course."

And Theia told me her husband did not return.

"You heard them through the door," de Bruijn observed.

"Yes."

"They must have been talking loudly."

"They were arguing. Again. I'm not certain about what. It must have been about her continuing to sing. I heard him yell 'I forbid it!' and she screamed back 'Who are you to order me so!' He answered 'I am your husband. The man you married! And I forbid you to contact him in any way.' Then there was a loud crash. She threw something at the door, or at the wall close by."

"She threw something?"

"Oh, Theia is always doing that. You could decorate a parlor very nicely with all the statuettes, teacups, dishes, and vases she has destroyed during her fits."

"So, if you heard the object break by the door, I assume it did not hit Mr. Drake."

"She never aims at him. She wouldn't dare. In any case, that was all I heard. I decided I would retrieve my wrap on the morrow and returned to my quarters."

"Who was the *him* that Mr. Drake referred to?"

"I have no idea. Perhaps Mr. Thackery, the assistant manager of the Grand? I would not be surprised if Theia spoke to him about extending her performances, even though Mr. Drake had said absolutely not."

"Life with the Drakes must be a challenge."

"All this is just a small part of it. And Yvonne would do any-thing to protect Theia."

They had reached the snoozing elder in the rocker again, and she stopped talking. When they were well past, she continued, "It's very strange, the two of them. There are times when they act more like sisters or friends than mistress and maid. And as for Mr. Drake..." An emotion he couldn't quite identify in his tired state—fear? disgust?—twisted her mouth, then disappeared. "I suppose I should feel sorry for him. But he is really no better than her. In any case, come the first of the year, I shall shed the lot of them, and all their petty little intrigues will no longer be any of my concern."

"How so?"

She looked at him, eyes shining. "I have a position as a singer with the Grand Opera House company."

"Congratulations, Miss Green! You are making your way in the world, it seems."

"I am." She radiated joy.

"Have you told the Drakes?"

"Why bother? They have no hold on me. She will no longer be singing professionally, in any case." Miss Green spread her arms out from her sides. "The Golden Songbird's wings will be clipped. I, on the other hand, am preparing to fly." She dropped her arms back to her sides. "Now, I must be going, Mr. de Bruijn. I have rehearsal with Señor Rubio, preparing for *The Lily of Killarney*. You see, the Drakes may not like that I continue my voice work with him, but they cannot stop me."

Chapter Fifteen

DECEMBER 23

"You are on your way to see Mr. Rubio?" Suddenly, de Bruijn was no longer tired. "What a perfect coincidence. May I accompany you? I would like to talk with him, get his side of the story." He hoped she would say yes. Otherwise he would have to trail her to the location and wait for her departure so he could corner Rubio afterward. "I shall be brief and not take up your valuable practice time."

"Why, of course, Mr. de Bruijn!" As they approached the elevators, she added, "I am certain he will talk with you. It is only fair you hear of the injustices *she* has heaped upon *him*."

"Would you happen to know where he is staying?" asked de Bruijn. He twisted the bell to summon the nearest elevator.

"Señor Rubio has rooms on the second floor at the Grand Opera House." She beamed de Bruijn a smile tinged with triumph. "You see, he will also be working at the Grand come the first of the year. And that, I assure you, has nothing to do with coincidence!"

He raised his eyebrows at the "non-coincidence." He also wondered at her tone. There was something more behind it. Could it be she saw working with Rubio, against Theia's wishes, as a way to turn the tables on the diva? Or could there be something more between Miss Green and Señor Rubio than a love of music and a new employment status at the same theater?

The elevator arrived with passengers and the operator, so he decided to hold his questions. From the elevator they exited directly into the busy reception area. He suggested a carriage for the short distance, thinking the enclosure would give him the opportunity to query her further. But Miss Green said, "Oh, let's walk!" and set a brisk pace toward the exit.

Once outside, the fresh air slapped him awake like a cool, sea-scented hand on the face.

"Have you been to the Grand before?" she asked him.

"I have," he said.

She continued as if she hadn't heard him. "It's not far. On Mission, between Third and Fourth. Honestly, I don't know why Theia insisted we take a hack there for practices. It's all of a ten-minute walk. Less, if one puts a little speed into one's step."

The crowds on the sidewalks certainly didn't hinder Miss Green's speed. De Bruijn resigned himself to saving his questions for later. After all, he was about to meet the mysterious Luis Rubio. Much would become clear, he hoped, once he had a chance to question the pianist.

They entered the Grand Opera House, with its perfumed fountain in the center of the vestibule, the skylight above causing light to dance upon the waters. Miss Green paused in her flight up the stairs to the second floor to greet the opera-house assistant manager, Mr. Thackery, who shook de Bruijn's hand as thoroughly as if he was priming a pump.

"We are so delighted that Miss Green will be joining our stock company!" he enthused. "She has the potential to scale the heights of the city's operatic artistry, we have no doubt."

Miss Green cast her gaze down demurely. "Mr. Thackery, you are too kind."

De Bruijn saw she was as capable at dissembling and playing modest, switching from self-assured and forthright to shy and retiring, as the situation dictated. *Yes, she will go far, if she can play this game successfully.* She could even best Theia, he thought, if she kept her head. He suspected the Golden Songbird had become so accustomed to being the center of the universe that she could not go back to singing in the shadows, even if she had to.

Thackery wagged a playful finger at Miss Green. "You have much rehearsing to do, if you are to be ready for *The Lily of Killarney* come February."

"I will be ready." Miss Green looked at him with wide, earnest eyes.

"Of course you will." Thackery beamed at her. He switched his attention to de Bruijn, a small frown replacing his broad smile. "I hope you are not here on 'official business,' Mr. de Bruijn."

"Not at all, Mr. Thackery," de Bruijn assured him. "Nothing to do with the opera house."

"Good, good." His pop-eyed gaze slid nervously to Miss Green.

"And nothing to do with Miss Green," de Bruijn said. "Merely a tangential matter." He changed subjects to prevent further questions. "I understand you have some new artists on the second floor and a new exhibit of paintings as well."

"Oh yes!" Thackery looked enormously relieved. "Do take your time and look around. We are ever supportive of the arts here, as you know." He bowed to Miss Green. "A pleasure to see you, Miss, as always."

"As always, Mr. Thackery," she twittered.

They parted ways, Thackery heading down the stairs, Miss Green resuming her rapid ascent with de Bruijn. "You are quick on your feet, Mr. de Bruijn," she commented. "How did you know about the new exhibit?"

"The newspapers," said de Bruijn, thinking he would have to sit down with Thackery at some point and delve into the night of Theia's performance. According to Mrs. Stannert, Thackery had witnessed Rubio's humiliation and was present when the bird was put in the cage.

Miss Green fairly flew along the open hallway, de Bruijn a couple steps behind. She halted before the last door at the end of the corridor and tapped with her umbrella. She called out with a lilt in her voice, "I'm here!"

A quick tread inside, the door opened, and de Bruijn found himself face-to-face with Señor Luis Rubio at last.

On first glance, and on second glance as well, he did not look the sort of man who would get himself thrown out of a hotel or accost a woman like Mrs. Stannert on the streets. Any accosting, de Bruijn thought uncharitably, would more likely be disguised within the coils of courtship ritual and flattery. Some part of his mind whispered: *You don't even know the man, yet you judge?* He credited the upwelling of instant dislike to Leland's remark about Rubio's penchant for nubile young women. He tried to take a mental step back and simply observe without bias but found it impossible to do so.

Rubio was impeccably groomed and gleaming—his dark, silver-winged hair brushed and meticulously styled, with one curl falling across his temple. He was undeniably handsome in that dashing way that seemed to set female hearts aflutter. He looked the sort of man who would spend an inordinate amount of time in front of a mirror before presenting himself to the world at large. The smile with which he had opened the door had faded rapidly. He was now assessing the detective with an expression that echoed de Bruijn's own growing aversion.

Miss Green chattered on as if oblivious to the tension between the two men. "This is Mr. de Bruijn. He has some questions about when Theia dismissed you so rudely. This is your chance to tell him your side of things. He also wants to know more about that awful row you had with Mr. Drake in the hotel afterward."

De Bruijn stepped forward, pushing himself closer to the threshold. Rubio retreated one step, still holding onto the half-open door.

"I am investigating an incident that occurred later that night," de Bruijn said, "and speaking to everyone who had access to the music room in the Drakes' suites."

"The bird and the dress," added Miss Green. "You know. I told you about it."

Rubio's face grew darker. He took Miss Green's wrist and pulled her gently inside, blocking de Bruijn's entrance. "Investigating? Are you with the police?"

De Bruijn shook his head and prepared to present his business card. "I am a private investigator. Employed by Mr. Drake."

"Then we have nothing to say to you!" he snapped. He slammed the door in de Bruijn's face, nearly clipping him in the nose.

The temper de Bruijn thought he had tamed long ago flared up, hot and sudden. He stepped back and raised his walking cane, ready to smash the ornate door panel with the head of the stick. Then he checked himself. He stood, unmoving, willing his heart to slow to a normal pace. On the other side, he could hear their voices, muffled, but clear enough.

"Luis! Why did you do that? You have nothing to hide!" That was Miss Green.

"Did you talk to him, this private investigator?" And that was Señor Rubio.

"But of course! And why not? He only wants the truth."

"He works for the Drakes. He will not want the truth. He will only be looking to ruin whomever they have already decided is guilty. Probably me."

"No, he's not like that at all. Besides, you have done nothing wrong."

"Ah, *mi querida*." Now the fury in Rubio's voice was gone, replaced with a caress. "Say nothing more to him. It is dangerous to play this game with the Drakes and their hirelings. Let us set this quarrel aside. Come, we have much to do today."

The last sentence was barely distinguishable as they walked away from the door.

De Bruijn, loath to slink away, leaned against the nearby wall and reviewed what had just transpired and his next steps. He was tempted, now that he felt he could face the man without smashing his face in, to knock on the door and try again, firmly but politely. However, a meeting with Rubio might go better without Miss Green. He might have less reason to bluster if there was no audience. Besides, de Bruijn wanted to stay in Miss Green's good graces. The way she spoke up for him to Rubio was touching, and he sensed a possible ally in her. Keeping her on his side was worth giving a shrug now and trying again later.

At least, he now knew where Rubio lived.

De Bruijn decided to find Thackery, who was never one to hold back on gossip. He might have insights into the Drakes, as well as Rubio's firing. And perhaps insight into the nature of Señor Rubio and Miss Green's relationship.

His mind snagged on that final thought. His memory turned to her words at the hotel, along with the shine in her eyes and the softness that enveloped her face whenever she said Rubio's name. De Bruijn finally realized what he would have seen earlier, if only he hadn't been so damnably tired from being up all night and distracted by Miss Green's enthusiasm and energies. The clues were there. Her use of Rubio's given name just now, her fierce defense of him despite evidence of his temper and propensity to violence. *Miss Green and Señor Rubio. Theirs is not a simple work relationship, nor is it a simple dalliance or flirtation on her part.*

She is in love with him.

Chapter Sixteen

DECEMBER 23

After leaving de Bruijn's office, Inez hurried to the elevator, wondering as she did so whether it would be quicker to take the staircase. Luck was with her, though, as the elevator was already on its way when she twisted the bell for service. The door slid open and she joined a woman, not much over twenty by Inez's estimation, with the most marvelous hat. Inez complimented, the woman demurred, and they exchanged introductions. The young woman was Mrs. Morton Whitney-Smith by name, and recently wed, Inez surmised, given the pleasure with which she announced her married name. They exchanged pleasantries before both exiting on the second floor and turning in the same direction. "Are you attending the tea, Mrs. Stannert?" asked Mrs. Whitney-Smith, eyeing Inez's understated, dark outfit with some dubiousness.

"I am Mrs. Drake's piano accompanist," said Inez.

She actually clapped her hands. "Oh! That is marvelous! Do you give lessons?"

Pleased at her response, Inez gave the young matron one of the store's trade cards. Inez had tucked some into her purse, thinking that the design—a bluebird perched on an Oriental-style vase holding roses, ferns, and other greenery, complete with a wave of notes wrapping around into a scroll—might appeal to the ladies' sensibilities. *We might gain a little more business from this event.*

The door to the parlor was whisked open by a solemn-faced member of the hotel staff. The melody of feminine voices washed over them, punctured by the tinkling sound of silver on china.

"Mrs. Whitney-Smith and Mrs. Stannert," said Inez's companion to the attentive doorman. She turned and gave Inez a wide smile. "I would like to speak to you more about your business. So, you own a music store? *And* sell Oriental antiques? How fascinating!"

"Mrs. Whitney-Smith, so glad you are here." Theia's voice rose above the rest. She floated toward them, the dove-gray silk flowing about her, slim silver and gold bracelets banding one wrist, a silver fan dangling from the other. Her hair was done up in a complicated knot, wound in and around with small white flowers. All in all, she appeared as majestic as a queen presiding over her domain.

Theia seized the young matron's hand and drew her farther inside. "I have been so anxious to meet you, and here we are at last! My husband speaks so highly of yours. I believe you and I shall end up fast friends." She drew the young woman's arm into her own. Mrs. Whitney-Smith, apparently dazzled by Theia's warmth and welcome, did not resist. Theia continued, "Come. You are sitting at my table. I shall show you where."

Mrs. Whitney-Smith lingered, with a backward glance at Inez. Theia clapped her hand to her bosom, bracelets tinkling. "Oh! Let me have a quick word with Mrs. Stannert."

The young woman brightened, eyes focused across the room. "Of course, Mrs. Drake. I see the Misses Finsilver and Price over there by one of the windows. I shall go say hello to them. I haven't seen them since my wedding four months ago."

The moment Mrs. Whitney-Smith was out of earshot, Inez said, "So there is assigned seating? Where would you like me to sit, then?"

"Let me see." Theia glanced around the room and Inez realized, with a sting of irritation, that Theia had completely forgotten to include her in the seating arrangements.

Theia pointed, and said with relief, "The table over there has an empty chair for you."

Inez looked at the table, shoved inconspicuously in a back corner, occupied by three women dressed in black punctuated by bits of lace about their collars, heads bent toward each other. It took no great intellect to realize Theia was directing her to the private servants' table. Inez turned to Theia, already drawing a breath to offer her a piece of her mind, but Theia had drifted away, chasing after Mrs. Whitney-Smith.

"You won't get away with this," muttered Inez through her teeth. Then she tried to calm herself. *I must remember. This is all for the "greater good." After all, I have masqueraded as worse. At least no one at that table will throw a drink in my face or pull a gun on me. And I may learn a thing or two. Servants are sometimes more forthcoming with each other when their masters and mistresses are not around.*

Inez moved toward the table. The women had broken off their conversation and were watching her approach. With their small black hats trimmed modestly with tidy feathers and beads, their all-black outfits, and bright, inquisitive eyes, the three reminded her of nothing so much as a murder of crows.

Inez said demurely, "Good day to you all. I believe I have found my place." She lowered herself onto the chair. A teacup and saucer, along with a small plate of finger sandwiches—identical to the setting before each woman—was already before her. Inez looked around the room, as if agog at all the finery. "This is quite the tea, wouldn't you say?" She set her purse on her lap and pulled off her black kid gloves.

"You must be Mrs. Whitney-Smith's private maid," said the one on her right, who also appeared the oldest. "How wonderful that at least *one* of the younger set carries on with tradition. So many now just go where they will, by themselves or accompanied only by their friends, as if being married well and wealthy gives them exception from proper behavior."

Inez nodded vigorously. "I know exactly what you mean." She looked around the table. "I am Mrs. Stannert. And you?" They rapidly went around the table offering their names and the names of their august employers. Inez tucked the identities of her compatriots away for future use: Warner to the right, McLaughlin across the table, Casey to the left.

Casey, who seemed the youngest, added with a discontented Irish lilt, "This is hardly a proper low tea. Why did Mrs. Carrington Drake announce it as such in her invitations? If this was a proper low tea, there would not be tables and place cards and all this folderol. The ladies would have armchairs, with the little side tables for their cups and saucers. The hostess would hand around the cups. There would be tea, yes. But there would also be biscuits, little cakes, and rolled bread-and-butter only, not all these"—she looked down at her plate with annoyance—"little sandwiches. Sticky cakes and frostings. This is *not* a proper tea."

"And that is not the only thing that is not proper here," said Mrs. Warner. She bent her head toward Inez. The other two copied her, drawing Inez into their circle. "We were just chatting about the hostess," continued Warner. "She has quite the history."

"I understand her husband, Mr. Drake, is the publisher of a local paper. The title escapes me. But then, I'm not much of one for the papers." The lie slipped glibly from Inez's lips. "I know the missus is a singer, quite famous. But I fear I know little more." She reached for the china teapot in the center of the table and poured some into the delicate flowered cup in front of her.

Mrs. Warner, who appeared to be the ringleader, raised her own cup to her lips. McLaughlin and Casey did the same with theirs. Inez copied their movements. Warner sipped and said, "Famous, yes, but in this city not just for her singing." The three tittered, their small laughter circling the table like carrion crows sensing something delectable and decaying below.

"Well, I never!" exclaimed Inez. "What, then? I have heard nothing of her past."

"You would have needed to be in the city for many, many years to know what I am about to tell you," said Mrs. Warner. "Nowadays, with that rich, handsome husband of hers, one must be careful of what one says to whom. I heard the mister say that to my mistress, just the other day. He insisted she come to this tea and warned her to watch her tongue. So, what I am about to say stays here, amongst us at this table. It could mean my position, if it were known."

Casey, McLaughlin, and Inez nodded solemnly.

Warner continued, "The mister, mistress, and I came to San Francisco in the fifties. The mister, he was one of the lucky ones who found gold in the mountains. And what's more, he's managed to hold onto it, which not all did. Be that as it may, Miss Carrington, as she was then, sang at the Melpomene in the late sixties. This was before the Grand Opera House existed. My mistress went once or twice and I with her. The Melpomene fancied itself as one of the 'better places.' However, the women who worked there did not have high moral standards."

Inez rolled her eyes. "Actresses," she intoned. "Dancers. Singers. Those in the theater trade."

"Exactly!" piped up Miss McLaughlin excitedly.

"So," Inez prodded, "are you saying Miss Carrington was one of *those* women?"

Pinky extended, Warner placed her cup daintily on her saucer and picked up a cucumber sandwich from her plate. The others, including Inez, followed suit. "Well, I'm sure I can't say for certain. But the mistress said something about Miss Carrington and the Melpomene manager. She didn't say straight out, of course, as she is much too much the gentlewoman. But I gather there were carryings-on in that direction. Some suspected it, but not the manager's wife, apparently. And *that* was when the mister told my mistress to hold her tongue."

Silence greeted this pronouncement, and they all chewed their sandwiches thoughtfully.

Warner swallowed. "And then, just like that, Miss Carrington disappeared. The theater had to cancel all her upcoming appearances and suffered as a result. She was popular, was Miss Carrington. Such a beauty, none will deny that, and a beautiful voice." Warner picked up a cake. Everyone else at the table did the same.

Casey examined the cake between her fingers critically. "Gone all those years and then waltzes back. Bold as brass." She then muttered, "Sticky frostings. At a low tea."

Inez bit into the overly sweet cake, thinking that yes, the sticky frosting was a bother. However, she was willing to put up with it in return for the earful of gossip she was consuming while trying to keep crumbs from catching on the black wool of her bodice. "So, that was it for Miss Carrington. Gone, and now returned as Mrs. Drake, with a rich husband in tow."

"Well, she might have come back before then," said Warner. "Soon after she disappeared, couldn't have been much more than a week or two later, the butler insisted he saw her in the company of a nice-looking young foreign gentleman. How he knew the gentleman was a foreigner, he didn't say."

Now *that* gave Inez pause. She thought of de Bruijn. Nice-looking? Certainly. Young? Well, ten, twelve years ago, they were all young. Foreign? He had that "air" about him. A quaint courtesy both charming and rather Continental. And he had a name no one could pronounce.

"So, no one knew who this mysterious foreign gentleman was?" she asked.

Warner shook her head and McLaughlin did the same. Casey was busy trying to wipe the frosting from her fingers with her napkin.

"A mystery, then," said Inez.

"And not the only mystery. Back then, there were whispers that Miss Carrington had a sweetheart waiting in the Comstock silver fields. Not that it stopped her from making 'friends' here."

"Who was he, I wonder?" murmured Casey. "She wouldn't give a fig for some poor miner, I imagine. Only a wealthy man would do, I expect."

"Well, Mr. Drake made his fortune in silver," said McLaughlin, eyeing the last quarter sandwich on her plate. "Most likely it was him."

Casey sniffed. "I wonder if he knows about her past here in the city."

"And if he does know, does he care?" countered McLaughlin. "I hear he may be a bit of a blackguard himself."

Inez arched her eyebrows as high as they would go. "Is that so?"

McLaughlin nodded vigorously.

"Pray tell," nudged Inez.

"So." McLaughlin gathered herself, seeming pleased at being the center of attention. "My missus, she helps the mister when it comes to the ins and outs of business. She has a head for figures. A clever woman, my mistress. I heard her telling the mister she didn't want him to have anything to do with Mr. Drake and his business dealings. She said Mr. Drake made his fortune in Comstock silver, but there was suspicion it was not entirely on the up-and-up."

A surprised murmur rounded the table.

"She used those very words!" said McLaughlin. "And she said she thought there was stock manipulation at the heart of it. As I said, my mistress is a clever woman, and the mister listens carefully to what she says because she is invariably right."

Warner interrupted, "Well, a man and his money, who cares how he comes by it? Half the city's gentlemen play the stocks. By *my* mister's accounts, most of them lose. He says those that don't have an 'inside track' on what's on the rise and what's on the fall."

Inez and the others looked at her agape. "Well, I'm only telling you what he said," said the lady's maid defensively. "So, for Mr. Drake, that's one thing. But her, that's a different story. Mrs. Carrington Drake has him and his money, but she'll never truly be accepted."

Just then, a crystal *ting-ting-ting* drew everyone's attention to the front of the room. Theia Carrington stood by the grand piano, one graceful, gloved hand holding a goblet, the other poised with a silver spoon. "Thank you, everyone, for attending and gracing my little tea."

Inez could have sworn she heard a soft snort from Casey.

"And now," Theia continued, "to the entertainment. I have a collection of songs for the season, which I hope you will enjoy. For this, I shall need the services of my accomplished accompanist Mrs. Stannert, who is one of the most gifted pianists I have had the pleasure to meet. Mrs. Stannert, will you join me?"

Three mouths fell open and three faces flushed as Inez wiped her fingers, set her napkin by her empty plate, and picked up her purse and gloves. "Ladies, it has been a pleasure," she said to her dining companions. As she rose from her chair she added sotto voce, "As Mrs. Warner said, what was said here, at this table, goes no further."

She raised her eyes to Theia and, smiling through the polite anticipatory applause fluttering through the room, moved toward the piano and the diva.

Chapter Seventeen

DECEMBER 23

Inez left after the tea, satisfied, if not full. Her purse was empty of business trade cards, and she felt sure that at least a few of the women, or their husbands or representatives, would visit the music store in the future. Mrs. Whitney-Smith had even asked if they had another piano in stock like the one Inez had played. How soon, Inez wondered, could Welles set his hands on another Broadwood? Or perhaps he could convince Mrs. Whitney-Smith that a Steinway was just as good, if not superior.

A glance at her pocket watch reassured her that she could make suppertime at Mrs. Nolan's boardinghouse if she was quick. Inez paid Mrs. Nolan board so she did not have to subject Antonia or herself to her complete lack of cooking skills. Mrs. Nolan had received a little financial assistance from Inez at a much-needed time and was happy to keep Antonia in sourdough bread pickle-and-cheese sandwiches for midday and supply both of them with a hearty nighttime meal.

No sooner had Inez set foot in the dining room than Mrs. Nolan, who was serving, turned a disapproving eye upon her. "And where have you been keeping yourself these last few days, Mrs. Stannert?"

Mrs. Nolan was never one to mince words, which Inez found refreshing. At least, most of the time. However, having had nothing that day but a couple quarters of sandwiches and a bit of cake topped with too-sweet frosting, Inez was in no mood to be driven into guilt.

"Very busy," she said, settling at the table. "And I have missed your splendid cooking, as a result."

Somewhat mollified, Mrs. Nolan passed her the bread bowl. "You will be here tomorrow for Christmas Eve supper? It will be roast beef. And Christmas is roasted goose! No one should be supping alone on Christmas Eve or Day." She added, "Since the wee one is visiting away, if you have a guest you wish to bring in her stead, it is quite permissible. The holidays, and all."

Inez pondered, the warm, homemade sourdough enticing her with its tangy aroma. Her first thought was of de Bruijn, who would no doubt be one of those poor souls who "supped alone" on the holidays.

"Perhaps," she hedged.

The room-and-boarders—three ancient gents, two male schoolteachers, a young married couple, and two women of indeterminate middle age—turned curious gazes her way.

"And perhaps not," Inez modified, thinking de Bruijn might prefer his own company to the inquisition he'd probably face at Mrs. Nolan's table.

She added, "Christmas Day sounds lovely. I shall be otherwise engaged Christmas Eve." Theia had told Inez to arrive at the hotel mid-afternoon Christmas Eve so the party could journey to the Cliff House in the same carriage for the private dinner and performance.

Mrs. Nolan served up a substantial meal of baked ham and boiled bacon and cabbage. Inez ate while dodging intrusive questions regarding her personal life served up by the renters. One of the ancients at the table went so far as to ask, "Might your 'perhaps guest' be a person of the male persuasion, Mrs. Stannert?"

Inez chewed, swallowed, and answered, "Perhaps."

After the meal Inez escaped, thoroughly satiated, and decided to walk home to help her meal settle. It was dark by then, and she was glad for the revolver in her pocket, although she doubted she would need it in this part of town. Carriages squeaked and creaked in both directions on the street, carrying their inhabitants homeward or to some of the varied entertainments offered by the city.

One hack, instead of rolling by, slowed and matched her pace. It pulled a little way ahead, into the pool of dark between two streetlamps, and stopped at the curb.

The carriage door swung open, but no one descended. Not the rider nor the driver.

The back of Inez's neck prickled in alarm. She halted on the sidewalk and glanced around. She was the only pedestrian in sight. Her hand slithered into her pocket and curled around the grip of her small revolver as she debated. Go forward or back?

A familiar voice floated out from the carriage interior. "Mrs. Stannert, may I have a few minutes of your time?"

With a sigh she transferred her hold from the gun to her cloak lapels and approached the waiting vehicle. The driver hopped down from his perch to give her a hand up.

"Mr. de Bruijn, you gave me quite a turn just now," said Inez, once she was inside with her cloak tucked neatly about her. "Were you waiting for me all this time outside Mrs. Nolan's boardinghouse, while I had supper? You could have knocked on the door."

"I had no desire to intrude. And I knew you would come out. Eventually."

He shifted in his seat across from her. "I have some things I need to discuss with you. Is there someplace we can talk privately, away from the hotel?"

Inez thought. She would not dare suggest her rooms above the store. All it would take is one set of eyes attached to a prurient mind to set tongues a-wagging.

"My store is closed, but we could talk in the office in back," she offered. "If you want to be doubly careful, have the carriage let me off in front. Go a block or so, leave off there, and come through the alley to the back door. If you feel it necessary."

"That sounds like a good plan." He knocked on the panel at his back with his cane. The carriage squeaked to a stop and de Bruijn told the driver, "Corner of Kearney and Pine."

Once inside the music store, Inez noted Welles had managed to procure a grand piano for the showroom. She commended him silently and thought maybe she would take a turn on it once she and de Bruijn had concluded their business.

She hurried through to the office and had time to light two oil lamps before she heard a tapping at the back door. After she let de Bruijn in, they sat at the round table in the central meeting area. He removed his hat and smoothed a hand absently over his neat mustache and beard. He still looked very tired, and she hoped he had at least napped in the carriage while she wolfed down Mrs. Nolan's feast.

To get the conversation started, Inez asked, "Have you made any progress? For my part, I had a most illuminating conversation with several ladies' maids at the tea this afternoon."

"I am interested in hearing about anything you think is relevant. But first, I have an ethical issue to discuss with you."

"Ethical issue?" She was bemused. "Whatever do you mean?"

"It has to do with our sharing of information. Have I ever showed you my standard contract?"

She shrugged. "There's never been reason to."

He reached inside his sack coat, pulled out a set of folded papers, and unfolded them. He extracted one page and placed it on the table for Inez to read. "Third paragraph," he said.

She squinted at the small type, sighed, excused herself, and went into her private office to retrieve her reading spectacles. She also retrieved a bottle of brandy and two glasses.

"Would you like some?" She gestured with the glasses.

"Perhaps after we finish our business."

"As you wish. For me, it's business concurrently." Inez poured herself a measure. She took a sip, savoring the warmth and the caramel-like fruitiness, adjusted her spectacles, pulled one of the lamps a little closer, and read:

Information gathered during the investigative process and end results shall be shared periodically with the client, and only with the client, unless otherwise directed by the client to share such information with the client's designees as specifically set forth in subsection 3(a) below.

She looked at him, over her glasses. "What are you saying? That you cannot share information with me, but I am free to prattle on to you?" The pleasant fullness of the meal and glow of the alcohol fizzled. "Is our so-called collaboration to be a one-way street?"

He tapped the paper. "Please continue reading, Mrs. Stannert."

It is understood that the aforesaid stipulations shall not bar the undersigned from engaging the employment of certain qualified individuals to assist the undersigned in gathering necessary intelligence to forward the enquiry. In such cases, the undersigned may share certain aspects of the investigation and/or information that he deems necessary to assist such individuals in their assigned tasks. It is understood that the undersigned shall take into account the discretion and the reliability of such individuals so as not to jeopardize the investigation or the client...

Inez leaned back. "So. You wish to, what, hire me?"

De Bruijn took the paper back and replaced the lot inside his jacket. "Mr. Drake let this portion of the contract stand. Sometimes I have clients who, upon reading, will strike it out and insist I do everything myself." He shrugged. "That can make a case more difficult or take longer to solve. Mr. Drake hired me on the spot. I do not believe he read the contract in detail before signing. In any case, this leaves me free to hire qualified associates, at my discretion."

She repeated "You propose to *hire* me?" and gave a little laugh.

He stared at her. "As I said, I am faced with an ethical dilemma.

I believe that, between us, we can settle this matter of the dress and bird fairly quickly. Particularly if we are able to pool our knowledge and orchestrate our movements."

She shook her head. "All this for a dead pet and a dress she could replace ten times over. Doesn't it strike you as odd?"

He didn't answer.

She stared back at him, then sighed at the stubbornness lurking beneath his excessively polite exterior. "Very well," she said abruptly. "Have you a dollar?"

He frowned. She held out her hand, palm up, fingers wiggling impatiently. "Give me a dollar, Mr. de Bruijn."

He retrieved his wallet and, after some digging about, handed her a silver dollar. She held it up, saying, "Thank you for paying my fee, Mr. de Bruijn. I am at your service now."

Some of the tension left his face. "If you are at my service, Mrs. Stannert, so am I at yours. I am honored to consider you a colleague in this matter."

Mollified, she said, "So. Who should start?"

"I had an intriguing interview with Miss Green," said de Bruijn. "And, I met Mr. Rubio. At last. Not that our conversation lasted longer than half a minute."

He summarized what he'd learned from Miss Green...

About her plans to leave the Drakes at the first of the year and join the Grand's repertoire company—

"Oh, Theia won't like that at all," said Inez.

—about her assertion that Mr. Drake returned to the music room after the debacle with Rubio, and that the Drakes had a loud argument that involved broken crockery of some sort—

"I remember now, a hotel maid was cleaning up a mess by the door!" Inez exclaimed. "It looked like bits of porcelain from a small statuette or some such."

—about Miss Green's belief the couple were on the outs concerning Theia's leaving the stage, and how there was no love lost on Miss Green's part toward the Drakes or Yvonne—

"It sounds unpleasant all around," said Inez. "No wonder she's anxious to leave."

—about Rubio living on the second floor of the Grand Opera House—

"How cozy!" Inez responded sarcastically.

—and about his own suspicions regarding Miss Green and Mr. Rubio's relationship.

Inez frowned. "Really? What makes you think that?"

"After he refused to speak to me and slammed the door in my face, I heard them talking inside. He addressed her as *mi querida*—my dear."

"Did he now."

"There were other indications. I blame my lack of sleep for not realizing this earlier." He shook his head. "I shall try to talk to him another time, when Miss Green is not around. I may have better luck then."

"He is one person I hope to never see again. Now. Let me tell you about the tea."

Inez told him how the ladies' maids were convinced Theia would never be welcomed by the city's elite, and how Graham was similarly viewed. "Although, he may have an easier time of it. Where there is money, there is influence and power," said Inez. "I suspect he will be more accepted in business than she will in high society."

He frowned. "That will sit hard with her."

Inez continued, "I also heard that when she was at the Melpomene a decade or more ago, she was involved with the manager. She mysteriously disappeared, only to reappear briefly with, and I quote, 'a nice-looking young foreign gentleman.'" She watched him closely as she spoke. It was then she saw it: a sudden stillness to his posture, his eyelids gone to half-mast, as if he was bored or in contemplation.

Or hiding his thoughts from view.

She leaned forward, intrigued. Had she caught him at last? Could this be his "tell?"

She thought perhaps it was. So she pushed a little harder.

"That was you, wasn't it? Were you working on some kind of case involving her or were you and Miss Carrington…?" She let the question hang.

His eyes opened. If secrets had been swimming below their surface, they were gone from view now. "What you are asking has nothing to do with the current situation."

"I beg to differ," she countered. "If, in the past you and Theia had, let us call it, a relationship, it is bound to influence how you perceive her now and how you view events and actions surrounding her. And *everything* in this case revolves around Theia. You cannot be impartial, Mr. de Bruijn. Your past with her, whatever it entailed, will color everything you see and hear."

He shook his head and stood. "Excuse me, Mrs. Stannert, but it has been a long day."

She held up a hand. "One more tidbit, Mr. de Bruijn."

He waited, one hand gripping his cane, the other in his coat pocket. He looked ready to bolt out the door.

"Rumor had it that she had a sweetheart in the Comstock. Some of the women thought it might have been Mr. Drake. But others thought it wasn't. If there was someone else and she ended up marrying Graham Drake instead, might there be a lover spurned in her past?" She tilted her head. "Was it you?"

He pulled the brim of his bowler down a little. "Really, Mrs. Stannert. I didn't think you were the type to indulge in sentimental fiction and dime novel romances. No. I was not in that area during that time. Now, about tomorrow, before the gathering at the Cliff House. Will you be at the hotel? Or here at the store?"

Rebuffed again. But this time, at least, he had answered with a testy but blunt "No." And she believed him. She also forgave him for the snide comment about dime novels. After all, she had wanted to provoke a response from him. Besides, how could he possibly know her reading tastes ran to Shakespeare and Milton?

She said, "Tomorrow, I shall need to be at the hotel in the afternoon. We are all leaving for the Cliff House together. And you?"

"I would like to be at the Cliff House event. It is not the best of places at night. I wonder why he set the party there. Before then, if there is time, I hope to find someone who can verify that Jacob Freeman was not at the Palace after his shift ended. First, however, I must speak with Mr. Drake and get to the bottom of what happened after the altercation in the music room."

He hesitated. "Mrs. Drake has one version of events: that Mr. Drake disappeared for a drink, at the hotel or elsewhere. Miss Green has another: that he returned to the music room, where the Drakes had an energetic row. It will be interesting to see what he says. Whether his story matches one or the other or is entirely different. I would also like to speak to Mr. Rubio tomorrow, if I can. I've yet to hear his account of what happened that evening or ascertain his whereabouts that night."

"Mr. Rubio, indeed," she said dryly. "So, is he your top suspect?"

"He and..." de Bruijn hesitated again.

"Yes?"

"Mr. Drake."

"Yes!" said Inez. "I have been thinking of him too. It cannot be easy, being married to Theia. If they fought that night and he went off to drown his sorrows, I can imagine he might be capable of a bit of revenge. Too, there is Yvonne. I got a glimpse of how Theia treats her when they think no one else is nearby: a round of verbal abuse with a sudden pivot to effusive praise. I can imagine the strain, not knowing whether that raised hand will bring a slap or a caress. Who knows what resentments Yvonne is carrying and for how long this has been going on? She and Theia have been together for quite a while, it seems."

"At least twelve years. They were both employed by the Melpomene at the same time."

So you did know Theia back then! Inez quelled the spark of triumph of having extracted a tiny, inadvertent confession from de Bruijn.

"And do not forget Miss Green," she continued. "Given what

she told you, I'd say there is considerable resentment between her and Theia. Miss Green was out and about when the Drakes were fighting. What was to stop her from sneaking back into the room when all was quiet?"

"It's possible," said de Bruijn, "although I think Miss Green is unlikely. She is on the verge of a new life. Why jeopardize it?"

"Hmm. Good point. And what was it that Miss Green heard Mr. Drake say just before the vase or what-have-you hit the wall? Something like 'I forbid you to see him.' Who did he mean? The Melpomene manager, perhaps?"

De Bruijn shook his head. "Keep in mind, we only have Miss Green's interpretation of the conversation. And even if she heard correctly, how could this unnamed person relate to the destruction in the music room? I'm more interested in the timing, as to who was where that night. As for the Melpomene manager, Mrs. Drake is performing at the Melpomene in a few days. It doesn't make sense for Mr. Drake to say, 'Don't talk to him.'"

"Or perhaps he was referring to someone else from her past? Don't forget the mysterious spurned lover from the Comstock," added Inez.

De Bruijn moved toward the back door. "Good night, Mrs. Stannert."

"Oh! You almost forgot this." Inez picked up the silver dollar from the table and, holding it out, walked to de Bruijn. When he didn't move to take the coin, she boldly grabbed his gloved hand and placed the silver dollar firmly in his palm.

He looked at her, brow furrowed.

"To help pay for the carriage ride to my store. After all, it must have cost you a pretty penny, waiting out in front of Mrs. Nolan's for me to appear." She smiled. "Good night, Mr. de Bruijn. Perhaps we'll be lucky and uncover the avian murderer on the morrow."

Chapter Eighteen

The morning of Christmas Eve found de Bruijn up at daybreak. But he had no interest in admiring the long shadows of buildings that stretched from the east, reaching toward the Pacific, nor the brilliant winter-blue sky overhead. Instead, he was waiting, impatiently, for Graham Drake to respond to the message he had given a hotel porter for delivery at the not-unreasonable hour of eight in the morning.

He spent the time going over the notes he had made on the case. He had questions for Graham Drake, oh yes. He debated if it would be better to approach the issues obliquely or head-on. He decided that being blunt would be best. If Drake decided to fire him for asking a direct question, that and his reaction to the question itself would tell him what he needed to know. Truth be told, he would not mind seeing the back of this investigation.

With the dawning of the sun, it had also dawned on him that Mrs. Stannert was right when she said he could not be impartial. His past interactions with Theia, long ago though they were, affected his ability to remain impartial. Whenever discussion turned to the singer, his reaction was to rise to her defense. It was not to anyone's advantage that he was unable to see clearly. And

Theia was not the only person he felt honor bound to defend. There was Jacob Freeman, whose biggest sin was apparently being in the wrong place at the wrong time—and perhaps having the wrong color of skin.

A knock at the door disturbed his ruminations. He answered it to find Toby, the Drakes' personal messenger, with a folded, wax-sealed paper on his silver salver. "From Mr. Drake, sir," he said. "Mr. Drake asks that you open it right away."

Inside was a curt message that Drake was available: now. It concluded "I leave for the office by half past the hour and will have no more time until after Christmas Day."

De Bruijn was glad he had caught up on his sleep because the tone of Drake's note—bordering on ill-mannered—would have otherwise been difficult to surmount. He checked his pocket watch. Eight-fifteen. He swore silently to himself.

"I'm to bring you to the suite," said Toby, his dark eyes anxious.

De Bruijn nodded and stepped out, locking the door behind him. "Back staircase," he said. Since minutes were at stake, there was no time to wait for the elevator.

Emerging on the second floor, they hastened to Graham Drake's rooms. At the door, Toby murmured, "I'll leave you here, sir. I have other messages Mr. Drake wants me to deliver this morning." He turned and vanished down the hallway.

The door was opened after a single knock by a harassed fellow who, judging by the clothes brush in his hand, was Graham's valet. Inside, Graham's voice rose, frustrated. "I told you that telegram had to be posted last night."

Another voice answered, "The telegraph office was closed when I got there, sir."

"Damn it!" snapped Graham. "I'm sure the city has more than one Western Union office!"

De Bruijn gave his name to the valet, who announced him.

He stepped inside to see Graham buttoning his waistcoat and glaring at a young man with tidy sideburns. Most likely his personal secretary, de Bruijn thought. Graham, still focused on the underling before him, finished with, "Well, man, go do it now!"

The unnamed, red-faced secretary tucked a crumpled paper in his jacket and hurried past de Bruijn, eyes averted as if by pretending the detective was not there, he would be invisible as well. Graham turned his impatient gaze on de Bruijn and gave him a curt nod. He said to the valet, "That is all, Charles."

"But, sir, your coat…" Charles gestured with the brush to a handsome black wool coat hanging by the door.

"It'll do. This is a private conversation."

The valet removed himself to an adjoining room, shutting the door behind him.

"Well, de Bruijn. Have you fingered the miscreant?" Graham finished buttoning his waistcoat and checked his cuff links.

"Not yet."

Graham's irate focus swerved from his cuffs to de Bruijn. "Why not? This shouldn't be a difficult task for someone of your vaunted caliber."

"After you escorted Miss Green to her room, you returned to the music room."

Graham reared back, as if de Bruijn had hit him. His face flooded with puzzlement, then ire. "Who told you that I… Was it that damned porter? The one who probably caused all this trouble to begin with? If he was listening outside the door—"

"Why do you insist on pinning the trouble on Jacob Freeman?" de Bruijn asked. "There is no proof that he has done anything wrong."

"Ha!" barked Graham. "They are always trouble. That sort." *That sort.*

"What do you mean?" De Bruijn was quite certain he knew, but he wanted to hear Graham say it.

Graham stared at him. "De Bruijn. You're a foreigner, right? You were not here for the War."

The War. He means the War between the States.

Before de Bruijn could answer, Graham said, "I thought not. So you don't understand how it was. If you'd been in New York in sixty-four, as I was, you would have seen how they drafted us, but let that sort alone." He sneered. "If you don't keep on them, their true nature comes through. Untrustworthy. Lazy. Mrs. Drake, she thought to give him a chance, since he came highly recommended. As did you, de Bruijn."

De Bruijn saw it all now. Drake's distrust of Jacob Freeman was all emotion and prejudice, with deep roots to his past and no basis in fact. The best way forward was not to argue, but to focus on gaining clarification.

"When you returned to the music room, how long did you stay?"

He bristled. "What business is that of yours?"

"I need to know everyone's movements that evening, and what happened when," said de Bruijn. "When you leave out or misrepresent your whereabouts or events, it leaves me with an incomplete picture, which makes it all the more difficult to bring this issue to a close. You still want a resolution, I assume? You still want me to uncover who killed your wife's pet and destroyed her dress?" He didn't wait for an answer, but returned to his original question. "So, you returned to the music room, and Mrs. Drake was there?"

"Yes!" snapped Graham. He advanced on de Bruijn, who stepped quickly to one side. But Graham only reached for his coat. "It had to be that porter," he muttered. "Or Yvonne. She was next door."

He pinned the detective with an intense stare as he put on his coat. "I never trusted that woman. She makes Mrs. Drake's hysteria worse. I've told my wife that after the first of the year, I would get her a proper lady's maid." He made it sound as if it would be as simple as ordering an overdone steak back to the kitchen to be switched with one that was properly cooked.

De Bruijn said, "Hysteria? Are you saying your wife has a medical condition?"

Drake pulled on his coat. "I told you before, she is high-strung. Recent events have made her yet more unbalanced, I fear. I have enough troubles with the newspaper, let alone—" He stopped. It was as if a door slammed shut.

De Bruijn knew his time was shrinking, even as the skeins of the conversation became more complex. "Your troubles with the newspaper. Could they be involved in any of this?"

"Any of... You mean the dress and bird business? Absolutely not!" His attention was now on the double-breasted buttons of his coat. "It couldn't be," he muttered. "I forbade her to..." A second time, he stopped.

"You were heard to say that you forbade her to see someone. Apparently, a man. What was that about?"

Drake's face, already flushed, darkened further. "It was a private discussion. One with no bearing on your investigation."

"Why don't you let me be the judge of that." De Bruijn added, "Everything you say is between us. It goes no further."

Drake took a deep breath and closed his eyes, as if to gain control. When he reopened his eyes, he focused his gaze on the mirror on the hallstand. "That evening, I found out she had been talking with the assistant manager of the Grand Opera House, behind my back, about returning next season. I confronted her and said absolutely not. She became irrational."

He picked up his top hat and settled it carefully on his head. "I will not have her going against my wishes in this regard. She thinks she can change my mind through her tantrums, sulking, or cajoling, but that is not the case. My decision is final. Our lives will move forward. She will accommodate." A note of menace wreathed his final words.

Some of what he said rang true, some did not. Lies mixed with the truth. Often the most difficult falsehoods to ferret out were dressed so. Still, it would be simple enough to inquire of Thackery at the Grand and see if the tale was true or not.

De Bruijn said, "Mrs. Drake's next appearance is tonight at the Cliff House, correct?"

"Correct."

"I think it best if I were there."

"I think it best if you were not," said Drake. "The guests are my business associates. I do not see the purpose of having you there. Your investigations are better directed at the hotel staff. Or perhaps at my wife's maid."

"Will Yvonne be at the Cliff House? With your wife?"

"Of course. She helps her prepare for all her appearances." Drake pulled out his pocket watch—a heavy gold object, with a gold watch chain anchored with a gold nugget. He clicked it open.

"Then it seems to me—"

"Charles!" shouted Drake. The door to the adjacent room popped open, and the valet hurried in.

"Time's up, Mr. de Bruijn." Drake put his pocket watch away and chose an ornate gold-headed cane from a collection on the stand. "Our conversation is over."

He glanced at the valet, who was hovering at his elbow, holding out a pair of black gloves. "Charles, Mr. de Bruijn is leaving." Drake took the gloves and began to pull them on. "Show him out."

Charles moved to the door and opened it, saying, "Mr. de Bruijn?"

Left with little choice, de Bruijn bowed stiffly to Graham Drake and headed for the exit.

Drake called after him, "I cannot imagine what useful information you gleaned from this conversation. And I don't like the direction of your questions. I suggest you find a way to wrap up your investigations, and soon." As the door closed behind him, de Bruijn heard Drake say, "Goodbye, Mr. de Bruijn. And Merry Christmas."

———

De Bruijn was still in a black mood by the time he reached the Grand. Deciding to deal with Luis Rubio first, he took the stairs two at a time to the second floor. He could hear voices inside, an intermittent murmur. At his knock, voices ceased. Hurried scuffling was followed by silence. De Bruijn was not in a frame of mind to wheedle or be polite.

Switching to Spanish, he said in a tone he seldom used but which few ignored when he did, "Señor Rubio. It is Mr. de Bruijn. I know you are there. If you do not open this door immediately, I shall call for Mr. Thackery. Furthermore, if you refuse to answer my questions, I shall bring the police into the matter, a step I am certain you wish to avoid."

This last statement was a calculated risk, but de Bruijn suspected Rubio, given his family's stature and his prior time spent in the city jail for assault, would not want to deal with the local constabulary again so soon.

"*Un momento.*" Rubio sounded a little breathless.

De Bruijn wondered what was going on inside. He hadn't heard the piano nor any singing, so not a lesson.

The subdued voices, the rustling of what he thought was cloth or clothes, the sudden silence. Had he caught Rubio and someone else, perhaps Miss Green, in a compromising position?

Or perhaps a different woman was inside? No sooner did de Bruijn think this than he felt certain it was the case, given what he had been told by the Palace night manager, Adams.

The door opened, revealing Rubio in a green-and-red paisley smoking jacket, tossed on over a half-buttoned white shirt and dark trousers. Behind him, de Bruijn caught sight of the messenger, Toby.

De Bruijn surmised Toby was spying for Rubio, acting as the pianist's eyes in the Palace, keeping track of the Drakes' activities, and perhaps running messages to Miss Green as well. Then, he took in Rubio's flushed countenance and the messenger's averted face. Toby furtively tucked his shirt into his trousers before reaching for the jacket on the arm of a parlor couch.

And the light dawned.

Rubio turned to Toby and said in a haughty tone, "Deliver the letter to none but Señorita Green." He pulled a coin from his trouser pocket. "For your service."

Toby nodded, not looking up as he took the silver half-dollar. De Bruijn stood aside to let him exit. The messenger glanced at de Bruijn as he passed, shame gilding his smooth features. De Bruijn noted he held no missive in his empty hands.

De Bruijn's dislike of Rubio metamorphosed into disgust. Not for the illegal acts which he suspected he had interrupted—after all, there was little he had not seen or heard of in his investigations— but for a perceived abuse of power. The amusement on Rubio's face did not improve de Bruijn's evaluation of the pianist.

Rubio gave an exaggerated bow and waved de Bruijn in. He then he strolled over to a sideboard, buttoning his shirt all the while, and asked, "Would you care for a drink, Señor de Bruijn? A whiskey or a brandy, perhaps? I have sherry, if you prefer."

At nine in the morning? De Bruijn shook his head.

Rubio poured himself a drink. "So. You are from the Continent?"

"Why do you ask?"

"Your Spanish. Fluent. But different, in subtle ways. Accent mostly. But that is not why you came pounding on my door at this hour of the day. Now that it is just us two, I will answer your questions as best I can. I have someone coming in half an hour for voice practice. Until then, my time is yours."

"Is that someone Miss Green, perchance?"

Rubio lifted one eyebrow. "No. She comes in the afternoons." He paused. "For a longer session." He smoothed his hair back from his forehead, the silver in the black like threads of ice in the night. "And today she is busy. She must go with the Drakes to the Cliff House for tonight's event, as I am certain you know."

De Bruijn decided to forge ahead. "I want to know what happened at the Grand and afterward on the night of the twentieth. The night you were fired by Mrs. Drake."

"I am sure you have heard it all from those who were there. Señorita Green, Señor Thackery, and that woman, Señora Stannert. Do you want me to parrot what you already know?"

"I want to hear your version of events," said de Bruijn.

Rubio sighed. "Well, let us at least sit down." He went over to the couch. De Bruijn followed him over but stayed standing.

"Is that the way it is to be between us? Very well." Rubio took a swallow of his sherry, then said, "After the performance, which was a full house and which I thought went exceedingly well, Señora Drake sent me packing in front of many. It was most humiliating."

"And then?"

"Then? They all left and I secured quarters here from Mr. Thackery."

"And then?"

" I went out to celebrate."

"Celebrate. That is a strange choice of words."

"Ah, well. You are employed by the Drakes, *sí*? Then you can understand what a joy it is to no longer be required to bow and scrape every moment to them."

"Explain."

Rubio held up his glass as if to admire the pale color of the liquid. "The Golden Songbird is not easy to work with. From the very beginning, when they hired me in Denver, we had our artistic differences in interpretation. But, despite what you have probably heard from others, I do not think that was the reason for her deciding to give me the back of her hand." He glanced at de Bruijn, something sly in his expression.

De Bruijn said, "So, the reason was?"

"Upon our arrival here in San Francisco, the lady propositioned me."

De Bruijn did not bother to hide his disbelief.

Rubio raised his hand. "I would swear upon my mother's grave this is the truth, only she is still very much alive. I could swear upon the Bible, if you prefer. No? Then you will have to take my word for it, because I doubt Madame Drake will confirm what I say."

"And why would she fire you? Did she tire of you that quickly?" de Bruijn snapped.

"Ah, the lady has a champion. Another heart dangling from the bracelet about her wrist. No, Señor de Bruijn. You see, I declined her invitation. As politely and delicately as possible. After that, it was only a matter of time. She could hardly abide to look at me. The writing, as you say, was upon the wall. However, I thought the dismissal would come from Señor Drake, a man-to-man parting of the ways. I was taken off guard after the recital. I tried to cajole her, talk to her. My mistake. I should not have bothered. She was done with me." He placed the glass on a nearby table.

De Bruijn, still digesting this information and trying to decide whether to believe Rubio or not, pressed on. "So, after you obtained an apartment here, you went out to drink. Where did you go?"

"Many places," said Rubio vaguely. "I cannot recall them now." His dark gaze settled on de Bruijn. "If you are looking for me to supply an alibi for my movements that night, I regret I cannot."

De Bruijn tried a different tack. "I understand you resided at the Palace Hotel in the past. I am certain you could find your way in without being noticed, if you wished."

"If I wished." He leaned forward. The soft material of his smoking jacket whispered. "However, despite what you think of me, I am a gentleman. I would not sneak into the hotel, like a petty thief, to destroy her pet bird and dress. It is beneath me. So, I swear to you, again, I did not return to the hotel."

"Not until the next morning," said de Bruijn.

He nodded. "I went back then. Or tried to. Walked up to the front door, and they did not let me in. It is probably just as well. I was determined to demand the money the Drakes owed me and tell Señor Drake he was in danger of being cuckolded. Upon sober reflection in the jail, I realized it would not do to speak against Madame to her husband. He is a powerful man. I know the type. He would rather squash the messenger than hear the message."

He sneered. "I suppose I have *that* woman, Mrs. Stannert, to thank for my time of reflection. You know, of course, Madame hired her to take my place. Do you know that this Mrs. Stannert threatened to kill me? If I am discovered with a bullet in my back, look to her first."

De Bruijn compressed his lips, thinking briefly of Mrs. Stannert and her occasional penchant for violence. "So, if what you say is true, you believe Mr. Drake has no knowledge of his wife's behavior?"

"Who knows what he thinks, what secrets they keep from each other and between themselves."

"And Miss Green? What does she know of all this?"

"If she suspects anything, she has not told me."

"Does Miss Green know of your other proclivities?"

Rubio stared at him, then threw back his head and laughed. When he finished, he said, "Señorita Green is such a charming miss. She holds herself to be so modern, yet cherishes old-fashioned sensibilities and notions."

"Old-fashioned notions such as love?"

"You are perceptive. Yes. And marriage. She thinks I will marry her, now that I am here and she will soon be free of the Drakes." He shook his head. "I suppose I must disabuse her of the notion. It would be a kindness. Besides, she grows tiresome."

De Bruijn was fed up with him. The feeling seemed to be mutual because Rubio rose, saying sarcastically, "I am glad we had this little chat, Señor de Bruijn. I imagine the Drakes would be happy if I were the villain of this story. But I am not. So, I suppose you must now continue your investigation as everyone else in the city celebrates the holidays. A pity."

De Bruijn ignored the dig. He wondered how women such as

Miss Green, and Theia, if what Rubio had said could be trusted, could find such a specimen attractive.

One last question, and then I am done with him. "Have you any thoughts on who might be the culprit? You were with the Drakes for much of their trip and their early days in the city."

Rubio tugged on the green velvet collar of his jacket, pondering. "Her companion, Yvonne. Or perhaps Señor Drake?" He opened the door to let de Bruijn out and before shutting it added, "As I said, who knows what he thinks. Or what happens between a man and his wife."

Chapter Nineteen

DECEMBER 24

The fact that it was Christmas Eve and well after dark made for no traffic on the long, straight Point Lobos Avenue leading out of the city to the beaches on the Pacific. On this wild coast, perched high above the waves, was their destination: the famous or infamous (depending on the time of day and one's opinion) Cliff House. The carriage holding Inez, the Drakes, Julia Green, and Yvonne rocked over the paved road, creaking as it rolled past San Francisco's cities of the dead. The only other outside sound was the whistle of the wind.

Inside, the single, side-mounted lamp sent shadows across the faces of the Drakes and Julia, who were sitting on the blue-velvet-covered bench opposite Inez. Seated next to the lamp with his top hat in his lap, Graham Drake wore an expression as opaque as his conventionally black evening suit and equally dark Inverness coat. Theia in the middle and Julia on the other end of the bench more than made up for his stoicism.

The two women shifted, rustled, touched the flowers in their upswept hair, fussed with the closures on their cloaks. For not the first time on the ride, Theia turned to Julia and snapped, "Truly, you had nothing better to wear than that old tired cape for the evening?"

Julia smoothed the crimson-colored wool with a white glove. "It has stood me in good stead for this long. Besides, we shall be shedding them as soon as we arrive." She added, "Unlike you, Madame, I do not have a different overcoat for every occasion."

This open criticism of Theia and her extensive clothes collection caused Inez to raise her eyebrows. Yvonne, squeezed between Inez and the singers' two small trunks, stiffened in apprehension as well. To Inez's surprise, Theia did not rise to the bait, but contented herself with a sniff. The carriage hit a modest bump in the road and they all swayed.

Theia angled herself toward Julia, saying, "Something in black would have been more formal. If you are at all interested in being more than a common variety-house *chanteuse*, you should invest in a proper wrap." She smoothed her own cloak, black cashmere heavily embroidered with silver thread.

"When *I* sing, I would rather the audience be transported by my voice, not by my costume," said Julia in an overly sweet voice.

"Ladies," said Graham wearily. "Please."

Inez had a feeling this wasn't the first instance of verbal swordplay he had been subjected to this Christmas Eve. When Inez had arrived at the Palace earlier, Theia was still getting ready in the music room. She had gushed about the dress fitting of the muslin, which would serve as a template for the final gown. "Miss Robineau is a marvel! So fast. So clever! She has promised the gown will be ready by the thirtieth. And the fabric is perfect!"

Even as she had heaped praise upon the seamstress, Theia heaped complaints upon Yvonne. Nothing Yvonne did pleased the diva, from how she had fixed her hair ("The flowers! They are hanging over my ear! I look like I'm peering through the underbrush!") to the state of her white gloves ("Look! A seam is loosening here!"). She even fussed over the bracelets Yvonne had chosen to go with her evening gown. Inez was glad the singer had not turned her sharp tongue in her direction. If she had, Inez thought she would be tempted to pull a "Rubio" at the piano and play with a heavy hand bold enough to upstage the opera singer.

The most she had done was to ask Inez to fetch Julia. "Why she keeps disappearing, I cannot say! Just go through the connecting door to Yvonne's sitting room. The door beyond leads to Julia's chambers."

Such summoning seemed more Yvonne's task, but after one look at the private maid's frazzled demeanor, Inez relented. She did as instructed and knocked. "Julia?"

"Yes?"

Inez opened the connecting door to find Julia adjusting the small parlor's fireplace screen. The young woman whirled around, startled.

"My apologies, I didn't mean to startle you," said Inez. "Theia is asking for you."

Julia had rolled her eyes. Inez suspected she was counting the days and hours until the end of the year.

The carriage rocked to a stop. "We are here," said Graham, with obvious relief. He turned to the women. "Ladies, keep in mind. Our guests tonight include important business associates and some of the most influential gentlemen in the city, including Adolph Sutro. Mr. Sutro and I go back to Virginia City, and I have conducted a number of business deals with him over the years. He recently bought the Cliff House, and we are holding the soirée here tonight at his request. I expect you all to be at your most charming."

It was the sort of admonition Inez might give to Antonia. In fact, she probably had said something similar to the girl shortly before they went for their evening's adventure to the Grand Opera House, the adventure that had led to this very moment.

He continued, "I have been assured rooms have been set aside for your needs." His gaze settled on Inez and Yvonne. "You two will take your supper there during the banquet. The entertainment begins after the meal. Mrs. Stannert, you will be called for then."

"As long as I can test the keyboard before we commence," she replied.

"I will make certain that is the case."

Stung from his dismissive tone, Inez reminded herself she was but a hireling in this situation. *No matter. It is just for the evening.*

Done with his lecture, Graham knocked on the roof of the carriage with his silver-headed cane. The springs bounced as the driver dismounted. The door opened, or rather was ripped from the hand of someone battling a stiff breeze. Graham exited first, followed by Theia and Julia. Inez, warned by their little shrieks and exclamations, gripped the hood of her overcoat tight about her face before setting foot on the step. The strength and icy temperature of the wind accompanied by a sudden spate of rain made her gasp. The damp, fierce cold gripped her inside and out.

How different compared to the summer days when she and Antonia had visited the Cliff House. Then, they had enjoyed lemonades on the veranda while watching the barking sea lions on Seal Rocks before exploring the beach and marveling at the foaming ocean breakers.

The entrance to the establishment on the headlands stood open, friendly lights inside. Inez plunged toward it, glad to escape what felt like a gale straight from the north. Once they were all inside with the small trunks, a gentleman came hurrying toward them.

"Welcome, Mr. Drake, Mrs. Drake, ladies! Captain Junius Foster, at your service, manager of the Cliff House. Mr. Drake, Mr. Sutro has told me of your joint business exploits during the glory days of the Consolidated Virginia. So pleased you are here and are planning to make our city your new home. Your guests have arrived and are already well along the celebratory path."

After conducting hasty introductions, Graham said, "If you would show my wife and her companions to the rooms you have set aside, I'll greet my guests and apologize for our tardiness."

That last, Inez thought, was an aside to Theia, who had had

them all tapping their toes and waiting while she had delayed the party by insisting Yvonne redo her hair.

Foster escorted the women through a central archway, saying, "I apologize for taking you through the common area, but it is the most direct path to the parlors I have arranged for you, and I can see you are all suffering from the cold. I suggest you avert your gazes." He ushered them past another large arch that lead to a magnificent barroom.

The others may have averted their gazes and shrunk within their wraps, but Inez devoured the scene with her eyes, wishing she could tarry and observe.

It was Saturday night, Christmas Eve, and Inez suspected that most of the men she glimpsed inside were there not because of the holiday but because of the day of the week. Smoke from a hundred pipes, cigars, and cigarettes billowed into the hall. She spotted a crush of gents jostling for space along the counter. Every table appeared occupied. Inez was willing to bet her bottom dollar that many who had circled up with elbows on the tabletops were engaged in games of chance. It looked a level of clientele that would have felt right at home in Leadville's Silver Queen saloon.

Her gaze snagged on the table closest to them as they passed. Four men in standard sack suits and bowler hats hunched over their closely held hands of cards. The elderly silver-haired and bearded gent facing her, his features lined and frowning behind his black-rimmed spectacles, glanced at her, then returned to studying his cards. He was, she noted, ahead of the others, according to the pile of chips before him.

Her unobstructed view of the interior vanished as several men came to the entryway, curiosity and avidity brightening their faces. One of them stepped into the hallway to inspect the huddle of women scurrying by. Inez pegged him as a knight of the green cloth. He was good-looking in that half-asleep, dissipated way some young men could pull off before the years and fast living grabbed them by the collar and shook them ragged. He sported a flashy red-and-black checked waistcoat, a green sack jacket, and a well-brushed derby hat.

A fellow gawper asked, "One a them pretties catch yer fancy, Farallon Finn?"

Farallon Finn grinned. A gold tooth flashed front and center in a mouthful of white, even teeth. He gave Inez an overt once-over, caught her gaze, and winked. "Some fine specimens of womanhood, and that's God's own truth. Brought them here for us, Captain?"

Captain Foster frowned. "Private party, Finn. Nothing to do with you and your kind."

"I'd pay a pretty penny for an invitation to that party." Finn smirked.

Inez was sorely tempted to stop and give the cardsharp a piece of her mind, but Foster prodded their group forward. The laughter of those lingering under the arch chased them down the hall and around a corner. Yvonne sputtered, "Hooligans!" Julia shook her head, and Theia sniffed, "Is this the level of clientele you encourage, Captain Foster?"

Foster set up a soothing murmur. "My apologies, ladies. The new owner will be changing things up. However, I should have taken you by the longer route, I see now."

A different chorus of men's voices gathered strength as they navigated another long passage. A flurry of waiters entered and exited a set of double doors halfway down the dim hallway. "Your soirée," Foster said, as he guided them around yet another corner. "And here we are!" he announced, opening one of a pair of dark-paneled doors for them. The four women entered, and Theia gave a dramatic sigh of relief.

Inez surveyed the room. The parlor was well appointed, with thick rugs, comfortable chairs and settees, tasteful paintings, and a brisk fire in a fireplace. Chandeliers dotted the ceiling at intervals, and two full-length mirrors stood to either side of the fireplace. Each mirror was well-lit by wall sconces. Foster walked to another set of doors at the far end of the parlor and opened one. A warm light beckoned from within. "This has been set up as a dressing room for your convenience. It has a parlor stove where you can hang your coats to dry."

He added, "All hallway doors to these rooms lock and can be bolted. I personally vouch for the safety of your rooms, this corridor, and the passageway to the banquet room. But it would be best, ladies, not to go a-wandering around the building unless you have a guide."

Two attendants appeared, hauling Theia and Julia's small trunks.

"Put them in the dressing room," Theia directed before dropping her damp cloak on the nearest chair.

Foster bowed again. "Madame Drake, Miss Green, I'll let Mr. Drake know you are here. How long before you ladies will be ready to join the guests?"

Theia wandered to one of the mirrors and examined herself, touching her hair, its careful arrangement now in disarray. "I will need half an hour, at least, to make repairs."

He bowed and left, along with the other men, closing the doors behind them all.

Julia removed her damp cloak gingerly and carried it into the dressing room. Yvonne retrieved Theia's discarded black-and-silver wrap and asked Inez, "Would you like me to hang yours?"

Touched, Inez said, "Thank you," and handed her the black overcoat.

Yvonne followed Julia into the back room.

Inez sat by the fire, removed her gloves, and flexed her fingers.

Theia remained by the mirror, fussing with the red roses pinned to her brown tresses. She called out irritably, "My hair, Yvonne. It's a mess. Come fix it. And I need my shoes!"

Yvonne emerged from the dressing room, holding slippers the same shade of pale green as her mistress's silk and satin dress.

Inez caught a flash of anger crossing Yvonne's countenance,

but all the maid said was, "Madame, do you want me to fix your toilette in the dressing room?"

"No time," said Theia. "Bring me a chair and do it here, by the mirror."

Inez wondered if there might be tea or coffee or something a little stronger available to warm her insides, now that the fire was doing its job of warming her feet and drying the hem of her cashmere dress. She smoothed her fichu, tied in a large bow at her neck. At least Theia had not protested her decision to alleviate her all-black garb with the frothy ivory lace.

A covered bank of windows on the far side beckoned. Inez stood, strolled over, and pushed aside an edge of the heavy damask drape. Night's darkness was complete, but she could see by the light falling from inside that they faced the wide veranda encircling the Cliff House. The rhythmic roar of surf pounding on rocks told her they faced west. Below the veranda were the cliffs that plunged into the edge of the ocean. She shivered and pulled the drapes closed as Julia said from behind, "Do you know who will be here tonight?"

Inez turned. Julia was standing with her back to the other long mirror. The ingénue twisted to examine the gathers and folds of her pink silk evening gown. The flowers in her hair were white. Inez thought the two singers made a good Christmas-themed pairing, wearing pale green and lightest of rose-pinks, with their similar skin and hair coloring.

"You heard Mr. Drake," said Theia. "Business associates. Crème de la crème of the city."

"I doubt the crème de la crème would be caught out here in the middle of nowhere on Christmas Eve," said Julia. "Did you see those men we passed? Is that your idea of the best San Francisco has to offer... Madame?"

Theia turned her head sharply toward Julia, just as Yvonne was attempting to pin another red rose into Theia's re-coiffed hair. "That's enough, Julia! Remember who you are talking to!"

Yvonne said, "Madame, please, sit still."

Julia sneered, then glanced at Inez. "Mrs. Stannert, you saw them. Don't you agree? What kind of establishment would allow such sorry dregs of humanity within their doors?"

Theia slapped Yvonne's hand away. Petals from the rose scattered on the floor. "Look at what you've done," she snapped. "This will not do at all. Get the pearls from my travel case. I'll have those in my hair instead. And hurry! Mr. Drake will be here soon!"

Inez observed the back and forth with interest. Whatever animosities and tugs-of-war existed between the two singers were no longer under wraps but on full display, and poor Yvonne seemed to be the lightning rod for Theia's displeasure. Inez wished she was anywhere else, including the watering hole of the Cliff House. At least she knew how to deal with drunks and lechers. Two women snarling at each other was a different matter.

A knock on the door shattered the moment, and Graham Drake's voice wafted through: "Are you all decent? Mrs. Drake, Miss Green, are you ready? It's time. Supper will be served shortly."

"One moment," sang out Theia. She grabbed her opera gloves, her bracelets jangling, and scowled at Yvonne. "No time for the pearls! Go. Let him in."

Yvonne stumbled to the door and opened it. Graham Drake stepped in, brow furrowed, as if sensing the tension in the air. Julia moved toward him. The frown on his face eased, and he smiled. "Miss Green, you look lovely. Do the rooms meet with your approval?"

She answered with a distant formality that Inez thought was quite unlike her. "Thank you, Mr. Drake. They are quite satisfactory." She looked at his proffered arm and seemed to hesitate but finally took it.

Theia moved to capture his other arm. "How are your guests?"

"In a celebratory mood and becoming more lubricated by the moment," he answered. "It promises to be a jolly evening."

He looked at Inez. "Mrs. Stannert, I'll send someone for you when the time comes."

As the threesome moved to the doorway, Theia said, "I hope the meal isn't too heavy. I cannot sing well after a heavy meal."

"My dear, this is not the opera house and your audience is, in the main, not musical experts. You could sing 'Jingle Bells' and they would give you a standing ovation."

After the door closed behind them, Yvonne and Inez released simultaneous sighs and looked at each other. Inez said, "Come. Take a chair by the fire. You haven't had a moment to sit since we arrived."

Yvonne approached slowly and lowered herself on the very edge of a plush-covered chair. She knotted her shaking hands together, then released them to smooth her skirt. Inez found herself softening in sympathy toward the beleaguered maid. *If she was the one who wreaked havoc on Theia's dress and bird that night, I would not blame her a whit.*

A knock on the door had Yvonne rising from her chair but Inez said, "Let me take care of this." She called out, "Who is it?"

"Ladies, we have your suppers," was the response.

Inez's stomach rumbled in a very unladylike manner. She smiled encouragingly at Yvonne, who gave an uncertain smile back. "Ready?" Inez asked.

"Oh yes," said Yvonne fervently. "I believe I am near faint with hunger. It has been a long day since the morning meal."

Three waiters marched in, wheeling carts before them. As they lifted the plate covers, Inez was glad she was not singing, if a heavy meal was an enemy of the voice. Oyster soup, terrapin soup, clam chowder, oysters on half shell, fried oysters, Eastern cod fricassee, chicken liver brochette, canvasback duck, frogs' legs sautéed with mushrooms, asparagus, new potatoes, French peas, an entire tray of fancy cakes, and coffee.

"What may I offer you to drink?" inquired a waiter. "The banquet includes Mum's champagne, but we also have a wide variety of beverages, including lemonades and hot drinks."

Inez hesitated. She yearned for a glass of wine, and some brandy for the coffee.

Yvonne's eyes were wide as the dinner plates. Inez saw the same uncertainty on her face.

Inez made up her mind. "Wine. Please choose whatever you have that will suit the meal. And brandy, please. For the coffee. For medicinal purposes, to counteract the cold outside."

The waiter did not bat an eye. He turned to Yvonne. "And you, madam?"

Yvonne gripped the seat of her chair. "Wine would be nice. And sherry, please." She glanced at Inez and almost smiled. "For medicinal purposes."

The waiters disappeared and one returned with a good red wine and a bottle each of sherry and brandy. Inez began to warm to the hospitality, and even Yvonne's eyes lit up.

Conversation focused on the food, which wasn't difficult as there was so much to enjoy and exclaim over. Inez, sensing a golden opportunity to delicately delve into the relationship of maid and mistress, formulated a plan even as she strove to keep conversation light and put Yvonne at ease.

After they had worked their way through the feast and sampled tiny portions of several cakes, Inez felt the time was right. By that point, Yvonne had had nearly two glasses of sherry. It could have been more, Inez thought, since Yvonne kept tipping small amounts into her glass so it was never completely empty. Whether due to the liquor, the warmth of the fire, the pure sensory enjoyment of food, the light back-and-forth, or some combination thereof, Yvonne's posture was more relaxed and her face more animated than Inez had seen it before.

Cradling her delicate china cup of coffee-plus between two hands, Inez said, "May I speak frankly for a moment, Yvonne? This may be the only time you and I will have the opportunity to do so."

Yvonne paused, sherry glass halfway to her lips, then slowly nodded.

Inez continued, " From what I observe, Mrs. Drake does not treat you as well as you deserve to be treated. In my opinion."

Yvonne lowered her glass, untouched, eyes downcast. "Madame has been under considerable strain lately."

"And as a result, so have you," said Inez gently. "I see how much she depends on you."

"Yes." Her voice was low. "It has been difficult. To hear her talk about others, it is the hardest. You heard the praise she gave of the dressmaker, Mrs. Robineau? Madame did not say any of that to her. Only berated her for the sleeves being too tight, the bodice not fitting well. Madame is always so. She says one thing, then turns around and says the opposite. One never knows where one stands."

Inez wondered briefly what Theia had said about her, then dismissed it. "In that case, I shall lay my cards on the table. I have an offer for you. If you should decide to leave the Drakes' employ, I have a dear friend, a very kind young woman, who recently lost her only close living relative. I am certain she would welcome you as a companion. She currently has no one."

Inez thought of Carmella Donato, who had led a sheltered life and was now living alone in the large house she had shared with her brother. "She needs someone like you in her life, someone steady and mature, who can help her navigate the world," Inez continued. "But what is most important is that she has a kind and open heart. I could introduce you after the new year. If she does not suit you, you have my word that I shall help you find a less stressful position than the one you currently endure."

"Thank you." The words were barely above a whisper. "Being Mrs. Drake's companion has never been easy. But lately, she, the situation, it has been nearly impossible. I'm not certain how much more I can take." She tipped a little more sherry into her nearly full glass. "I am grateful to you. However, I do not see myself giving notice."

Inez relaxed, glad she had read Yvonne correctly. The woman yearned to escape but did not know how to do so. Inez reached out and patted Yvonne's hand. "Give notice? Must you? Why not just leave? Start anew? Whatever you owe Mrs. Drake, my guess is you have repaid her many times over with your loyalty and your constancy. Your silence in the face of mistreatment. Your unending patience. Your discretion. How many years have you been with her?"

"Many. More than ten." Yvonne then shook her head. "I don't think I can leave."

"Whyever not? No matter how close you two once were, it is clear she now takes you for granted. It is worse than that, actually. She dumps all her disappointment and her anger into your lap. Or on your head. Of *course* you can leave her. I will help you. After all, this is not an 'until death do we part' arrangement, is it?"

She didn't reply but hunched her shoulders, making herself smaller.

Inez said as kindly as she could, "Yvonne, this is *your* life. Isn't it time for you to *live* it?"

Yvonne looked up at last. Something behind those pale eyes shifted. It was as if clouds had parted, revealing a blue sky of hope.

A tap at the door gave way to a voice in the hallway. "Mrs. Stannert? The banquet is over. Mrs. Drake asked that I fetch you for the recital."

"One moment," called Inez. She rose, checked her hair in one of the mirrors, then smiled at Yvonne and moved toward the door. "Please reflect on what I said. I meant every word, every offer. I do not like to see you, or anyone for that matter, suffer such mistreatment."

With that, she left Yvonne with her sherry and her thoughts.

Chapter Twenty

DECEMBER 24

The boom of loud male voices in the banquet room hit Inez like a physical blow after her quiet conversation with Yvonne in the women's parlor. Head up, shoulders back, Inez assumed a professional air as she entered the room. Graham Drake rose from the head of the table, saying, "Our talented pianist, Mrs. Stannert, has arrived. Thank you for your time on this eve of the holiday."

He lowered his voice as he escorted her to the piano where Theia waited, looking irritated. "This is for my wife, you understand. When she heard of the gathering I had planned, she insisted on singing for the company. I've told her as I am telling you, the music should proceed briskly, as the guests are more interested in cigars and cognac than carols tonight."

No wonder Theia is annoyed.

Inez said, "Of course, Mr. Drake. As you and Madame wish."

She sat at the piano, a parlor grand which had seen better days, and ran soft, experimental scales followed by the opening bars from "Ave Maria." She said to Theia, "It is not perfect but will have to do."

"None of this is perfect," muttered Theia, adjusting the seam of her long gloves and pushing her bracelets up to anchor them in place. "However, let us see if we cannot bring the music of the angels to this den of iniquity. Shall we begin?"

Inez launched into the opening chords of "Joy to the World." Theia's voice caught the melody and soared to the heavens, circling above the long table, bringing an end to the conversation. From there, it was forward with the same repertoire they had played for the Palace Hotel tea. The pieces rolled out one after the other, with pauses for polite applause between the numbers.

During those pauses, Inez observed the audience, at least those at the near end of the table, including Miss Green. From time to time, the young singer unfurled her fan, whispering behind it to the robust gentleman sitting next to her, who seemed quite happy to be receiving her attentions. Inez wondered who he was.

Scanning the other guests between "Good King Wenceslas" and "It Came Upon a Midnight Clear," she recognized the polite, slightly glazed look from the times she would play an extended classical piece on the old piano at the Silver Queen saloon. Back then, such expressions were her signal to switch to popular tunes such as "Shenandoah," "Mollie Darling," or "Down by the River Liv'd a Maiden." In this venue, Inez was constrained to march along through the dozen or so musical numbers Theia had prescribed. She hoped none of the gentlemen would nod off partway through, which would certainly not go down well with the diva.

Drifting along on the music and the bracing yet soothing effects of several cups of coffee and brandy, Inez startled when Theia touched her shoulder and murmured, "Ave Maria."

Inez glanced up, surprised. "Now? What about—"

Theia, tight-lipped, shook her head.

Inez discarded the last two carols on her mental list and moved into Theia's pièce de résistance. The shuffling and murmurs from the audience died at last, as the listeners finally gave their complete attention to the music. Afterwards, the applause was enthusiastic and sustained. Theia bestowed her glittering triumphant smile upon them all, waving one gracious arm in Inez's direction. Inez rose from the piano bench with a half-curtsy.

Graham approached, beaming. "My Golden Songbird!" he announced to the room at large, taking Theia's hand. He continued, "Perfect, my dear, as always. And most excellent, Mrs. Stannert." He began to draw Theia away, saying to all, "Gentlemen, I am certain the ladies would like to retire now so we can talk about business and other topics not to feminine tastes."

"What about Miss Green?" came a bass rumble.

In the midst of lowering the keyboard cover, Inez looked up in surprise. The speaker was the robust gentleman, standing now and smiling at Graham. "We have not heard from the young songbird here. I think, it being Christmas Eve, we could handle one more song." He turned to Julia. "What about it, Miss Green?"

Julia smiled modestly, fluttering her eyelashes. "Oh, Mr. Bert, I would not presume."

"No, no, Miss Green. One song would do us honor. It is quite all right," said Graham.

From Theia's fleeting grimace, Inez gathered this new development was *not* all right with the diva. She recovered quickly and said in a honey-sweet voice, "Yes, by all means. Miss Green has been under my tutelage and has *much* benefitted from my instruction."

Daggered looks passed between the two women, swift as lightning. Theia continued, with an indulgent flip of the wrist, "Mrs. Stannert will be happy to accompany you in whatever ditty you have in mind."

Inez sank back onto the piano bench, *not* happy about being thrust into a spur-of-the-moment, unrehearsed number with an unknown singer, charming as she might be, in front of a sizable audience. *It's a recipe for disaster and embarrassment, and Theia knows it.*

Julia, apparently of the same mind as Inez, moved to the piano and said, "Thank you, Mrs. Stannert. However, no need. I shall sing a cappella."

Theia interjected, "Remember, my dear, *chiaroscuro*."

Julia inclined her head toward Theia, but Inez, seated in the piano chair, could see that her expression was anything but subservient. The protégée faced the long table, hands clasped before her, and began to sing "What Child Is This?" Her voice, soft at first, expanded, dominating the room. The melodic line of the simple hymn soared, swooped, soared again, weaving a siren spell of terrestrial enchantment. No one moved—it seemed no one breathed—until the last note died. The room exploded into applause, the men pushing back their chairs for a standing ovation, punctuated by hearty cheers.

The robust gentleman who been seated by Julia, Mr. Bert, clapped loudest of all, before turning to the group and shouting over the din, "Isn't she magnificent? I am proud to announce Miss Green has signed with the Grand Opera House, beginning in the new year. We expect great things from her, our silver-throated songbird."

Inez just barely heard Julia beside her murmur, "Mr. Bert owns the opera house." She was looking at Theia, who appeared stunned. Graham seemed similarly nonplussed. *They didn't know.*

Recovering his composure, Graham strode over to Inez and Julia. "I shall escort you all back to the parlor. I expect the event will wind down soon. If it doesn't, I'll arrange to have you transported back to the Palace."

Graham didn't seem to notice the icy tenor of silence on the short walk back to the parlor.

Once they were inside and Graham had left, Theia exploded. "How dare you go behind my back! And what did you do to gain that position? I can guess, the way Mr. Bert was eyeing you. You are no better than a common whore!"

Yvonne, who had come out of the dressing room to greet them, froze by the door. Inez wondered if she should slip out the door and let the two women battle it out between themselves in relative privacy.

Rather than flinching, Julia responded with similar fierceness. "So you think that is the only way to get ahead, Madame? Is that *your* experience?"

Yvonne caught her breath, and Inez covered her mouth. *Oh my God.*

Theia's face went white. She rushed into the dressing room, brushing past Yvonne and almost knocking her off her feet. Inez heard the bolt on the other side slam home. An unholy quiet descended, leaving Inez, Yvonne, and Julia staring at each other. "How could you say such things to her?" Yvonne whispered. "After all she's done for you?"

Before Julia could answer, a tap sounded at the hallway door. Graham's voice floated in to them. "Mrs. Stannert, a word?" Glad of the interruption, Inez cracked the door open, wondering what he could possibly want and if he'd heard the commotion. He stood there, looking earnest. "I have a favor to ask, Mrs. Stannert. Mr. Sutro, the new owner of the Cliff House, asked if you would be willing to come back and play for a while longer. Christmas tunes, what have you. Light background music."

"Certainly, Mr. Drake." Relieved to avoid further fireworks, Inez excused herself to Yvonne and Julia and let herself out. Playing background music for men intent on drinking, smoking, and engaging in the male version of gossip would be relaxing. Especially compared to the alternative of waiting in the parlor room for Theia's eventual emergence.

On their way, Graham asked, "Did you know of Miss Green's plans?"

"She didn't tell me," said Inez. And this was true; she had heard it from de Bruijn.

Back in the banquet room, the atmosphere was much more relaxed. As Graham escorted her to the piano, he nodded at two men sitting by the head of the table. "That is Charles Butler, owner, or I should say, previous owner of the Cliff House. Adolph

Sutro is by his side. If they or anyone else asks you to play something in particular, please do so."

Back at her bench, Inez ran through her repertoire of seasonal carols and hymns, skipping "Silent Night" and "Ave Maria," having had her fill of them both. By the time she finished, the men were standing by the door in small knots. The gathering seemed to be slowly breaking up. She looked at Graham and he nodded in response to her unspoken question. She rose from the piano, glad to be done. After acknowledging the scattered applause, she turned down Graham's offer to walk her to the parlor. "It's only a few steps," she said. "I know the way by now."

She traipsed to the parlor, thinking that a short stroll outside on the veranda, even though it was bound to be cold and dark and most likely dank as well, would be a welcome change. She wondered if her three companions would be speaking to each other, or if the two singers were still in high dudgeon, with Yvonne stuck somewhere in the middle.

The room was empty.

The fire was blazing merrily along, so it had not been deserted long. Inez gathered her courage and knocked on the dressing room door. When no one answered, she peeked inside. The travel trunks were still there. Julia's gaped open, its contents scattered on nearby chairs. Inez wondered if Theia had gone so far as to throw Julia's clothes about, out of spite. Theia's trunk was shut and locked, as if its owner was prepared to leave. Yvonne was nowhere in sight.

Baffled, Inez went to the warming stove to retrieve her overcoat. That, too, was gone.

Frustrated, Inez said aloud, "So much for my outside perambulations." She wrapped her arms about herself and decided she might just as well explore the nearby corridors. She had her Smoot pocket revolver, so felt safe enough. Perhaps, she thought, she would run into the other women. Maybe they all went out together, although that seemed unlikely. And why take *her* overcoat?

She took her bearings and sallied forth.

It soon became clear the Drakes were not the only party celebrating at the Cliff House that night. From the uproar behind closed doors, the loud, drunken voices of men and women, and the occasional expletive as well as other sounds better befitting a bordello, Inez realized many of the late-night clientele were more of the Barbary Coast variety than the Nob Hill set.

This was confirmed when she turned to head back to the parlor and nearly ran into a young woman whose rouged cheeks, scandalous neckline, and potent perfume breathed more demimondaine than femme due monde.

The woman's scarlet lips parted in a grin. "Oops! Wrong way!" she said and twirled about, tripping merrily away. The heels of her fashionable shoes flashed gold in the dim light cast by the hall sconces. Perhaps, Inez thought, the rumors she had heard about favored sporting girls wearing golden double eagles for heelpieces on their slippers were more truth than rumor.

Two more turns and—

"Pardon," murmured a tall, slender man as he brushed past Inez.

Inez did a double take.

She'd seen his face but fleetingly—esthetically narrow, high cheekbones above a well-groomed, no-nonsense mustache, hair of a distinctive dark-red, almost mahogany, hue. He was not drunk, he was not leering, but he was a man on a mission as he strode away from her. *I know him. I've seen him before, but where?* Then, it hit her: the newspaperman who had appeared on the stairs of the Grand Opera House right before she and Antonia had taken their tour. The wild-haired, craze-eyed fellow who had demanded to see Graham Drake.

John Teague.

Only now he had shed his bohemian look, unkempt long hair, and shaggy beard, and appeared quite the proper gentleman.

What is he doing here? Tonight?

Intrigued, Inez reversed direction in time to see him disappear down a side hall. She hurried to follow. Was Teague planning to confront Graham Drake at his exclusive Christmas Eve gathering? If so, he was heading in the wrong direction. She slowed at the corner and peered warily around it. At the far end, he knocked on the door of what she assumed was a private room. At some invisible invitation, he entered. The door closed.

Inez moved to the runner rug that stretched the length of the silent, empty corridor—and hesitated. The lights were turned lower than in other areas she had ventured. Small tables punctuated the hall between the doors, each with a crystal ashtray. Inez hefted one, as she tried to decide what to do next. It was heavy, most certainly crystal, not glass. Setting it down, her decision made, she set her feet silently upon the carpet and advanced to the door John Teague had disappeared behind. She paused beside it, sweating a little lest the door fly open, and placed an ear close to the dark panel. She heard voices, male and female. The woman's voice was familiar. *Theia?*

The woman's voice rose higher and louder, tinged in desperation, and the words became clear. "John! Please, don't turn away from me."

Definitely Theia.

Inez glanced around. She didn't want to be caught lurking, ear glued to the door, by the room's occupants or by someone coming around the corner. She retreated to the next door down and twisted the handle experimentally. It swung open, revealing a room empty, but recently used. Flames guttered in the fireplace, shedding wavering light on a bed pushed against the back wall, its sheets tossed and crumpled. Inez discarded the images her imagination pulled up of what might have occurred on that bed. A table hosted two chairs and held two empty beer glasses. A murmur of voices rose and fell through the shared wall.

She picked up one of the beer mugs, shook out the few drops remaining, placed the rim flat against the wall, and set her ear against the bottom of the glass, screwing up her face in concentration. She hardly needed the facial contortions, as their conversation leapt out at her, strong and clear.

"We can't be seen here, Theia," John said. "What would Graham do if he found us like this?"

"I don't care! Please listen. I only care about you. It has always been you." The pleading in the diva's voice sounded sincere.

"No. I cannot. Don't do this."

"He wronged you. I wronged you. I made a mistake. I know that now. Please, let me make it right."

Inez had never heard the diva say the word "please" so often in such a short space of time.

"Theia, stop it. Let go." Teague sounded exasperated. Inez could almost imagine Theia clinging to his arm.

Theia said, "Back then, when I left you, I swear that I didn't know what had happened between you and Graham."

He sighed. "Listen, my current disagreements with Graham have nothing to do with all that."

"You have to understand, I didn't know what I was doing." A note of desperation had crept into the diva's voice.

"Look, Theia. You made your choice, a long time ago. The reasons I left the newspaper, the reasons I am fighting Graham with every penny I have, they have nothing to do with you."

Inez winced, thinking this was probably the worst thing anyone could say to Theia.

Theia gave a short, angry cry and said, "So. You don't love me anymore, is that what you are saying?"

"It doesn't matter how I feel. You are married to Graham. That can't be undone."

"After all these years, all this time that I have thought of you, longed for you. Well, then. Here. Take it!"

Take what? Inez pressed her ear even tighter against the smooth glass—almost as if, if she listened hard enough, carefully enough, she would be able to see what was happening on the other side of the wall.

"You kept this?" He sounded dumbfounded. "No. I'm sorry, Theia. I have to go now."

"You won't take it? Very well, then. Just like my heart, it now belongs to no one!"

A smart crack against the wall of her listening post caused Inez to jump and the beer glass to tumble to the carpet. Inez retrieved the glass only to hear the bang of a door hitting the wall in the next room. Fast, light footsteps hurried out and faded away.

That would be Theia.

After a space of silence, a heavier foot trod across the room and down the hall in the opposite direction.

That would be John Teague.

She cracked the door, saw nothing, and opened it wider just in time to see Teague's slender silhouette swing around the corner leading into the depths of the establishment.

"Well," she said to herself. "That was certainly operatic."

She wondered if the object that had hit the wall and set her ear a-ringing was still there or if the newsman had retrieved it.

There was only one way to find out.

She slid out of her room and into the one vacated by Theia and Teague. This chamber was different, with a made-up bed, a cold hearth, and a table for two, holding a low-burning oil lamp and the ubiquitous crystal ashtray. And there, on the floor by the wall adjoining her eavesdropping post, lay a small, dark lump.

She approached and picked it up.

One of Theia's bracelets. The one she had worn when Inez first met her at the Grand Opera House. Only then, it had anchored a thin gold chain that bound the diva's beloved yellow songbird to her wrist. A heavy gold clasp weighted a wide, intricate braid of woven material, thin as thread, gleaming in the subdued light.

Thin as thread.

Inez took the bracelet closer to the lamp and turned up the flame. Now she could see that the braid was not dark brown, but a dark red.

The same color as John Teague's hair.

Chapter Twenty-One

DECEMBER 24

Inez was pondering this unexpected development when she heard someone coming up the hallway. She twisted the lamp key to douse the flame and went to stand behind the half-open door, hoping whoever it was did not enter the room.

The flurry of footsteps grew louder, and she realized there were at least two people. A shadow flitted across the interior rug as they passed her room, and she heard Julia's distinctive voice say, "Must we really go outside for this? The weather—"

"Shh."

Inez could not tell from that single, drawn-out syllable whether Julia's companion was male or female.

No more was said, and Inez heard the door leading to the veranda open, bringing with it the sound of the sea, and then close.

First Theia, now Julia. Inez wondered if Yvonne would be the next to come traipsing up the passageway. She knew the identity of Theia's clandestine meeting partner. But who accompanied Julia? Someone Julia didn't want to be seen with, obviously. Or who didn't want to be seen with her.

Curious, Inez slipped out of the room to follow Julia and her companion out onto the veranda. If she "happened to" bump into them, she would say she was simply walking off the effects of dinner and the performance. She hurried to the egress and opened one of the double doors.

She gasped.

A westerly, straight from the Pacific, slapped her sideways, snatched her breath away, and chilled her to the bone. It buffeted her, as if trying to push her back inside, away from the veranda and its low railing fronting the sea. The roar of waves breaking on the rocks below drowned her senses and made her unsteady on her feet.

A hand seized her elbow from behind.

She yelped in surprise.

A male voice shouted in her ear, "Mrs. Stannert! Stop!"

The man drew her back into the hallway, then circled to shut the door. The crushing sound of the sea softened.

Inez set her arms akimbo, indignant at the familiarity of a stranger.

He turned, and her planned reprimand dissolved into bewilderment.

The dour-faced, silver-haired cardplayer from the Cliff House barroom pulled off his black-rimmed spectacles, rubbed his eyes, and straightened his shoulders. With the frown and accompanying creases smoothed from his face and his posture no longer stooped, Inez recognized de Bruijn.

Finding her tongue, she said, "Mr. de Bruijn! How did you do that? Gray your hair and so on? A most excellent disguise. I did not recognize you at all. But what are you doing here?"

He glanced about. "I could ask you the same. This is not a section of the Cliff House where I would expect to find a proper woman such as yourself. However, we should not linger where others might find us."

"Follow me." Inez led him back to the empty room where she had found the bracelet.

She lit the lamp wick with matches left on the table. Once the light penetrated the gloom, he shut the door. She faced him, her back to the table.

De Bruijn remained by the door. "I cannot stay long," he said. "To answer you, I was following Luis Rubio. I believe he came this way, but perhaps not. The layout of the building has changed since the last time I was here some years ago."

A chill that had nothing to do with the weather breathed down her spine. "Rubio is here? At the Cliff House? Now?"

De Bruijn nodded. "I thought he might show up tonight. He knows Mrs. Drake's schedule of appearances, just as we do. I came on a hunch, but it paid off when he appeared and set to drinking. Then, he left and I followed. Or tried to. Aside from that, I wanted to be sure everyone in your party was safe."

Inez said, "I was in this room when Julia passed by with someone. I don't know who."

"What were you doing here?" He shook his head. "Never mind. We can discuss that later. Did they go outside?"

"Yes. I was heading after them when you stopped me. Do you think Rubio is with her?"

"Possibly. No, make that probably." He tapped his walking stick once on the floor, looking at the wall as if he could see through to the outside. "I should check the promenade. There are so many exits and entrances in this building, it may be a lost cause."

"I'll go with you."

He seemed about to reply when a jumble of exuberant, slurred exclamations echoed up the hallway. Inez froze and saw de Bruijn do the same.

The door to the room next door opened and slammed shut. A male voice bellowed, "The party's gotta be here somewhere, boys. Let's keep lookin.'"

Inez sucked in her breath. *I heard that voice earlier tonight. Farallon Finn.*

She twisted around to quench the lamp, but de Bruijn was

suddenly next to her, spectacles in place, murmuring, "Apologies in advance, Mrs. Stannert."

He put an arm around her waist, pulled her close, and, to her utter astonishment, kissed her with vigor.

Inez floundered in a sudden flood of... *Now, just what do you feel anyway?* queried some small, snippy part of her consciousness. That little voice was quickly overwhelmed and didn't have a chance, swept away by the sudden rush of heat rising inside her. The hand she'd instinctively raised to his chest, preparing to shove him away, would no longer do her bidding. In fact, its traitorous fingers were clamoring to do quite the opposite and pull him in, closer still.

Somewhere beyond her roiling emotions, she heard the door to their room open and crash against the wall, followed by an incredulous hoot. "Whoa-ho! What have we here?"

De Bruijn relaxed his embrace, and Inez's eyes flew open. Until then, she hadn't even been aware she had shut them. His face, so close to her, so serious in its mien, telegraphed a silent warning. His expression shifted, and the dour frown and furrows in his face reappeared, adding years to his appearance. His shoulders slumped and the stooped posture returned. Dizzy and breathless, she still had the wherewithal to marvel at his ability to flow back into character.

Keeping hold of her waist, he addressed the interlopers in a low, rough voice, very unlike his own. "Occupied. Move along."

The door started to close, but a shadowy figure pushed it open, saying, "Well, well, well." The man stepped inside, into the light. An unmistakable gold tooth flashed in a calculated-to-charm grin. "It's the old codger who damn near robbed me blind at poker earlier tonight," said Finn. "And he's got a Christmas present for me. Right thoughtful of you, grandpa."

From within the protective circle of de Bruijn's embrace, Inez appraised the men.

Finn plus two companions, although it had sounded like more when they were carousing in the hallway.

Guns?

She didn't see any on display. But they all looked like the kind of roughs who might have something special tucked up sleeves or stowed in jacket pockets.

"I dunno, Finn," said one of his chums. "She don't look like a good-time girl to me."

The grin, if possible, widened. "Which makes it my lucky day. She's just the way I like them. Wrapped up neat and tight. All in black, like she's waiting for the right fella to come along and let her loose. She's no common soiled dove, I'd lay odds on it. No sirree, this is something special, just for us."

Inez sensed de Bruijn's grip on his walking stick tighten. She knew the havoc he could wreak with that simple weapon. She also suspected the group would not give him a chance to attack first.

It's up to me.

An unnatural calm, paired with a heightened alertness, descended on her. Details like the embroidery on the red buttons of Finn's waistcoat and the curve of the side of de Bruijn's neck in the lamplight appeared to her with crystal clarity. She brought her mouth to de Bruijn's ear and whispered, "Not yet. Follow my lead, and you'll know when."

With that, she finally gave her hand permission to push him away. He retreated a few steps, obviously reluctant to leave her side. She smiled at the men across the room. "Gentlemen, welcome. The truth is, I was bored with him before we started. So glad you came along to rescue me." Her gaze flicked from one to the other before settling on Finn, the obvious leader.

Finn licked his lips. "Well, now. We can start celebrating the holiday in style." His eyes strayed to her bodice and lingered there before traveling up to rest on the knot of ivory lace at her throat. "Yessirree. Wrapped up tight with a nice big bow."

Anger began to hum in her head, threatening her focus. She leaned back against the edge of the table, the fingers of one hand furtively exploring the tabletop behind her until they touched the object of her search.

Wait. Just a little longer.

With her other hand, she toyed with the lace bow, pulled slowly on one end, loosening the knot. She gave Finn her most seductive smile and purred, "Then you better come untie me, don't you think?"

Finn advanced, his grin widening.

De Bruijn, who, she judged, had been positioned so that he saw the tabletop and her machinations, took another step away. Finn's cohorts stationed themselves to either side of him, their eyes on Inez, stupid lust slapped on their slack faces.

Finn halted in front of Inez. Close enough that she could smell the waves of alcohol and garlic on his breath. Close enough for her next move. All she needed was the right moment.

Finn looked aside at de Bruijn. "How about we let you watch, old man? You can pay for the show with that sawbuck you won from me at the table." He snickered.

One of Finn's partners slung a companionable arm over de Bruijn's shoulders and said, "So, Finn, you plan on sharing?"

"After I'm through, I don't see any harm in giving you boys a turn. The spirit of the season and all. Just don't ride her too hard, because I might be ready for another go when you're done."

You filthy bastard.

Inez's rage, simmering throughout the exchange, came to a full boil.

As he turned back toward Inez, she slammed the crystal ashtray into his jaw, fast and hard, aiming for that gold tooth.

The howl that erupted from him was eminently satisfying. The spray of blood that splashed her face and her gown, not so.

For good measure, and because she thoroughly loathed men like him, she hit Finn again, just below the sternum.

He went down.

Twin thuds and a duet of groans elsewhere in the room told

her de Bruijn had dealt with the other two men, as she had hoped he would.

"On your stomach!" She kicked Finn in the ribs to punctuate her command.

He spasmed and rolled over, dribbling blood and bits of broken teeth.

The gold tooth, she was pleased to note, lay in a puddle of pink-tinged saliva. She rooted in her hidden pocket, finally untangling her pocket revolver from Theia's bracelet. Stepping close, Inez set the heel of one shoe upon the delicate web of bones on the back of Finn's hand. She wished she had a gold piece mounted to her shoe heel, like the lady of the night she had spotted earlier. That, she mused, would have been a nice bit of justice.

Inez applied a little pressure.

His twitching fingers stiffened.

"That's right," she cooed. "You want that hand to stay in good shape, don't you, so you can keep fleecing the greenhorns and taking unfair advantage of the women who are unfortunate enough to cross your path in the future."

She was rewarded with a small whimper.

"Oh, I know your kind well," she said through gritted teeth. "I've dealt with men like you before. Cheats. Liars. Bullies. Confidence men. Taking advantage of the naïve and the weak. Taking advantage of women."

Wonder of wonders, a "Please, ma'am," a little slurred due to missing teeth yet clearly audible, burbled up from the floor.

The red haze of wrath began clearing from her mind. She allowed herself a glance toward de Bruijn.

Finn's friends were also facedown on the floor and unconscious or close to it. The detective was binding their arms behind them with their own leather galluses. She took her foot off Finn's hand and set the muzzle of her gun against the nape of his neck. There was a terrified squeak, worthy of a mouse, and he blubbered, "I meant no disrespect."

Bully, con man, and a coward as well.

She flipped up the back of his jacket and removed the pistol from his waistband, reaching behind her to place it on the table. "Of course you didn't. And you won't be 'disrespecting' any other woman for a while, will you? Perhaps never again." She twisted the muzzle a little. "Here's my advice, free of charge. Pay first. Play later. And only with those ladies from the line who are interested in a financial exchange with you. Oh, a final word to the not-so-wise. Treat every woman as if she is a lady, even if you think she isn't."

A pair of worn boots appeared on the periphery of her vision. De Bruijn's words floated down to her. "We should go."

She nodded to show she had heard, then continued to Finn, "This is what you will do. You will lie here, quietly, and count to one hundred slowly. I assume you can count that high, since you probably count cards in your line of work. After that, you may quietly rise, free your friends, and quietly depart. Not a word to anyone of what happened here. After all, you three wouldn't want it nosed around how you were bested by a frail woman and a doddering old man, yes?" She straightened up and pocketed her gun. "Agreed? Please nod yes."

He nodded. Slowly.

"Excellent." She turned, grabbed Finn's firearm, lowered the wick in the lamp, and headed to the exit, saying, "Merry Christmas, gentlemen."

De Bruijn was at the door, checking the hallway. "It's clear."

Out in the hallway, the door closed behind them, she handed the gambler's firearm to de Bruijn. "Do us all a favor and toss that over the railing into the sea, if you would."

De Bruijn pocketed it, searching her face. "That blood is not yours, correct? You are not injured?"

She'd forgotten about the backsplash, but a quick examination of her lace-bow fichu, now splattered with a Christmasy red, was a colorful reminder. "Egads. I need to clean up." She hurried into the room next door. "Leave the door ajar for a little light," she said. A water pitcher, still partially full, stood on the bedstead, but there was no towel.

Untying the lace collar, she muttered, "I never want to see this again and it's ruined anyway." She soaked it and scrubbed her face before dabbing at her bodice. "Oh bother! Never mind. I'm glad Theia insisted that I wear black." She glanced at de Bruijn. "How do I look?"

"As you were." He stared at her oddly.

"What is it? Out with it!"

"Was all that necessary?"

She bristled. "What? I didn't break his hand. And I didn't shoot him, although I was sorely tempted. If I had, others would have heard and who knows who would have shown up to see what the racket was. And you, I would never have thought of using braces as restraints. I shall have to remember that." She looked him over. "I'm glad you jumped into the fray, although I was sure you would. I just wasn't certain how much of an expert you are at hand-to-hand combat." Remembering their kiss, she permitted herself a smile. " I have to say, you acquitted yourself most proficiently in that area. On all accounts."

He looked away. "I did not mean to take liberties. I had no time to explain—"

She waved a hand. "No need to apologize, de Bruijn, I rather enjoyed it." She added, "I must say, you continue to amaze me at the most unexpected times."

He didn't reply; his expression remained unreadable. Finally, he said, "It is probably much too late to find Rubio. Or Miss Green. But I'll venture out and take a look around. Do you need to return to the banquet?"

" I'd better get back to the parlor they set aside for us. It's not far."

"I'll escort you. What if you run into others such as Finn?"

"You should know by now, I can take care of myself. I know the way back, and I'll be careful. See if you can find Rubio."

As they left the room, she stopped him with a hand on his sleeve. "We must talk tomorrow. I know it's Christmas, but I'll be in the music store office, going over accounts all afternoon." She winced. Said aloud, her plans sounded so empty. She continued, "Would you care to join me for Christmas dinner? The landlady where I board said I could bring a guest. We could talk before or afterward."

She thought he was on the verge of declining, but instead he said, "Thank you. Perhaps after we talk."

She released him. "Be careful."

He walked toward the veranda, stopped, and turned around. "Did you really threaten to kill Rubio?"

"So you've spoken with him. I suppose I did. I have a bad habit of saying such things when attacked. I don't wail and faint. I fight."

He gave her a small smile. "So I have seen. And you do it very well." He straightened his hat, said, "See you tomorrow afternoon, Mrs. Stannert," and went out onto the veranda.

Inez wasted no time returning to the parlor. She hoped she could slip inside, that everyone was still out running about, skulking around, taking the air, whatever the excuse or reason, and that she could sit by the fire and collect her wits.

But no sooner did she open the door than four heads swiveled her way. Mr. Drake stood by the fireplace. Theia and Yvonne were in chairs on either side of the fire. Theia sobbed, her hair a mess. Yvonne, her fists in her lap, looked wound tight as a spring. One more twist and Inez sensed she would fly apart. Captain Foster was there as well, much to Inez's surprise. The atmosphere in the room was tense, nearly explosive.

Captain Foster was the first to speak. "Thank the heavens, Mrs. Stannert, you're safe!"

She wondered if he knew of her exploits. *No. How could he?* "Why yes, I just took a turn around the building and got a bit lost. I didn't mean to worry anyone. I would have ventured outside for air, but my cloak was gone." She realized then that Theia wore it draped over her shoulders.

"Where is Miss Green?" Inez asked.

Graham Drake jerked forward, an oddly mechanical movement, his face stiff, unreadable. A tic began to twitch under his left eye. "There's been an unspeakable accident. Miss Green, she..." He stopped, seemingly lost for words.

Foster continued, "A horrible, sad affair, Mrs. Stannert. It appears Miss Green fell from the veranda. Or perhaps jumped. The railings are low, something I have wanted to rectify. So it could be an accident, it could have been deliberate. She fell to the rocks below. She...is..."

"Oh say it!" wailed Theia. "Just say the word! She is *dead*! You all talk this way and that. You say she fell, she jumped, but how? Why? No! I tell you, someone *pushed* her over the rail. She was wearing *my* cloak. Whoever did this must have thought she was me! It could have been *me* on the rocks below!"

Chapter Twenty-Two

After leaving Mrs. Stannert, de Bruijn ventured out on the veranda, clutching his hat against the fierce breeze. The wide planks were empty. Staying close to the walls of the building, he approached the nearest corner, thinking to make a circuit of the outside in search of Rubio.

The west-facing promenade came into view, and he stopped. The porch, far from being deserted, had a small crowd milling about. Flickering lanterns lit shadowy figures, most of them peering over the railing, some pointing down at the steep, rocky cliffs that gave the roadhouse its name. He was tempted to approach, linger about the edges, and find out what the disturbance was about. It was not unknown for some unfortunate soul, too drunk to see straight or perhaps with a little help from a more sober ruffian, to tumble over the railing and onto the rocks.

De Bruijn then recalled the ruffians he had recently left counting to one hundred and decided it would be more circumspect to leave. Besides, he would most likely not find Señor Rubio now. If the pianist had come to meet Miss Green, their meeting would have been brief by necessity, since the young singer would have had to return to the parlor before she was missed.

In any case, if Rubio had departed, de Bruijn would know soon enough. He had hired a dependable set of eyes to watch for just that event.

The investigator took a nearby door and made his way back to the front of the Cliff House, avoiding the more public areas.

The size of the crowd at the entrance matched the crowd at the back, and the attendants were busy helping departing parties into various rigs and hacks. Eagle-eyed Pete, the doorman de Bruijn had engaged, hurried up to him. "Would you like your carriage back to town, sir?" he said, loud enough for others to hear, then lowered his voice. "He left, not fifteen minutes ago."

De Bruijn believed him. Pete had an almost preternatural ability to keep straight a multitude of faces and names, which made him invaluable to Cliff House management as well as to the investigator.

Resigned that his quarry had yet again slipped away, de Bruijn nodded and slipped Pete a single. The paper note slid from palm to pocket with nary a crinkle.

"I'll get your hack," Pete announced and started to turn to the carriage house.

"A moment," said de Bruijn. "Do you know what happened on the west veranda?"

Pete scratched one of his sideburns. "Someone went over the second-floor railing. Body's hung up on the rocks just above the beach. Captain Foster came out here, looking for volunteers to go down and bring 'er up." He lowered his voice. "Rumor has it's one of the doxies that was here tonight. Poor mite, Christmas Eve and all, maybe it was too much and she decided to end it, eh? Anyhow, things are quite a muddle right now. Not good for business and the Captain isn't happy. There're more than a few folks cutting holiday celebrations short and heading back to the city. Mostly the kind who don't want to be questioned too closely when the coppers come, if you get my drift, sir."

De Bruijn certainly did get the drift, and he decided it would be best if he left as well.

On the way back to town, he pondered the fate of the Cliff House. Compared to what it had been during his previous stays in San Francisco, the business had taken a tumble in reputation. Once the destination of wealthy San Franciscans and even U.S. presidents, it was still fairly staid during the daytime, when it catered mostly to tourists and the less wealthy locals. But once the sun set, those who preferred the night for business and entertainment crept out to its isolated reaches.

He wondered what had led Graham Drake to think the Cliff House was a proper venue for a gathering of "the better sort" on Christmas Eve. He only hoped that Drake and the ladies would retreat to the city before news reached them of the death on the cliffs below.

It seemed he had just reached his rooms, washed up, and retired when the knocking at the door began. Usually he awoke at once, clearheaded and alert, but his sleep— what there was of it—had been disturbed and restless. He blamed it on the unsettling events of the previous evening and the odd, unexpected interlude with Mrs. Stannert.

Now, here he was, on an early Christmas morning. At least, it must be morning, given that he had returned to the hotel after midnight. The sky, through the scrim of lace curtain, was neither blue sky nor gray mist but had the hesitant air of being just short of dawn.

He got up, threw on a dressing gown, and went to the door with the persistent tapping just beyond. "Who is it?" he called through the solid panel.

"Sir, a message, from Mr. Drake, sir."

Recognizing Toby's voice, de Bruijn opened the door. "It must be serious business for Mr. Drake to send you down at this hour."

Toby's tan uniform looked as if he'd just stepped into it neatly pressed. The only evidence he had been roused and sent out at this unholy hour was the state of his hair, uncombed, with unruly curls sticking out above his ears. "Yes, sir. It is. The police are here, questioning the Drakes. Mr. Drake wants you present as soon as possible. He asked I wait for you."

Thoroughly awake now, de Bruijn said, "A moment." He closed the door, retreated to his bed chamber, and donned his clothes as quickly as possible. Recalling Toby's cowlicks, he took an extra few seconds to comb his hair, beard, and mustache before emerging. "Let us go, then."

The lights were blazing in the music room when they arrived. Graham was pacing by the unlit fireplace, clenching and unclenching his hands as if he wished there were a neck he could strangle. Theia, weeping, and Yvonne, stiff and silent as stone, occupied armchairs on opposite sides of the cold hearth. They appeared as a matching set of bookends with Graham trapped between them.

Theia looked up at de Bruijn's entry, her eyes red-rimmed. She appeared terrified and, de Bruijn thought, older and more helpless than he had seen her to date. "Oh, Mr. de Bruijn! Thank heavens you are here."

Yvonne glanced at him but said nothing.

Graham swung around and said, "Toby, go back to your room."

Toby threw de Bruijn an apprehensive glance. It was almost as if the scene between the messenger and Señor Rubio rose up, ghostlike, summoned by the boy's anxious fears. The investigator wished he could say, "Your secret is safe with me," but, of course, that was out of the question. All he could do was nod encouragingly and hope that conveyed all he could not say.

The minute the door shut, Graham said tersely, "It's Miss Green. She apparently threw herself over the rail at the Cliff House last night. The police are here, in her room right now."

Theia rose, hands clutched before her. "Julia was wearing my cloak. I lent it to her when she misplaced her own. She went outside and, and…"

"Enough!" Graham's voice cracked like a whip. "The girl is dead."

Theia shrank down into her chair.

The connecting door to Yvonne's room opened. Detective Martin Lynch, of the San Francisco detective force, entered the music room, dressed slapdash in street clothes. He held a crumpled paper in one hand. A uniformed policeman and Adams, the hotel's night manager, followed.

"Mr. de Bruijn," said Detective Lynch. "Top o' the morning to ye." The words oozed sarcasm. De Bruijn suspected Lynch, dedication to the job notwithstanding, was not happy about being dragged away from a warm bed at this hour and on this particular holy day. His suspicion was confirmed when Lynch continued, "However, I think you'd agree this is not the way to start Christmas morning. Mr. Drake wanted you present. He said he'd engaged your services." He raised his ginger eyebrows and waited for de Bruijn to elaborate.

De Bruijn was saved from having to answer when Graham said, "I told you, Detective, I hired him to help with a trifling matter that has no bearing on this whatsoever. Matters of a business nature."

Lynch nodded without taking his gaze from de Bruijn. "So you say, Mr. Drake. And a better private investigator would be hard to find, in my estimation. Certainly the only one I can think of who would roust himself to stand by his client before the first bells of Christmas morning." He glanced over at the uniform and the night manager. "Mr. Adams, please wait outside with Officer MacKenzie here. I will be done in short order with this sad business, and perhaps we will all be able to retire and gain some rest before the sun rises."

Adams said, "What shall we do with Miss Green's possessions?" He sounded faint.

"Leave them be for now," said Lynch. "There's no reason to move them."

The two men went into the hallway, Adams throwing glances nearly as nervous as Toby's toward de Bruijn.

Once they were gone, Detective Lynch let out a long sigh. "Gentlemen, please sit. It will be better for what I have to say."

Graham Drake looked as if he wanted to object, but Theia held out a hand and said, "Dearest, sit by me."

He sat on the edge of the love seat by Theia's chair. De Bruijn took a straight chair where he could observe everyone's faces. He noticed the Drakes were still dressed in formal evening wear, probably the same they had worn to the Cliff House.

Once everyone was settled, Lynch said, "I believe this paper, found in Miss Green's wastebasket, serves to at least partially explain the events of tonight. But I hope one or more of you might know more about the particulars."

He smoothed out the paper on the top of the grand piano, then read aloud, "I will be brief and direct. I am horrified and upset by what you said to me earlier. Such words should never have been spoken, ever. You must know, I cannot go on living like this. Knowing the lie that I now know is you…" He looked up. "That is all it says. The last words are scratched out. The paper was crumpled and thrown away."

He surveyed them all and said again, with heavy emphasis, "*I cannot go on living like this.* My question is, do any of you have thoughts on who Miss Green was writing to? What the matter in question might be?"

De Bruijn watched Graham's face close up as his hands did the same. Yvonne licked her lips, clamped them shut, and twined her fingers together, hiding them in her lap. Theia's gaze skittered from one face to the other, settling on de Bruijn, pleading.

He was nonplussed by the intensity of her gaze. *What does she want from me?*

Silence reigned supreme.

Lynch's penetrating stare moved from Graham, to Theia, to Yvonne, lingering on each. They twitched beneath his inspection but said nothing.

He finally continued, "From my brief interviews at the Cliff House, I am thinking the lass took her own life. 'Twould not be the first time such has happened. I will return and speak again with

Captain Foster and the attendants who recall seeing her. However, that seems to be the consensus, and this"—he held up the discarded note—"supports that notion. But, if this is so, I would like to know why. I'll say right now, I'm not discounting that whoever she wrote to might have had a hand in hastening her to her end. With that in mind, can any of you tell me if Miss Julia Green might have had a beau? Someone she was, ah, intimate with?"

"Luis Rubio!" Theia burst out.

Lynch frowned.

Shock replaced Graham's defiant expression. He rounded on his wife. "Spreading gossip is beneath you, Mrs. Drake. Miss Green is dead and you smear her reputation?"

De Bruijn had hoped to talk to Lynch privately about Rubio, but now he saw no choice except to speak up. "I believe Mrs. Drake is right. Miss Green and Mr. Luis Rubio were more than mere acquaintances."

Graham's attention jumped to de Bruijn. "Why did you not tell me this?" he snarled.

Lynch held up a hand and addressed Yvonne. "Miss...Marchal, is it? Did you know of this?"

Yvonne looked down at her hands as if meditating or praying, then at Detective Lynch. "It could be true. Mr. Rubio joined us in Denver as an accompanist to Madame. I saw him and Miss Green together on many occasions. So I wondered..." She faltered.

Lynch scrubbed his face with one hand, muttered, "Jesus, Mary, and Joseph," then said, "Apologies, ladies, for the blasphemy. Thank you all for your cooperation. I may return to speak to you. Mr. de Bruijn, I'd like a private word with you now, if you will."

Graham rose without glancing at his wife or anyone else, said, "I'll be in my rooms," and left. Yvonne hurried to Theia, who seemed on the point of fainting. "Madame, let me help you."

"Oh, leave me alone!" Theia cried. She gathered her skirts around her and fled into her own chambers, slamming the door behind her.

Yvonne drooped, then straightened and turned to Lynch. "My chambers are joined with Miss Green's. Is there anything I should do?"

"Not at present. The door is locked between your rooms and hers. We'll hold the key for now, just to keep anyone from going through her effects. Has Miss Green any family who should be notified?"

"She was quite alone. Madame took her in, trained her. Madame always said she thought of Miss Green as a daughter. She..." Yvonne covered her mouth and seemed to struggle to hold something back. She finally said weakly, "Such an awful thing to happen. So young. Why would she kill herself? Life is a gift."

"I hate to say, but many never seem to stop and consider what a permanent solution it is for dealing with life's sufferings." Lynch shook his head. "Listen to me, going on like a priest. I'll light a candle for Miss Green today. Miss Marchal, you might do the same."

"Merci." Yvonne headed to her rooms with her slow, soundless tread.

Lynch jerked his head toward the door and de Bruijn followed him into the hallway where the night manager and policeman waited.

Adams approached. "Is there anything we should do at this point, Detective Lynch?"

"Nothing more today. 'Tis Christmas, and I believe we have what we need to proceed."

"I hate to ask, but I will need to let Mr. Leland, the Palace's manager, know. Has this anything to do with the hotel?"

Beneath his ginger mustache, Lynch's mouth twisted into a humorless smile. "You and Mr. Leland can rest easy on that account. Miss Green's death took place at the Cliff House. The only tie I see is that she was residing here."

Adams bowed his head. "Thank you. Such a terrible thing, the death of Miss Green. She was quite a light during her short time here and seemed to have a bright future in the city."

Lynch turned to de Bruijn after the manager departed. "So, we'll make this short, Mr. de Bruijn. I hope to get a few winks before the missus shakes me awake for morning Mass. What can you tell me about Miss Green and Luis Rubio?"

De Bruijn chose his words carefully. "I had occasion to speak separately to both of them. I believe Miss Green fancied herself in love. I do not believe the feeling was mutual, although I believe Luis Rubio was fond of her. They were both slated to join the company at the Grand Opera House starting in the new year." An unexpected pang of sorrow swept through him. "Miss Green had much to look forward to and seemed excited about what the future would bring. It is difficult to see her taking her own life, even in the face of a love affair gone sour." He suddenly recalled an offhand comment from the young singer. "She confided she was afraid of heights. If that was the case, why would she choose such a manner for her death?"

Lynch waved a tired hand. "Who knows what might have gone through the lass's head last night. The Cliff House. At night." He shook his head. "Didn't Mr. Drake know the reputation of the place? And to take the ladies there. He may be one of the richest men in the city right now, but that is hardly the decision of a man with half a brain. I know he is a client of yours, but still."

"I should add, Detective, that Señor Rubio was at the Cliff House last night. I was there, unbeknownst to the Drakes, following him. It seems like too much of a coincidence to ignore. I regret that he gave me the slip." Regrets at this point were meaningless, he told himself. "Also, Miss Green apparently met with someone who did not want to be seen. It could have been Luis Rubio. Too, he left soon after the body was found."

" And did you observe this meeting between Miss Green and her mystery visitor?"

"No," admitted de Bruijn. "It is hearsay, from someone who heard but did not see them."

"Hearsay from who?"

De Bruijn did not like the direction of the detective's questions. He hesitated, trying to work out if there was a way to be truthful without mentioning Mrs. Stannert by name.

At that moment Officer MacKenzie, who was anxiously checking his pocket watch, interjected, "Pardon, Detective, will you need me to return with you to the station after this? My shift is over, and me mam is expecting me to take her to early services."

With a start, Detective Lynch pulled out his own pocket watch, examined the time, and swore softly under his breath. "You're dismissed, Officer MacKenzie. I've got to drop this bit of letter off at the station before I head home myself."

The officer touched his brim and hurried off. Lynch started to follow and de Bruijn stopped him. "A quick question. Am I right in thinking you know of Señor Rubio?"

"The Rubio family is well known. An old family, with not inconsiderable influence."

A non-answer. De Bruijn pressed, "Do you know of Luis Rubio's...proclivities?"

"Proclivities is it?" Lynch sounded amused. "There's not many 'proclivities' I don't know of, given my years in the force, most of them on the Barbary Coast." He looked hard at de Bruijn. "I'd not like to get crosswise of any of the Rubios in this case, unless we find someone who will swear on a stack of Bibles they saw Luis Rubio catch the girl by the waist and heave her over the railing. Proclivities or otherwise, the Rubios protect their own. If they sense we are sniffing after one of theirs, one quick ticket across the bay to the train station and *pffft!*" He snapped his fingers. "Gone! Before you can say Jack Robinson."

He glanced down at the paper in his hand. "Miss Green's own words in her own hand is enough for now. Perhaps we'll take another look through her room later. Unless something else comes up—something concrete, mind you, not the musings of one of those whiskey-soaked sots who frequent the Cliff House after midnight—then we will set aside the idea of Señor Rubio being anything more than the agent to a broken heart. For now."

He headed toward the stairs, adding, "You might offer up a prayer for the young woman on this day of all days. She seems to have no family to mourn her passing. Perhaps God the Father might take pity on her poor tortured soul, forgive her this mortal sin, and allow her to sing with his angels."

Chapter Twenty-Three

DECEMBER 25

When the church bells rang at six o'clock Christmas morning, Inez awoke and lay motionless, listening.

How could they sound so exuberant? It was not even dawn. Not a hint of the light yet to come.

And Julia Green was dead.

Inez turned her head toward the window. A mist or a light rain coated the glass beyond the half-open curtain. The clack of hooves and squeak of wheels on cobblestones heralded the arrival of the thin light from a carriage lantern that slid across the mottled moisture on the pane.

She sighed and shifted from her back to her side, her heels bumping the iron frame of the too-short bed. In Antonia's absence, Inez had abandoned her bedroom farther back in the flat and had taken to sleeping in Antonia's room, which had a window overlooking the street. Alone in the apartment, knowing that below their rooms stretched the empty, dark music store, she didn't like being tucked away at night, unable to see the front of the building and the street.

Particularly last night, when ghosts and fears crowded her feverish imagination.

She pulled Antonia's feather pillow over her eyes, trying to block out the memory of the nightmare at evening's end at the Cliff House. Breathing in the sweet, sweaty scent of the girl, Inez found she missed Antonia more than she wanted to admit. And right then, in the predawn, with the pillow shutting out sight and sound but not the reality of death, she missed her Leadville lover, the Reverend Justice B. Sands, and her long-absent son, William Stannert, who had just turned three years old a continent's width away. God help her, she even missed her charming scoundrel of an ex-husband, Mark Stannert.

At that moment she missed them all with an ache that extended to her very toes.

She suspected the bottle of brandy, full when she'd brought it with her to bed and now half empty on the nearby nightstand, had something to do with the ghosts and sorrows that surrounded her in the predawn, whispering their regrets to her. The tumbler standing next to the bottle glinted, still partially full. She could drain it dry, close her eyes, and slide into forgetfulness for a while longer.

She hauled back hard on the unexpected feelings, like pulling on the reins of a runaway horse. *Enough. I have to focus on today.*

Still, she couldn't shut out the awfulness of the previous night. The frozen shock that had descended over her, like a suffocating blanket, at the news of Julia Green's death. Her first coherent thought had been a denial: *She can't be dead. I just heard her voice, less than an hour ago.* But she kept her mouth shut and kept her peace. The wiser course had seemed to be to sink into the chair next to Yvonne and follow the maid's lead by fading into the wallpapered background and observing. The Drakes occupied center stage in the drama, supported by Captain Foster, his aides, and an off-duty San Francisco policeman who had happened to be taking a little pre-holiday cheer in the bar.

Inez hadn't seen Julia's corpse but had heard Foster conferring with the men who brought it up, had heard them say, "She didn't have a chance, hit the rocks hard, head split like a melon."

Yvonne, next to Inez, must have heard as well. She had risen from her chair and dashed to a spittoon in the corner of the room to be sick.

There were questions with no answers: How did it happen? When? Why?

As she listened, Inez realized that the men were circling in on an agreement that Julia must have jumped of her own free will, intending to destroy herself. This, despite Theia's loud insistence that, dressed as Julia had been in Theia's enveloping silvered velvet cloak, it could have been murder, with Theia as the target.

Theia could be right.

Inez groaned and sat up. The pillow tumbled to the floor.

The bells were silent. She thought she must have dozed off again, because morning had arrived to flood the small bedroom with light. Craning her gaze upward, she saw that Christmas Day had brought a brilliant blue sky, clear of clouds.

She threw back the covers, set one bare foot on the braided rug, and through sheer will propelled herself upright and standing. She immediately sat back down to don a pair of heavy woolen socks and then padded out into the apartment. First, she'd stoke the fire in the small stove, heat a large kettle of water, grind coffee beans. The water would serve for making at least one cup of coffee, maybe more. Between downing the coffee—black, strong, bitter—and scrubbing herself down with copious amounts of lukewarm water, Inez felt she could face the rest of the day.

At least the Drakes had given her Christmas off. Thank goodness. She just didn't think she could face the Drakes and Yvonne so soon. However, de Bruijn would be coming by later.

Inez paused in the act of tying her everyday corset. *De Bruijn.* That kiss from the previous night. All business, or something more? Too early to tell, she decided. They were colleagues, certainly. She then wondered if he knew about Julia's demise. The Drakes would probably have told him. He might even be roped into an investigation of her death.

Once dressed, Inez returned to her kitchen table. Theia's bracelet, woven from Teague's hair, waited patiently, curled like a small snake. She dropped the bracelet in the same hidden pocket that carried her Smoot revolver. She had decided she would bring the weapon with her from this point forward, no matter what.

She retrieved hat and gloves, left the apartment, and descended the stairs to the small, street-level vestibule. Bypassing the overcoat Theia had "borrowed" from the previous night, she grabbed her cloak. Even though the music store was only twenty steps or so from the street-level door of her apartment, she would not venture outside without the accoutrements of a proper lady.

The street was quiet, stores shut up tight for the holiday. Using her key, Inez entered, calling, "Good morning, Mr. Hee," so as not to startle her employee.

The curtain to the alcove where John Hee spent his time repairing instruments twitched aside. He emerged, looking surprised, with a bowl and chopsticks. "Mrs. Stannert! I was not expecting you. No church? On Christmas?"

"No church for me today, Mr. Hee." She turned to the Christmas tree by the entrance and touched a paper streamer hanging from one brittle branch. Dried needles scattered to the floor. If Antonia were at home, Inez would have insisted they attend the First Unitarian on Geary. But being alone today, and considering the events of the previous night, she could not imagine warbling hosannas to the highest. She turned back to Hee. "I have much to do in the office. Matters have piled up while I've been engaged by the Drakes."

"Mr. Drake came yesterday," said Hee. "Bought another vase."

"You found him one to match the oxblood?" Inez exclaimed.

"A *Langyao hong*. Yes. Not exact match. But good."

"Good enough, then." Inez felt guilty at the zing of satisfaction that sparked through her.

"For Christmas gift. For his wife," said Hee. He continued to stare at Inez, a small frown creasing his smooth features. "Mrs. Stannert, you have breakfast?"

"What?" Then she realized he was asking if she had had breakfast. She recalled the now-stale bread in the bread-safe upstairs and what was probably a slightly moldy chunk of cheese in her much-depleted larder. "I am used to surviving on coffee. I will eat my fill at Mrs. Nolan's Christmas supper this evening."

Hee disappeared behind the curtain. Inez started toward the back office, stopping to admire the Steinway grand now occupying pride of place in the store. "I shall have to try this out later," she remarked to the air. "A gift to myself, after I tackle the books and correspondence."

"Mrs. Stannert, here." Hee had re-emerged from his alcove and was holding a different bowl and spoon out to her. "Breakfast. Happy Christmas."

Inez looked at the proffered bowl of what looked like mush. "Why, thank you, Mr. Hee. Um. What is it, may I ask?"

"Congee." At her puzzled expression, Hee tried again. "Jook. Rice porridge." He extended the bowl. "Sorry, not warm. But good for breakfast."

Touched, she took the bowl and spoon. "Thank you." Casting about for something to offer in exchange, she said, "I am going to make coffee in the office. Would you like a cup?"

"Coffee." He made a face, then looked contrite and shook his head. "Happy Christmas."

She bowed her head. He did likewise. She added, "Mr. de Bruijn will be by later today. Remember him? If he comes to the front door and you see him before I do, please let him in."

He nodded.

Satisfied she had done what she needed to do, and touched by John Hee's "Christmas breakfast," she went to her office and settled in to lose herself in the columns of numbers—income, outflow, moneys owed, bills to be paid.

The jook was long gone, a third cup of coffee gone cold, and the day on the wane when Inez stood to stretch and consider. The music store's business was picking up, which was good, but the moneys owed them on credit had ballooned. Not unexpected around the holiday, but this year was excessive. That sudden upwelling could be traced to one account: the Drakes.

It was clear. She would have to ask Graham Drake to bring his account up-to-date. The two vases themselves, the piano leases, they added up. And he had apparently been by twice more to purchase small but expensive Oriental statuary.

Inez had yet to tackle her "personal" business books, the accounting of the various small women-run businesses that she championed. She was about to take a break and test out the Steinway when she heard a tapping from the front of the store, quick steps, and the "clunk" of the bell over the door. Subdued murmurings accompanied the double tread of two people. Inez moved toward the main room of the store, calling, "Mr. de Bruijn. Excellent timing."

John Hee retired to his alcove, leaving de Bruijn to make his way. His somber expression told Inez the detective knew. Nonetheless, she asked. "You have heard about Miss Green?"

His mouth was a hard line through the short, neat beard. "I have."

Inez indicated a chair at the round table. He sat, put his cane aside, and removed his bowler hat with care. She went to her office and returned with two glasses and a bottle of whiskey. The brandy, alas, was upstairs in Antonia's bedroom and unavailable. She didn't ask if he wanted any, simply poured a measure for them both. She sat across from him and held up her glass. "To Miss Green. A young woman with fortitude and talent. A singer who will not sing again in this world. May her spirit soar in the hereafter, since it was cut far too short in this life."

Throughout her tribute, de Bruijn kept his eyes on the tumbler before him. When she finished, he picked up the glass and touched it to Inez's in silent acknowledgment. They drank. Inez set hers down, empty, noting that de Bruijn had barely touched his.

She crossed her arms on the table. "I heard what happened when I returned to the ladies' parlor at the Cliff House. They were talking about suicide. I do not believe for a moment that she took her own life."

"Nor do I." He nudged his whiskey glass away. "The Drakes called for me, well before dawn. Detective Lynch was in the suite, searching Miss Green's room when I arrived." He told Inez about the half-finished letter and what it said.

Inez frowned. "*I cannot go on living like this.* So melodramatic. The sort of thing a young woman would declaim when confronted with, oh, infidelity or some such. In fact, it sounds like something Theia might say." She sat up straighter. "Do they know for a certainty that the letter was penned by Julia?"

The moment Theia's name left her lips, de Bruijn had started shaking his head. "I do not know if they have other samples of her handwriting. But I'm not certain it matters. The assumption of suicide was made and 'proof' found. This being Christmas Day, with Miss Green having no kin, I can well believe her death will merely be noted in a few column inches in the city's newspapers."

"But probably not in Graham Drake's *San Francisco Times*," said Inez dryly. "I can't imagine the Drakes would want to advertise that Theia's protégée met such a horrifying end in such a setting. Besides, Graham knows Mr. Adolph Sutro from Virginia City, and Mr. Sutro has just bought the Cliff House. I don't think that's public knowledge yet. Sutro is quite the force in town, buying up land here and there. I can imagine Graham would want to cultivate his favor here."

She gazed at de Bruijn thoughtfully, taking close note of his appearance. Every hair was in place. His dark-gray suit had been carefully brushed, as had the gray felt bowler hat. One well-manicured hand lay still and steady on the table, fingers only inches from the tumbler of whiskey. By every indication, he was under control. But the subtle set of his eyes as he focused on the glass of liquor before him, the compressed lips, the almost pre-ternatural stillness, gave him away. He was, she thought, holding himself together by sheer will.

It occurred to her that when de Bruijn had stopped her from following Julia out onto the veranda, he had perhaps inadvertently sealed the singer's fate. If she had followed Julia outside, she would have most likely seen the young woman and her mystery companion and might have interrupted the flow of events that led to Julia's death.

Inez steeled herself. *What is done is done. Now, to the next item of business, which will not be pleasant, nor easy.* "There is more you should know about the events at the Cliff House. Something that happened before I heard Julia go by. I was in the hallway, heading out for some air, when I heard Theia in one of the rooms. In fact, the room you and I were in when we were, ah, interrupted."

His gaze snapped to her.

She held up a hand. "Yes, I know. Coincidence. Serendipity. Call it what you will. In fact, I was following John Teague." She stopped. "Did I tell you about Teague?"

De Bruijn shook his head, looking baffled.

So, he doesn't know about this part of Theia's past, apparently. "He is a newsman, but I don't know much about him," she said. "I first saw him at the Grand Opera House after Theia's appear-ance. He was making quite the fuss, demanding to see Graham Drake, intimating that Mr. Drake was not who he seems, and insisting that, as a newsman, Teague saw it as his duty to tell the world. There's clearly some conflict between him and Drake. At the Cliff House, Theia and Teague met, and it was obviously a prearranged meeting."

She closed her eyes, pulling up bits of the overheard conver-sation. "Teague told Theia that his 'current disagreements with Graham' had nothing to do with what happened 'back then.'" She opened her eyes. "Teague did not elucidate on those past events. I'm guessing Theia knew what he meant, because she did not press him in that direction."

"How did you hear this conversation?" De Bruijn's tone was sharp.

"I eavesdropped," she said matter-of-factly. "If you want to know how, I shall explain later. But every word they said was clear. I did not mishear nor am I embellishing. Anyhow, Teague said that he left the newspaper for reasons that had nothing to do with Theia. I'm assuming he was employed by *The San Francisco Times*? A guess on my part. What is not a guess is that John Teague and Theia have a past history. And she still carries, or carried, a torch for him."

De Bruijn sat back in the chair, his hand sliding away from the glass before him. "How did you reach these conclusions?" His tone was distant now, professional.

"It was what they said and how they said it. And, there is more." *In for a penny, in for a pound.* "Theia tried to hand him an object, saying 'Here, take it!' When he refused, she said, and I quote, 'Just like my heart, it now belongs to no one.' She then threw it at him, but it hit the wall. She is prone to throwing things, you know. I went into the room after they left and retrieved this." She pulled out the hair bracelet with its heavy gold clasp and set it on the table.

He looked at it as if afraid the piece of jewelry would poison him if he touched it.

Inez continued, "Hairwork from John Teague's hair, which is a very distinctive red."

"I thought hairwork was only used in memento mori." He finally picked up the bracelet.

"Mourning jewelry, certainly. But it is also used in keepsakes by those with a special affection for each other." She cleared her throat. "I propose to find out more about Teague."

De Bruijn let the bracelet drop from his fingers. "What connection could this possibly have with the events of the present?"

She blinked. "You mean the bird, the dress, and Miss Green's death?"

"Yes." The answer was terse.

He clearly wanted to get back to the matters at hand. Inez was willing to let it drop. She had said what she meant to say.

"Perhaps nothing." She frowned. "However, it involves Graham Drake. More and more, I feel he is hiding a great deal. He had access to the room where the initial mischief occurred. He was unaccounted for at the same time all of us women were wandering about the Cliff House. In retrospect, that was quite stupid of us, given the Cliff House's after-dark reputation, but oh well."

"I should have been there," said de Bruijn grimly. "I suggested to Mr. Drake that I attend, but he turned me down. Hence my lurking in the shadows, as it were. So, tell me, how did the evening progress, after you arrived? Were you at the banquet itself?"

She told him how they had cooled their heels in the nearby parlor room until Theia and Julia were called in for dinner. She debated telling him about her conversation with Yvonne but decided to skim over it for now. "I was then brought in to play for Theia, as expected. What I did not expect was that Miss Green also took a turn singing, solo, without accompaniment. It was then that I realized what an accomplished vocalist she is. And at such a young age, not yet fully matured into her voice. Such a loss." She continued on with the scene between Theia and Julia, adding, "Not unexpected, given the circumstances." She explained about her solo turn at the piano and finished with, "When I returned to the ladies' parlor, it was empty."

He raised his eyebrows. "Yvonne was gone as well?"

"No Yvonne. No Julia. No Theia. And my coat had disappeared." She frowned. "Theia said Julia had lost hers, so she gave her own to Julia, then took mine instead. I don't quite understand why. Anyway, I went out myself and, well, you know the rest. When I returned after your and my set-to, everyone was back. Mr. Drake claims he had also been out wandering about, searching for us. So, who is to say? Who is to say whether he, oh, took a shine to Miss Green and propositioned her? She wrote a letter to him, his vanity was wounded, his temper got the better of him. Possible, don't you think?"

He picked up his whiskey at last and drained it. "The thought had occurred to me. He seems to have little patience with his wife these days. Theirs does not seem to be a happy marriage. And I've seen him look at Miss Green in a manner that makes me wonder."

"Yes. I have seen that too." She hesitated, then blurted out, "I don't trust Graham Drake." There. She'd said it. "I don't like how he treats others. He can be all charm but then turn mean as a snake. I sense he has quite a temper. Perhaps even a violent disposition. I don't like him."

"And there is Yvonne." His dark, unreadable gaze settled on her. "You say she was absent at the same time."

"Yes." At this admission, Inez sighed. "Theia treats her most cruelly. And Graham doesn't hold her in very high esteem either."

He made a dismissive gesture with the glass. "Yet, she stays loyal. Finally, there is Rubio. He was at the Cliff House. And he is, or was"—he set the glass down—"involved, if you will, with Miss Green."

"Goodness, yes." Inez clasped her hands together, staring down at them. "What a mess." She looked up. "Señor Rubio. Did you, by chance, catch up with him afterward?"

He shook his head. "He left the Cliff House before me, but after Miss Green's accident. I searched for him earlier today. He's not at the Grand Opera House. He might be at the Rubio family manse. I have no way of finding out at present."

"You know where the Rubios live?" She was surprised he had ferreted out that information, on Christmas Day no less, and followed up on it.

"City directory, Mrs. Stannert."

"Well, of course." *No magic there, simply common sense.*

He continued, "I have a question to put to you. I asked last night, but I would like to discuss it further with you now."

"And that is?"

"You admitted that you threatened to kill Mr. Rubio earlier."

"Well, yes. He attacked me!"

He nodded, then continued, "When you are being rational, Mrs. Stannert, I could not ask for a better partner in this investigation. But…this other side of you."

She bristled. "What other side?"

"Your impulsiveness. Your temper. I am afraid that, someday, it will get the best of you, and I shall have to bail you out on manslaughter."

That did it.

Stung, she grabbed the whiskey bottle and poured herself another shot, ignoring the disapproval in his eyes. "My temper, as you call it, has saved me many times, when I have had no one to call upon but myself." She set the bottle on the table with some force, picked up her glass, and glared at him over the rim. "I can play the damsel in distress, if the situation calls for it. But that is all it is. A part to play. And not one I am overly fond of performing."

She put her glass back down, still full. "What about you, Mr. de Bruijn? What part do you like to step into? I think it must be the savior. You come riding in, eager to save the frail and helpless. Theia sees this in you and plays to that side, I wager. And what about Drina Gizzi, Antonia's mother? What little I know of her, she took care of herself and her daughter and managed for quite a while even under the most desperate of circumstances. But I'll bet you viewed them as needing your protection—mother and daughter, alone in the dangerous world. Is that how it was? Well, I am neither frail nor helpless, nor do I ever intend to be. I don't need to be saved, de Bruijn. You will never need to bail me out or ride to my rescue."

She saw she had hit a bull's-eye, and reminded herself he was an ally, not an enemy. She softened her tone. "My apologies. I presume too much. It has been a difficult day for us both. At the Cliff House, we worked well together. I could not have handled those three ruffians alone. You could not have, either."

"As you said, Mrs. Stannert, you presume. On many accounts." He kept his gaze steady upon her. "You don't know what I am capable of. And I agree, I do not know that much about you and your capabilities. So perhaps I presumed as well."

Given his admission, she decided to take another step forward, open the door, and extend an olive branch. "You know, Mr. de Bruijn, I woke up today, thinking of my times in Leadville and before. Thinking of my husband. Being married to Mark Stannert was no bed of roses, I assure you. In many ways he was a cad. But he always treated me as his equal, for which I am thankful."

Inez looked at de Bruijn, determined to make him see her as she was. "I hope you eventually will come to view me as an equal as well. I will probably never have your skill in detecting and disguises, but I believe I have certain qualities and strengths that complement yours." She smiled, aiming for a lighter tone. "And now, before I am tempted to sup on whiskey and little else for Christmas dinner, what do you say to accompanying me to Mrs. Nolan's, where a holiday feast awaits us?"

Chapter Twenty-Four

DECEMBER 25

Once de Bruijn had expressed his concerns about her temperament and Mrs. Stannert had started in on him, he accepted his fate, sat back, and listened. It apparently didn't occur to her that she was exhibiting the very behavior that he had wanted to bring to her attention: strike first, think later.

At least, she had not decided that his transgression rose to the level of her throwing her drink in his face. He felt he had made his point and, once she had time to think on it herself, she would see he was correct. The jabs at him and his motivations were, he decided, merely indications as to how closely he had hit home. And in the end, she had apologized and insisted he join her for Christmas dinner at her boardinghouse.

He readily accepted her invitation, primarily to show there were no hard feelings—but also because the thought of returning to take Christmas dinner alone in the Palace Hotel dining room or in the gentlemen's "Grille Room" did not appeal. Besides, he was curious to see where Mrs. Stannert and Antonia were boarding. He wondered if they might actually take up lodgings there at some point. His long-ago glimpse of their current living arrangements had revealed rooms sparse and devoid of anything but transitory necessities. Hardly a home. Hardly a place to raise a young girl.

Once he was sitting amongst the lodgers of Mrs. Nolan's boarding house, he began to see why Mrs. Stannert chose to stay in the apartment over the music store. Mrs. Nolan had placed him across the table from Mrs. Stannert, wedged between two elderly boarders who seemed intent on delving into the facets of his "relationship" with the "widow Mrs. Stannert" as one of them put it.

Pausing over the roast goose, string beans, and mashed potatoes, the fellow to his left poked de Bruijn's sleeve with an arthritic finger. De Bruijn bent in his direction and the elder whispered with breath redolent of port, "She's a handsome woman, that widow Mrs. Stannert. Quite the catch. And available! You could do far worse, and she needs a husband. She has a daughter, Antonia, you know. Or is Antonia her niece? Oh, doesn't matter. Woman and girl, alone in the world, they need the protection and guiding hand of a proper gentleman. And you seem like a very proper gentleman! We are delighted she brought you to us for inspection. You have our full approval to proceed!"

De Bruijn merely smiled, thinking that it was just as well that Mrs. Stannert, who was in conversation with the landlady, Mrs. Nolan, hadn't heard. The glances Mrs. Stannert shot him from time to time across the table made him suspect that the landlady was urging her to similar effect. The gray-haired woman—who could set a fine table, he'd grant her that—alternated low-voiced comments to Mrs. Stannert with filling plates, declaiming on the lovely holiday weather, and skewering him with eyes curious and approving by turn.

The room-and-boarders took turns peppering him with questions as enthusiastically as they peppered their goose and gravy. He responded politely when the questions seemed harmless and evaded when they became too personal. Once they found out he was a private investigator who specialized in "finding the lost," table conversation veered to local, unsolved cases and current scandals trumpeted from the headlines of the local papers.

All in all, these were topics he was much more comfortable addressing.

That is, until the gentleman to his right said, "Now here's one I just heard about from the local constabulary when I was taking my constitutional this morning. A young woman fell over the rails at the Cliff House last night. Only some say"—he leaned over his plate, the napkin tucked into his collar coming perilously close to tangling with his mince pie—"she was murdered."

De Bruijn and Inez locked eyes. She paled noticeably. One of the women down the table yipped in dismay and dropped her knife to her plate with a clatter. Mrs. Nolan jumped in her chair and snapped, "None of that. This is Christmas, if you please. Scandal-sheet gossip is not proper talk for the table."

The conversation swung back around to the weather and conjectures as to whether it might rain over the next few days. Once the mince pie was consumed and after-dinner coffees imbibed, de Bruijn and Mrs. Stannert offered their thanks to Mrs. Nolan for the feast and to the boarders for their company and conversation, and the pair made good their escape.

It was dark by then, and de Bruijn insisted on walking Mrs. Stannert back to the store.

"I'm always glad for the walk after dinner. It requires some promenading to settle Mrs. Nolan's repasts." The whites of her eyes flashed at him as she glanced his way. "In case you didn't notice, Mrs. Nolan keeps a teetotaler house. Although, as I'm sure you realized, the odd bottle of port manages to make its way inside now and again, the explanation being that it offers medicinal relief against arthritis and the restless sleep that comes with age. My, it is chilly tonight. Do you mind, Mr. de Bruijn, if I take your arm?"

"Not at all. I should have offered earlier." He did so now, and she snaked a hand through the crook of his arm, pulling herself close to his side.

The sudden stirring of feelings that he had thought long tamped down shouldn't have surprised him, but it did.

Seemingly unaware of her effect upon him, she continued, "Speaking of drinks of a more alcoholic nature, would you be interested in joining me for a brandy when we return?"

The drowsy weight of the heavy meal evaporated. The words of her invitation were straightforward enough, but the way she said them...

Is she offering more than brandy? He looked at her for clues. She gazed straight ahead, a faint smile curling the corners of her mouth.

"Just a glass, to wrap up the evening," she said. "And it would be nice to have your company for a little longer, Mr. de Bruijn. I don't mean to make light of recent events. Last night was so horrible, so sad. Yet I confess, I almost feel in a holiday frame of mind right now, or at least more philosophical about life than I did when I awoke this morning. It must be the roasted goose."

She sobered. "Tomorrow we shall be back at it, I assume. You will be looking into Miss Green's death. How could you not? We both agree that she did not seem as if she was in the depths of despair, prone to suicide. As for myself, I would dearly love to have a few minutes or an hour to myself in Miss Green's room, if I can figure out how."

"What would you hope to find?" he asked.

"I am not certain, but the police most likely did not do a very thorough search, given the hour of the day and what so handily appeared in the trash basket. I believe she was a young, attractive woman, perhaps struggling with a love affair, certainly at odds with Theia. And who knows about Mr. Drake? They have all been traveling together for a while, including Rubio. Could be all kinds of things going on, behind the scenes. Too, Mr. Drake has his own entourage—his valet, his business manager, the young messenger he sends scurrying hither and thither. We know so little of them. Well, perhaps *you* know, but you've not shared that information with me, if so."

She looked at him expectantly. She was so close he could feel her breath on his cheek. "I have been negligent in my reports to you," he said, thinking of Toby and Rubio, and wondering how much to tell her and whether to be blunt or more circumspect in his suspicions. "I shall have to correct that. But in any case, I do not think any of them are connected to the recent sad events."

She shrugged. Her forearm, snugged between his arm and frock coat, shifted with the movement, almost like a caress. "In any case," she continued, "if Julia was involved with someone, I imagine there would be correspondence. Notes from admirers, for instance. What woman would not cherish those and keep them safe? Perhaps she had a journal or a daybook where she recorded her thoughts. I should like a look around. So." She pulled him to a stop and turned to face him. "That brandy. Are you tempted?"

Tempted? Of course he was. And her eyes told him that she knew it.

"A brandy would be excellent." He smiled down at her. "It is Christmas, after all."

She smiled back, her gloved hand resting, gentle and promising, on his sleeve. "Good. I have an excellent bottle, up in the apartment."

The apartment.

Antonia was off on holiday.

They would be alone.

He wondered what he had just agreed to and whether he would regret it later. The wisest course at this point would be to have the drink—he'd accepted her invitation, after all—keep the conversation light, and keep his distance. However, de Bruijn felt it would not take much encouragement for that distance to dissolve and for him to throw his customary caution to the wind.

As they approached the store, she slowed, then frowned, perplexed. "Strange. The store lights are on. It's far too late for Mr. Hee to still be about."

She gave the door a push. It yielded, with a strangled note

from the bell. Inside, the alcove curtain parted and John Hee appeared. He hurried toward them, the worry lines in his face fading into relief, his bowler hat gripped tight, his western-style overcoat over his shoulders.

"Mr. Hee." She slipped her hand from de Bruijn's arm. "Is something wrong?"

He stopped before them both, his eyes darting from one to the other.

She stepped aside, increasing the distance between herself and de Bruijn.

John Hee's attention settled on de Bruijn. "Detective. Good. You are here. Mr. Drake came before dark, very insistent, very unhappy. He ask, asked, for," John Hee took a deep breath. "He want to know where to find an opium room. With no Americans."

While de Bruijn digested this unexpected development, Mrs. Stannert exclaimed, "An opium den! Certainly you refused to say anything. Told him you didn't know."

"I tell him place." The tenses and articles were slipping from Hee's usually careful speech. "Better, I think, to know where he is."

The music store assistant looked back at de Bruijn. "Detective, you come. I show you where place is. You take him away."

"I'll go with you." Mrs. Stannert, arms crossed, faced them both with a stubborn expression that put de Bruijn in mind of Antonia.

"No!" The exclamation burst simultaneously from John Hee and de Bruijn.

De Bruijn added, "Mrs. Stannert, think on what you are saying. Chinatown at night is dangerous. I am certain I am telling you what you already know when I say that no decent woman dares set foot there at night, not even the Methodists who run the mission there. As for entering an opium den, it is truly madness, beyond the pale, for you to consider it. We are not talking about the back alleys of Leadville. An opium den is… Have you ever been in one, seen one?"

"No," she retorted. "Have you?"

"I have." He did not want to waste time arguing with her. Every minute gone was another minute in which Graham Drake could be sinking into oblivion, or worse. "If what I have said does not convince you, consider this. If he were to see you with us, he will know you know his weakness. No good can come from that. He is a proud man, who views himself as superior by virtue of his wealth and position. Such men do not handle shame well, especially if they feel shamed before a woman. He might take it out on you—in what form we can only guess."

The stubbornness on her face only intensified.

He added, "There is no time to discuss this. The first priority must be to get him out and get him back to the hotel as inconspicuously as possible."

She threw up her hands. "I don't understand. Why save him at all?"

"He owe you much money, Mrs. Stannert," pointed out Hee.

"He is my client," added de Bruijn.

She sneered. "Save the husband from his sins, save the wife from the truth. You cannot protect them all, Mr. de Bruijn." She turned away and walked toward the grand piano. "Go. Both of you. No need to return when you are done."

De Bruijn was certain that last was directed at him, even though she finished with, "I shall close up the store, Mr. Hee."

As the door shut behind Hee and de Bruijn and they turned toward Chinatown, de Bruijn caught the faint notes of "What Child Is This?" drifting out. Less than a half-block's journey, and the music died away past hearing.

With the music gone, all the "what ifs" and "might have beens" of a late-night private moment with Mrs. Stannert faded away as well. De Bruijn set the unexpected pang of regret aside and turned his focus to Graham Drake, somewhere in Chinatown.

He hoped they were not too late.

Chapter Twenty-Five

DECEMBER 25

De Bruijn lengthened his stride to catch up with John Hee, who had hurried ahead. "When did Mr. Drake leave the store?" the detective asked.

The store assistant shrugged. "Two hour ago?"

De Bruijn hoped Drake was not far and not insensate from the drug. Theia's husband was a large man, and he would not be easy to support, much less carry, even with John Hee's help. They walked up Kearney, skirting the edge of Tangrenbu, the Chinese quarter of the city. Multistory wood and brick buildings loomed over them, and metal balconies and canvas canopies jutted out from storefronts sporting lanterns of various shapes and sizes, dark or dimly lit. De Bruijn's and John Hee's shadows stretched long from those faint lights, wavering on the cobble streets as they passed, merging and parting from the shadows of other passersby. Those they encountered did not look up, but kept their heads down, giving the two men a wide berth.

Hee stopped short of Portsmouth Square, now empty, its trees black silhouettes, and pointed up Clay Street. "This way."

De Bruijn paused, eyeing the blocks rising ahead. "Where are we going?"

Hee pointed again up Clay, then held up three fingers.

Three blocks. De Bruijn consulted his mental map of Chinatown. "Sun Louie Sun Hong, Mr. Hee?" he asked, using the Chinese street name.

Hee nodded, adding, "Spofford Alley, Detective."

"Your English is much better than my Chinese," said de Bruijn.

A quick smile escaped Hee's lips but he only said, "Come."

As they trudged uphill on Clay, de Bruijn scoured his memory for the entities that called Spofford Alley home. A grocery store and saloon catering to whites was at the corner of Clay and Spofford. Within the alley itself was a joss house. Keeping company with that temple of worship were various laundries, general stores, small candle shops. A carpenter and a painter, several tailors. The Ghee Kong Tong had their hall there. Finally, several houses of prostitution. Nestled among them was a gambling house and an opium den catering to Chinatown residents, but not, to de Bruijn's knowledge, outsiders. He tightened his grip on his walking stick, its weight and heft both comfort and protection.

As he walked, de Bruijn was reminded again how the Chinese quarter was, really, just like any other part of the city: people worked, ate, and slept here. They quarreled, they shopped, they looked for friendship, for connection, for family. They kept different customs and spoke a different language from others in the city but lived and breathed the same air. They all celebrated the joys and suffered the sorrows and pains of life. And for some, those sorrows and pains drove them to seek solace in opium.

Graham Drake apparently was no different in that respect.

Usually, the district was busy day and night with commerce and entertainments of all kinds. But not tonight. De Bruijn ascribed the stillness of the streets to the Christian holiday.

They entered Spofford Alley. Only a flickering light, here and there, showed from the upper stories of the various lodgings or leaked beneath the doors. As they went by the joss house, he saw a pale figure—clearly a woman, clearly half dressed, lean out of a second-story window, two buildings away. She looked their way, then disappeared. They passed the door leading to the house of prostitution and John Hee stopped by its neighbor, a stout door without a sign, blank and varnished black. Hee said, "I go in first, and come back for you. You have money?"

"How much?"

"Enough to open doors, let us in, and let Mr. Drake out."

De Bruijn fished out his wallet from his waistcoat. He bypassed the small change and held out a five-dollar gold piece. "Enough?"

John Hee eyed it dubiously. "You keep. Pay me back later."

He removed his derby hat, pulled the long queue from under his collar so it hung down his back, and knocked on the door, saying to de Bruijn, "Wait."

A narrow panel on the door slid back and lantern light leaked out, only to be replaced by a pair of shadowed, suspicious eyes. John Hee leaned in close and spoke in rapid Chinese that confounded de Bruijn's small knowledge of the language.

The panel slid shut.

De Bruijn heard several bolts being pulled back. Hee turned to de Bruijn and repeated, "Wait." The door creaked open, just wide enough for Hee to slip inside, then slammed shut.

De Bruijn waited. And waited.

A tapping far above his head, followed by "*Sssss*, handsome American!" caused him to look up. The same woman he had seen previously—at least he thought it was her—was back at the second-story window of the adjacent building, wearing even less than before. Two other women crowded the window with her, grinning down at him. "American!" said one in a loud whisper. "Come!" They all beckoned to him and pointed to the door leading to their premises. He shook his head. With disappointed hisses, they vanished inside.

Just then the door before him creaked open and Hee leaned out. "Now. We take Mr. Drake. But quiet. Talk to no one, Detective."

De Bruijn, his walking stick in hand, entered cautiously. It was not that he didn't trust John Hee, but entering without knowing exactly what awaited on the other side set him on edge. Once he was inside, a wiry man, small in stature, materialized from behind the door, locked and barred it, and resumed his station on a nearby stool.

Hee led de Bruijn down a long, narrow passage. Another door and another guard waited at the far end. As they approached, de Bruijn became aware of two things: the muffled sound of music from the East, played with strings and a drum, and the faint, sweetish scent of opium, tangled with the heavier one of tobacco.

Apparently Hee had smoothed the way, for the guardian nodded once to Hee, who nodded back. The guard stamped on the wooden floor. De Bruijn heard another bolt drawn back, more locks opened, and the heavy door swung in slowly. They entered what was clearly a room dedicated to gambling, full of tables crowded with silent men, most in the garb of the Orient. A raised platform in one corner held the band. On the tiny stage, a woman in traditional attire played a three-stringed guitar while a man accompanied her on an erhu, a two-stringed Chinese fiddle. A third musician beat on a small Chinese drum with two sticks.

From what de Bruijn could see, the favored game appeared to be "than" or "tan." At each table, a dealer would take a seemingly random handful of Chinese bronze coins from the pile before him, slam them on the table and cover them with an inverted bowl, all under the watchful eyes of the players. The players made bets on whether the number of coins under the bowl were odd or even. There were other bets that could be made, but as with most games of chance, the house inevitably became rich and the players poor.

As they wove their way past the tables, de Bruijn felt he might as well be a ghost. No one spoke, and the only sound was the music, the clash of coins, and the clack of the bowls. No one looked at them in surprise, suspicion, or curiosity. Even the band kept their gazes averted. It felt that they were being purposely ignored, as if the word had been spread: *Do not look at the men*

passing through. If we do not see them, then they have not been here.
He wondered how much John Hee had paid for their invisible
passage. Whatever the amount, de Bruijn determined the music
store assistant would be paid back, with interest.

Reaching the stairs at last, Hee gestured without words: Up.

They climbed the stairs—almost as steep as a ladder—which
brought them to the second floor. Another hallway of doors faced
them, with a single door at the end. At this door waited a man. De
Bruijn guessed he might be the proprietor or manager, as he was
more richly dressed than the others they had seen thus far. That,
plus the fact that he faced the two of them squarely, his eyes never
leaving them as they approached. His satin skullcap gleamed as
he and John Hee leaned together, conferring in low voices. The
smell of opium, sweet and heavy, lay thick at this end of the hall.

Finally, John Hee turned to de Bruijn. "He is inside," said Hee.
"We are to take him out down the back stairs. No one must see
him until he is out of the building. It is for the safety and well-
being of those here." He lowered his voice. "The law says, Chinese
are not allowed to smoke opium with a white man present. If a
white man is present, all can be arrested."

De Bruijn nodded that he understood.

The proprietor turned and knocked on the door. The door
opened silently, and de Bruijn and John Hee entered.

The first thing de Bruijn noticed was the thick haze of smoke
filling the room like the worst of San Francisco's fog. The second
thing was the bunks, lining both sides of the room, filled with
unmoving forms. The room was dark, interrupted only by the
small, flickering lights of gas jets used to heat opium pipes. John
Hee touched de Bruijn's sleeve and pointed to the rear of the
room, blocked from sight with a heavy curtain. "There."

When they reached the curtain, John Hee stood aside. "Better
it is you," he said.

De Bruijn steeled himself, trying not to take too deep a breath
of the near-suffocating miasma, and pulled back the curtain.

In this alcove, separated from the rest, a lamp burned. Dim, it still shed more light than in the greater space outside. So de Bruijn saw everything.

Graham Drake, half dozing in an opium daze, sprawled upon a wide, raised platform with several large cushions at his back. His unbuttoned shirt hung open, revealing a torso marked with the unmistakable pits from a long-ago ravaging case of smallpox. The scars blanketing his torso made his pockmarked face, now in repose, look almost smooth and scar-free. De Bruijn wondered briefly where the man's undervest had gone, but he quickly set the thought aside as a trivial concern.

It wasn't the scars, the lack of undervest, nor even the opium pipe dangling from Graham Drake's loose fingers that gave de Bruijn pause. Rather, it was the two Chinese prostitutes, half-clothed and drowsy, lying to either side of him.

De Bruijn thought of Theia. Thought of his promise to himself to never interfere in the affairs of men and their wives.

It didn't help.

The contempt he felt for Graham bloomed like a fever in his chest. He strode into the room, leaned over Graham, gathered his shirtfront in both hands and jerked him up to sitting. "Mr. Drake!" He tried not to shout.

Graham opened his eyes. His pupils were pinpoints. De Bruijn gave him a shake.

"De Bruijn?" The words emerged slow, mystified.

"We need to get you out of here. Now." De Bruijn buttoned up Graham's shirtfront, reattached the collar, which was hanging loose, and decided to forgo the cuffs. Besides, the cuff links were nowhere to be seen. He hitched the braces up over Graham's limp arms. De Bruijn spotted Drake's waistcoat and his overcoat, hanging on pegs on the wall. "Mr. Hee, would you please help me. The faster we get him dressed, the sooner we can leave."

Between the two of them, they finally had Drake more or less presentable. There was no hat to be found, but at least his shoes were lined up against the wall, under the overcoat.

"Out now, through back door," said Hee.

Leaving the two women still on the mattress—eyes unfocused, limbs loose—the threesome staggered to another door of sturdy proportions, leading to a small landing. Two oil lamps on the wall showed the top and bottom of a steep, narrow staircase. Since they could not go three abreast, John Hee went first, facing backward with a steadying hand on Graham's chest, while de Bruijn hooked one of Graham's arms over his own shoulders. In this manner, they managed to get down the stairs without incident, but it wasn't easy. Graham Drake was not a small man. And, despite the time spent in boardrooms and offices, he still had a muscular build.

At the bottom was one last door, unlatched and unattended, and thus, de Bruijn suspected, closely watched by unseen eyes. The three men exited and stood, at last, outside. The narrow pathway, hardly more than a gap between buildings, stank of offal. John Hee said, "We go to Stockton. Easy to get a hack. You take him back to hotel."

After lugging Graham Drake down the steep stairs, de Bruijn didn't have the breath or the wherewithal to offer a better plan. As the two half carried, half pulled Drake the block or so to Stockton Street, de Bruijn asked, "How much money are you owed?"

John Hee shook his head. "None. Mr. Drake, his wallet is back there. He paid."

"As well he should," said de Bruijn.

Luckily, transportation was quick in coming. After de Bruijn hailed an available hack, John Hee said, "Good night, Mr. de Bruijn," and before de Bruijn could thank him, he had turned a corner and vanished.

The driver was willing to help de Bruijn load Graham into his vehicle. "A little too much merry-making on the holiday?" he remarked.

"Too much for my taste," said de Bruijn, adding, "To the Palace

Hotel." He thought quickly. Going in the main entrance would not do. Too many eyes. Too many wagging tongues. Best to go by one of the back ways. "The Jessie Street entrance," he finished.

"The one for employees?"

"The same."

"You're the guv'nor, guv'nor."

De Bruijn sat across from Graham, folded his hands atop his walking stick, and stared at the disheveled man before him. Now was his chance. He might get more from Graham while the man's mind was clouded than when he was himself again and on his guard.

Graham groaned and rubbed his eyes. "Where am I?"

De Bruijn leaned forward. "You are on your way back to the Palace Hotel. You were found in Chinatown. Do you recall that? You were in an opium den."

Graham groaned again.

"Why did you go there?" de Bruijn pressed. "Was it because of Julia? Or your wife?"

Graham shut his eyes tight, then turned his head into the corner of the carriage.

"She was so much like Theia…" His voice sounded small, lost. "So beautiful. I, I didn't think she would… I didn't mean to…" He began to weep. "Do you know how long it has been since we have been together as man and wife? She avoids me. I tried. I tried."

This was not what de Bruijn wanted to hear. Nor did he want to be trapped in the carriage with this sobbing man.

He braced himself and plunged on. "Julia fell to her death on the rocks below Cliff House. You remember that, surely. What can you tell me about that evening? Were you there when it happened? Had the two of you been having an affair, and you could not take her rejection?" He was spinning wild tales, he knew. But with Graham in an opiated state, where dreams and nightmares collided, de Bruijn hoped that one or another of his queries would penetrate the fog.

"The bird. I gave her that damned bird. It was a gift." The sobbing stopped, and some of his pugnaciousness leaked through. "Goddamn it, I could strangle her. And him. I should strangle him as well."

The words sent all of de Bruijn's internal alarms jangling.

Graham drifted into semiconsciousness. Using the head of his walking stick, De Bruijn tapped the man's knee. "Whom are you talking about? You want to strangle whom?"

The carriage creaked to a stop. The driver's voice penetrated the coach. "Want help getting him out, guv'nor?"

"Yes, please." Resigned, de Bruijn waited for the driver to open the hack door for them.

What had he learned on this short ride? Apparently, there had been something between Julia and Graham. Or Graham had wanted it so. She or Theia or perhaps both of them had rejected his advances. There was a "he" and a "she," both unnamed, who Graham wanted to throttle.

And the bird.

Could Graham have killed the bird? Started the whole series of events rolling to this moment? If he was clever, it could have been. Hire a detective, point the investigator this way and that, always out and away.

The driver helped them to the service entrance and accepted the five-dollar gold piece cheerfully and with surprise.

"Thank you for your help, and Merry Christmas," said de Bruijn.

"Oh, this makes it a very merry holiday for the missus and me, thank you, sir," said the driver.

After the carriage pulled away, de Bruijn walked Drake into the service entrance. He propped him up against the wall, but Drake slid to the floor with a moan and sat there. The detective looked around, thinking. It was several flights of stairs to the second floor—difficult to maneuver Drake by himself. He spied a hotel telephone on the wall by the staircase, clearly there for the employees to contact other parts of the building.

Whom could he call for help? Whom could he trust?

A night porter came down the stairs and de Bruijn asked, "Do you know how to ring the baggage room?"

The man looked from de Bruijn to Drake, almost invisible in the shadows, his head bowed. "Too much to drink," said de Bruijn, hoping the smell that clung to their clothes would pass as tobacco, and that the porter did not have an intimate knowledge of opium and its scent. The porter picked up the speaking tube, turned the crank a number of times, then presented the tube to de Bruijn, saying, "You know how to use one of these?"

"Yes."

"You speak and listen through this end here."

"Yes, yes, thank you."

De Bruijn held the hollow opening of the tube to his ear in time to hear a tinny, laconic "Yeah?"

He moved the handset to speak into it. "This is Mr. de Bruijn. I work at the Palace as an investigator. We spoke some nights ago. Is Jacob Freeman there?"

After a pause the tinny voice of the night baggage supervisor responded, "Not here."

"Not working tonight?"

"Not working at the hotel anymore."

For a moment, he thought he'd heard wrong. "Pardon, what did you say?"

"Freeman's gone. Sacked."

That he heard. "What? When did this happen? Who fired him? Why?"

A staticky, impatient sigh crackled through the line. "Early tonight. When he came on shift. Night manager. Adams. Dunno why."

Dismissed. On Christmas.

De Bruijn broke the connection and swore in vicious Dutch. His spontaneous outburst in his native tongue warned him that he was slipping out of control. He leaned his forehead against the polished wooden box of the telephone and closed his eyes, pulling his thoughts together.

Graham's slurred voice floated up to him. " De Bruijn? Is that you? Where are we?"

De Bruijn turned to him. "We are inside the Palace Hotel, at one of the employee entrances. In your current state it seemed best to avoid the reception area and the rising rooms."

"Good man." Drake struggled to his feet. "To my room. I need to sleep."

"You need more than that," said de Bruijn under his breath. "We shall have to go up several sets of stairs."

"Of course." Graham lurched sideways. "Help me. Damn floor keeps tilting."

De Bruijn moved forward and allowed the drugged man to drape an arm over his shoulders. They climbed the stairs, one by one, Drake's weight shifting side to side, throwing de Bruijn off-balance. The investigator braced one hand on the near wall, while Drake clung to the steel bannister on the other. Nearly at the top of the first long set of stairs, de Bruijn had a sudden mental picture of releasing his hold on Graham, perhaps giving him a shove with one elbow, and letting him tumble down the stairs to what would be a certain death.

That his anger gave rise to such thoughts only made him doubly determined to deliver Graham to the suite, safe and sound.

After that, the chips would fall where they may.

But one of his first items of business afterward would be to find night manager Adams and uncover what had led to Freeman's sudden dismissal.

They emerged on the second floor and de Bruijn propelled Graham toward his chambers.

They halted in front of the door. "Your key?" de Bruijn asked Graham.

Graham patted his waistcoat, then his overcoat. "My wallet. Where's my wallet?"

"Gone," said de Bruijn. "To pay for your retrieval from the opium den. You got off lightly, Mr. Drake. Now, how to get you inside. Might your valet still be awake?"

"Found it." Drake tugged a key out of his trouser pocket, much to de Bruijn's relief.

De Bruijn fit the key to the lock and opened the door as quietly as he could. They entered the private parlor, all dark. A dim light spilled from inside the bedchamber, the door half ajar. De Bruijn allowed himself to hope that the valet had left on the lamp or perhaps left the fire in the grate burning on the assumption that the master would turn in late and need a guiding light. Graham Drake still leaned, a heavy weight, across de Bruijn's shoulders. Together they walked, or rather de Bruijn walked and Graham stumbled, to the bedroom.

They entered, and there, sitting on the edge of the bed—

Theia.

With Mrs. Stannert beside her.

In one hand, Theia held a crumpled whiteness, a paper or handkerchief. With the other, she gripped Mrs. Stannert's hand tightly. Her long hair was unpinned and in disarray around the shoulders of her dressing gown. Rage, exhaustion, and disgust chased each other across her mobile face.

As for Mrs. Stannert...

If looks could kill, the gaze she leveled at him and Graham would have dropped them on the spot.

Theia released Mrs. Stannert's hand and stood up in a soft rustling of material. Graham lurched backward, pulling de Bruijn off-balance and nearly sending them both to the floor.

She approached, gliding noiselessly, like a wraith or one of the furies. "How could you do this to me?" she cried. She held up her fist. In it, the whiteness resolved into a balled piece of paper. She threw it at Graham and it bounced off his chest. He clutched his breast as if the balled projectile had been a bullet through his heart.

"You. You and Julia. " Her voice trembled. "After all of…this! You brought me here, when I told you I didn't want to ever come back to this city! You insisted I stop singing. You have choked me, taken my life away! And then, this. This!"

Graham Drake stammered, "Theia, I–I never meant to… It was just…"

She stepped forward and her crazed eyes widened. De Bruijn could only guess that she had caught a whiff of the heavy scent that lay over Graham like a blanket of guilt.

Theia shoved Graham in the chest, hard. De Bruijn grabbed him so he would not fall.

She continued, voice rising, "And you've been to one of those hideous places. After you promised in Denver that you would never, ever again."

"Theia, Theia," Graham moved out of de Bruijn's reach and attempted to embrace her.

She collapsed in his arms, weeping uncontrollably. "And you left me all alone. I was here, all alone! "

Graham's arms tightened about her.

Mrs. Stannert rose from the bed and de Bruijn saw her slide her small revolver into the pocket of her dress. He had not even registered she had it out.

Theia pulled away from Graham, rounded on de Bruijn, and pointed a shaking finger at him. "Get out!" She looked at Mrs. Stannert. "You too. Get out!"

Passing de Bruijn, Mrs. Stannert murmured, "Best we leave and let them sort this out. It's none of our affair. Or at least, it shouldn't be."

He followed Mrs. Stannert out of the bedchamber and through the parlor as Theia continued to berate Graham with ever-increasing pitch and volume. They had just reached the door to the hallway when a crash behind them announced that Theia had thrown something more substantial than a ball of paper.

Once in the corridor, they both leaned against the wall. Mrs.

Stannert pushed back strands of hair that had slipped out from the knot at the nape of her neck. "So, you and Mr. Hee found Mr. Drake, I see."

"It was best you did not go with us," said de Bruijn. "We were lucky to have Mr. Hee there. It would not have been safe at all."

"Best I did not go, in more ways than one. Shortly after you left, I received a telephone call from the hotel. Theia had asked them to tell me to come, right away, that it was urgent. I hadn't even finished the conversation when a hack pulled up outside the store to bring me here."

He drew a hand over his eyes, wondering if the opium fumes he had breathed had addled his brain. "What happened? Theia said she was alone. Where is Yvonne?"

"That is a very good question, Mr. de Bruijn." Mrs. Stannert folded her arms and stared out over the dark, silent space of the hotel atrium. "Yvonne has disappeared. Vanished."

Chapter Twenty-Six

DECEMBER 26

After de Bruijn and Mrs. Stannert went their separate ways, leaving the Drakes to fight it out between themselves, de Bruijn stormed into the night manager's office to demand an explanation regarding Freeman's dismissal.

"He was discovered carrying a roast chicken from the kitchen at the end of the previous night's shift," Adams said.

"Christmas, and you sacked him over a chicken?" De Bruijn was incredulous. "Was this your decision, Mr. Adams?" He felt certain it was not, but wanted to see how the manager responded to a direct question.

Adams straightened a pile of papers on his desk, then moved the stack from one side to the other, without looking at de Bruijn. "Upper management gives us considerable leeway when it comes to handling matters on our shifts and for matters relating to guests and employees during those shifts."

"But Freeman wasn't even on your staff. He was only working nights until certain problems were resolved."

"Irregularities," said Adams, seemingly apropos of nothing, almost as if answering a different question. He added, "We strive to provide faultless service and luxurious appointments to our guests. Nothing can be allowed to blemish the good name and the prestige of the hotel."

It didn't take much to grasp what Adams was dancing around but not saying. "This is Mr. Drake's doing, isn't it?" said de Bruijn.

A sharp inhalation, then a sigh of surrender was the response. After a moment's silence, Adams said, "It would be best if you address your concerns to upper management."

"Oh, I certainly will," said de Bruijn.

When he awoke in the morning, his first act was to use the telephone in his room to arrange a meeting with hotel manager Warren Leland. He set it for later in the morning, allowing himself enough time to prepare for the day and collect his thoughts. A scrubdown removed most of the lingering scent of opium smoke and a clean suit of clothes took care of the rest. De Bruijn was in his office, finishing breakfast and making a few notes to himself, when a knock on the door gave him pause. The quality of the knock, deferential but determined, was familiar.

If he had any doubts as to his visitor, Toby's soft voice on the other side of the door put them to rest. "Mr. de Bruijn? Are you there? Mr. Drake wants to see you, sir. Soon as possible. Now, if you can."

De Bruijn stood up from his desk and began buttoning his waistcoat, calling out, "One moment, Toby."

He turned to the bay window as he finished with his waistcoat and attached his pocket watch. The rain, which had been a mist when he had risen, was increasing. Clouds in dark bands in the distance promised more on the way. Just like the weather, his plans for the day were shifting. He would have preferred to speak to Drake after talking with Leland, but now it appeared the order of his meetings would change. He donned his checked sack coat, retrieved his bowler and walking stick, and went to the door. Toby, who had been leaning against the wall outside, straightened up. "Thank you for waiting," said de Bruijn.

"No, thank *you*, sir," the messenger said fervently. "I'm just glad I don't have to tell Mr. Drake you weren't available."

"It looks to be a dark day," said de Bruijn, testing the waters as they walked toward the elegant curve of one of the grand staircases.

"Yes, sir," said Toby, almost inaudibly. Then louder, "Mr. de Bruijn, do you know Yvonne is missing?"

"I do. She is still gone, then?"

He nodded. "Your card says you're a 'finder of the lost.' Are you going to find her?"

"I will, if asked."

"I hope that happens. Yvonne being gone has Madame in a mad fret, and then with Miss Julia—" He caught his bottom lip with his teeth, as if he regretted having said even that much.

"I know about Miss Green. A true tragedy," he said gently. "I will do my best to find Miss Marchal." *And delve further into Miss Green's death as well.* De Bruijn added, "It might help if I knew where to find Señor Rubio."

Toby's footsteps faltered. "D'you think he might know where Yvonne is?"

"I don't know. Both he and Miss Marchal vanished at more or less the same time. Perhaps there is a connection. Perhaps not. But I believe he might know more about Miss Green."

"Miss Julia, she was always nice to me." Toby sounded forlorn, and de Bruijn got a glimpse of how lonely and chaotic life among the Drakes must be for him.

He looked sideways at de Bruijn. "You might find Mr. Rubio at the Baldwin Hotel. He keeps another set of rooms there."

"Thank you, Toby." De Bruijn glanced at him. "Some people think being a good detective involves magic. That uncovering clues and finding who, or what, has been lost is a matter of mind-reading or prestidigitation. Not so. Many times, it is people who care, people of good character and an observant eye, who point the way."

A blush darkened Toby's light-brown complexion and he said, "Please, don't tell him, sir, that I told you about the Baldwin."

"Another thing about investigative work: we keep our sources to ourselves."

They stopped in front of the door leading to Graham's office, and Toby rapped with a white-gloved hand. Inside, Graham barked, "Enter!"

Toby opened the door, announced, "Mr. de Bruijn, sir," and closed the door after the detective, leaving the two men alone.

"De Bruijn." Graham, behind the expanse of desk, half rose and waved perfunctorily at the empty chair on the other side. As de Bruijn approached, his nose was assaulted by a masculine fragrance, heavy on the citrus. The overapplication of cologne, paired with Graham's precisely pressed three-piece suit, suggested Drake had also tried to erase every trace of the night's events. All that lingered were deep lines of exhaustion haunting his drawn, pocked features.

The investigator hardly had time to sit before Graham pulled open the top drawer of the desk and extracted a check. He set the draft in front of de Bruijn. "For services rendered, with my thanks. Consider the terms of our contract fulfilled, the issues resolved."

Stunned, de Bruijn picked up the check and scrutinized the amount. As if reading his mind, Graham said, "The total is above and beyond what we agreed upon. For reasons of…" His gaze, which had held steady on the detective, now jittered to the side, then returned. "For taking upon yourself certain tasks that, while not within the scope of our contract, were greatly appreciated." He pushed back his chair and stood. "I will pass along my satisfaction with your assistance and praise your discretion to Mr. Leland." He held out his hand.

Still in disbelief, de Bruijn rose, ignoring Graham's offer to shake. "Our contract gave me until the end of the year to find the person who destroyed your wife's dress and pet bird."

"And it is to your credit that those troubles were wrapped up quickly, with days to spare." He lowered his hand. "The miscreant has been dealt with."

"If by miscreant you mean the porter Freeman"—De Bruijn kept his tone steady and neutral, with effort—"you have the wrong man."

"We are done." Graham's voice had the quality of granite.

"What of Miss Green? She was under your protection, a member of your party. Surely you want to be certain, beyond a doubt, what caused her death. Whether it was accidental or—"

"The police came by early this morning. They went through her room again. Nothing more was found. They are satisfied that she took her own life."

"What about the note?"

Confusion broke through the stubborn set of his face. "Note?" Then, comprehension dawned. Shoving his hands into his trouser pockets, Graham moved from behind the desk to stare out the rain-pelted window. "The note you refer to only supports the conclusions of the police. There was no new information to be gained from it."

"Did you show them the note?" de Bruijn persisted.

Graham did not look around. "My wife threw it into the fireplace. It is gone. What is done is done. Bringing it up now would bring only discord and grief."

And more scrutiny to you, thought de Bruijn.

He made one last attempt. "What of Miss Marchal? Is it true she is missing? If so, that is most disturbing. First Miss Green's death, then Miss Marchal's unexplained disappearance."

"I never had much faith in Yvonne. I suspect she poisoned my wife's mind against me. Recently, Theia had begun to lash out at her as well. And then Julia," he stopped and shook his head. "Miss Green would jump in, taking one side or the other. I do not mean to speak ill of the departed, but those three women were at each other's throats, changing alliances, bickering constantly. There was hardly a moment's peace amongst them. Given Miss Green's sudden death, Yvonne probably decided it was in her best interests to leave without making a fuss and then did so."

"Without packing?"

Graham glanced at him sharply. "Who said she did not pack? And how did you know about Yvonne in the first place?"

De Bruijn hesitated. He did not want to admit Mrs. Stannert had initially provided him with the information. As far as he could tell, the Drakes were still ignorant of his connection to the music store owner. Nor did he want to implicate Toby.

Graham's shoulders sagged. "Of course. Knowing such things is your stock-in-trade. I salute your investigatory powers. However, you needn't concern yourself with us any longer. Our business is no longer your business. Good day, Mr. de Bruijn."

De Bruijn took his leave, Graham's check clenched in his hand. He had considered leaving it on the desk, in a gesture of…what? The total was no more than small change to the Drakes, he was certain.

And, it had occurred to him there was someone the Drakes owed, someone whom he perhaps could recompense secondhand—Jacob Freeman, unfairly dismissed, on Christmas. Perhaps he could be persuaded to accept half the total? Or perhaps there was a way to send the sum to Freeman anonymously? The former Palace employee was a proud man, de Bruijn knew.

However, and here was another thought: perhaps he could hire Freeman occasionally to help him with his work. There were parts of town and various businesses that, no matter what de Bruijn did, he would always stand out from the crowd. The possibility of paying Freeman with Drake's money appealed to de Bruijn immensely. Of course, the payment for that part-time employment would never replace the salary and tips he'd received as a Palace hotel porter.

These ideas occupied him on his way to Warren Leland's office. He was five minutes early but decided to knock rather than wait. He hoped he could, after meeting with the manager, find Mrs. Stannert and alert her before she waltzed, unawares, into the Drakes' domain.

Hearing out de Bruijn's protests about Freeman's sacking and de Bruijn's suspicions that the Drakes were ultimately behind Adams's actions against the porter, Leland was sympathetic, but firm. "I'm sorry, but what's done is done," he said, echoing Graham Drake. "Any employee can be dismissed for any reason by a manager. That is the way it works."

"But Freeman is innocent. He had nothing to do with the dress, the bird."

"And the guilty party is?"

De Bruijn had no answer.

Leland added, "Mr. Drake is a powerful man with powerful friends. He and his wife are valued guests at the hotel. I understand they are looking for a suitable residence to purchase in our city. But that will take time, so I expect we shall need to make them comfortable and welcome in the Palace for some months yet. Do you understand what I am saying, Mr. de Bruijn?"

"And Jacob Freeman must pay the price for their continued comfort. Do you know the ostensible reason for his dismissal? He took a roasted chicken, left over from Christmas Eve. If you gave notice to every employee who took home table scraps that night, you would have no one to cook, serve, or cater to your guests on Christmas Day."

"We will give him a good reference. It is the least we can do, under the circumstances."

"Do you know that Mr. Drake dismissed me this morning as well?"

Leland's eyebrows rose.

De Bruijn continued, "He said I had fulfilled my contract. And I suppose you have heard of the death of Mrs. Drake's protégée, Miss Green."

"Indeed. Sad. Very sad. May God rest her soul. The police detective in charge, Detective Lynch, talked to me about it earlier this morning."

"I am not convinced Miss Green took her own life."

"Well, I am certain, knowing you and how you work, you feel duty-bound to chase down every trail until you are satisfied all possible explanations have been explored. However, I don't believe you were given that charge, were you?"

"I was not," de Bruijn admitted.

Leland nodded. He twisted in his chair and gathered two folders from the table behind him. "Don't blame yourself, Mr. de Bruijn, for any of this. I am certain you did all you could, and more, for the Drakes and their people. Now, since it sounds as if you are currently at liberty"—Leland set the folders before de Bruijn—"a couple of concerns have arisen here at the hotel that could benefit from your special expertise. We will, of course, pay your usual fee."

Chapter Twenty-Seven

DECEMBER 26

Where is Yvonne? Did she disappear of her own volition, or is there some treachery afoot? Is she even alive?

The questions lingered in Inez's mind as she fell asleep in the early hours of the morning. They were still there when she awoke the next morning to gray skies and slick streets. The weather, that topic of eternal interest to Mrs. Nolan and her boarders, offered up a cold mist of rain that floated through the air, coating everyone and everything. The gentle moisture caused feathers on ladies' hats to droop, unwound the carefully dressed curl at the end of gentlemen's mustaches, snuck under collars of lace and linen alike to breathe gently on necks, and settled into the smallest break between sleeve and glove to cool the wrist.

Inez lingered over her toilette, glad she did not have to appear at the music room until later. Today she and Theia were to start work on a series of "popular ditties," as Theia called them, for the Melpomene Theater performance.

That, at least, had been the original plan.

Now, given Julia's death, Yvonne's sudden absence, and the stormy goings-on between the Drakes, it felt as if all plans and schedules were in abeyance. Still, no one had said anything different. No messenger had arrived with a change of instruction, so Inez decided she would proceed until told otherwise.

But that didn't mean she was going to proceed as if nothing had changed.

First, she planned to talk to John Hee to find out what had happened the previous night in Chinatown.

Second, she was going to arrange to speak with Graham Drake as soon as possible and, well, not demand, exactly, but firmly and politely request he pay at least *half* of the considerable outstanding balance the Drakes owed the store. She was not going to get into the position of a few businesswomen she knew who had fallen into insolvency because they hesitated to press their wealthy, well-connected clients for payment. Inez had no such hesitations, although she promised herself she would be circumspect in her demands. Above all, she was determined to do all in her power to stave off a similar fate for D & S House of Music and Curiosities.

Third, she hoped to talk with de Bruijn. They needed to plan their next steps.

Finally, later in the evening, she would host her usual collection of Monday evening card players—musicians to a man, except for the newsman Roger Haskell, whom she intended to corner. Haskell had information about fellow inkslinger John Teague, and Inez was determined to extract what he knew, over cards or afterward.

Thinking about all this, she fortified herself with sourdough bread and butter, grateful to the ever-vigilant Mrs. Nolan for the simple repast. The boardinghouse proprietor had slipped her a small round loaf and a chunk of butter before she and de Bruijn had left. "I know you are probably in need of breakfast victuals," she'd whispered. "You are thin as a rail. Breakfast, Mrs. Stannert, is more than a cup of coffee or tea."

With a good hour yet before she had to think of leaving for the hotel, Inez decided to go directly to the store, review the inventory statements, and catch John Hee when he arrived. Intent on locking the door to her private premises, she was only peripherally aware of the carriage sitting in front of her shop.

It wasn't until a voice called out "Mrs. Stannert?" that she whirled around. A top-hatted gentleman with well-groomed, flowing white whiskers and a salt-and-pepper mustache was exiting the carriage's open door.

"Mr. Sutro?" She smiled, polite but puzzled by his presence. "Good morning."

"Good morning!" The greeting came out sounding more like *Guten Morgen*. He glanced up at the sky. "Well, it would be a better morning if not for the incident at the Cliff House night before last." A thick German accent pressed over his words. "That is the kind of thing I intend to stop, once I put my hand at the helm of the place. I will bring it to greatness and civility again, make it into a respectable resort. Once I set my mind on a goal, it is only a matter of time before it becomes a reality." He smiled at her, the gleam in his eye alerting her to the fact that he was, perhaps, speaking of more than real estate.

Suddenly wary, she said, "I am preparing to open the store. Would you like to come in?"

"*Ja*. Very much."

She unlocked the door and escorted him inside. While she hung her oilcloth coat and umbrella by the front door, he looked about with a calculating eye. She could sense him taking stock of everything, from the building's construction, to the Oriental oddities and curios, to the various instruments and neat stacks of sheet music.

He said, "Do you know, Mrs. Stannert, when I first came to San Francisco in the early fifties, I had a store on Long Wharf. I sold this and that, everything from turpentine and tobacco to soup plates and classic music. Variety, give the customer what they want, and then what they do not *know* they want until they set eyes on it. That is the key."

"I agree completely. Now, can I help you in some way today? I hope I did not keep you waiting out there long."

"Not long, not long at all."

She wondered about that. Wondered if the carriage had been patiently idle while she meandered through her morning meal.

He continued, "As it happens, after your recital, I inquired of Mr. Drake, and he said, you, a widow, also own a music store. Forgive my asking, but you are a widow?"

"Yes, that is true." She was not about to clarify that she was a "grass widow," parted from her husband not by death but by divorce. Still, it put her on guard that he knew this much about her. She had heard that Adolph Sutro had a penchant for widows. In fact, one of the musicians she knew—dreadful gossip that he was—had explained to her the reason Sutro and his wife lived in separate residences in the city. Apparently, Mrs. Sutro had caught her husband sharing a hotel room with "the ninety-thousand-dollar-diamond widow," a woman fond of wearing diamonds with her widow's weeds. Mrs. Sutro had to be restrained from breaking a bottle of champagne over the head of her husband's companion.

Sutro doffed his top hat. "I have always had the utmost respect and admiration for women such as yourself, who look to make their mark in the business world." He fished in the hat lining and held out one of her store trade cards with a flourish. "Mr. Drake provided this to me."

Inez looked at the card. "Indeed. As you can see, we carry a wide variety of goods ourselves, although not as varied as your store on Long Wharf, I expect."

"Perhaps not. But you have what I need."

Another double entendre? She gave him a tight-lipped smile and kept her tone cool but polite. "That would be?"

"I would like to buy a piano. Perhaps more than one. They add such grace to a house, don't you agree, Mrs. Stannert? And we could use better instruments at the Cliff House, as I'm certain you are aware."

Her cool smile warmed. If he wanted to buy a piano or two or three, who was she to dissuade him?

Besides, he knew Graham Drake, and John Teague knew Graham and Theia, and Graham, Sutro, and Teague had Comstock connections. It was too tempting an opportunity to pass up. A chat with Mr. Sutro might shed some light on questions as yet unanswered.

"I would be delighted to show you what we have in stock," Inez said. "Of course, we can always order for you. I have catalogs as well." She led him to the grand piano in the center of the showroom. "This Steinway is a wonderful instrument. The Steinways received the highest awards at the International Exhibition in Philadelphia five years ago, for best pianos as well as best pianoforte material."

She pattered on a bit about the construction of the soundboard and the instrument's depth, richness, and volume of tone. He nodded encouragingly, but the way he watched her made her suspect his mind was not truly on the piano and its qualities. She finally slowed down and said, "Excuse me. I do hope you don't think me forward for asking"—she drew one finger along the curve of the lid—"but I am curious about your connection to the Drakes. I know Mr. Drake made his fortune in the silver fields. I understand you did as well."

He raised his salt-and-pepper eyebrows, looking pleased. "You have heard of me?"

"Of course. You and your amazing tunnel. The Sutro tunnel is a true engineering feat."

Now he looked surprised. "You know of my tunnel?"

She nodded. "Was Mr. Drake part of that effort? Is that how you came to know each other?"

"Indeed. 'Lucky Duck' Drake and I go back a long way. Our stories, much the same. It is true the silver in the Comstock made him rich." Sutro moved toward her, a smile blooming over his genial face. "My tunnel made him richer."

"Is that so?" She casually circumvented the piano, putting its bulk between them.

"Why do you ask?" The calculation was back in his eyes. He leaned on the highly polished lid, facing her. She winced inwardly, hoping his cuff links would not scratch the finish.

Inez crossed her arms on the lid, careful to keep just her elbows on the wood. She tried to look hesitant and delicately embarrassed. "May I be frank with you, Mr. Sutro? With the hope that you will forgive me and hold my concerns in confidence? You know I am employed by the Drakes as an accompanist, but they have also run up quite a large balance at my store. With your past experience as a merchant, you know how that can go. Be that as it may, and between this, that, and the other, they now owe me a great deal of money. I hesitate to press my case to Mr. Drake, not wanting to offend, but I want to be reassured that he is what he seems." She held her breath to see if he accepted her explanation.

He threw back his head and laughed—a wide open, warm sound. "*Ach*, my dear Mrs. Stannert, do not worry about Mr. Drake. He is exactly as you see. He made his wealth the way many did—kept watch on the stocks and kept his ear to the ground, alert for when to buy, when to sell. He may have started in the mines, but such energy could not be contained underground. When I met him, he was high in the Miners' Union." He sobered. "I think, unlike me, he has forgotten his past."

"What do you mean?"

"He owns a newspaper now. He fights the unions. I tell him, make the workingman and unions your friend. If they become your enemy, your luck will change. Graham Drake is a smart man. A wealthy man. He was lucky from the start." He shook his head. "His partner less so."

She pricked up her ears. He strolled around the piano, closing the distance between them. She straightened up, ready to step back if needed. "His partner?"

"A newsman. What was his name? Irishman. McTee? *Nein.* Teague! Yes, that was it. They were a pair. But Lucky Duck held onto his riches. Teague made a bad bet, held onto stock too long, lost everything. Then Graham married the Golden Songbird. Now the Drakes are here and he bought that newspaper." He shrugged. " I told him, better to buy land. Real estate. But does he listen?"

Before Inez could pursue that further, he said, "A man's passions, there is no going against them. For me, it is land. Art. Books. Beautiful things. Speaking of beautiful things and listening, I enjoy music but have no talent. Would you do me the favor and play this magnificent piano, so I may hear this tone, depth, and, what did you call it, richness?"

"Of course." She made to move past him.

He took her arm, stopping her. "A classic piece. A waltz perhaps."

She looked down at his hand, then up at his expression. He was smiling again.

She returned his smile. "Certainly, Mr. Sutro. Whatever you wish." She hoped she wasn't overplaying her hand.

That seemed to be an acceptable response, because he released her. She moved to the piano and sat down, rearranging her skirts and her thoughts. It didn't take long before she knew exactly what she wanted to play for Herr Adolph Sutro. A sprightly tune poured forth, her fingers almost waltzing across the keys. The music, with its happy shimmering lilt, seemed to bring a sunshine of its own into the gray, mist-filled world. She played with gusto and a light hand, finishing with a flourish, the final notes dancing in her head like motes in a sunbeam. When she twisted around to gauge his reaction, his hands were folded over the top of his cane, marvel in his eyes.

"Strauss. *An der schönen blauen Donau.*"

She stood and smoothed her skirts. "So, what do you think?"

"*Sehr schön.*"

It was the tone, more than the words, that told Inez her rendition of "The Blue Danube Waltz" had not only made its point, but sold the piano. "*Vielen Dank*, Herr Sutro."

The bell over the entry door clanked irritably, and store manager Thomas Welles entered with John Hee close behind.

Hidden beneath his umbrella, Welles was muttering deep in his oilcloth overcoat. "Damn umbrella is as worthless as—" The umbrella tipped back, and he stopped in his tracks. "Morning, Mrs. Stannert."

John Hee slid around him and headed toward his alcove.

Welles struggled to close the umbrella, saying, "I thought you'd be in the office."

Inez moved away from the piano. "I've been busy, making a sale." She introduced the two men, adding, "Mr. Welles will be happy to draw up the papers of sale and discuss delivery with you. I have tasks that require my attention in the back. It has been a pleasure doing business with you, Mr. Sutro. I hope we can do so again in the future."

She held out her hand.

He took it and said, "I hope for the same, Mrs. Stannert." After glancing at Welles, standing some distance away, he ventured closer and lowered his voice, "Perhaps a private concert at my little cottage out at Land's End? Or over champagne at the Baldwin Hotel?"

She raised her eyebrows.

He added quickly, in a louder voice, "We can always discuss this later. And no need to start a line of credit for me. I shall arrange to pay upon delivery." He winked at her, then turned to the store manager. "Mr. Welles, where shall we talk?"

"The back room has a table," said Welles, escorting him away.

Inez hurried to John Hee's alcove, knocked on the wall next to the curtain, then drew the curtain back. "Mr. Hee," she whispered. "Last night. What happened?"

Hee looked tired, bags under his eyes, even more subdued than usual. "We found Mr. Drake. Mr. de Bruijn took him back to hotel."

"That's all?"

"All I know. The rest, you must ask the detective."

She retrieved her waterproof coat, grabbed her spare umbrella, decided to forgo galoshes for the quick walk to the hotel, and advanced outdoors.

At some point, the mist had decided to get serious and was now a determined rain, nothing light and gentle about it. Inez was glad that the Palace was not far and that her waterproof was as sturdy as her walking shoes. Even so, she knew the hems of her dark-gray wool skirts, which extended below the hem of her coat, would be sopping wet and darker still by the time she reached the hotel. She just hoped her hat, also dark gray with a circle of soft gray feathers about the crown, would survive the damp.

She walked quickly, head bent, trying to hide from the wind that whipped splashes of rain into her face. Item one, talking with John Hee, was checked off her list. She reversed items two and three, deciding she would dodge into de Bruijn's office before continuing to Theia's music room. She wanted to find out if de Bruijn had learned anything of value from Graham the previous night. Drake had been incoherent and Theia's rage all-consuming. Their spat, if one could call it that, had been a sight to behold. Once she and de Bruijn had left and she had mentioned Yvonne's absence to him, they had parted ways. She suspected he had been as exhausted by events as she was by that time.

But now it was a new day—and time to determine the next steps. She decided she would not allude to their personal inter-actions of the previous evening, specifically her invitation and his acceptance vis-à-vis an exploratory tête-à-tête. The moment had passed. It was time to move on to more urgent matters.

Upon reaching the hotel, Inez decided she would simply do as she had done before: pop up unannounced and catch him in his office.

She spotted him as she stepped out of the rising room. He was approaching the elevators, apparently on his way out, oilskin coat over one arm, furled umbrella in hand, distracted frown on his face.

"Mr. de Bruijn," she called out. "May I have a few minutes of your time? In your office?"

The unfocused look in his eyes quickly cleared. "Certainly, Mrs. Stannert. I thought I might try to find you at your store. I am glad to see you here now."

"You can always use the telephone to call," she remarked, falling in step by his side. "It could save you a trip for nothing."

"I have other reasons for going out, but yes, you are right."

Once inside his office, she took one of the leather visitor's chairs and gestured to its match, catawampus to hers. "I have much to tell you, but first, what happened last night?"

He sat, removed his hat, and leaned the umbrella against the chair. "John Hee was very helpful. I'm not certain I would have been able to extract Mr. Drake without his considerable assistance."

"So, it *was* opium. The smell was quite overwhelming when you two made your appearance."

He nodded. "I had to send my suit out for airing. It is completely unwearable. At least for the parts of town I plan to visit today."

"Did you learn anything from Drake?"

"It appears we are correct in that he fancied Miss Green. I am still not clear as to whether she returned his affections. Which does make me suspicious about what might have transpired between them at the Cliff House, if they did meet privately."

"As to whether Julia was inclined toward him, I believe I can shed some light, if we are to believe what I saw last night," said Inez.

She explained that when she had arrived at the door to Theia's chambers, per the singer's behest, the woman had pulled her with a frighteningly strong grip through her private parlor. Inez had barely avoided knocking over one of the two oxblood vases standing guard by the parlor fireplace before Theia dragged her into her sleeping quarters. From there, the diva had unlatched the connecting door into her husband's bedchamber, insisting Inez accompany her. The two bedrooms were conjoined, and Inez had glimpsed Graham's private parlor, just beyond.

Inez continued, "Yvonne's disappearance completely unnerved her. Theia said Yvonne left early Christmas Day to attend Mass and never returned. She called me late because Yvonne and Graham had 'vanished,' and she could not bear being alone at night. By the time I arrived, Theia was close to hysteria. She seems to think Yvonne is somehow involved in all the goings-on, even Julia's death. I asked her about it, but she was not clear as to why she believed that."

He frowned. "Yvonne involved in Miss Green's death?"

"From what Theia said, the antagonism between Miss Green and Yvonne ran deeper than we realized. And now Theia thinks Yvonne may even be bent on harming *her*."

"That sounds preposterous."

"I agree. I almost fear for her sanity. She seems to suspect everyone of evil. She mentioned Rubio and indicated she is afraid of Graham—which is interesting, given how she reacted when he finally showed up." Inez eased back in her chair. "She seemed convinced someone was after her. I showed her my pocket revolver, just to calm her, and told her nothing would happen while I was with her. We were in Graham's room for, oh, perhaps an hour. During that time, she showed me a note she found in her husband's chambers, purportedly written by Miss Green. It was much in the vein of the partial draft found by Detective Lynch in the trash can. That letter should probably be turned over to the police."

He shook his head. "Too late. It apparently has been destroyed."

"What?" She gripped the arms of the chair.

"I spoke with Graham Drake earlier today. He said Theia threw it into the fireplace. He could be lying, I suppose. We only have his word for this."

"It sounds like Theia," muttered Inez. "She does like to throw things. Although it seems very handy, doesn't it, that the note is now nothing but ashes. In any case, it sounds like we shall never know if the handwriting of the note matches the draft."

She sat up straighter. "Also, I was able to question Adolph Sutro when he stopped by the music store this morning to buy a piano. He knew Graham well in Virginia City and said Graham and Teague were once business partners." She explained about the Comstock, and how Drake's star rose while Teague's fell. After she finished, she frowned. "But how does Theia fit into all this? A love triangle, and she decided to go with the moneyed man and is now having second thoughts, perhaps? If Theia is correct in supposing Julia was mistakenly killed, this might have a bearing on things. Perhaps Graham found out Theia intended to see Teague and was consumed with jealousy. It wouldn't be the first time a husband tried to murder his wife over a thwarted love affair. We should try to find out more about this."

De Bruijn looked at her, his expression grave. "I have information for you as well. This morning, Mr. Drake thanked me for my services and dismissed me."

Inez gasped.

He continued, "He clearly did not want me to delve into Miss Green's death and Yvonne's disappearance. Yet, I cannot walk away."

"Neither can I," said Inez. "It's not right."

De Bruijn leaned forward. "If you remain with the Drakes and continue to be my eyes and ears, we could work together to bring justice to the situation. If you do so, you must be careful. Particularly since I now have new cases that will take me away for stretches of time. Do you see what I am saying? You will, for all intents and purposes, be on your own."

Chapter Twenty-Eight

DECEMBER 26

You will be on your own.

De Bruijn's caution echoed in Inez's mind as she took the stairs down to the second floor and made her way to the Drakes' suite.

The vast, central court below was jammed with departing guests and their stacks of luggage, and carriages and hacks of every variety. Sharp-edged sounds of transport bounced off the marble pavement: metal-shod hooves clicked, harnesses jingled, wheels squeaked and clacked, and carriage doors clapped shut while the calls and chatter of drivers and guests rose up with painful clarity. The dissonance was accompanied by the pervasive odor of manure from the horses who circled through on their rounds. The smell and sounds rose, having no escape route, locked as they were within the hotel's vast central chamber topped by the opaque glass roof.

Inez hurried along the open arcade of the second floor, holding her breath, thinking that the guests waiting for conveyance below probably wished they could wait in the open air of Market Street instead. She covered her nose with one gloved hand and used the other to knock on the door of Theia's music room. A Palace Hotel chambermaid opened the door, dark eyes wide and cautious. Inez figured she must have been inveigled into acting as doorkeeper. "Ma'am?"

Inez could see Theia, deep inside the room, swathed in shimmering gold fabric and ivory lace. She held her arms out slightly from her side while the dressmaker, Clarisse Robineau, stood on the fitting platform and pinned and measured, fussing about the short, demi-sleeves of the dress, the tools of her sewing trade scattered on a low, nearby table. The dress forms stood silently in their rows like sentinels guarding a queen.

"Have I arrived too early?" called Inez from the threshold, certain that she had not.

A regal half turn of the head was followed by, "We are finishing up here. My husband has been waiting for you. He wishes to speak to you first, before we begin today."

"How propitious," Inez said under her breath. "I wish to speak to him as well."

Theia continued, "His office is three doors down." She gave a little twist of her wrist to indicate direction, otherwise remaining stock-still.

Inez reversed direction and, counting the doors, braved the malodorous air of the gallery above the open court once again. A smart rap on the panel summoned a man of pale, attentive mien.

"Who is it, Charles?" That was Graham, from somewhere inside.

Inez said, "Charles, you may tell Mr. Drake that Mrs. Stannert is here to see him, per Mrs. Drake."

"Mrs. Stannert," he announced, opening the door wide.

Graham Drake stood as Inez entered. "Good day, Mrs. Stannert. I have business I wish to discuss with you."

"As I do with you, Mr. Drake."

He waited until she sat in the visitor's chair and then lowered himself back into his seat. She thought he had the look of a man who'd had a rough morning. In fact, although more finely dressed and better groomed, he reminded her of the men who would straggle into the Silver Queen, her saloon in Leadville, when the doors were first opened. Men whose haggard faces showed they were having trouble facing the light of day after struggling with too many demons in the shadows of night. Not to put too fine a point on it, but Graham appeared to her as a man sorely in need of a drink.

"Mrs. Stannert, if you don't mind, I shall begin." He set his elbows on the blotter and steepled his hands. "Mrs. Drake would like you to take up residence here, in the hotel, through the end of the year."

Inez opened her mouth to protest.

"She wants you close by, given recent events. You would stay in Yvonne's room."

Inez closed her mouth, mind racing. Here was a golden opportunity, presented to her on a platter.

Graham continued, "She cannot bear being alone. Particularly at night. She trusts you. Hence this request."

She could not believe her luck. Be possessed of the key to Yvonne's room along with an invitation to linger inside? Where she would be free to snoop through the companion's things, without having to sneak around? And if she recalled correctly, Yvonne's room connected to Julia Green's chambers. The police had absconded with the connecting door key, true, but what of that? She was no expert at the black art of lock picking, but given a stretch of uninterrupted time, she was certain she could manage. Hatpins, hairpins, and time would do the trick.

Yes, this would suit her purposes better than Graham could possibly imagine.

However, I must not appear too eager to accept. He will expect me to protest this additional intrusion on my time.

She fixed him with a graze both stern and sympathetic. "I can appreciate how Mrs. Drake must be feeling, what with her companion missing and her protégée departed from this life." Inez gave as deep and sorrowing a sigh as her stays would permit.

"Such a sad and sorry situation. However, your request is problematic. I have neglected my business during this busy time of year and was planning to catch up this week during the time I am not scheduled to be here or at the performances."

His steepled fingertips pressed against each other so hard they turned white. "We will pay you well. And there will be times when Mrs. Drake has engagements. Teas, luncheons, I believe. You will not be expected to attend. It is only to the end of the year."

"What if Yvonne should return?"

"I doubt she will. But if she does, and we decide to re-engage her, you will be released from those obligations."

She tipped her head, as if considering his words, and let him hang a moment. "I believe I can see my way to helping you, then. But I have a few conditions."

"Let's hear them."

"I am engaged this evening, so I will not be able to arrive until close to midnight."

He nodded.

"I cannot perform the duties of a personal maid—style Mrs. Drake's hair, help her dress, maintain her wardrobe, and so on. For that, you will have to find someone else."

"I'll speak to the hotel manager about hiring a hotel maid. I imagine one of them would be willing to take on those tasks. What else?"

"This next involves pecuniary matters." She cleared her throat. "We very much appreciate your patronage at the D & S House of Music and Curiosities, so please do not take offense with what I am about to ask. Our costs have run unusually high this month. I am asking customers with accounts above a certain level to pay their balances before the end of the year. I am hoping you will do the same."

"I see."

"And," she added, "I would like to be paid, up front, for these additional responsibilities."

Silence stretched between them. He searched her face. "Is that all?"

Inez nodded, returning his scrutiny with equanimity. His light-blue eyes, she noted, were quite bloodshot.

Graham said, "If I agree to your terms, and clear the books of what we owe you, you will do this for us? For Mrs. Drake?"

"I will." *And with pleasure.*

"When do you want to be paid?"

"Now."

That seemed to surprise him, but not for long. "Do you have the amount?"

"Do you have a telephone?" she responded. It was a leading question, because Theia had called her the previous night from the suite. "If you have a call placed to the D & S House of Music and Curiosities, my manager, Thomas Welles, will provide the total. If you want a breakdown of the charges, I can bring a written accounting back with me tonight."

"Then we need only discuss your fees for your additional services."

She smiled. "I am certain we can come to a satisfactory agreement."

———

In the end, it was, to Inez's reckoning, an *extremely* satisfactory agreement.

She returned to the hallway with two checks: one made out to the store, the other made out to her personally. The payments tucked safe in her satchel with her sheet music, Inez proceeded to the music room, confident she would be able to deal with whatever Theia might, well, throw at her.

The same chambermaid answered the door. Behind her, Inez could see Theia, now dressed in an elegant sea-green tea gown with ivory lace cascading down the front from neck to hem. The singer was talking to Clarisse, who was nodding, her carpetbag clutched to her like a shield. Right inside the door, a porter waited with the dressmaker's work trunk.

Inez smiled at the maid and said, "I am expected."

She entered in time to hear Clarisse say, "Madame, I will do the best I can."

"A few alterations should not tax your skills," said Theia.

"Adding more lace as you wish, yes, I can do that easily enough, once I purchase more. And adjusting the armscye and bodice, yes, I am able to accomplish those things in time. But the other changes, they may sound simple, what you request, but they will change the line of the dress substantially, and require I buy more material. The tucks and drapes, the panniers, and I do not quite understand why you want—"

Theia cut her off. "The longer you stand here and gabble at me, the less time there is. You have four days. The dress must be done in time for my appearance on the thirty-first. I shall see you in two days, for what I hope is the final fitting. Now, the sooner you go, the sooner you can get it done, yes?"

Clarisse bowed her head and hustled to the door. She almost bumped into Inez, and startled, looked up. She said low-voiced, "Mrs. Stannert! I am glad to see you. I must speak with you soon." She glanced over her shoulder at Theia, who stood with arms crossed, chin tilted upward. "In private. *C'est tres importante.*"

Inez suspected that the last-minute changes to what had to be an expensive gown were exhausting Clarisse's available funds. "I will cover what you need," she murmured. With an upwelling of bank balances in her future, she felt confident she could help Clarisse make this last hurdle. The dress, from what little she had seen, was a marvel. Surely more business would flow the dressmaker's way after Theia wore it on the stage before an audience that could number in the thousands.

Theia watched as the dressmaker scurried out, trailed by the porter with the trunk. "You may also leave," she said to the chambermaid in a tone suited for speaking from a royal throne.

The chambermaid wasted no time in exiting the room.

Theia dropped her regal pose and turned to Inez with a sigh. "You would think I asked Madame Robineau to toss it out and start over! A few changes, some minor adjustments to bring it into this winter's fashion. That is all. I cannot understand what her problem could possibly be."

You cannot understand because you have probably never threaded a needle in your life. Inez bit the inside of her cheek to keep her thoughts unvoiced. Instead, she said, "I have spoken with Mr. Drake and agreed to spend nights here, though I am not certain what my role is, exactly. Companion? Night watch?"

The diva approached, fingers twined in the lace at her bosom. "I would feel safer at nights, with you here."

This struck Inez as odd, given that Graham's bedchamber was on the other side of the wall from hers. But then, it seemed Theia could not count on him being "at home" evenings.

Theia continued, "The little gun you showed me last night. You said you had pockets added to your gowns so you could carry it with you everywhere."

"Not *everywhere*," hedged Inez.

"Do you have it with you now?"

Inez wondered at this line of questioning but saw no reason not to answer honestly. "Yes. It seemed prudent, what with Señor Rubio's whereabouts unknown, Yvonne's odd disappearance, and Miss Green's sad, untimely death."

"So you do not believe she killed herself!" said Theia triumphantly. "I have told Graham over and over, and I tried to explain to the police, I gave Julia my cloak after she misplaced hers. Yvonne was there, she saw me do it. Someone approaching Julia from behind would think she was me. We are of the same height, the same figure."

Inez tried to stay sympathetic but felt her mouth twist in irritation, despite herself. *Why must it always be about you?*

Inez's expression must have registered with Theia, because the singer's face fell and she looked away. "Julia had such promise. The poor child. I do not mean to sound insensitive about her death. I know it is a tragedy. I saw her promise, from the very start. That is why I wanted to take her on, in the first place. I believed that, with time and an expert guiding hand, she could become an outstanding soprano. But young women, their hearts so often distract them from their art." Theia pulled a dainty linen square from the fabric belt at her waist and dabbed at her eyes.

She paused mid-dab, staring at Inez. "It could have been Señor Rubio. He knew I was there, singing that night. He could have been lying in wait, looking for an opportunity."

"It is possible," said Inez cautiously. Was Rubio's ire at being disparaged and dismissed so intense that he would contemplate murder? He was hotheaded. De Bruijn had not discounted him. However, Inez was far more troubled by Graham Drake, who seemed to have more motive to be shut of Theia or Julia. She could imagine him thinking how much simpler life would be without his volatile wife. As for Julia, it would not be the first time a man turned killer when a woman he fancied spurned his advances.

Theia's eyes widened. "It could have even been Yvonne." Her hands crept to her throat. "She has changed lately. I have caught her staring at me with the strangest expression. Could she have come to hate me? Could resentment have festered inside her until she took it out on my poor sweet little pet Aria and my favorite gown? And then, at the Cliff House, thinking Miss Green was me, crept up behind her in the dark and gave her a shove?"

The same could be said for Graham, Inez thought. But Graham had hired her to essentially guard his wife. Would he do so, if he intended to kill Theia?

Inez knew the answer: He would hire her to direct any lingering suspicion away from himself. He would hire her because he would not believe that she—a musician and a businesswoman of modest means and demeanor—was capable of protecting his wife.

A little prickle of fear whispered up her spine.

Inez gave herself a shake.

If that is true, how little he knows me.

She did not like the direction her thoughts or Theia's verbal wanderings were going. It was time to retreat from all the what-ifs and return to the matters at hand.

"Perhaps we should focus on the pieces you wish to perform at the Melpomene," said Inez. "We have all afternoon, but I will need to leave by suppertime. I will return later tonight, before midnight."

"Very well. But first, can I see it?"

Inez frowned. "See what?"

"Your little gun."

Inez wondered at Theia's near obsession with the revolver but put it down to the diva's conviction that dangers lurked about every corner. She extracted the weapon from her pocket and showed it to Theia, pointing the muzzle down and away from them both, her finger set firmly on the frame, well above the trigger itself.

Theia stepped closer, peering at it. "Where does one find a little pistol like that? What is it called?"

"It is a Remington Number Two Smoot Patent revolver," Inez said patiently. "I bought mine a long time ago, not here in San Francisco. But one need only look in the city directory under Guns and Gunsmiths to—" Realization dawned. "Theia. You are not thinking of buying one, are you?"

"Of course not. It just reassures me to know you have it with you. Knowing you will be in Yvonne's old room with your little pistol, I will sleep much better at nights."

Theia turned and walked toward the piano. "Now, you are right. We should get to work. With Christmas over, I have been rethinking the repertoire for the Melpomene. We will keep 'Ave

Maria,' of course. However, I was not altogether satisfied with your rendition at the Cliff House. We shall keep at it until it is perfect."

Chapter Twenty-Nine

DECEMBER 26

Inez had so looked forward to the Monday gathering of penny-ante poker players in the back room of her music store. Almost all were musicians—young, bright-eyed, eager to make their mark in San Francisco's brutal, mercurial music world. She figured they would be a breath of fresh air after the insular environment of the Drakes' rarefied universe. But even their lighthearted gossip and intense but harmless quarrels over the odd copper penny bet couldn't keep her mind from wandering to the recent events at the Cliff House and the Palace Hotel.

Her thoughts swirled in counterpoint to the musical pieces she and Theia had slaved over for the upcoming Melpomene appearance. The selections Theia chose for the theater appearance were quite a switch from the soulful Christmas music they had played before. She had pelted Inez with sheet music for last-minute replacements, saying, "You will need to spend time familiarizing yourself with these. They are quite outside your usual oeuvre, I imagine."

Little did Theia know that, thanks to Inez's many hours humoring musical requests at the Silver Queen saloon, she was quite conversant with "Listen to the Mockingbird," "I'll Take You Home

Again Kathleen," and their ilk. Still, Theia had her own vision of how the songs should be sung and played. As they bent to their task, Inez was struck by how the diva projected meaning and emotion into the most trivial of tunes. Her "Clementine" actually brought a lump to Inez's throat. Judging from the tears swimming in Theia's light-brown eyes, the singer was overcome as well. But those tears vanished with the piano's dying notes, leaving Inez to wonder how much of the performance was heartfelt and how much was artifice.

Then again, that was one of the imponderables about Theia.

Now, in the comfort of the back room of her music store, with friendly conversation and a cup of coffee with just a touch of brandy, she should have been able to relax at last. But that wasn't the case.

Snatches of lyrics kept interrupting her concentration. *I'll think of him never, I'll be wildly gay, I'll charm ev'ry heart, and the crowd I will sway*—this snippet from "I'll Twine 'Mid the Ringlets" seemed to sum up Theia's final words to John Teague at the Cliff House. *Ninety years without slumbering, ticktock ticktock, his life's seconds numbering, ticktock ticktock*—the faintly ominous refrain from "Grandfather's Clock" wouldn't leave her alone.

"Your deal, Mrs. Stannert." Thomas Welles was looking at her curiously.

All the eyes were on her. She glanced down at the deck of cards before her and sighed. "Gentlemen, I will have to cut this evening short. Next week, I assure you, all will be as it was."

William Ash said, "Need time to recover from the holiday, Mrs. Stannert? It's a busy time for us as well." He glanced around at his compatriots. "We spend our time from Thanksgiving to New Year's racing from one end of town to the other. All the theaters, restaurants, high society, and what-have-you suddenly want to hire musicians. It'd be nice if they could spread their events throughout the year. But we'll take what we can get, when we get it." He turned to Roger Haskell, the newsman and only non-musician of the bunch. "Did your nephew like the flute?"

"Oh, the little heathen was delighted. Unwrapped it and gave a whoop loud enough to deafen us all. My sister was less enthusiastic. I told her music would be a good civilizing influence. I think she took that as a criticism of her parenting." He shrugged. "Speaking of civilizing music, Mrs. Stannert, how are you doing with Mrs. Carrington Drake? Doesn't she have another appearance before her finale at the Grand on New Year's?"

"The Melpomene on the thirtieth," said Inez.

Chatter broke out around the table as the winners, pocketing their handfuls of change, gleefully ribbed their friends who were going home with lighter pockets.

Inez leaned over to Welles and Haskell, who were sitting nearby, and said, "If you gentlemen would stay afterward, I need to speak with you. It won't take long."

The musicians clattered off, full of energy and debating which watering hole they would stop at to while away another hour or two. Inez retrieved a more expensive brandy from the locked cabinet in her office and poured measures for both men.

Haskell nodded approvingly and set his cigar in a nearby ashtray, which someone had apparently purloined from the Bella Union. "What's on your mind?"

"Since you both know of the Drakes, I want you to be aware of what is going on. Perhaps you have some insights." She glanced at Welles. "A bit of store business first. Mr. Drake has paid his bill in full, so we can begin restocking without worrying about coming up short. Aside from that, there have been some disturbing events in the Drake entourage. Did you hear what happened to Theia Drake's protégée, Miss Julia Green, at the Cliff House on Christmas Eve?"

Welles nodded soberly. Haskell's brow furrowed. Inez summarized, finishing with, "Her death is deemed a suicide. I am not convinced it is so. To top it off, Mrs. Drake's longtime companion, Yvonne Marchal, disappeared on Christmas."

"Foul play?" asked Haskell.

"Unknown. However, much has happened that is out of the ordinary, and Mrs. Drake has some"—she wrinkled her nose— "concerns? Fears? She is used to having a female companion close by, so Miss Marchal's absence is adding to her distress. As a result, I was asked to take a room in the Drakes' suite until the end of the year, to keep her company. I agreed."

Welles paused in the process of lifting his glass, surprise filtering through his normally somber aspect. "You did?"

"It's only for a short while," said Inez. "And Mr. Drake is paying me very, very well."

"So you sold your soul to the devil for pieces of silver, eh?" said Haskell.

"Hardly my soul," snapped Inez. "Merely my presence. Why would you even say that?"

"I thought you championed the cause of the common workingman."

"Common working folk. I do not discriminate between the sexes on that issue."

"Just keep in mind that, since taking over the *Times*, Drake has been doing his best to break the backs of the union shops in his newspaper," said Haskell. "It's stupid and pigheaded of him. But all the owners of the big local newspapers are watching him closely. If Drake can get his workers to accede to lower pay and longer hours, the other owners will probably try to do the same. We can't let that happen."

"My arrangement is completely separate from his business doings," said Inez sharply.

"So you say, but then you were curious about John Teague and his connection with Drake, right?" Haskell dug into the inner reaches of his waistcoat and pulled out a much-folded newspaper. "You're looking for *the truth*? Well, here you go." He handed the paper to her.

Welles drained his glass and stood. "Since the topic of conversation has shifted from the music store to local papers and politics,

I'll take my leave. The missus is expecting me." He handed Inez an envelope. "Since you're returning to the hotel tonight, you might as well take this with you. It's the details of the Drakes' account, in case he wants to see the numbers."

After plucking his overcoat and hat from a hook by the back door, Welles added, "I'll take care of the store. You can leave me instructions or call on the telephone. I'll keep an ear out for the ring."

She pocketed the envelope and unfolded the newspaper, which was little more than a four-page broadsheet. The masthead read: *The Truth.* "Thank you, Mr. Welles. I'll do that. Please give my best to your wife."

As the door swung shut behind her store manager, she scrutinized the small type beneath the title: Volume 1, Number 1. Published by John Teague. "So, *The Truth* is a new business venture for Mr. Teague?"

Haskell leaned over and tapped the dateline. "This is from about a month ago. When word came down that Drake had bought *The San Francisco Times,* Teague was all set to quit, but Drake beat him to the punch and fired him. Rather than hire on at another paper, Teague decided to pick up the pen and do battle with Drake and the other local bigwigs."

She returned her attention to the sheet in her hand and read aloud. "I begin the publication of *The Truth* because I want free expression. I have no expectation that I shall be able to slay the dragons of greed and dishonesty which master this town. But I hope to foil them." She looked up at Haskell. "Oh my."

He raised his eyebrows.

She looked back down. "And here Mr. Teague says, 'Being a journalist, and nothing else, I have no political ambition and have no place in the society column to lose. Moreover, I have no wealth to be robbed of.'" She returned her gaze to Haskell. "So how does he afford this newspaper gambit of his?"

"A handful of loyal subscribers and believers. Some savings. Does it on a shoestring out of his boardinghouse room, I daresay."

She returned to his screed. "I do not look for the approval from Nob Hill, nor from those who sit in presidential splendor in the Palace." She stopped reading and commented, "He does not pull his punches. The Drakes are ensconced in the presidential suite at the Palace Hotel."

Haskell leaned back in his chair. "No secret there."

Inez continued reading aloud. "It will be my pleasure to interfere to the extent of my ability with their freebooting and happiness, and pull off their masks of artifice and arrogance to reveal *The Truth* beneath." She scanned the rest of the page, then turned to the middle spread. "And on it goes. So, he writes and publishes this by himself?"

"Yep. He doesn't suffer from a loss of words. Some say he's a wild slinger of abuse and vituperation. In reality, he's the most conservative and charitable of men, but his conservatism is on the side of the downtrodden and his charity begins with the poor and the honest workingman."

Inez thought of Haskell's own vociferously pro-labor newspaper, *The Workingman's Voice*. "That explains your friendship."

Haskell nodded. "I met him when he breezed into town about ten years ago. I even hired him now and again to write an article or three before he signed up with the *Times*."

The newsman scooted a little closer and pointed at one of the narrow columns of text. "He sharpens his pen further in. Such as here: 'Consider the character of the men who are held to be the most eminent among us, including those newly arrived in their coaches of stolen silver. In our city, our pirates do not mount the scaffold, but receive political and social rewards for their prowess as they pilfer and steal.'"

"He's asking for trouble," said Inez. "Is that what he wants?"

Haskell shook his head. "I advised him to take it easy in his first issue to attract more readers, but that's never been Teague's style. It might look like he is indicting Nob Hill as a whole, but certain thrusts he makes are definitely meant for Drake."

"And he gets away with this?" Inez asked, a little astonished.

"Well, probably only a hundred or so in the city are actually reading *The Truth*."

Inez folded the paper slowly, thoughtfully. "I'd like to chat with Mr. Teague. Where do I find him?"

"I'll give you his address," said Haskell. "Be sure to mention me. He'll talk more readily if he knows I sent you."

Inez retrieved a pencil and handed it to him along with the folded newspaper. "Write the address there. Do you know where he was before he came to San Francisco?"

"Virginia City." Haskell scribbled an address in a nearly illegible hand. "That's where he knows Drake from, I'd wager. When I asked Teague, he was tight-mouthed, but since Drake made his fortune there, it's a logical assumption. I've not bothered to dig into it. None of my business." He shot her a look from under his bushy gray eyebrows. "Please don't do anything that'd destroy a beautiful friendship between two old newsmen. By my sending you to him, I'm giving him assurance that you're sailing in under my flag, not Drake's."

"I will tread lightly," she assured him.

They said their goodbyes and Inez closed shop, preparing to return to the Palace Hotel. She had packed and sent on a modest traveling trunk with attire she would need for the next few days. Theia had said "simple black" would do for the Melpomene engagement. "For the last appearance at the Grand, you may wear something more elegant," she had added.

"Something *not* black?" Inez had asked with an unintended note of sarcasm.

"Certainly. It will be New Year's Eve. A time of new beginnings. I will be in gold and silver, so wear something that will complement but still be appropriate."

Inez understood. She was being asked to don an evening gown that would not outshine the singer on her last night center stage.

Upon arriving in the hotel's reception office, Inez asked for a key to Yvonne Marchal's room. The clerk handed it over without a murmur. Clearly, Graham Drake had paved the way.

Upstairs, she hesitated, wondering if she should check the music room, perhaps even tap on Theia's door, to let her know that she had arrived. It was midnight. The diva kept early hours. Inez presumed Theia was already abed, so she decided against it.

In case Yvonne had returned, she rapped softly on the door to the companion's rooms.

No response.

Inez went in, thinking it would be wise to be prepared if Yvonne returned to gather her belongings in the dead of night or if someone else, more sinister, came by and gave the doorknob a try. She decided to keep her revolver close at hand, just in case.

She was pleasantly surprised to find someone had thoughtfully left lamps burning in the small parlor and the bedchamber beyond. Her trunk was waiting in the sleeping quarters. Although it was late, Inez explored the rooms, including taking a peek into the adjoining water-closet. All the while, she thought about its former occupant.

Yvonne had ostensibly left to attend Mass on Christmas morning and had not returned. It didn't sound as if she had decamped with any luggage. Many questions swirled through Inez's mind. Where had she gone for service? Saint Patrick's was nearby, as was Saint Ignatius. More distantly, there was Saint Mary's Cathedral, which had the wealthiest and most aristocratic congregation, or so she had heard. Then she thought of the dressmaker, Clarisse, who was also of the faith, and who admitted to having known Theia "back in the day" when she was Miss Carrington at the Melpomene. Perhaps Clarisse had known Yvonne then as well. In any case, Inez thought, whether through past history, common language, or common faith, the two women had seemed to have a bond in the here and now. Perhaps Clarisse might have recommended one house of worship over another, or even invited Yvonne to attend Christmas morning services with her. Inez decided she would ask Clarisse about Yvonne, next time she had a chance.

She strolled over to the little desk, lifted the top, and aimlessly opened and closed the drawers, which were empty. Had Yvonne left that morning, intending to come back? Julia Green had died just the previous night. Had the protégée's death so shaken her that she simply abandoned everyone and everything, shed her "old way of life," perhaps, to move on, unburdened, to a new one? Or did guilt propel her out the door with a fierce desire to disappear?

Or, had someone made certain that she would never return to the land of the living?

And if Yvonne had secrets to keep from prying eyes, where would she hide them?

The question came to her, it seemed, from somewhere outside herself. A little voice, murmuring in her ear. Inez slowed her perambulations and moved to the middle of the parlor. She turned in a circle, slowly, her arms wrapped about herself to guard against a sudden chill that, she was sure, existed only in her mind.

Yvonne, the invisible. Yvonne, the set-upon. The whipping post and confidante of the high-strung diva. Scorned by her mistress's husband, ignored and discounted, or at the least taken for granted, by the rest of the Drakes' entourage. Everyone has secrets, Inez reasoned, and with all Yvonne had heard, seen, and been subjected to, she probably had more than most.

Where are they, Yvonne? Where did you hide them?

Not in the parlor. Too public, too open to discovery.

Inez moved into the bedchamber. The closets were empty, awaiting Inez's wardrobe. Yvonne's two trunks, modest in size, were stacked neatly in a corner. The bed was freshly made.

If she left Christmas morning with the intention of returning, then whatever she might have wished to keep private could still be hidden.

It would be close at hand, so she could rest easy at night. Inez opened the cabinet under the nightstand, peered under the bed, under the cloth draping a small table, and under the dust ruffles of the over-stuffed chair. She explored the chest of drawers.

Close at hand.

It would probably be a simple hiding place, for who would come searching the companion's bedchambers in the normal course of things? Inez sat on the edge of the bed, thinking.

Close at hand.

Surely, it wouldn't be as obvious as...

She snaked a hand down between the goose-down mattress and the sturdy oak headboard. Her searching fingers touched an object that was neither. She gripped the edge of what felt like a book and pulled. The scrapbook, which announced itself as such with ornate letters on the front of the worn leather volume, slipped from her grasp to land with a thump on the rug. She picked up the splayed volume, dislodging loose bits of ephemera. Inez gathered them up—several advertisements trumpeting the appearance of "The Golden Songbird, Mrs. Carrington Drake" at this or that theater and a handful of letters, their envelopes slit neatly open.

Curious, she thumbed through the album's pages. Most were filled with articles and announcements of Theia's appearances, carefully snipped from newspapers, along with programs. These were interspersed with trade cards, leaflets, the odd pressed flower, and a few yellow feathers, perhaps from Theia's pet bird. The first few pages, she noted, featured clippings from the Melpomene Theater. From there, the clippings evolved to Virginia City. Inez perused a short announcement heralding the "upcoming nuptials of Mr. Graham Drake and Miss Theia Carrington." The last page included a Denver theater program for the RENOWNED (in all capitals) operatic singer Mrs. Carrington Drake, appearing with San Francisco pianist Luis Rubio.

Next, Inez picked up the envelopes. They were all addressed in the same hand and directed to Theia Carrington in Virginia

City. Since the envelopes had been previously opened, Inez had no qualms about choosing one at random, pulling out the letter, and reading it.

The missive opened with "Dearest Songbird of my heart."

Letters to Theia? In a scrapbook kept by Yvonne?

Intrigued, Inez shifted closer to the lamp on the nightstand to read. The single page, front and back, overflowed with impassioned entreaties and vows of eternal devotion in language both elegant and intense. Inez thought if *she* had received such a letter, she would have flung caution to the wind and risked reputation and more to fly to her lover's side. And so it continued, to the closing declaration: "Never doubt the faithfulness of your beloved, most devoted scribbler of words, John."

John Teague?

The turns of phrase, the command of the written word—she had seen their like just a few hours earlier in *The Truth*.

It had to be him.

"So, Mr. Teague," Inez said to the love letters on her lap. "I wonder why Yvonne has your letters to Theia. And just when it was that you wooed the Golden Songbird. And what of your past partnership with Graham Drake? I believe you and I shall have to have a chat. And soon."

Chapter Thirty

DECEMBER 27

The next morning, Inez awoke to the creak of a door opening. She lunged upright in bed, momentarily confused as to where she was. She heard Theia's voice, alert and impatient, in the parlor beyond. "Inez, are you still asleep? We have much to do today! When did you get in last night?"

After preparing for bed, Inez had spent almost two hours reading the rest of Teague's letters to Theia. Some were very long. She had thought to explore the scrapbook further but had fallen asleep with the papers scattered over the coverlet.

Now, Inez hastily gathered the letters and other bits of loose memorabilia from Yvonne's scrapbook, calling out, "Good morning to you, too, Theia. I arrived a bit after midnight but did not want to disturb you. We are practicing early today?"

Footsteps approached. Inez hastily crammed the papers inside the album before stuffing the book underneath the bedclothes.

Theia appeared at the threshold of the bedchamber, dressed, coiffed, arms crossed. Inez made a mental note to retrieve the key for the connecting door at the first opportunity and to be sure the door was locked at all times.

"Early? This is hardly early. It is nearly eight o'clock. And didn't

I tell you yesterday? We must start our work early because later we are meeting with Mr. Thackery at the Grand about my New Year's Eve recital."

"This is the first I've heard of it." Inez made another mental note: Apparently moving into Yvonne's room also entailed adopting Theia's early-to-rise habits and being at the mercy of the diva's schedule. Inez continued, "The sooner I have some privacy, the sooner I can be ready."

Theia retreated, saying, "I'll be in the music room. Breakfast is waiting for us both. It will probably be cold by the time you come out."

"Start without me, Theia. Coffee is all I require at this time of day."

After the connecting door snapped shut, Inez rose and dove into an abbreviated version of her morning rituals. Along with a quick wash-up, she gave herself a stern talking-to. "You are being paid for this, so be civil, " she muttered to herself as she pulled on clean black stockings and common-sense garters.

"This is your best chance to find out more about Julia," she added as she whipped on drawers and a chemise.

"And perhaps more about Yvonne," she continued, as she pulled on and tied her corset with practiced fingers.

"Perhaps I can discover more about 'Lucky Duck' Drake as well." On went camisole, petticoat, and half boots.

"You can handle this," she told herself. "Early mornings and all. It's just for a few days." Her simple dress—black, of course, with no-nonsense schoolmarm-style white collar and cuffs—was fastened in record time.

Inez brushed her hair and twisted it up, stabbing the resultant knot with more than enough hairpins. "It's only a few nights," she repeated, reassuring the overly stern face in the mirror. She noted her normally olive skin was paler, the slight lines between her eyebrows deeper. And was there more silver in her dark hair than a month ago?

She leaned forward, eye-to-eye with her image. "I will do this," she said fiercely. Julia was dead, most likely slain. The porter Freeman had been unfairly fired. And malice, perhaps even murder, stalked Theia.

"I want justice," said Inez to the mirror. "For all of them. Is that too much to ask?"

She spun away from her reflection, replaced the scrapbook in its hiding place between headboard and mattress, and pulled her Remington Smoot from the bedside drawer and pocketed it. Inez then headed toward the music room, hoping the coffee, at least, would still be warm.

———

Inez tried to push Teague's letters from her mind during practice with Theia, but she found it nearly impossible. Had Theia ever seen the letters? Or had Yvonne waylaid them, hidden them from her mistress? If so, why?

They slaved over "Happy Young Heart" for some time, with much frustration and little progress. Theia stopped Inez again, saying, "Lightly, sprightly, Inez! Make the music dance. This piece should be upbeat, not a funereal dirge!"

Inez had had enough. All she wanted to do was toss Sullivan's music out the window and bang out some angry Beethoven. "I must rest my hands," she said, closing the keyboard lid. She stood and stretched, asking, "I'm curious. I recall you said that you sang at the Melpomene in the past. Was that before or after you met Mr. Drake?"

"Before." Theia twisted the string of pearls around her neck. "I met him shortly thereafter."

"Here in San Francisco?"

Theia glanced at her sharply, then strolled to her line of dress forms, stopping in front of her lavender walking suit. "No. We met in Virginia City."

"Did Yvonne go into your service after you married?"

Theia picked at the neckline of the lavender outfit, then turned to Inez. "Why all the questions?"

Inez said demurely, "Well, I *am* living in Yvonne's rooms. I find myself wondering about her. How long she has been with you, whether she came to you through your marriage, or if you knew each other from before. I just cannot fathom what would make her leave you like this." She watched Theia for a reaction.

A shadow flitted across Theia's face. "I am also at a loss to understand. I have known Yvonne a long time. We shall leave it at that." She glanced at the mantel clock. "This would be a good time to stop. We shall take a light meal before going to the Grand. I do not want to be late to this meeting."

After a lunch of tea sandwiches, Theia retreated to her private rooms to change with the help of one of the hotel's chambermaids. Inez pitied the young servant who scuttled in and out as if she expected to be beaten about the shoulders. When Theia emerged, cool and collected, in her lavender suit and dark violet coat, hat, gloves, and umbrella, Inez was ready with her own jet-black coat, hat, gloves, and umbrella. Given that the sun outside the bay windows was shining with its customary hard-diamond winter brilliance, Inez suspected the umbrellas would be superfluous, but one never knew.

"It's a beautiful day," announced Theia, handing Inez the key to the music room. "We shall walk."

Inez stifled a sigh, wondering how far Theia would push the limits of treating her like a maid. *Only a few more nights.*

The walk to the Grand was short. Theia kept her gaze straight ahead, a small smile playing about the corners of her mouth. Inez was certain the diva was aware of the admiring glances sent her way by the men passing by. *Always center stage, even on the sidewalks.*

At the Grand, Theia walked through the lobby and entrance hall as if she owned every inch of its black and white marble floor. She led Inez down a side passage to a door on which was lettered: E. P. Thackery, Assistant Manager. Theia pointed to a long, olive-green-upholstered sofa outside the office. "You can sit and wait for me here."

Bristling at the singer's tone, Inez planted the ferrule of her umbrella onto the plank floor. "I prefer to stand."

They locked eyes and a silent war of wills ensued. Theia finally broke ranks with a shrug and a dismissive "Suit yourself, Inez." She turned away and went inside the office. As the door snapped shut, Inez heard her say, "I'm here for Mr. Thackery."

Inez strolled the hallway, gazing on framed posters of past shows, including *Faust, Oliver Twist,* and *The Beggar's Opera,* which hung side-by-side with *Richard III* and *Hamlet.* After a while, Mr. Thackery and Theia appeared. The assistant manager was saying deferentially, "Of course, Mrs. Drake, I shall certainly be willing to entertain the possibility. We would be honored. But first, you understand, I must talk with your husband."

"Of course." The two words were so sharp that if they were glass, their edges could have opened a vein. Inez guessed the conversation had not concluded as Theia had expected: the singer was clearly seething.

Thackery's eyes lit on Inez and his nervous expression brightened into something like relief. "Mrs. Stannert, what a stroke of luck that you are here. You came with Mrs. Drake? Yes, yes, of course you did. In any case, your timely appearance saves me a trip to your music store. May we speak?" He turned to Theia and said, "I have just a small spot of business with Mrs. Stannert. It won't take long. " He indicated the sofa. "Please, make yourself comfortable."

Theia surveyed the couch as though it had insulted her. "I prefer to stand," she said, mirroring Inez's words and defiant air.

He cleared his throat and repeated, "This won't take long," and waved Inez in. They passed a young man, who was fighting a losing battle with the paperwork on his desk. Inez thought he must be the assistant to the assistant manager because Thackery said to him, "No visitors until Mrs. Stannert and I have had our little talk. If Mr. Rubio shows up again, keep him at bay until we are done." He hustled Inez into an inner office, fussed a bit pulling a chair out for her, then circled his desk and sat with a heavy sigh. "I suppose you know I am in quite a bind with this latest request of Mrs. Drake's."

Inez realized he assumed she was in Theia's confidence. Rather than disabuse him, she merely tut-tutted sympathetically and said, "Quite the conundrum for you, Mr. Thackery."

"Conundrum is absolutely the perfect word for it, Mrs. Stannert." He closed his eyes and massaged his temples. "The tragic business of Miss Green, I cannot tell you how shocked we were to hear of it. And now, Mrs. Drake has renewed her, ah, I would call it a demand but I do not wish to be unkind, to extend her contract and return to our stage after the first of the year. Of course, I cannot offer her anything until Mr. Drake agrees, and he has made his position clear."

"Retirement at the end of the year," said Inez, striving for an understanding tone.

"Exactly." He spread his hands. "She has put me in a difficult position. He is her husband and manager. I felt I had to remind her, although I tried to be circumspect, that any agreement with the theater must be made with him. That he speaks for her."

"Of course. How very awkward for you."

"Perhaps you can be my confederate, help smooth the troubled waters. I have no desire to distress Mrs. Drake, but that is how business is conducted. She, of all people, knows this."

"I will do what I can, Mr. Thackery." *Not that I can do much in the next few days.*

He stroked his mustache. "Thank you. I am glad you have no such complications, Mrs. Stannert, and that you and I can deal directly without, ah, intermediaries."

What is he driving at? She nodded and waited.

He plunged in. "I have a business proposition for you. We, that is, the management of the theater, hope you will consider being an accompanist for us, as the occasion may arise."

Inez blinked, surprised. "Me?"

"Mr. Bert, owner of the Grand, heard you play at the Cliff House. He was, in his words, 'transported.' He asked that I speak with you."

"This is unexpected." Inez thought of the store, her side business interests, Antonia, and all the tasks "hanging fire" until she could wiggle free from the Drakes. Did she really want, or need, to take on another responsibility? But...it was very tempting. "I am honored by your interest, of course. However, surely you are not short of accomplished pianists. I heard you hired Mr. Rubio, for instance."

"Oh yes, Mr. Rubio." He picked up a pencil from his desk and began twiddling it in his fingers, not looking at Inez. "Well, I will be straight with you, Mrs. Stannert, as I know you have had some unpleasant interactions with him. You will understand when I say he is notoriously difficult to work with and unreliable. We took him on because Miss Green insisted, and we saw great things for her. Such a tragedy," he repeated.

The pencil's movements ceased, as in deference to the dead, then began again. "Please. Do consider our offer. We know you are busy with your business and what-not, and as we are eager to make this a long-term relationship, we would not take advantage. Each appearance would be individually negotiated to mutually agreeable terms. Now, now, no need to answer right away." He gave a little laugh. "Particularly if you are inclined to say no. Just tell me you will think it over and give it your serious consideration. That will satisfy us for now. We can always talk further after the new year."

"Very well, Mr. Thackery, thank you for extending this opportunity to me. I shall, as you say, think it over and give it serious consideration." She rose and smiled. "Will that do as an answer for the present?"

He also rose, his toothy grin flashing out from under his mustache. "For the present."

She held out her hand. He leaned over and shook it. She added, "I plan to keep your offer to myself. No mention to the Drakes, in any way, shape, or form. I am employed by them until year's end, and it is all I can think of until my contract with them has ended."

"Absolutely understood." He opened the door for her and then hurried through the office to open the outer door. "Until New Year's Eve, then."

Inez exited the office, feeling almost guilty. Here she was, with an offer from the opera house which she wasn't at all certain she wanted, and there was Theia, begging for a chance to sing again, a desire that was all but a pipe dream. *How unfair life is, sometimes.*

Then, she thought of Julia Green. There would be no more opportunities for her.

Life is unfair, and capricious and cruel as well.

Out in the hallway, Inez looked about. *Where is Theia?*

She was not sitting on the sofa. She was not examining the hallway posters. But, in the direction of the lobby, Inez could hear two voices, raised in heated disagreement. Theia and—

Rubio.

Oh no.

Inez hurried toward the kerfuffle. She entered the entrance hall in time to hear Theia cry, "How dare you!"

The two of them, singer and pianist, faced off by the staircase to the second floor. They reminded Inez of nothing so much as two peacocks from Woodward's Gardens, circling each other, flamboyant feathers fanned, ready to strike.

Luis Rubio sneered, "You cannot accept it, can you? You are a has-been, Theia. Julia may be gone, but you"—he pointed at her—"will vanish as surely as if the waves had taken you instead of her. I wish they had. She had the will, she had the voice. She was twice the singer, many times the woman you will ever be."

Theia struck him hard across the cheek. Inez gasped, thinking the blow would certainly have drawn blood if not cushioned by the purple glove.

Rubio's head snapped back, and just as quickly, he grabbed her wrist.

"Unhand me, you, you debaucher!" Theia tried to yank away.

"You insulted me once, in this very place, on the stage," said Rubio, still holding on. "And now, again. This is the last time."

"Stop it!" Inez shouted, hurrying forward.

"Inez!" Theia turned frantic eyes her way. "Thank God you're here." She cut back to Rubio. "Mrs. Stannert carries a gun! She will shoot you if you do not let go of me, right now."

Rubio's rage wavered. "You lie."

"She does not," said Inez, silently cursing Theia's tongue. "But I hesitate to waste a bullet on you. This entire scene is ridiculous. Let her go."

Closing in on them, she prepared to employ her umbrella— again—as a weapon against him. The wave of alcoholic fumes wafting from the pianist nearly set her back on her heels. "You are drunk!" she said to Rubio with disgust.

"What is going on here?" Thackery's voice boomed out, startling them all into silence.

This impressed Inez a great deal. She had not pegged Thackery as the booming type. Yet, here he was, striding toward the three of them, his face red as a tomato, his impressive walrus mustache only adding to his indignant expression.

Rubio dropped his hold on Theia and stepped back.

She retreated as well, nursing her wrist. "He attacked me!"

"*You* attacked me, Madame. Verbally and then physically. I merely was trying to stop you from hitting me a second time," retorted Rubio.

Thackery looked from one to the other, and then at Inez. She said, "When I came on the scene, they were already arguing."

The assistant manager sighed. "Mrs. Drake, I am sorry for what appears to have been an unpleasant encounter. Señor Rubio, we will talk now. In my office."

Rubio straightened his cuffs, gave Theia and Inez a last withering glare, and started toward the back of the theater, with Thackery on his heels.

"I do not think I can walk back to the hotel," said Theia, her face pale.

"The walk will do us both good," said Inez. "Besides, we can talk."

"You sound just like Yvonne," said Theia, falling in step beside Inez. As they crossed the foyer, she regained some of her spirit. "A has-been! He called me a has-been! How dare he."

"No doubt he was searching for the words that would wound you most deeply." *And it seems he found them.*

"Oh, what do you know of him? I spent two months putting up with his insufferable attitude. His rages and his drinking. And all that time, he and Julia—" she bit her lip. "I shall not speak ill of the dead. It would be most unkind."

Inez was tempted to say, "And you would know 'unkind.'" However, she refrained and waited to see what else Theia would say. As she expected, Theia rushed in to fill the silence.

"Oh, the poor girl. You must think I'm cruel and selfish, that I hardly give her a second thought, but it's not true. On the one hand, I believe we must carry on, for what else can we do? On the other hand, I wonder about what happened. Whether someone killed her, mistaking her for me. Or if she killed herself. There are no answers, I suppose. With no family to claim her, it will be up to Mr. Drake and me to determine her final resting place. Most likely it will be here, in San Francisco." She sighed. "I suppose I shall have to go through her things. Or perhaps the hotel would take on the task."

"I could do so, if you wish. Is there anything in particular you'd want me to look for?"

"Oh no, Mrs. Stannert. I couldn't ask that of you." She paused before they exited the building, looked about, then stepped closer, lowering her voice. "One more thing. Two nights ago, with Mr. Drake and the letter. I regret you witnessed our disagreement. He and I have come to an understanding. He has been under a lot of pressure with his newspaper, and I had not realized things had come to such a state with him. His relapse into a previous weakness, and what I uncovered about him and Julia… I realized I must change my ways, truly, and be a more accepting wife, try to help him in his struggles. After all, he is not the only husband who has strayed. Do not tell anyone, and promise that we shall speak no more of it."

"Very well. And we shall not speak of it." Inez parroted Theia's words, thinking her promise provided wiggle room for dissecting events with de Bruijn, should she so decide.

Theia sighed, as if a weight had been lifted from her. "Thank you, Inez. Only a few more days, and you shall be able to return to your quiet existence, without all our dramas."

Inez couldn't help but feel she was being manipulated. Theia's little confessions, her sudden self-awareness, all seemed completely out of character. Inez scrutinized the diva's face, but saw nothing aside from a faint blush of apology.

They stepped out onto the sidewalk. Theia remarked, "It is a beautiful day. And I have much to think about. I believe I will take a stroll to compose myself."

Inez felt she could do with a little air herself, under the circumstances. "Where shall we go? To Woodward's Gardens?"

"I'd prefer to walk by myself." She clasped one of Inez's hands in both of hers. "Thank you for coming to my rescue. I should know by now that responding to Señor Rubio's malice only feeds his vindictiveness."

"I am glad Mr. Thackery showed up when he did. It is he you should thank, you know."

"You're right. And I will." Theia released Inez's hand. "I imagine you have much to do, what with the upcoming performances and your music store. Shall we reconvene later this evening for another run-through?" With a small, diffident smile, Theia turned and walked away.

Thoughtful, Inez watched as the lavender- and purple-clad figure joined the other pedestrians headed north toward Market Street. Yes, this was a definite sea-change in Theia's attitude. And so suddenly.

Much too suddenly. She is up to something. And whatever it is, it cannot bode well.

Chapter Thirty-One

Inez stared in the direction Theia had gone, debating what to do next.

She could go to the music store for her copy of *The Truth* or hunt up Teague and try to wheedle more information from him about the Drakes. She had to admit, she was anxious to talk to the newsman.

But suppose Theia was of the same mind? At the Cliff House, the diva had stormed out in high dudgeon after her clandestine meeting with the newsman. Inez suspected Theia regularly employed such *Sturm und Drang* techniques to soften up her "victim" before circling around later for another try at getting her way. Señor Rubio was the only one who appeared immune to her approach, the only one capable of giving her a dose of her own medicine. Also, Inez suspected Theia had been lying about why she wanted to go off on her own. The diva had some purpose in mind, Inez was certain. And what better smokescreen for visiting her former lover than professing a renewed affection and interest in her husband?

So perhaps, Inez thought, the visit to Teague should wait. Instead, she could visit Clarisse Robineau's shop to see what the dressmaker wanted to discuss and question her about Yvonne's possible whereabouts.

Or, she could return to the Palace Hotel and attempt to "unlock" the door to Julia Green's rooms. What Theia had said about having the hotel pack up Julia's possessions lent an air of urgency to the last task.

Finally, she was tempted to explore the diva's private rooms—the risk being Theia might return unexpectedly and catch her.

Inez felt that the answers lay somewhere in the interconnected rooms at the Palace Hotel. She sensed them closing in around her, waiting for her to uncover the definitive clue and to ask the right questions before revealing themselves.

The best course of action, she decided, was to return to the hotel now, while she had the chance to nose about. She could always beg off sometime in the next couple days, pleading a business emergency, and escape long enough to run Teague to ground and to meet with Clarisse.

Inez hurried back to the Palace. As she approached the suite with its many doors, she realized that getting into Julia's room would the most difficult task. She was no expert lock-picker.

Halting by the door leading to Yvonne's chambers, she spotted one of the army of hotel maids emerging from a room down the hall. Carrying an armful of folded towels, the young woman turned and locked the door behind her.

Inspired, Inez grabbed the doorknob, rattled it, then clapped her hands to her cheeks and said loudly, "Oh dear!"

Just as she hoped, the chambermaid approached. "Can I help you, ma'am?"

Inez pasted a bewildered expression on her face. "I just realized, the key to my rooms is inside. I am the new musical accompanist for Mrs. Drake. She and I were going over some music in my little parlor when I had to leave. She promised to lock up behind me." Inez prattled on, willing the chambermaid to realize what she was asking, without actually saying the words.

To Inez's relief, the chambermaid pulled out her skeleton key. "That's all right, ma'am. It happens all the time." She unlocked the door, adding, "The hotel has extra keys if this happens again. Just ask at the office."

Inez said quickly, "The connecting door between my rooms and the music room will be locked as well. Could I borrow this?" She plucked the key from the maid's hand. "I won't be a minute."

She zipped inside, closed the door on the maid's startled face, and hurried over to the door connecting the tiny parlor to Julia's rooms. Inserting the master key, Inez prayed it would work on interior doors as well as the hallway doors and gave it a turn. The latch withdrew with a click. She twisted the crystal knob and the door swung open. The shadow forms of furniture loomed in the dim parlor interior. A half-open door, probably leading to the bedchamber, leaked a small sliver of light onto the parlor rug. Inez shut the door and went to return the maid's key.

"Thank you so much!" she gushed, and handed the maid a coin from her pocket along with the key. "I will keep in mind what you said about the duplicates."

Inez didn't know how much time she had to explore Julia's rooms. But with Theia's remark about having the contents removed, there was no time to delay. Once inside Julia's quarters, Inez lit a lamp on an occasional table, turned it low, and looked around. The room had a forlorn air, even though it had been unoccupied for just a couple of days. One of Julia's hats waited on the love seat, along with a matching pair of gloves.

A lump rose in Inez's throat. She closed her eyes a minute to focus.

She remembered Julia as she'd last seen her in this room, right before they all left for the Cliff House. When Inez had knocked and entered, she had caught Julia adjusting the silk-embroidered fire screen. The singer had stepped hastily back, a furtive, almost guilty look on her normally open face.

Had she hidden something behind the screen?

Inez moved the fabric screen aside, and peered into the firebox. Ashes showed that it had not been cleaned recently. She picked up a nearby poker and stirred the clumps and ashes around the andirons. One piece refused to fall apart. She drew it onto the hearth to get a better look at it—a crumpled piece of paper.

She picked it up with the merest of fingertips, glad to see it was not burned, merely wadded up and thrown away. Was this what Julia didn't want anyone to see?

Holding the crumpled paper up and away so as to not scatter light-gray powder on her dark skirts, she carried it to a table where she set it down and smoothed it flat. A small sheet, about the size of her hand, with one ragged edge, it had apparently been ripped out from a book. At the top was a date: December 24, 1881, the day of the Cliff House event. A penciled scribble below, in which penmanship surrendered to emotion:

I would never have known if we had not come here. I would never have known if I hadn't spoken to Y/M. HE is vile, but SHE is worse!

That was all.

She turned the paper over to be sure, but it was blank.

Who was "he?" Graham Drake? Luis Rubio?

And "she." Could that be Theia, or perhaps Yvonne? Did Y/M stand for Yvonne Marchal?

Inez shivered.

She glanced around, wondering if a draft was sneaking in under a door. Shadows flickered in the wavering flame of the lamp. Inez turned in a circle in the silent room, her long skirts rustling like dead leaves in the wind.

Thoroughly spooked, she replaced the poker, moved the screen back into place without bothering to sweep up the ashes now littering the hearth, and hurried to the connecting door. She peered through the open crack, careful to keep her ash-stained fingers from touching anything.

No one was there.

But what else did she expect?

She wasn't sure.

She quenched the lamp and quit the hushed chambers, the crinkled, dusty page clutched tight in her hand.

Chapter Thirty-Two

DECEMBER 27

Inez checked the mantel clock in Yvonne's rooms...or rather, the rooms that were now hers for the interim. She had time to get to the music store before it closed if she didn't dally. She folded the ash-smeared paper into neat quarters. It seemed best to secure the page in her office safe, for now. Losing the young singer's last, anguished written words, or having them fall into the hands of others, was a development Inez wanted to avoid. The store would be a far better place to keep it than her hotel room.

She tucked the small square into her coat pocket, dropped the keys to her room and the music room into her reticule, and stepped forth. It was almost suppertime. The perfect time to catch John Teague at his boardinghouse.

She swept into the store as Thomas Welles was finishing up a sheet-music order for a customer. After smiles and salutations all around, Inez said to Welles, "When you're done, I would like to speak with you." Then she headed for her office in the back. The piles of paperwork on her desk, growing ever deeper, made her sigh. She unlocked the safe and placed the folded page, hardly more than an inch all around, in one of the drawers. She then extracted her private ledger to determine how much she could lend to Clarisse.

Welles came back as Inez was preparing to write a check to the dressmaker.

"Has a Mrs. Robineau been by at all?" Inez asked, as she carefully penned the date.

Welles leaned against the open door. "Twice today. Once yesterday."

"I'm not surprised." Inez nibbled on the end of her ink pen, considering the amount. One hundred dollars should be more than sufficient for completing Theia's dress. She hoped. Once Theia had her evening gown and all the hubbub had calmed down, Inez determined that she and the little dressmaker would have a frank talk about a payment schedule. She prayed that when Theia came out onto the stage of the Grand Opera House for the last time, all the society women would be so dazzled by her gown that they would demand the name of the dressmaker.

Inez signed the check, tore it carefully from the register, and waved it to dry the ink, saying to Welles, "I am going to leave this for Mrs. Robineau for the next time she comes in. You can tell her I will be difficult to reach, but I would like to speak with her. If nothing else, I will be at the Grand Opera House on the thirty-first and could meet with her after the performance." She slipped the payment in an envelope, sealed it, added the dressmaker's name to the front, and handed it to her store manager.

"I'll put this in the register," he said. "By the way, John plans to work late tonight and probably tomorrow night too. He got a shipment of goods in today. Needs to look the pieces over and determine their prices."

Inez nodded. "As long as he is comfortable locking up the store, then I see no problem with that." She rose. "I must go. Thank you for taking on the extra hours and keeping things running smoothly."

"Happy to do so. You'll be glad to hear that we've seen a surge in customers in the past couple days. Several from a ladies' tea before Christmas and a minor stampede from the Cliff House event." He scratched his chin. "I guess that's the silver lining of working with the Drakes."

"At least some good has come of all these troubles," she said, thinking she would gladly turn it all away if doing so would restore Julia Green's life.

With the winter sky fading to a soft gray-blue, Inez stopped at her apartment to collect the hair bracelet Theia had thrown at Teague and the copy of *The Truth* with Haskell's notation of Teague's boardinghouse address. Checking the street and numbers, Inez saw it was too far to walk at this time of day. Stuffing both items in her reticule, Inez returned to the street and hailed a hack, heading west up Pine. When she disembarked, she was gratified to see Teague's neighborhood appeared neat and altogether working-class respectable. Mostly likely her revolver could stay hidden from view for this venture.

She marched up to the door of the two-story boardinghouse and knocked loudly, thinking that since it was suppertime, *someone* would be around to answer. Only twenty or so taps of her foot later, the door was opened by an older man, napkin tucked into his collar, two tufts of hair jutting out above each ear below his bald dome.

On hearing she was looking for John Teague—she waved her copy of the newspaper at him, as if that would serve as a pass to entry—he said, "A matter of *The Truth*, eh?" He scratched his neck, as if the napkin itched. Inez noted printer's ink staining the cuticles of his otherwise clean hands. "He's at his office."

"Which is where?"

"O'Bannon's, on the corner."

She looked up and down the street. "Which corner?"

"O'Bannon's on the corner," he repeated, a touch impatiently, then jerked his thumb to the left before closing the door.

She backed down the steps and took off in the direction he had indicated, wondering what sort of place O'Bannon's might be. Restaurant, she hoped, and not a saloon. A woman entering a restaurant would be tolerated. Entering a saloon, not so.

At the end of the block squatted a worn wood-frame building, a sign under its awning announcing O'Bannon's on the Corner. From the looks of it, and she'd seen many of its ilk in her checkered past, this was an establishment where alcohol was the primary commodity, not food.

She had to know if Teague was inside. Since she had no male companion to enter what was traditionally a men's venue and inquire for her, she would have to go in herself. Inez squared her shoulders and pushed the door open. The inside, she was surprised to see, had more the appearance of a well-kept restaurant, boasting as it did good lighting, tablecloths, a few amateur landscape paintings, and a well-swept floor. Even so, the inevitable L-shaped bar, with its array of spirits behind and spittoons before, made clear its true purpose.

Customers claimed most of the tables and a good length of the bar. Many of the men were eating supper, but all stopped, with their spoons, forks, or cups upraised, and stared at her. She halted just inside the entrance. Also staring at her were two figures behind the bar—a man and a tiny woman, whom Inez hazarded were the barkeep and his wife, or possibly his sister, as they wore identical expressions of astonishment.

John Teague, at a table by the wall, was one of the few not to look up. He had a mess of papers in front of him and was scribbling away, head bent, completely focused on the page before him. A bottle of whiskey and bowl of soup at his elbow looked untouched. Inez stepped forward. "John Teague? I must speak with you."

He lifted his head and frowned, puzzled. Inez waggled her copy of *The Truth* at him. The small woman emerged from behind the bar and marched with a determined foot up to Inez. She pointed to the door behind Inez. "Ladies' entrance, around the corner!"

"I did not know. My apologies to all." And with a last, imploring glance at Teague, Inez went out the way she came in. She circled to the side of the building, where a small, neatly painted sign read

Ladies' Entrance, along with an arrow pointing to the only door, as if one needed further instruction.

Inez dutifully entered to find the woman who had ordered her out of the saloon standing there, arms crossed over her apron bib, a scowl folding her face. "A proper woman, such as yourself appears to be, should know better than to just waltz in the front door of such a place as ours. Mrs. O'Bannon, that's who I am. I cook and I serve. But not the liquor. Mr. O'Bannon does that, which is only right and proper. Will you be having something to eat? I have soup and bread." It was said in an accusatory tone, which allowed only one answer.

"Yes, please. That would be lovely. And coffee." Inez meekly took the table indicated in the small, but tidy, back room. There were tablecloths here as well, she noted. She was the only customer.

Mrs. O'Bannon might have read her mind, because she said, "Usually the room is only open for lunch for the ladies and families. Now, you want to speak to Mr. Teague, you say? And who might you be?"

"Mrs. Stannert," she said. "He will not know my name, but please tell him it is a matter of"—she grasped on what the fellow at the boardinghouse had said to her— "a matter of *The Truth.*" She set the newspaper on the table, masthead side up.

Mrs. O'Bannon's fierce expression softened a bit. From marble to, perhaps, sandstone. "Well, if it's *The Truth* you're after, then, the coffee is on the house. I'll fetch Mr. Teague for you." She turned and left.

Teague arrived at the same time as the woman barkeep. She carried a tray with *two* bowls of soup, plates of thick-sliced bread, and cups of coffee. And two napkins. Teague nodded at Inez and sat at the table. Inez noticed that his appearance, which had been considerably smoothed down and sartorially improved when she glimpsed him at the Cliff House, was beginning to come a little undone. He had the beginnings of a beard, his hair could have used a careful combing, and his jacket hadn't been brushed lately. But he still glowed with the internal intensity she recalled from when she first saw him on the stairs at the Grand Opera House.

Mrs. O'Bannon tut-tutted and fussed at him. "You didn't touch your soup out in the main room, Mr. Teague. It was sitting on your table for more than an hour, and now it's stone cold. Here's a fresh bowl. Living on bread and whiskey won't help you write any faster."

Teague sighed, with a trace of good humor. "Ah, Mrs. O'Bannon—"

"No back talk, now," she said. "I want to see only empty dishes when you're done." She exited to the barroom, pulling the door closed and shutting off the murmur of voices beyond, enclosing the two of them in the silent room.

Teague pushed his papers aside and tucked the napkin into his collar. "Don't be disappointing Mrs. O'Bannon," he said. "She's not a woman you want to defy. Particularly on matters of digestion. Now, who are you, Mrs. Stannert, and how can I help you?"

Inez sipped her coffee, hot and strong, just as she liked it, before reaching into her reticule and extracting Theia's bracelet, woven from Teague's distinctive rust-red hair. She set it on the table and said, "I am looking for the truth about Graham Drake. For Theia's sake."

He paused, soup spoon raised, then slowly set the spoon down and picked up the bracelet.

"She sent you here? With this?" Behind the shock in his voice, Inez thought she detected a note of wistfulness.

Inez refrained from answering. Since she couldn't answer his direct question honestly, she wanted to see what he would say next.

He looked hard into her face. "Have we met before? And how did you get this?" The bracelet dangled from his slender fingers, the heavy gold clasp inches above his soup bowl.

Inez said, "We have met. Once. On the stairs of the Grand

Opera House. Before Christmas." She laced her fingers together. "Mr. Thackery was giving you a piece of his mind and you were responding in kind."

"Oh yes. You and the wee girl were on the stairs with that rodent of a man. I remember now. But you haven't answered my other questions." He put down the bracelet and picked up his spoon.

Inez spread her napkin on her lap. "I run a music store on the corner of Pine and Kearney, the D & S House of Music and Curiosities. In addition, I was hired to be Theia's accompanist for her remaining appearances. Did you know she is retiring from her singing career at the end of the year?"

He raised his eyebrows, but said nothing.

"Not by choice," Inez added. "I believe Graham Drake intends to turn her into a politician's wife."

He snorted. "We'll see about Mr. Drake and his ambitions. How did you find me?""

"Roger Haskell, a colleague of yours, frequents the store and knows me well. He gave me your address, and a fellow there told me you were here, at your office. If you have doubts about me, ask Mr. Haskell."

"I know Roger." He tore off a piece of bread and sopped it into the soup. "So. What brings you to my 'office,' Mrs. Stannert?"

She tried the soup. The stock, stew-like in consistency, was pleasingly peppery and thick with tender pieces of beef, carrots, potatoes, and turnips. "I have become Theia's confidante." She nodded at the bracelet, letting him draw his own conclusions.

"You have? What happened to that woman who is always with her? What is her name now?"

"Yvonne Marchal." Inez was sure he was testing her, that he knew the name of Theia's companion as well as she did. "Yvonne is one of the reasons I am here. She has disappeared, but that is not the worst of it. The Drakes' entourage has been plagued with distressing incidents. The evening you and Theia met at the Cliff

House, her protégée, Miss Julia Green, fell from the veranda to the rocks below and died."

She set her spoon down, stomach tightening. "Julia was wearing Theia's cloak at the time." She explained Theia's belief that Julia was killed in her stead. She concluded, "Theia is terrified and I am concerned. I have seen her with her husband. Not a happy union, from what I can tell. So, I am wondering." She cleared her throat. "I know you and Mr. Drake were business partners in the Comstock, back in its heyday."

"You seem to know a great deal for someone who has just recently been brought in," said Teague.

"Is Graham Drake the kind of man who would terrorize or harm his wife?"

Teague stopped eating, pushed the bowl away, and leaned over the table, soup spoon clenched in a tight fist. "Has he hurt her?"

"I can't say. Not for certain. But there is much tension and discord between them. Enough that I, a relative newcomer, can see it."

"Ah," he muttered. "The truth will out. Perhaps the time is now." He leaned back in his chair, balancing on the two back legs, bright blue eyes raking Inez. "Since Roger Haskell sent you to me, I will accept that you are bona fide and here out of concern for Theia. For what would be your game, otherwise? Certainly 'Lucky Duck' wouldn't have sent you. He has nothing to gain by having me reveal his secrets to you."

He brought the chair back down with a thump. "Very well. You come looking for the truth of Graham Drake, and I shall give it to you. It reflects badly on me and my casual attitude toward the getting of lucre in my early days, but even worse on him. Whereas I very much regret what happened, he does not and continues to pile silver upon gold in a manner fit for Mammon. And who cares about a penniless newsman, in any case? But the wealthy and prominent, their Achilles' heels are a different matter. I would very much like to see Graham Drake fall from a well-placed arrow. It cannot come from my hands, however."

"Well, here I am," said Inez, breaking off a piece of bread to butter. "I am listening. And, as I said, if what you tell me can shed light on these fears of Mrs. Drake's, whether to reassure or to warn, it is all to the good."

"Here is the short version, then. Drake and I met in Virginia City, where I had a fairly successful newspaper and he worked in the mines. Ah, but he had a quick mind, clever and devious by turns, and rose swiftly in the union hierarchy."

"I understand you both made fortunes there," commented Inez. "That you both played the stocks. Only at some critical juncture, you held on too long while he sold at the right time. Thus, his star rose and yours fell."

He pulled the soup bowl back toward himself. "And how do you know all this?"

"Mr. Adolph Sutro told me a little. He also frequents my music store and is an associate of Mr. Drake's." *Frequents* was a stretch, but he had said he would return, and she could see the name made an impression.

"Sutro? That old scoundrel. I should come visit your music store sometime, Mrs. Stannert. What with your caliber of customer, I might find plenty of fodder for *The Truth*."

His face darkened, "Last year, Sutro and Drake sold their Sutro Tunnel Company stock on the sly while the price was high. Then prices tumbled. They were the only ones to make it out with profits intact. The unions, who invested early at Sutro and Drake's encouragement, suffered great financial loss, along with the other investors."

He brooded over his soup, and Inez returned to her own meal, giving him space to think.

He finally said, "You may be wondering, so I will tell you, I do follow Graham's financial adventures. Call it a sickness, or a compulsion. I am amazed how he succeeds over and over, yet it does not seem enough. But you wished to know of more ancient matters. In my defense, what I tell you next, others were involved in similar schemes. At the time it seemed almost a game, a sport, to ferret out news of discoveries of new ore bodies and impending strikes before they were widely known. Those who had inside knowledge and could move quickly upon it could increase their initial investments, sometimes ten times over."

"You speak of stock tips and such?" asked Inez, taking a casual tone lest she sound too eager. "Nothing new there. This is San Francisco, after all. Insiders, stock manipulation, what-have-you."

"But in Virginia City, where the Comstock was, we were on the ground floor. I had a fair bit of capital back then." He shrugged. "Inheritance. I was not always as you see me now. Graham and I came together because he was anxious to make his mark. He was well-placed in the mine and had the ear of one of the owners, while I had the funds. We both hoped to make our fortunes from silver. A third joined us as well. You see, at this particular mine, when a promising vein was found, the miners were forcibly kept below ground until the owners and the investors in the know could position themselves. Only then would an announcement be made."

He glanced at her to see if she understood.

She said, "So you are saying that when you were alerted, you bought early while the price was low. Once the word was out, the stock price would then..." She spiraled a finger upwards.

He nodded. "For example, in early 1868, the miners at one of the levels of this mine agreed to be prisoners belowground in return for triple pay. When they were released, the news went out about a discovery on their level. The stock, which had been trading at thirteen hundred dollars a foot two days earlier, shot to twenty-two hundred."

"Impressive."

"So, we had a system. When Graham or the other fellow was 'detained' belowground, I would buy stock for the three of us. Of course, they paid me what I fronted them, once the stock price rose. We did this several times. Graham had a nose for business and made other investments as well. He no longer needed my capital, although we continued to work together. He moved up shaft, from miner to manager and eventually to part-owner. I was a newspaperman, through and through and had ambitions in that direction. But then, there was trouble."

"What kind of trouble?"

He smacked the table, flat-handed. "Graham double-crossed us. A rumor of a strike led us to increase our holdings, but Graham knew it was all a lie, a rumor floated just to drive up the stock. He sold at the peak of the buying frenzy. I and the third man held on." He shrugged. "Like fools, we had thrown nearly all we had into that strike on Graham's say-so. When the tide turned, I had all I could do to scrape together enough to keep the paper going. The third fellow swore he'd get even. That was a mistake. The next day, he was found at the bottom of one of Graham's mine shafts. Neck broken. Accident?" He shook his head. "Not to my way of thinking. But what could I say, without betraying my part in the scheme?"

Inez touched the bracelet. "What about Mrs. Drake? How did she fit in?" Remembering the gossips at the tea, Inez added, "I understand you two were sweethearts, at one time."

"We were engaged," said Teague flatly. "This was back when we were still working the scheme and all of us were wealthy. Graham fancied her, too, but Theia chose me." He shook his head. "Even now, I cannot call her by her married name. She is Theia Carrington and will always be so to me. When I first met her in Virginia City, Theia was an actress, a singer, who wanted more." He sighed and looked away at the seascape hanging on a nearby wall.

"She wanted the world at her feet. Virginia City was too small for her, so she went to San Francisco, promising to return. That's when I gave her that." He gestured to the bracelet. "She gave me a fob for my watch chain. I still have it, fool that I am. But then, she kept the bracelet."

"Why didn't you go to San Francisco with her?" Inez asked. "You were rich. San Francisco had the stock exchange."

"I needed to stay in Virginia City, where I could keep the scheme going and the silver piling up. And, there was my newspaper. Ink flows in my veins, and I couldn't just turn my back on it. So, Theia was still in San Francisco when I lost everything. Of course, I told her of my reversal of fortunes. She sent me a telegram saying she would come back, not to worry, she would give me the means to regain the wealth I had lost."

"Really?" Inez allowed her skepticism to blanket the word.

He laughed. "I know. I have to admit I wondered at that. But I didn't care. We'd be together. That was all I wanted. However, when she finally arrived, she had that other woman, Yvonne Marchal, in tow and an empty purse. I told her the money didn't matter to me. I guess it did, to her." He stirred his coffee absently. "When Theia came back, she was different. I can't say quite how. Almost as if the spirit had been sucked from her. Then, Graham stepped in."

Teague sighed, put the spoon down, and lowered his face, gripping his hair with both hands. Finally, he looked up. "I've often wondered if Graham didn't double-cross us, just to have a chance at Theia. Maybe he knew her better than I did. Knew she would marry for money, not for love."

Inez hated to ask, but she felt she had to. "Did you write letters to Theia when she turned to Graham? To try and win her back?"

He spread his hands wide, futility in the empty palms. "Seven. Ten. She never answered. I gave it up. She married him, they left, and I tried to put her out of my mind." He let his hands fall. "You must have wormed your way into her confidence very far indeed if she talked to you about those letters."

"I don't think she ever saw them," said Inez gently.

He looked shocked. "Why do you say that?"

"I found them hidden in Yvonne's possessions. As I said, Yvonne has disappeared. At Theia's request, I am staying in

Yvonne's room as a surrogate companion. Since Yvonne's belongings are still there, I've been looking for anything that might shed light on why she left and where she's gone." *Or if she's even still alive.*

"I never did trust that woman," muttered Teague. "I wouldn't put it past her to pour a little honey about Drake in Theia's ear and a little poison about me."

"There is one more thing I should tell you." Now that Inez knew how things stood between Teague and Graham, she felt safe imparting the information. "Apparently Graham was having an affair with Miss Green. Or perhaps he desired to do so, and she rebuffed him."

"Is that so." Teague sounded grim.

She nodded. "In either case, Miss Green is now dead. And Theia found out about them." Inez clasped the cup of now cold coffee between her hands. "So, I'll ask you again. From what you know of Graham and with what I've told you, do you believe Theia is in danger from him?"

Teague looked at her bleakly. "I know what Graham was capable of in the past. I know he has become a ruthless businessman who is intent on destroying the lives of those working on his paper, all to increase his own bank account and show the world that he can bend them to his will. But I have no knowledge of the goings-on of man and wife. You have more insight into that than I do. So, Mrs. Stannert, the question is, what do you believe?"

Chapter Thirty-Three

DECEMBER 27

After her sobering conversation with John Teague, Inez decided to retreat to the Palace Hotel. She considered making a stop at the store first to drop off the bracelet and the newspaper, but it was well after suppertime and Theia expected her that evening.

Inez was troubled by what she'd heard about Graham Drake. Who would guess such a violent past lay under his polished exterior? Other men, fashioned by the West and its rugged times, might not even raise an eyebrow at his doings, and Inez had met her share of such wolves lurking amongst the sheep. Still.

This was different.

After hearing of the Comstock confederate who had "accidentally" fallen down a mine shaft, Inez felt she had to seriously consider the possibility that Graham had killed Julia. He had reasons for doing so, either knowing who she was or mistaking her for his wife. His retreat into opium could have been due to his shock at finding out that he had killed not Theia but Julia.

And Yvonne—could she have witnessed the event and, in fear of retribution, deliberately vanished?

Or might her lifeless body be found tonight, tomorrow, or the next day, and her death ascribed to a "misstep" or from falling out, say, a window?

Inez decided that she would find de Bruijn before going to the music room, discuss what she had discovered, and engage his help in uncovering Yvonne's whereabouts.

The line of hacks disgorging and taking on passengers at the Palace Hotel moved slowly through the grand circular driveway. When Inez finally disembarked from the hired cab, the two carriages in front of hers simultaneously emptied. A large cluster of men and women, all waiting for transport and dressed to the nines for an evening event, moved in to claim the vehicles. Standing with them—a part of the group, but apart at the same time, was de Bruijn.

Surprised, but pleased to see him, Inez called, "Mr. de Bruijn, a word, if I may?"

He turned toward her voice, and her heart turned over with a quick, unexpected leap.

Attired in fine evening wear and a handsome overcoat, he fit right in with the knot of high society types preparing to depart. She was gratified to see that he, in turn, looked pleased to see her. With a quick bow and word to those closest by, he excused himself and moved toward her. "Mrs. Stannert, good evening. All is well?"

"Well enough. And you? You are going somewhere?"

He adjusted his top hat, glancing at the next line of hansom cabs drawing up to the curb. "My attendance is required at a wedding tonight."

Inez scrutinized him, thinking she could not recall ever seeing him dressed so formally. The overcoat fit as if tailor-made, as did his swallowtail coat. The rest of his apparel toed the line for a formal evening event: black silk vest, cut low; a white cravat; simple gold shirt studs; pale kid gloves; and a walking stick that, in design and no doubt cost, was several notches above the one he usually carried. His hair, beard, and mustache appeared freshly trimmed and groomed to perfection. He looked like an aristocrat setting off for a royal reception.

She said, "I believe hobnobbing with *le beau monde* suits you." In truth, he carried himself in his current persona with complete ease. It dawned on her that, perhaps for the first time, she might be seeing the "real" W. R. de Bruijn.

His faintly European accent and Continental manners dovetailed perfectly with his appearance in a way that one not "born and bred" could not possibly emulate. Inez, raised in the rarefied air of New York City wealth, intuitively recognized it. And she couldn't help but wonder what life journey had led him here, to being a private investigator at the westernmost edge of the American continent, and whether his journey had been as extreme as hers.

The warmth in his smile extended to his steady brown eyes. "When 'hobnobbing,' as you put it, one must take care to blend in, wouldn't you say?"

"You are on the job, then."

He nodded. "A new case. Not the best time to be away, I know." He looked her over, his smile disappearing. "Is something amiss?"

"We should talk tomorrow. There is much to discuss."

His gaze turned troubled. "I will be out of town for a couple of days." He glanced at the neat piles of trunks and baggage arrayed near the travelers.

"You are going away?" She swallowed her dismay. "Well then, I shall be brief. I spoke with John Teague. He and Drake have a history, and Theia is part of it. I believe Mr. Drake has blood on his hands."

His eyes widened in alarm. "Do you mean—"

"Oh, not recently. Well, perhaps recently, but I can't prove anything. Actually, I think it likely that he, he's the one who…" She could not say it, not in the middle of the grand concourse of the Palace Hotel, with people ebbing and flowing about them and the clatter and shouts of carriages coming and going. "I believe Yvonne holds the key to what has happened here."

"Mrs. Stannert—"

"And I believe Julia knew something as well."

" Mrs. Stannert, I—"

"I want your help in finding Yvonne, since I am trapped with Theia from now until doomsday, practicing for her last two appearances."

Out of the corner of her eye, she noted that the majority of the party had embarked. Only a small number of gaily dressed partygoers remained, waiting for the next wave of carriages. One such personage, a young belle, was staring at de Bruijn and Inez. The investigator, standing as he was with his back to the group, could not see the woman's slight pout, her mauve fan twitching in her gloved hand. Inez saw and turned her full attention and energy upon the detective.

She added, "I have moved into Yvonne's rooms until the end of the year."

"What??" His concern became alarm.

"Theia apparently cannot manage on her own, without someone to prop her up. Since Yvonne is gone…well, here I am. The Drakes are paying me well for my time and it does give me access to Yvonne's rooms and Julia's as well. I will do what I can while I am there."

He started to shake his head.

She continued, resolute. "I'll hire you to find Yvonne Marchal. Surely you can invent some reason to return tomorrow."

"Inez."

His use of her given name stopped her.

He continued, "I cannot do anything about this right now."

"Oh. Of course. You are under contract and 'engaged' elsewhere." The words came out so derisive she wanted to bite her tongue.

"I am." He sounded almost apologetic. Almost.

Inez saw the pouting belle in mauve break away from her cohorts and head their way, her long cloak and skirts swishing along the marble pavement with a purpose.

He added, "I will be back by the thirtieth, at the latest. We will meet and work out a plan. Do *not* take any chances." Emphasis deepened his voice. "Do *not* aggravate Graham Drake. In fact, do not engage with him at all, if you can avoid it. Now that you are staying in the suite, if there is danger from that quarter, it will be doubly so. And if you can pacify Mrs. Drake, keep her calm, all the better. I will be in the audience for both performances, I promise you."

By then, the pouter was at the detective's side, her fan flipping up and down, fluttering against de Bruijn's sleeve. "*Monsieur* de Bruijn, *excusez-moi de vous interrompre,* but a proper gentleman does not abandon the lady he has promised to escort."

Inez noticed with a twist of malicious satisfaction that *la belle jeune femme*'s French pronunciation was atrocious.

De Bruijn turned toward her and said in a soothing voice, "My apologies, Miss Wellington. You are, of course, correct, and I am sadly derelict in my duties." He then added with a hint of old-world courtesy, "Mrs. Stannert, may I present Miss Wellington. And Miss Wellington, may I introduce you to Mrs. Stannert." He turned to his companion. "Mrs. Stannert is also a guest in the hotel."

Inez smiled at her, more or less politely.

L'enfante petulante just sniffed and tapped de Bruijn's sleeve again. "Freddy says we must go."

Sure enough, a young man was hanging out of a carriage window, waving his topper at them, while the remaining trunks and hatboxes were being loaded and secured in the trunk.

De Bruijn turned once again to Inez, saying, "Please keep in mind what I said, Mrs. Stannert. I wish you a good evening." His words were neutral, but his eyes said much more.

Mademoiselle Prétentieuse pulled on his arm all the way to the carriage. De Bruijn helped her negotiate the step and gave Inez a final encouraging nod before entering himself.

As the carriage pulled away, Inez indulged herself for one

moment, imagining hurling vulgar insults in French and a few in German for good measure at the peaches-and-cream-complected face of the beautiful and no-doubt sinfully rich Miss Wellington. In her mind, Inez saw that perfect rosebud mouth rounding into an O of confusion and stupidity. Inez turned on her heel and headed toward the elevators. *Ridiculous. I am better than that. Besides, if I were to hurl insults at anyone, it would be at de Bruijn for. . .*

For what?

For not dropping everything, including his current investigation—whatever that might be—to run to her aid? And wasn't that the very behavior she had disparaged him for, just a few days ago?

Inez squared her shoulders and lifted her chin, determined that she would continue her own investigations as best she could during her free time. There was Yvonne's scrapbook, for instance. What more did those pages hold? Perhaps tonight she could give them a more careful examination. She wondered if she should find a way of getting Teague's letters back to him and question him further. As for Yvonne, how much history did Theia and Yvonne share? Perhaps by gently and carefully questioning Theia, Inez could uncover more about their relationship and the companion's background.

Too, she could explore Julia's rooms more thoroughly during the nighttime hours. If she dared.

And Theia and she would have two back-to-back performances: Melpomene on the thirtieth and the Grand on the thirty-first.

There was much to do.

Inez stopped at the music room and knocked. "Theia? Are you there?"

Quick footsteps from inside, and the door flew open. "At last! Where have you been? I said we would resume our work after supper. I was not assuming you would be taking a late meal at a soirée or a ball. I planned that you would be back here an hour ago. More. "

Inez's initially protective feelings toward Theia began curdling under her barrage. "I needed to stop at my store and attend to business." Suddenly, all the put-upon feelings of the past week came boiling to the surface.

Inez faced the diva matter-of-factly, speaking equal-to-equal. "If you want me back by a certain time, you need to tell me. I cannot read your mind."

The diva jerked back as if Inez had struck her.

Before she could respond, Inez continued, "I am here to help you. To be your accompanist. To be your confidante, if you wish. I am not your servant. I am not here to be whipped by you when you are out of sorts. We have three more days to work together. Three days for me to help you give the most wonderful performances of your life. My hope is, when you leave the stage at the end of the year, those who have seen you here will forever speak of you in admiring tones, praise your talent, your charisma, your beauty, and your singing. Thus, when you are invited to the houses of the city's most wealthy and powerful as the wife of the publisher of *The San Francisco Times*, they will greet you with the respect and reverence that *you* deserve and have earned."

Theia's mouth formed into the perfect O Inez had envisioned on Miss Wellington's face, just a short while ago.

Inez walked toward the connecting door that led to her private rooms, shedding her gloves. "I'll just put my things away, and we can begin. Which pieces did you want to start with tonight?"

Chapter Thirty-Four

They worked long and late, well after midnight. After they went through the entire program for the Melpomene several times, Theia announced it was "good enough."

"Are you certain?" Inez asked, taking advantage of the break to stretch her fingers and rotate her wrists. This was the first time in her experience that Theia was willing to settle for less than perfection. Privately, Inez thought that some of the popular pieces could still use a little smoothing out.

Theia flipped a hand dismissively. Then, almost as if she could read Inez's thoughts, she said, "This is the Melpomene Theater, not the Grand Opera House. We needn't concern ourselves with being perfect. The audience will be happy if I sing ditties they can hum along to. We are not venturing out with Rossini, Verdi, classic opera. Gilbert and Sullivan is as sophisticated as I dare." She paced to the fireplace, looked at the mantel clock with its ever-mindless tick-tick, then paced back. All evening she had seemed preoccupied, restless.

"I suppose I cannot expect Mr. Drake back tonight," she said. She sounded forlorn and irritated at the same time.

Inez tensed, her fingers digging into the palms of her hands.

A vision of Graham Drake, awash in opium, flashed through her mind. "Do you think he's returned to Chinatown?"

She laughed mirthlessly. "I think he is still at the newspaper. Unless he's gone looking for 'entertainment' of the female persuasion in other parts of town." She wrapped her arms around herself, her mouth in a thin line. Then she shook herself. "Enough! Tomorrow and the next day, we shall go over the pieces for my last performance. New Year's Eve, at the Grand. That *must* be perfect. You've looked over the program for the recital, I assume. A little Gilbert and Sullivan, which we have already worked upon. We shall revisit 'Ave Maria' and '*Dove sono*,' as well as some of my favorites from *Cosi fan Tutti*, including '*In uomini in soldati*' and '*Come scoglio*,' and we mustn't forget '*Una voce poco fa*.' Oh dear, that's right. We have not worked on those. That was with Señor Rubio." Her voice curled around his name with scorn and her hands curled into fists.

"I could not believe his behavior today. The bastard!" She swiveled angry eyes at Inez. "We shall stop for tonight. It is already late. Tomorrow morning is my last fitting for my gown. We shall practice after that."

Inez offered to put out the lights and secure the music room. That way, she could be certain that the door—*all* the doors— were locked. She waited until Theia retired to her private rooms. When she heard the door bolt snick into place, she checked that the music room door to the hallway was also locked. She picked up a hand lamp, extinguished all the others. The only light was from the lamp in her hand, from the subdued glow of dying embers in the fireplace behind the screen, and from the moon outside the bay windows. The dresses on their displays picked up the moonglow, their bright colors now faded into black, grays, and white. It was a ghostly army of invisible women, arrayed before her. At that moment, the slim line of light beneath the door leading to Theia's chambers winked out.

Bringing the lamp with her, Inez passed through Yvonne's

parlor, and opened the door connecting to Julia's rooms. She could swear the rooms had begun taking on the dusty, deserted smell of places long closed-in and abandoned. It must, she thought, be her imagination. It had only been a couple of days.

Inez was determined to explore Julia's rooms more thoroughly. The page she had found in the fireplace had been torn from a small book. A book with dated entries.

A journal. Or a pocket diary.

Given the size of the crumpled sheet, she thought it might be a daybook Julia could carry with her and keep from prying eyes, of which there seemed aplenty. She would hide it well when not carrying it, particularly since her quarters connected to Yvonne's. Inez had seen for herself that Julia and Yvonne did not always see eye to eye. Plus, Yvonne seemed to have Theia's interests and well-being first and foremost in mind.

So, if Julia wrote down her thoughts, the book would be easily accessible but hidden. But where?

Had the police found it?

If so, she thought she would have heard, from de Bruijn at least, since he had spoken with Detective Lynch.

It must still be here. Somewhere.

She tried the small writing desk first, with its many little drawers and cubbyholes, even though she felt certain this would have been the one place the police would have searched thoroughly. Her investigation yielded an ink bottle, a sharpened pencil, a neat stack of stationery, a copy of *Peterson's Magazine,* and a recent edition of the San Francisco newspaper *The Call.* She shuffled through all the paper but found nothing.

She moved on, checking anywhere she thought a small book might be hidden. Under the seat cushions of the chairs, behind the hanging pictures, and behind the clock on the mantel. She even lifted the edges of the rug and peered inside the decorative urns and the vases holding potted ferns.

Nothing.

Finally, she moved on to the bedroom. Here, the curtains were partly drawn back, allowing light from the street below to filter in.

Looking around, Inez felt exhaustion seep in, the long day and intense hours at the piano taking their toll. *I can't finish the search tonight. I'll have to return tomorrow.* Her gaze skimmed over the armoire, night table, and chairs, and the modest number of hatboxes and travel trunks lined up neatly against one wall.

Inez went to the armoire and opened the center door to reveal an array of drawers. The top one yielded stockings, corsets, camisoles, and other "unmentionables." Finding herself loath to plunge her hands into Julia's intimate apparel, Inez muttered to herself, "If such is the case for me, it must have been doubly so for Detective Lynch and his crew."

She put the lamp on the nightstand, then returned and began to gently push the items aside. Nothing hidden in the bottom or back of the drawer. She then picked up each of the three, stiff-boned corsets in turn. It was, of course, the bottom-most corset that yielded results: two small pocket journals and, folded on top of them, a formal employment contract between Julia and the Grand Opera House.

Triumph washed away exhaustion. Inez moved to the bed and perched on the edge. She set the contract aside and leaned closer to her lamp to better see the entry dates of the two journals. The first one was from the previous year, 1880. The second, from the current year. Inez thumbed to the end to check the date of the last entry.

From the depths of the parlor, a doorknob rattled, the sound loud in the silent chambers.

Inez froze, one hand gripping the daybook, panic shooting through her. "Hell and damnation," she whispered.

Who would be at Julia's door, well after midnight?

She hurried to shut the armoire door, then returned and doused her lamp.

The scrape of a key in the lock was as much a warning as a

shout, and she recalled the maid's words: "The hotel keeps extra keys to all the rooms."

And then, there was no more time to think.

No time to dash back to the safety of her own quarters.

Her hand swept the bedcover in a desperate bid to gather the scattered items. Her fingers closed on one of the daybooks, and she heard a muffled thump as the other hit the floor, somewhere.

The parlor door creaked open. A narrow beam of light from the hallway sliced in like an arrow through the parlor and the bedroom, casting a faint illumination on the heavy drapes.

She mouthed another curse, not daring to even whisper.

No time to try to retrieve it. Only time to hide.

Holding the one daybook, Inez dropped to the rug and wiggled past the dust ruffle of the bed, pulling her skirts around her, striving for absolute silence. She flattened herself, chin to the floor, and did a quick scan of the floor that she could see. The fallen daybook was nowhere in sight. *I must have given it quite the whack.* She put her cheek to the cool hardwood floor and held her breath against the dust, praying she wouldn't sneeze. Praying that the intruder, whoever he or she was, did not stay long and did not venture into the sleeping chamber.

The hallway door closed and the narrow beam of light on the floor vanished. Some rustling ensued, then a wavering light danced on the slice of floor she could see beyond the dust ruffle. The person had brought a candle, Inez reasoned. So, they were planning on staying a while. Her palms flat on the floor, Inez bit her bottom lip and waited.

Footfalls—she could not tell if they were men's or women's—advanced into the parlor, then stopped.

Did I shut the connecting door to Yvonne's rooms?

She could not remember.

Now she *really* began to perspire.

The footsteps started up again, their slight vibration rising through the floorboards into her hands and the side of her face.

Candlelight wavered, as the person moved about the parlor room. The unmistakable sounds of drawers being opened and shut, and the rustle of papers followed. *So, first the desk. Just as I did.*

Part of her longed to wiggle closer to the dust ruffle and see who was searching, just as she had searched. If she had had to choose, she would have bet on Graham Drake. Possibly Theia. Or even—given the hour, the hesitation, the furtiveness—Yvonne. She could also not discount Luis Rubio. Somehow, she doubted that his official banishment from the hotel was enforced by all, at all hours.

As she pondered, she heard a short sigh from the direction of the parlor—the exhalation so quick and low, it was not possible to tell whether male or female. The footsteps advanced, growing louder, and the wavering light grew brighter. Inez shrank inward to the center, pulling her feet up ever-so-slightly, clutching the daybook to her.

The trespasser entered the bedroom, Inez guessed, but did not come to the side of the bed where she could see the feet. It sounded as if the person stopped at the foot of the bed. No more sound, only the shifting of shadows and light as the candle was held from side to side.

A crinkle of paper above her reminded Inez she had left the contract lying on the bedcover. The flickering light moved, reaching under the bed and then retreating as the person bent down and straightened back up.

The fallen daybook.

Inez hoped it was the older of the two journals.

To Inez's everlasting relief, the person then retreated, candlelight dimming, footsteps fading. Sounds ceased, and the candlelight disappeared. Everything went dark. The hall door squeaked open, bringing with it the arrow of hallway light. Another squeak, the arrow vanished, and the hall door was locked with a click and a scrape.

Inez waited a few minutes, arms trembling, before wiggling out from under the bed. She stood shakily, wiped the dust from the front of her dress, and slid the journal into her pocket. Groping for her lamp, she debated. Light the lamp? Try to find the connecting door in the dark? Inez imagined herself bumping into one of the standing urns, sending it clattering to its side and rolling noisily along the floor.

Then she realized she had left the matches in the music room and had nothing to light her lamp with, so that was that. She could open the curtains, but what if someone were to return later and notice?

Oh, to hell with it.

She fumbled her way to the drapes, drew them back, and surveyed the room. The additional light confirmed her suspicions. The contract, which had been on the bed, and the second daybook, which had tumbled to the floor, were both gone. Grabbing up her lamp—she was not going to leave *that* behind—she rushed into the parlor. The connecting door, thankfully, was closed, so at least she hadn't given herself away in that regard. With an overwhelming burst of relief, Inez hurried into her sanctuary, closed the door behind her, and wished she had the key.

What was to say that whoever had been lurking would not return and try the door, just to see if it was truly locked? Inez retrieved a straight-backed wooden chair from the bedroom and dragged it to the interconnecting door, jamming the back of it under the doorknob.

Only then did she go into the bedroom and remove both the daybook and her revolver from her pocket. The gun she kept on the nightstand, where she could grab it if need be.

She opened the daybook to the first page.

January 1, 1880.

Inez snapped it shut. She wanted to hurl it across the room, but that would be discourteous to the memory of the deceased.

Whoever came in after me reaped the reward of my snooping.

She swallowed her despair. *It would have been better had I not gone in at all!*

Who could it have been, she wondered. Perhaps Graham, looking for anything Julia might have left behind that tied him to her. Such as entries in a journal.

She set the old daybook on the stand beside the gun, hoping the interloper did not put two and two together and come looking for her with questions she could not answer.

Chapter Thirty-Five

DECEMBER 28

Inez emerged the next morning feeling hungover from the previous night's adventures. It didn't seem fair, she thought, that she should suffer such aftereffects when she had come away empty-handed. Or nearly so.

Her mood was not lifted by the scene that greeted her in the music room. The chambermaid, who now seemed tasked with helping Theia in the mornings, stood by the fireplace, hands clasped before her, as if trying to blend into the wallpaper. Clarisse was there, her traveling dressmaker's trunk open nearby. She was carefully pulling layers of tissue off a well-swathed garment. Theia hovered anxiously over her, saying, "Did you fix the bodice? And the sleeves? And did you add—" She looked up at Inez. " Inez! Good morning!"

No jibes, Inez noted, about the "late" hour of her rising. "Good morning, Theia…Mrs. Robineau."

Inez spotted a shimmer of gold-and-silver material emerging from the paper. Curious, she started to move closer. Theia moved toward Inez, blocking her view, and said with a smile overflowing with charm and apology, "I kept you so late last night, working so hard, I am sorry."

Theia apologizing? Inez wondered what was going on. Before she could respond, Theia continued, "Clarisse and I will be busy for two or so hours. This would be an excellent time for you to take a breath of air, perhaps visit your store. I know you worry about it. Let's reconvene for lunch, shall we?"

The dressmaker said piteously, "Mrs. Stannert? Would it be possible to have a word?"

Inez cut her off, but not unkindly. "I left a note in an envelope for you at the music store. I believe it has what you need."

She dodged further conversation by hurrying back to her temporary quarters to snatch up her outerwear, her gun, Julia's 1880 pocket diary, the copy of *The Truth*, and Theia's hair brace-let. The bracelet and the little journal would go into her safe at the store, joining the single sheet of paper she had uncovered the previous day.

An hour or two away from the hotel sounded heavenly. It felt as if the walls were closing in upon her, even in the large, airy music room, and she was happy enough to escape.

Inez exited the hotel and began walking toward Montgomery, her mind turning over the list of possibles who might have taken a surreptitious sneak into Julia's rooms. Would the front desk be able to tell her who had obtained a key during the midnight hours? And if she asked, would that get back to Graham Drake? Then Inez wondered if he possessed a master key to *all* the rooms in the suite.

A terrifying prospect. But not an impossibility.

Suppose, she thought, Drake had had too much to drink or smoke one night and breached Julia's apartments, either here in San Francisco, or in Denver or—

"*Buenos días*, Mrs. Stannert."

Inez's thoughts scattered, and she nearly fell off the curb in her haste to step away from Luis Rubio, who had somehow snuck up beside her.

Her hand dove into the coat pocket holding her revolver. He

caught her elbow. Whether to steady her or prevent her from pulling the firearm, he succeeded on both accounts. "Careful, Mrs. Stannert, careful. It would be a nasty fall to those cobblestones on such a busy street."

Fall to the stones. Inez suddenly imagined Julia, smashed on the rocks below the Cliff House.

"What do you want?" she snarled.

He withdrew his hand and raised it, placating. "My apologies. I did not wish to startle you."

The hell you didn't.

"May I walk with you a ways? Across the street, one or two blocks, is probably far enough. I shall make certain you do not suffer from any missteps. You see, I have decided. We must talk."

She gave him a savage glare, taking in his appearance. He was dressed neatly, with a man-about-town air. Hair combed, hat seated at a rakish angle. He seemed a little drawn and tired, perhaps from past overindulgences, but not drunk or raging.

Inez switched her attention to the busy street in front of them. "I am not interested in talking with you."

Just then, the road cleared and Inez joined the pedestrians, Rubio in attendance. Thoroughly annoyed, she decided to go on the offense. "Is that what brought poor Julia to her sad end? A 'talk' with you, overlooking the Pacific?"

He glanced at her, surprised.

"I know you were at the Cliff House that night," Inez said. "You were seen before and after she fell."

"I heard it was an accident. You are saying it was not?" He shook his head. "Why aren't the police looking into this?"

"Oh, don't toy with me!" she snapped.

"Toy with you? Never, Mrs. Stannert. I treat you with all seriousness. Which is why I have come to extend the olive branch and ask for a, shall we say, cease-fire."

She looked at him in astonishment before stepping up—very carefully—on the far curb. "Whatever do you mean?"

"I mean the windows."

"Windows?" Whatever she was expecting him to say, it wasn't that.

"Windows smashed with bullets, which lead to windows smashed with bricks. Enough is enough. Let us stop, before someone gets hurt. After all, what have I done to you?"

It was as if she had stepped into a world where they spoke different languages. "What on earth are you talking about? As to what you've done, well, to begin with, you accosted me on the street when you were blind drunk—"

He shrugged. "I was drunk. I admit it. But you, in turn, threatened to kill me. I did not think you were serious." His dark eyes swept to her coat pocket. "Then yesterday, you admitted to carrying a gun. After that, well, how could you believe you would get away with it?"

"Get away with what?" She was thoroughly annoyed now.

"Now *you* are toying with *me*. Not a wise move, Señora." He glanced around. "We will draw attention, standing at the corner like this. Let's not make a spectacle of ourselves. You have not been to your store since yesterday afternoon, but you are heading there now, yes?"

A chill breathed on her neck. "How do you know?"

"I know a great deal. I know you are staying in Yvonne Marchal's rooms at the Palace, for instance. I know Madame kept you practicing until well after midnight last night. She has no heart, that one. Be careful of her. What happened to me could happen to you. Or worse."

She found his statement alarming but also bizarre. Trying to make light of it, she snorted. "You are persona non grata at the Palace, so I know it isn't you lurking at keyholes. Have you set your spies to watching me?"

He looked at her, eyes heavy-lidded. "If I truly wanted to get into the Palace, into any room there, I could. Remember that. And remember my offer of a truce. We are currently tit for tat. Let's stop before something more serious happens. Not all accidents involve an ankle twist on the streets."

"I still have no idea what you are talking about, Señor Rubio." They had reached the corner of Sutter and Montgomery.

He stopped, faced her, and tipped his hat. "Demur if you must. Our ways part here. Good day, Señora. It's a pity about the windows."

Baffled, Inez watched him walk up Sutter. She eased her grip on the gun in her pocket, palm sweating inside the kid glove. With a growing sense of dread, Inez quickened her pace to Pine and turned toward Kearney. Only a block to the music store, but it seemed so far away.

The storefront, with its large display window, came into view.

But there was no glass pane.

Only shattered glass on the ground.

Chapter Thirty-Six

DECEMBER 28

Dismay erupted from Inez in the form of a very unladylike word.

She hurried up the block as fast as her long walking skirts would allow and arrived, panting. Welles was out front, sweeping glass shards from the walkway. A large piece of heavy cloth, which looked suspiciously like the drape used for their showpiece grand piano, covered the empty gap. She asked, "What happened?"

Welles paused in his cleanup and leaned on the broom. "Hoodlums heaved a brick through the window late last night. Smashed it to smithereens, then ran. Good thing John Hee was still here when it happened."

John Hee had come to the door, satchel in hand. "Hoodlum," he said, raising a finger. "Only one."

And I know who it was.

"Did you report this to the police?" she asked Welles.

Her store manager scratched the back of his neck. "Talked with them this morning. Not much we can do. I told John he could go home, get some rest. He stayed here all night to keep thieves away."

She turned to John. "Thank you, Mr. Hee. Did you see who did it?"

John Hee shook his head. "Saw him running away. Only one."

She sighed. "Any damage to the items on display?"

She listened as Welles enumerated. Two Oriental vases. Several tabletop-size statuettes. Three silk, Oriental fans received a dusting of glass. A drum, which received the full force of the heavy brick, had taken a beating. "I will try and fix," said John Hee. "Tomorrow."

"The items are in the back," said Welles.

Inez and Welles went inside to discuss the next steps. Despite the gaslights being on inside, the interior was positively gloomy with the window blacked out.

"Get another pane of glass as soon as possible. Today, if you can," she said. "Thank goodness, Mr. Drake paid up on his account. We have funds to spare." Then, because Rubio's mysterious "tit for tat" comment still bothered her, she added, "It seems all kinds of mayhem erupted recently. Did you hear anything about windows being shot out?"

"Oh yeah." Broom in hand, Welles stepped up onto the display platform, now empty, to give it a good going-over. "In fact, Luis Rubio stopped by earlier to commiserate over the mess here. He mentioned that last night, late evening, someone fired a pistol at his window at the Grand. He keeps an apartment on the second floor, where the opera house rents out rooms to artists and musicians."

"So he was particularly sympathetic to our plight," she said grimly. "How kind of him."

"Yeah, well, he and I agreed on one thing. That we'd both love to wring the necks of those responsible. Not that the two events have any connection."

"At least none that I can see," said Inez, truthfully enough.

She went into the back to calculate the losses and draw up a list of items to display, once the new glass was in place. Nothing too valuable. Nothing too breakable. In case someone decided to take another potshot at Señor Rubio's window and he blamed her, despite her protestations of innocence.

Inez thought of all the glass windows on the exterior of the opera house. It could have just been a hoodlum having a lark. *Or...*

She thought of Theia's curiosity about the pocket revolver. *Surely not. Surely she wouldn't do something so unwise.* Yet, Theia seemed to often act on impulse and from emotion. What if the Golden Songbird's well-known propensity for "throwing things" had evolved into "shooting at things," or even people?

Inez decided she would, at the first opportunity, ask the diva if she had gone out on her "walk" the previous day with the express purpose of purchasing a weapon.

With a start, Inez pulled out her silver pocket watch. *Late!*

Theia had asked that she be back in time for the noon meal and here it was, five after noon. Abandoning her reckonings on the damage, she grabbed her coat and gloves and rushed to the front of the store.

"I'll most likely be gone for the next couple of days," she told Welles. "Two more events with Mrs. Drake and then 1881 is over and I can focus on the store." *And I can start making the rounds of all the women who count on me, see how last year worked out for them and what they foresee in 1882.*

"Don't worry, Mrs. Stannert. John and I will take good care of things. The missus and I plan to be at your appearance at the Grand. We'll give the accompanist a standing ovation."

Inez almost ran over Clarisse getting ready to enter.

"*Ça, alors!*" the tiny dressmaker squeaked, then, "Madame Stannert. I must speak to you, it is of greatest urgency."

"There is an envelope waiting for you," Inez said. "Ask Mr. Welles. What you need to stay afloat to the end of the year is inside."

"*Merci.* I am so grateful."

Inez spotted an empty hack and waved it down. "Now, I have a quick question for you. You know Yvonne Marchal well?"

"From long ago," said Clarisse, hand on the doorknob.

"She went to church Christmas morning, but didn't return. Have you seen her?"

"Christmas morning?"

Inez, focused on the carriage pulling up to the sidewalk, turned to look at Clarisse. She was biting her lip. Suspicious, Inez asked, "Was Yvonne at your church that morning for Mass?"

"Ah, it is a big church. So many people, and on Christmas." Clarisse pulled the door open slowly, set one small foot over the sill. "I do not know where she is. Perhaps she is gone away?"

"Ma'am?" That was the hack driver. "Where to?"

Inez muttered under her breath. There was no time to interrogate the dressmaker, and besides, on the street was not the place to do so. "To the Palace Hotel," she told the driver. Then, to Clarisse, "You and I must talk. And soon."

"Of course. But it is so busy right now. The dress, I must finish it. You know Madame Drake, how she is." Clarisse brightened, "After the new year, yes? We will talk then?"

The driver had dismounted and extended his hand to help her into the carriage.

Over her shoulder, Inez called out to the dressmaker, "Will you be at the Grand for Mrs. Drake's final appearance?"

"Of course. I want to see Madame in her dress."

Inez nodded. If necessary, she would find a way to corner Clarisse after the show. "Perhaps we can meet then. I am concerned about Yvonne."

She sat just as Clarisse said, "Madame?"

Inez stayed the driver from closing the door.

Clarisse's eyes were wide. She seemed trapped, frozen on the threshold. "Do you think she is in danger?"

"Perhaps," said Inez. "That is why, if you know where she is, it would be best to tell me. I might be able to help her."

Inez settled back and the door swung shut. Her last view of Clarisse as the carriage jerked into motion was of the dressmaker staring at her, purse clutched close to her chest as if it held a world's treasure inside.

Upon returning to the music room, Inez found Theia in her elegant dressing gown, dining alone, oyster fork in one hand, ink pen in the other. "Hello, Inez," she said without looking up from the sheet of paper before her. "I recommend the consommé and the pâté. The oysters are magnificent, as always."

Inez, expecting a storm of outrage at her tardiness, was nonplussed. *I just never know what to expect from her.* Looking around, Inez realized that although Theia dined solo, she was not alone. The Palace chambermaid tasked with helping Theia with her dresses and her hair stood by the hearth, hands clasped. The Drakes' messenger, Toby, stood by her, shifting from foot to foot. Inez wondered how long they had been waiting there.

Theia scratched out a line from the list on the paper and set the pen in the ink bottle. She waved the paper, simultaneously drying the ink and catching the messenger's attention. "Please deliver this to the manager of the Melpomene. Tell him this is the program. No more changes."

Toby took the page. "Should I wait for a response, ma'am?"

"No need. There is nothing left to say. What is on the paper is what I shall sing."

"Will there be a decent piano there? And it will have been tuned?" Inez asked.

Theia nodded. "In my previous missive to the manager I said this was a necessity."

It bothered Inez not to have an opportunity to test the piano in its surroundings until right before the performance. However, Theia seemed to brush off the Melpomene performance as not particularly important. Inez was glad she had set hands upon the Broadwood at the Grand. At least that would be familiar.

After Toby left, Theia smiled brilliantly at Inez. "Come, Mrs. Stannert. It is the usual excellent Palace fare. You shall need your strength, for we will be working hard the rest of today. I must change into proper afternoon wear, now that Mrs. Robineau has left."

Inez sat, wary of the diva's cheery mood but determined to take advantage of it. "Very well, but first, I have a serious question for you." The singer, who had begun to rise, settled back down, eyebrows raised. Inez continued, "You were so interested in my pocket revolver, and all the particulars of its make and model. I feel I should ask, as a gun, no matter how small, is a deadly weapon. Did you buy one?"

Theia's hands flew to her chest. "Why, Inez, of course not! I did say, didn't I, that I would speak to Mr. Drake about it first. After all, I know so little, and it would not be proper for me to go to those places where you said they were sold. I hope he will consider buying one. I would feel safer having it about. After all, once your contract is finished"—her face clouded—"I shall be quite on my own until we hire another lady's companion or a permanent maid. I would like some means of protecting myself on those long nights that Mr. Drake is," her gaze slid to the chambermaid and she hesitated before saying, "when he is working late."

Inez picked up her bouillon spoon. So, Theia had spoken to Graham about the gun, but nothing had come of it yet. Or maybe it had. Maybe he had bought a firearm and, on impulse, decided to avenge his wife's humiliation at Rubio's hand.

Assuming he even knew about it.

Besides, Graham seems the sort who would prefer taking care of "difficulties" in person, face-to-face, not from afar.

She thought of Julia, how little effort it would have taken to push her over the railing that dark, blustery Christmas Eve. But if Graham was behind her death, who did he think he had tumbled onto the rocks? Julia or Theia? And if he intended to do away with Theia, might he be tempted to try again?

Theia leaned forward, frowning, "Dear Inez, you look quite peaked. Did you have breakfast? I recall you bolted out to attend to your business, and I imagine you did not stop to even have a cup of coffee." She waved at the various dishes on the table. "Eat! I need to dress, warm up my voice. You have plenty of time to sup and relax."

Inez recovered her appetite enough to make a credible dent in the meal, which was a good thing, because once they began working on the pieces for the New Year's Eve performance, they did not stop until the sun had finished its race across the sky and plunged into the Pacific, drawing twilight after it like a long dusky cloak. Then, they went through the entire repertoire for the Melpomene.

"Tomorrow," Theia warned her, "we shall do it all again. It will be our last chance." She looked out the window. "He is working late again," she said. "I shall have a light supper in my rooms. Shall I order for you?"

"I am still full from the earlier meal, but thank you." Inez stood wearily from the piano seat, feeling as though her lower limbs would never be straight again. "Regarding tomorrow. I will need a couple hours in the afternoon. I do not want to overdo, so close to your last two performances. And I must stop at the music store. I want to be sure certain problems have been dealt with."

Besides checking on progress with the replacement window, she planned to take Yvonne's letters and scrapbook to the store for safekeeping. After the close call in Julia's bedchamber, she did not want to leave anything at the Palace that might fall into the wrong hands. She also hoped de Bruijn might be back. She wanted to tell him about the windows, Theia's interest in firearms, and the letters to Theia that she had found in Yvonne's possession.

Theia started toward her rooms. "Of course. As it happens, I am meeting Mrs. Whitney-Smith tomorrow for tea. Shall we start early, stop about two o'clock, and reconvene after dinner for a final run-through?"

The expected answer was clearly "yes."

Inez retired to her quarters. She promised herself she would finish exploring Julia's rooms the next night. Tonight, she allowed herself the luxury of a hot bath. How sensible, she mused, to have a tub in each suite.

When she and Antonia first arrived in the city, they had stayed in the Palace Hotel. Inez had forgotten how convenient it was to have both bathrooms and water closets in each apartment. She sighed and sank up to her chin, letting the warm water slosh and soothe her.

"Wouldn't it be lovely to move back here," she said aloud. No cooking. Hot baths every night, if she wished. Closer to Antonia's school, assuming she returned. A little more distance from the store. She shook her head, annoyed. "Completely impractical and ridiculous," she announced. She closed her eyes and let her hands float, moving her fingers languidly through Gilbert and Sullivan's "I'm Called Little Buttercup."

Chapter Thirty-Seven

DECEMBER 29

The early part of the next day flew by. When Inez and Theia finished their run-through, Inez felt confident that the Melpomene recital would go smoothly. She headed to the store, where she found the new pane of glass in place, much to her relief. After that, it was off to the boardinghouse to bother Mrs. Nolan for a simple repast she could take back with her to the hotel.

"And when is little Miss Antonia coming back?" Mrs. Nolan asked as she wrapped a piece of apple pie, two slices of bread, and some cheese in brown paper.

"Very soon. Less than a week." Inez secreted the meal in her satchel.

"She's missed some school," said Mrs. Nolan reprovingly.

"True. I suppose she will have to work all the harder to make it up," said Inez, thinking she would have to decide, and quickly, whether Antonia would be returning to public school.

"And that gentleman. Mr. de…ah. I will butcher his name for certain. 'Tis a foreign one that does not roll off the tongue. Will we see him again?"

"Perhaps," hedged Inez.

"Such a gentleman! Knows how to dress and how to hold a fork and knife proper."

Not wanting to get involved in a discussion on de Bruijn's attributes, Inez thanked Mrs. Nolan and beat a hasty retreat.

Back at the Palace Hotel, she inquired at the front desk whether the private detective had returned. The clerk disappeared to "check with management," then reported he was not expected back until the morrow.

Inez willed herself to patience and asked for pencil and paper to leave him a message. In the hastily penned communication she noted they had much to discuss, closing with: *Events are moving apace, but I am not certain in which direction.* She hated to admit how "at sea" she felt. She hoped that, together, they could analyze the various pieces of the puzzle, which seemed scattered in many directions, and build a picture that made sense.

Taking the stairs to the second floor, Inez checked her pocket watch. If tea was the order of the day, Theia should still be chatting with Mrs. Whitney-Smith about hats or whatever society women chatted about. Try as she might, Inez could not envision the diva in that role, relegating her days to, what, charity works? Shopping? Gardening?

She headed to her temporary quarters, thinking she would have a private bite to eat and perhaps poke about a bit more in Yvonne's rooms. Upon opening the door, Inez heard a startled "Oh!" from the bedchamber, followed by the soft swish of skirts. Dropping her satchel inside the door, Inez called out, "Who is there?" A maid, surely. Who else would have a key to come and go?

Theia emerged from the bedroom, looking sheepish. "You have found me out, Inez."

Inez realized she had automatically reached into her coat pocket for her gun. She tried to calm her galloping heart. "What are you doing here?"

Theia wrung her hands. "I have been thinking. About Yvonne. We met at the Melpomene, and we were like sisters. Oh, we squabbled, but we survived together through the best and worst of times. For more than ten years. I keep wondering why she left. I find it hard to believe she is responsible for Julia's death, or that she wanted mine. I was hoping I might find a clue, a little hint as to what happened between us and why."

She looked at Inez beseechingly. Her eyes, light-brown with a hint of yellow, unnerved Inez, not the least because, try as she might, she could not determine if Theia was telling the truth or dissembling.

Theia continued, "We were all happy in Europe, even in Philadelphia. But once Graham decided we would move to San Francisco, everything changed. I thought about all this during my little stroll two days ago. The day you thought I was buying a pistol." She gave a sad smile, as if acknowledging the folly of her ways.

"It *is* curious that Yvonne would leave now, so close to the end of your performances," said Inez cautiously. "Did you have a falling out?"

"Yvonne, Julia, and I had our differences. It was easier when it was just me and Yvonne."

Inez noticed that Graham did not enter the equation of Theia's thinking.

Theia said, "It occurred to me, Yvonne was there at the Cliff House when Julia said such awful things to me. And Yvonne has always been so devoted, even during the worst of times. Could she have killed Julia, an impulse born from her loyalty to me? And then fled from guilt?" Theia looked down at her afternoon gown and smoothed the bodice. "I have not been kind to Yvonne lately. The stress of the situation. She is gone, and I cannot apologize to her."

She looked at Inez, almost as if she were pleading for understanding, for approval. "I am truly trying to atone for my sins, whatever they might have been. And I suppose I should have asked your permission before coming in, but you weren't around.

Now, I should give you a few minutes of respite from my musings before we rehearse a final time."

"I thought you were having tea with Mrs. Whitney-Smith," said Inez.

"She canceled, with many apologies. We will reschedule after the first of the year, when I will have plenty of time for such things."

"How did you get in? I have the key to both doors." Inez clutched her coat pocket, just to be certain.

"Ah well." She looked embarrassed at that. "Graham has a key that works on all the doors in the extended suite. I knew where he keeps it, so..."

"I see." That raised the possibility of Graham, or even Theia, using the key to come into Julia's rooms at whim. Another disturbing thought occurred to Inez. *I can have no expectations of privacy while I am here.*

Inez waited until Theia left. Then, for all the good it did, she locked her doors and went to take her simple meal in the chair by the fireplace. Glancing into the bedroom, she saw that one of Yvonne's trunks was open and the armoire door was ajar.

At least in one respect Theia had been telling the truth. She had been snooping around. Looking for something.

But what?

Inez glanced at the door leading to Julia's rooms. The chair was still there, propped under the doorknob.

Tonight I will see if anything might still be hiding in the room.

She held that thought through the hours it took to rehearse for the Melpomene.

They had just begun the opening arias for the Grand when Graham appeared, insisting Theia join him for dinner. "After all," he said, "the next two nights will be consumed with your performances. And remember, after your final appearance, we are joining the manager of the Grand to celebrate your career on the stage."

They swept out for a late repast, leaving Inez, for the first time she could recall, alone. It was an opportunity she might not have again.

Julia's room, first.

She took up a lamp, moved the chair from the door, opened it, and—

"Blast!" she exclaimed.

The room was empty. All trace of Julia Green, gone.

The bed was stripped, and the mattress spirited away, probably for airing. The armoire gaped open and empty. Even the rugs had been removed. Inez walked through the rooms, her footsteps echoing in the uncarpeted interior.

Where had Julia's belongings gone?

And who had made the decision to empty the suite?

It had to be Graham Drake. He was the one with authority to do so.

They can't erase her like this!

Inez wanted to protest. To say something, to someone. To demand that Julia's belongings be brought back, forthwith.

But to say anything to the Drakes would reveal that she had been in the rooms before they were emptied, and then had ventured back in once they were cleared.

She wished heartily for de Bruijn's return.

Chapter Thirty-Eight

DECEMBER 30

The next evening, while waiting at the Palace Hotel for the hack Graham Drake had reserved to take their party to the Melpomene, Inez surveyed the crowded reception area and the busy roundabout, looking for de Bruijn. She hoped to spot him among the hordes setting out for a Friday evening's entertainment in the city. Although if he did turn up, she had no idea how she would signal him without drawing the Drakes' attention as well.

However, he was nowhere to been seen. Wringing her fan between her hands, Inez reminded herself that he had promised to be at the Melpomene. She deliberately eased her grip on the fan, lest she break the ribs. *I have nothing to be nervous about. At least, for the performance.*

What had her on edge was the possible attendance of Luis Rubio and perhaps even John Teague. Inez couldn't decide who would be worse. If Teague came, he might make a scene, demanding to see Graham as he had at the Grand Opera House. And what would he say to Theia, if they happened to meet face-to-face? As for Rubio, Inez did not put it past him to sit front row, center, just to inject maximum annoyance or alarm into both her and Theia.

As the hack drew up with clatters and squeaks, Inez decided

that, once she walked onstage, she would not look out into the audience. If de Bruijn were there, he would be unobtrusive, she was certain. And if she happened to spot either Teague or Rubio, it would only break her concentration. If Graham Drake saw either of the men, more than just her concentration could end up shattered.

Inez recalled the last time she had ridden in a carriage with the Drakes to a performance—Christmas Eve, heading to the Cliff House. The undercurrents of the conversations had passed her by. Now, reflecting on Yvonne's protective vigilance, Julia and Theia's sniping, and Graham's impatience with them all, she wished she had listened more closely. But she had been an outsider to their circle, more worried about her anemic bank accounts and the shaky future of the music store than about the dark below-the-surface currents amongst the members of the party.

Now, just few days later, much had changed. The occupants were silent. No one even attempted to converse. The Drakes, once again sitting across from Inez, looked out their separate windows. They didn't acknowledge each other, Inez, or the nameless Palace chambermaid who had been conscripted to help Theia with her gowns and hair. Theia wore an indigo velvet cloak over her silk, satin, and lace evening gown of blue and green. Inez wondered if she would ever replace her "signature" black and silver cloak. But why would she? Julia had worn the cloak in death. Even a replacement would harbor dark memories.

The driver came to a stop and Theia broke the silence. "I shall be glad when this evening is over."

Graham finally looked at her. "All this time you've been saying you cannot abide leaving the stage."

"*The* stage. Not *this* stage."

"But you've always said the Melpomene is where you had your start, your leap into being the Golden Songbird. If you didn't want to sing here, you should have told me when the theater contacted us. You could have declined."

"I couldn't. I do owe the theater this. I just wish it wasn't at the end of my tour." She sounded wistful. "I had such aspirations when I first came here. Such dreams for the future."

"And look at what you've accomplished since you left and we married," said Graham. "Europe. America. You have been lauded everywhere."

"But now, it's all coming to an end. Because you say it must."

Graham sighed, an impatient exhalation. He glanced at Inez and the maid, trapped on the bench across from them, and said to Theia through gritted teeth, "Save your voice, my darling."

The door opened, and a doorman dressed in red said, "Welcome, Mrs. Drake, Mr. Drake. We've been expecting you."

Graham said in an emphatically upbeat tone, "You see, Mrs. Drake? Your public awaits you. Let's not disappoint."

He escorted Theia out of the carriage, leaving it to the doorman to help Inez and the chambermaid and to gather the small amount of baggage Theia had brought for the evening's event. Inez told him, "Take it to whatever room you have designated for Mrs. Drake." She said to the chambermaid, "Follow him."

The young woman threw her a grateful look. Once inside the theater's foyer, Inez found the Drakes conversing with a man dressed in evening wear and large in both height and girth. Inez joined them as the man shook Graham's hand, saying, "Eden Yates, sir, at your service. And at the service of your charming wife, of course." He turned to Theia. "My dear, it has been far too long since the Golden Songbird has deigned to grace my theater, much less our fair city, with her presence. I understand you are now in San Francisco to stay."

His tongue darted out to lick his lips, catching some of his mustache.

Theia said in the haughtiest of tones, "Yes, it has been a long time, Mr. Yates. Much has changed since those days." She turned to Inez, and Inez thought she saw a flicker of relief on her face.

"Here is my accompanist. Mrs. Stannert, this is Mr. Yates, the owner of the Melpomene Theater."

"Charmed." He bowed.

Inez smiled stiffly. She could not say why her antipathy was so sudden and unwarranted, unless it was that quick tongue lick. She thought of the Grand's assistant manager Thackery, with his eager-squirrel appearance. This Mr. Yates with his immense size and the random nature of his mustache reminded her of "Big Ben Butler," the famous male sea lion that claimed Seal Rocks as his domain. Just as with that sea lion, there was something slick and shiny about the owner of the Melpomene.

She offered him her hand. He seized it eagerly and stepped a little closer. "A lady pianist! Such a pleasure!" he barked. An image of the two-ton-plus marine animal lording it over his harem of much-smaller females flashed through her mind. She reclaimed her hand, resisting the temptation to wipe it on her coat.

He continued, "We have had women musicians here before, of course, including a banjo ensemble recently. They are a great draw for the clientele."

Graham said, "The ladies need time to prepare. We can discuss business while they do so."

"Of course, Mr. Drake, at your service. Just one more word with your wife, if I might." He turned to one of the red-jacket-clad men nearby. "Please, take Mr. Drake to my office. I shall follow shortly. Offer him a glass of my best."

He waited until Drake was on his way upstairs before he turned to Theia with a smile that didn't reach his small dark eyes. "My dearest Mrs. Carrington Drake, the changes you made to the program were so late, you put me in a bit of a bind. As I noted in our earlier communications, I wanted you to do something from your 'old days.' Something light and entertaining."

Theia drew herself up. Between the blue cape and the white

flowers in her hair, she looked positively regal. "I included several numbers from Gilbert and Sullivan. Very popular light opera."

He frowned. "I hoped for something from *The Black Crook.* And maybe a few verses of 'Champagne Charlie.' Just a couple of pieces, mind. I billed this appearance as a return to the cradle of your fame. People will be expecting it."

"Well, they can just *un*expect it," snapped Theia. "I haven't performed any of that rubbish since I left your theater. The list I sent you day before yesterday is what we will present. Nothing more."

Inez turned to Theia, eyebrows raised. Now *this* was the Theia she recognized. Not the demure, wistful, accommodating woman of the past few days, but the all-or-nothing, iron-willed diva.

Mr. Yates didn't quail but simply said, "Very well. Since you refuse, we shall see how it goes."

He looked at Inez. "I don't suppose you have 'Champagne Charlie' or anything from *The Black Crook* in your repertoire?"

Inez narrowed her eyes at him. "I am completely unfamiliar with those pieces." Which wasn't wholly true. She was pretty certain she had a nodding acquaintance with "Champagne Charlie," thanks to some of the more unsavory aspects of her past.

Theia wound her arm through Inez's and said to Yates, "Mrs. Stannert is a *classical* musician."

"I see." He raised his mammoth arms in a monumental shrug. "Well, the show must go on, am I not right, *mesdames*?"

The murmur outside the open doors grew louder. A crowd, mostly male, had gathered on the sidewalks and was getting restless. Two doormen barred the entrance but apparently not the view, for someone shouted, "Hey, there's the Golden Songbird. Songbird! Over here! I remember when you were Miss Carrington!"

Yates snapped his fingers at one of his assisting men-in-red and said to Theia and Inez, "Ladies, he will escort you to your room to prepare."

Once upstairs, the assistant said, "If you need anything, Mr. Yates' office is three doors down from yours."

The Palace chambermaid was waiting for them inside. Theia removed her cloak, handed it to the maid, and sank into the cushioned seat before the dressing table. She stared at her reflection and touched the flowers in her hair. "Are these too gaudy? Should I do the pearls instead?"

Inez glanced at the maid, clutching the cloak and apparently struck mute in terror that the question might be directed at her. "The flowers are perfect," Inez assured Theia.

The diva twisted a ringlet dangling by her ear. "I'd like some hot water. Not to drink, just for the steam." She stood and began pacing, humming. Scales would be next, Inez knew.

"I'll see if they can bring you some," said Inez. She slipped out of the room and, moving her fingers in her own warm-up, headed to Yates' office.

Preparing to knock, she heard Graham inside, saying, "No. I did not know."

Yates replied, "It was a long time ago, if that makes a difference. Please, have some more cognac."

Inez knocked. Yates called, "Enter!"

After delivering Theia's request, Inez added, "I would like to test the piano before the performance."

"Of course!" Yates hopped belatedly to his feet. Inez stepped to the side as the theater owner went out into the hallway and bellowed. Footsteps pounded up a set of unseen stairs.

She surveyed the office. An array of cartes de visite and larger cabinet cards—all portraits, from what she could see—filled the walls. Drake had stood when Inez entered and walked to the single window. He seemed focused on the wall of the neighboring building, but Inez noticed a muscle jumping in the line of his jaw.

Yates returned with an usher, instructing him to take Inez down to the stage. "What fer?" the usher asked, seeming clueless.

"To test the piano, you imbecile!" He turned to Inez. "Apologies, Mrs. Stannert. Now, off you go. I don't mean to be rude, but we gentlemen have business to conduct and I must be ready to introduce you in"—he glanced at the grandfather clock in the corner—"fifteen minutes."

A set of serpentine stairs emerged onto the backstage area. From there, Inez and the usher moved to the piano onstage. He held up a light for her while she tested the sound. It was, she had to admit, not bad for an instrument that had obviously seen much use. She had time for scales and a warm-up routine, then Yates was at her elbow. "Mrs. Stannert, if you'll join Mrs. Drake in the wings."

She crossed over to the area where Theia waited, the white flowers in the diva's hair making her look like a goddess awaiting the adoration due her. The curtain went up. The bright footlamps cast their light across the wood stage. Yates strode to center stage and began, "Tonight, ladies and gentlemen, we are very honored…"

Inez wondered if de Bruijn was out there, listening and waiting. Then, with one shake of her head, she wiped all extraneous thoughts from her mind. The two women smiled at each other, the music a bond between them.

Yates said, "Please welcome the Golden Songbird herself, Mrs. Carrington Drake!"

Head held high, Theia glided onto the stage and the applause mounted to the rafters.

Inez followed. Theia inclined her head, accepting the plaudits.

Inez took her seat and watched Theia, waiting for her signal. A nod.

Inez bent her gaze to the keyboard, and they began. Theia's voice was like a light in the dark, guiding through time and meter. Inez walked the piano accompaniment alongside. The prima donna steered the emotional color of each piece, with the piano providing the underpinning and reinforcement. From light opera, to popular ditty, to the more serious arias, the performance moved in its studied path. Time unrolled like a long skein of yarn, each composition flowing from future, to present, to past.

After the "Ave Maria" finale, Inez rested her fingers on the keys, the bravas and cheers washing over her, content in knowing they were meant for Theia. The perfection of the music was enough for her.

Somewhere amongst all the plaudits came the shout: "How about 'You Naughty, Naughty Men?'"

Then another shout, "Or at least a little 'Champagne Charlie.'"

Theia, suddenly close, put her hand on Inez's shoulder. Inez looked up, wondering if Theia would proceed with an encore, and if so, what. Inez didn't think the crowd would appreciate "*Dove sono*" as much as the audience at the Grand.

Theia's stage smile was in place, but Inez sensed she was struggling to contain her wrath. "Stand, bow, and we shall exit the stage," she said under her breath. "I have fulfilled whatever obligation Mr. Yates believed I owe him."

They moved into the wings where Yates stood, rocking on his heels, with an "I told you so" look on his face. Beside him, a young woman jittered in a scandalously skimpy costume consisting of tights and a short, full dress skimming her knees.

Yates said to Theia, "I was prepared, my dear. You needn't worry about the encore. Little Lily here is quite up to the task. I had her waiting, just in case." He turned to Inez next. "A pity you don't have the score, but I shall fill in on this one."

With that, he and Lily proceeded to the stage.

Theia said in controlled fury, "We are finding Graham and leaving. Now."

No sooner had they turned toward the backstage stairs than Graham Drake appeared. Looking as angry as Theia, he seized her arm. She hissed, "Stop it! You're hurting me!"

"We need to talk. Now. Upstairs." He glanced at Inez. "Alone."

Inez folded her arms, thinking of the little maid waiting in the changing room, who would no doubt be booted out for their "private talk."

Inez made her way to a door that emerged into the auditorium. She stood by the wall, listening as the last refrain of "You Naughty, Naughty Men" rolled out along with the singer's swaying hips and ticktock waving finger: "And when kind we'll say, oh, bless you, oh! you dear delightful men. We've no wish to distress you, we would sooner far caress you, And when kind we'll say, oh, bless you, oh! you naughty, dear, delightful men."

Inez was thinking the song would probably garner much approval at the Silver Queen saloon, when a movement at her side caught her attention. "Mr. de Bruijn!" A warmth unrelated to the heated atmosphere of the crowded theater spread through her. "You're here!"

"I said I would be." He watched the stage, where Yates and the diminutive Lily were taking multiple bows. "The program went well. But I assume this last is unexpected?"

She nodded. "I believe Theia and Mr. Yates have a fraught history. It's in what they say and don't say. I wonder—"

There was a sudden commotion, a scream offstage.

Inez breathed "Theia!" and bolted toward backstage with de Bruijn right behind her.

Chapter Thirty-Nine

Inez heard Yates, still on stage, bray to the audience through the cheers and applause, "Thank you all. I hope the evening met— no, *more* than met your expectations. We hope to see you at our upcoming performances of *The Black Crook* in the new year."

As she passed the wings, the curtain descended with exceptional speed.

A little farther, and there, at the bottom of the backstage stairs, Theia was in a crumpled heap on the floor, sobbing. Before Inez could react, Theia said, "Oh, Wolter!"

Wolter?

De Bruijn circumvented Inez and knelt by Theia, who immediately threw her arms around his neck. "Someone pushed me."

Inez examined the tableau. De Bruijn crouched by the diva, while she sobbed into his frockcoat. *Too cozy to be merely investigator and client.*

"Are you injured?" he asked.

"I could have broken my neck! My ankle, I think I twisted it."

"Who did this?"

"I–I don't know. I was standing at the top, ready to descend, and someone pushed me."

Inez heard shouting above. Graham and another man, their voices running together.

"Stay away from my wife, damn you!" That was Graham.

"Look at you, Graham. You are destroying everything you touch. The newspaper. And now your wife!" That sounded like John Teague.

Yates and Lily arrived at the foot of the stairs. Yates studied the scene with mild concern before turning to his petite singer. "Lily dear, please help Mrs. Carrington Drake and this gentleman—"

De Bruijn looked up.

Yates stepped back, shock stamping his wide face. "Mr. de Bruijn? What a small world! And to have our paths cross here, after how many years? Ten? Twelve? You, I, and the Golden Songbird, together again."

"Let us not speak of that now," said de Bruijn. "Mrs. Drake needs a place to recover. Perhaps a physician."

Yates became all solicitous business. "Lily, as I was saying, help Mrs. Drake to the chorus dressing room, the closest one, and keep her company. I must put an end to any impending fisticuffs. Then we can see about getting a doctor."

He stepped around Theia and hurried up the stairs, the treads shaking under his weight.

Inez rested a comforting hand on Theia's shoulder, while her mind whirled with questions.

The first was: Who pushed Theia?

The second: How did Yates and de Bruijn know each other?

The third...

She looked at de Bruijn. *He and I have much to discuss, but it will have to wait.*

"I shall get your maid for you," Inez said to Theia.

Lily jerked her thumb toward a room behind the stairs. "We'll be in there."

Theia moaned. "I shall be black-and-blue tomorrow."

With de Bruijn focused on Theia, Inez turned to the stairs, determined to see what she could learn on the second floor.

In front of Theia's dressing room on the second floor, Drake was being restrained by two theater attendants while Teague was being similarly kept in check. Yates stood between the two men, an effective blockade should one or the other tear loose from their captors. Inez hung back, not wanting to be seen. Not that anyone seemed to notice her, given the tense situation.

"Gentlemen," said Yates. "Not here. Elsewhere, if you must." He addressed Teague's restrainers with, "Please escort this one out the rear. No need to provide a free show by hauling him out onto the street. The alley is good enough."

Once he was gone, Yates said, "What happened, Mr. Drake?"

Graham jerked out of the attendants' grasp. "I came up here with my wife to discuss certain matters. In private. She pulled away from me and ran toward the stairs. The next thing I knew, I heard her scream."

"She says she was pushed," said Yates.

"By whom?" Graham demanded.

"She did not see. Then what happened?"

"I started to go after her, and this ruffian showed up out of nowhere—"

"Do you know this supposed ruffian?" asked Yates.

"He worked for me until I fired him."

There was a space of stubborn silence.

"Ah." From that one syllable, Inez could tell Yates suspected there was more to the story. "Do you think he could have pushed your wife?"

Drake set his jaw. "If he did, I'll make him wish he was never born. I want to take my wife back to our hotel. Now. She needs to see a doctor and rest."

"Of course, of course," Yates said soothingly. "It could be your wife is mistaken. She could have misjudged the stairs' location when she rushed down the hall. If you would wait downstairs, in the lobby, I can have one of my men hail a carriage for you. Best to avoid the rear entrance, of course."

"I'll wring his neck," muttered Drake.

"But not here," said Yates calmly, escorting Drake toward the front of the theater.

They had just disappeared down the main staircase when a voice said in her ear, "Fascinating. Someone that Señor Drake hates more than me."

She recoiled. "Señor Rubio! What are you doing here?"

He smiled. "I said I would come to the last two concerts. A very credible performance, Mrs. Stannert, however I think your interpretation of 'Una voce poco fa' could use some work."

She wanted to ask if he'd seen what happened but became aware of how quiet it was. Theia, Lily, and de Bruijn must have retreated to the chorus room downstairs. No one was in sight. It was just her, Rubio, and the steep stairs, only a few feet away, leading down.

Without turning her back on him, she retreated down the hall, saying, "I need to bring Theia's maid to her. We are leaving soon." She entered the dressing room and closed the door behind her with a sigh of relief.

Inside, the chambermaid was quaking. Inez said, "Mrs. Drake needs you downstairs. The fracas is over. Come with me."

Inez checked the hallway in both directions before they left the room. There was no sign of Rubio. She chided herself for her sudden onset of nerves. What did she think he would do? Attack her in the theater? *But if he was the one who pushed Theia, who knows what he is capable of?*

No sooner had she delivered the maid to the chorus room than Yates appeared, saying, "Your coach awaits, Mrs. Drake. Such an unfortunate way to end your days as the Golden Songbird. I hope tomorrow night's performance at the Grand is all you wish it to be. As you know, I have always had the greatest respect for your *many* talents." He gave her a little bow.

Theia, ankle resting on a cushion, gripped her handkerchief tightly. To Inez's surprise, she burst out, "Don't think you can manipulate me! The things I could say about you—"

"—Matter not a whit to me anymore, my dear." Yates glanced around the room. "And where is Mr. de Bruijn?"

"How should I know? He left."

Drake came in, and all conversation ceased. "Let's go," he said shortly. "We will get you a doctor once we're back at the hotel."

He turned to Inez. "Mrs. Stannert, Mr. Yates was preparing some papers for me. If you would wait here until they are done and bring them back with you, I'd be grateful."

So I am now messenger as well as lady's companion and accompanist.

But this would give her a chance to find out more about Yates's connection to Theia and de Bruijn. "Certainly."

Once the Drakes and the maid had left. Yates said, "Mrs. Stannert, would you prefer to wait here or accompany me to my office while I finish up the paperwork?"

"Your office," she said promptly. It would easier to ask questions if they were in the same room, she figured.

Once in and settled, Yates occupied himself with papers on his desk. Inez sat and looked around at his office, intrigued by all the images on the walls. Portraits as well as full-figure poses were featured. Here and there, a few men struck theatrical poses, but most of the photos were of women of a decidedly youthful age, in costumes ranging from togas to scanty above-the-knee garb. Scanning the cabinet cards pinned on the nearby wall, Inez focused on one, and she rose from her chair, unable to believe her eyes.

"Julia Green," she whispered.

It was her.

It *had* to be.

But in a costume Inez could never imagine Julia wearing. Bare arms, bare legs—or were those light-colored tights?—and an outfit that was hardly more than a camisole and drawers, albeit liberally spangled with fringe, beads, and lace. A shield and hal-berd were positioned by her side. She peered up at the viewer, head tipped coquettishly.

Yates glanced up at Inez's exclamation, and chuckled. "You and Mr. Drake came to the same erroneous conclusion. I agree, Miss Green bears an uncanny resemblance to the Golden Songbird in her youth. Even Miss Green remarked upon it."

There was so much to absorb in his short response, Inez didn't know where to start. So she began with, "That's Theia?"

"Ah, on a first-name basis with the soon-to-be-former prima donna?" He leaned back in his chair, which creaked ominously. "Yes, back in the late sixties, the esteemed Mrs. Drake performed the role of Stalacta, Fairy Queen of the Golden Realm, in *The Black Crook*. She was marvelous. But I will say she was equally fetching in her earlier role as the soubrette Carline, singing 'You Naughty, Naughty Men.'"

Still staring at the photo, Inez felt a chill begin to seep into her bones that was unrelated to the almost stifling air of the closed office. "Mr. Drake didn't know all this about Theia?"

"I believe not. At least he seemed very surprised."

"So, you told him what you've just told me?"

"Of course! He is her husband." He spread his hands. "I have nothing to hide."

Inez thought of Graham, face suffused with anger, saying to Theia after the performance, "We must talk." *Just how angry was he? Angry enough to...* Inez caught at another thread, knowing her time with Yates was limited. "You met Miss Green, then? She saw the photo?"

"Oh yes. She came here shortly before Christmas, looking for work after the first of the year. Explained she was Mrs. Carrington Drake's protégée. She saw the photo, exclaimed over it, and we chatted. Of course, I was entranced by her. I had to have her audition, hear her sing. Outstanding voice. So like the Golden Songbird, it brought me to tears."

Inez tried to marshal her thoughts and questions. "She signed a contract with the Grand."

"All my doing. It being so close to Christmas, I must have been feeling the spirit. I said her talent would be wasted here and she should approach Thackery, with my blessing. A crime, what happened to her."

"You heard about the accident?"

"Accident? You mean that nonsense about her taking her own life? Preposterous! Alive, vibrant, determined. She had no reason to turn to death." He tapped his large, bulbous nose. "I work with many young women here at the theater. I am familiar with their ways and their moods." He looked contemplative. "The Golden Songbird. Now, she was a handful. She definitely gave me a run for my money."

Something in how he said that last caught her attention. He was staring at the photo of Theia, resignation pulling his triple-chinned visage into a frown.

She decided to dig a little deeper. Yates did not strike her as dangerous. Not like Rubio. So she had nothing to lose by asking. "Just now, downstairs, Theia said, 'The things I could say about you.' What did she mean?"

He lifted his eyebrows, and the weight lifted from his expression. "Oh. It's all in the past. When my wife died five years ago, I buried my indiscretions. And the repercussions. I have paid for my sins and I don't see any reason to divulge the secrets of others. If you want to know what Mrs. Drake was referring to, I suggest you ask her."

"Or I could ask Mr. de Bruijn." She hoped mentioning his name would bring a reaction, but Yates didn't even twitch an eyelid. She persisted. "Was the good investigator involved in his official capacity, perhaps?"

Yates took the papers before him and sealed them in a large envelope. He leaned over the desk, saying, "If you would give these to Mr. Drake, please."

She reached out to take the envelope. He held onto one end. "I don't suppose I could persuade you to consider playing here at the Melpomene once in a while? You have a fine touch on the keyboard."

"I am happily employed elsewhere, thank you." She tugged the envelope.

He held tight. "You don't strike me as someone who has spent much time around the Drakes. You might be available later. Keep me in mind."

She slid the envelope from his loosened grasp and stood to leave. At the door, she hesitated. "You didn't seem overly concerned about Theia's tumble down the stairs. She claimed to have been pushed. Doesn't that trouble you?"

He stood as well. "My first thought on seeing her crumpled at the bottom of the stairs was that the Golden Songbird is still a very fine actress. My second was that she still retains her acrobatic skills of yore. Our early dramas involved athletic maneuvers on the part of dancers and singers."

"You think she was feigning?"

He shrugged. "She did not appear to be broken or bloodied. Those stairs have taken others by surprise. If what she said was true, she survived remarkably unscathed."

Inez turned to go, then turned back. "At the end of the performance, when the shouts began for Theia to sing tunes from her past, you knew she would decline. And you and Lily were so conveniently at the ready. Those men in the audience. Ringers?"

A small smile emerged from underneath the walrus mustache. "I suppose I have not paid for *all* my sins. Yet."

Chapter Forty

"It's time to lay our cards on the table," said Inez the next morning.

She sat in de Bruijn's office. She'd accepted his offer of coffee. They now faced each other across his desk, which held only a blotter and the cups and saucers. She wondered how he kept all the details of their meetings straight, without taking notes.

"I thought that was what we were doing all along," said de Bruijn. His overcoat was slung over the back of his chair, a clue that he was prepared to leave as soon as they were done.

She nodded at the smallish travel trunk waiting by the door. "Traveling again?"

"Not until after the first of the year." He gripped the handle of his cup but did not drink. "I promised to be at the Grand Opera House tonight, and I will. But I do have other business today that I must attend to first."

A hint to hurry it up, she thought.

"To the point, then." She leaned forward. "What is the connection between you, Theia, and the Melpomene?"

He exhaled, long and slow. "An old case. More than ten years ago. As I've said before, it has no bearing on what is happening now."

"I beg to differ." And she launched into what had happened the few days since they had last spoken. Her meeting with Teague and what he had said. How he and Theia had planned to marry after she returned from San Francisco, where she had gone to better her singing career at the Melpomene. How Teague had played an insider's game in the stock market with Graham Drake—and lost. How Theia had written she had plans to help him regain his fortune, but had returned to Virginia City from San Francisco penniless, "different," and with Yvonne in tow.

Inez added, "Graham 'Lucky Duck' Drake, on the other hand, prospered in the market and won Theia as well. Everything seems to point back to that time."

"What has this to do with Miss Green's death?" said de Bruijn, sounding a touch impatient.

"I found a page from Julia's diary in her fireplace, ready to burn. It said, *I would never have known if we had not come here. I would never have known if I hadn't spoken to Y/M. HE is vile, but SHE is worse!*" In her mind, Inez could see the sentences, scribbled without regard for penmanship, the pencil marks deep and dark as if Julia sought to brand the words into the paper.

Inez continued, "I am certain 'he' refers to Graham. I have to agree with her assessment. He *is* vile, despite all his money and fine manners. I initially thought Y/M was Yvonne Marchal, but was unsure about 'she' and had no idea what it all meant. Was 'she' Yvonne? Did Yvonne say something that revealed a side so heinous that Julia was appalled? Or did 'she' refer to Theia? I still do not know for certain. However, I'm now wondering if Y/M refers to Yates at the Melpomene."

He frowned. "Miss Green met Yates? She went to the Melpomene? When?"

Inez summarized what Yates had told her, adding, "He has a cabinet card on his wall of Theia, from her early days. She was dressed less than, shall we say, appropriately for the wife of a prominent newspaper publisher who wants to make his mark in society and step into politics. In the photograph, Theia looks *just* like Julia. Julia and Graham both saw it. Yates was very cagey as to what he told Graham and Julia about Theia. He clearly enjoys dropping little hints and letting the listener interpret as they may. For instance, he told me that with the death of his wife five years ago, he was now freed from the burden of his indiscretions and their repercussions."

De Bruijn sank back in his chair.

She glared at him, impatient with his silence. "He said this as he spoke about Theia and the theater. About the past. When I asked, Yates said I should ask you or Theia to explain. Now, will you tell me what this is all about or should I follow Yates's advice and ask Theia herself?"

"No!" He spoke with an urgency she'd not heard in him before. "Do not talk to her about this. You say Yates spoke with Mr. Drake about his wife's past at the Melpomene?"

"Yates said he did. After the performance, Graham stormed over to Theia, clearly angry, and they went upstairs to talk privately. Shortly thereafter, Theia fell down the stairs."

"Or was pushed," said de Bruijn.

Or pretended she was. Inez refrained from saying so out loud and continued, "Don't you see? Theia could be in danger from her husband. Or," she hesitated and said carefully, "he might be in danger from her, if he now has information she was determined to keep from him. It goes both ways."

"Are you saying he might have tried to kill her?"

"Or possibly it was Señor Rubio, seeing an opportunity and seizing it. To be fair, he has no love lost for Theia. I saw him. He was sneaking around upstairs and observed Graham and Teague having it out, apparently."

De Bruijn shook his head. "Wait. Señor Rubio was there? And John Teague as well?"

"Yes, but—" She stopped and decided not to confuse matters by dragging her ongoing problems with Rubio into their discussion.

"Did they appear upstairs before or after Mrs. Drake's accident?"

"I am guessing they were there before. But I don't know for certain."

De Bruijn passed a hand over his forehead. "What happened after the Drakes returned to the hotel that night? And this morning?"

"Nothing, as far as I can tell. I was delayed with Yates and came back by myself. The music room was empty, dark. I delivered Yates's papers to Graham, or rather to his valet. Graham was 'unavailable.' He might not have even been there." She frowned. "It's very odd. I didn't hear any screaming or fights. No objets d'art lobbed into the walls. I did see Theia this morning. She was in the music room, waiting for Clarisse to arrive with the dress she is to wear tonight. I told her I was stepping out for a while. She acted as if nothing had happened." *And not a bruise or limp in sight.*

Inez added, "I was hardly going to bring up last night's events if she wasn't."

"Follow her lead. That is the safest avenue of action for you right now. Do not confront Graham Drake, whatever you do. Do *not* put yourself in his way."

"Easily done," she assured him. "In fact, Theia told me he is busy today and will meet us at the theater tonight. Perhaps they are deliberately avoiding each other until this is all over."

"Anything else?"

Inez shook her head. She had decided to not go into Rubio's threats and the broken windows. Nor had she mentioned the intruder who had ventured into Julia's room or the disappearance of Julia's diary and all her belongings. She had decided to hold those particular cards close to her vest until the detective had answered her questions.

"It's your turn, de Bruijn," she said. "And you'd better not prevaricate. What happened at the Melpomene with you and Theia ten, twelve years ago?"

"I will tell you." He rose, coffee still untouched. "Later. After I speak with Mr. Yates."

"Wolter de Bruijn!" She banged the armrest of her chair with her fist. "This is the *last* time you trick me into babbling so much and then run out the door without telling me what you know!"

"Mrs. Stannert, investigations are my livelihood, and confidentiality is the bedrock of my profession. Before I say anything, I must talk to Mr. Yates."

"So, he was your client?"

"He was my client."

"And he, what, hired you to track Theia down? Find her? Being 'finder of the lost' is your stated occupation. What did she do, what did he lose to her? His heart? His money?"

"Enough," said de Bruijn through clenched teeth. "Say no more. I have several stops to make today, and now I have one more. Nothing will happen before tonight's recital, I am certain. However, if you or Mrs. Drake are threatened, do what you must. I advise you to scream for help first and be very chary about pulling out your pocket pistol."

"It's a revolver," snapped Inez. "There is a difference."

"Mrs. Stannert, I—" He shook his head. "I cannot say more right now. We will finish this discussion later."

Inez rose in an angry flurry of skirts. "I know when I am being dismissed. You need not see me out." At the door, she tossed over her shoulder, "I am counting upon you being at the Grand tonight. Señor Rubio will probably be there, and I wouldn't put it past John Teague to appear. Perhaps the scene at the Melpomene was just the rehearsal for whatever happens tonight. If it turns deadly, I make no promises regarding the use or not of my revolver. It seems to be the only thing I can bank on being at my side."

Chapter Forty-One

After her meeting with de Bruijn, Inez expected that the day would crawl by. Instead, the hours galloped in a mad stampede toward sunset before plunging into an abyss.

Theia spent most of the day in her private chambers, only coming out to go over "Una voce poco fa" with Inez. They ran through it several times, Inez wondering if Theia and Rubio had caught something she had missed in her execution at the Melpomene.

Theia finally nodded, apparently satisfied, and murmured, "Just so. Now, I must rest my voice while you rest your hands."

Inez repaired to the little parlor of her suite to pore over Yvonne's scrapbook and muse over the career highlights carefully collected and mounted within its pages. Inez thought how difficult it must be for Theia to close the chapter on all that she had worked for. Had she known this would be part of the bargain when she married Graham Drake? If she had turned to John Teague instead, though, she would not have had the opportunity to train in Europe, to travel and stand upon the stages, and to share the gift of her voice. A newsman stayed with his paper.

There were never easy paths in marriage, Inez thought. Her own marriage to Mark Stannert had been a whirlwind of a gambler's life: the constant travel, the new towns—each different, yet also the same. Always on guard, assessing the odds of making a killing or being killed, dancing on the edge of what was lawful and what wasn't, playing the parts that needed to be played to lure the high rollers and greenhorns to the table, chasing the dream that beckoned ever westward, looking for the place where the luck would always be good and the money easy. Chasing the dream that always stayed just a little ahead of them, whispering, inviting, seducing.

From what Inez saw in Yvonne's scrapbook, Theia had chased her dream and caught it. She had become exactly what she wanted to be: a prima donna, admired and applauded across continents.

And now, she was going to give it all up. Let her dream go, watch it fly away.

Inez shook her head and set the book aside to prepare for the final appearance.

Although she had yet to see it in its final form, Inez knew Theia's new gown was gold-and-silver. With that in mind, Inez had chosen carefully from her small selection of evening attire for her role as accompanist. She had settled on a maroon silk-striped cuirass-style gown from her Leadville days. A few years out of date, but elegant and understated. Most importantly, it had a pocket sewn into it for her revolver.

Tonight, of all nights, she was not going unarmed, even onto the stage.

At the last minute, Inez was called into Theia's bedchambers to quell a panic. "Where are my pearls?" Theia wailed. Her temporary maid stood by a wall, as if trying to make herself invisible.

"I thought you brought them with you last night, in case you decided to use them instead of the flowers," said Inez.

"Yes! In a box in the trunk!" Theia turned to Inez. "Would you fetch them please?"

Inez glanced at the maid, clearly terror-stricken by the diva's outburst. *No help from that quarter.* Inez surveyed the room for the small trunk. She couldn't recall if it was the same one that made the trip to the Cliff House or a different trunk. Her gaze traveled over the furnishings in the crowded room. There was the armoire, an occasional table with two overstuffed chairs covered with floral embroidery, another table, and a small ottoman-style table covered with a lace tablecloth and several cushions. Was that a hinge shrouded beneath the open lacework? Inez started toward it, thinking it might be the trunk in question.

Theia grabbed her hand. "Where are you going? It's over there."

Inez recognized the travel case from the previous night on the opposite side of the room. "Oh. I thought—"

"Never mind," said Theia. "I just realized, I have the perfect necklace. Graham gave it to me in France."

She hurried to her bedroom armoire, pulled out a handsome mahogany dressing case, unlocked it, and returned with a small satin box, which she handed to Inez. Inside, resting on blue velvet, was one of the most beautiful necklaces Inez had ever seen— pearls and diamonds, set in a tulip motif in silver and gold.

Theia turned her back to Inez. "Would you please put it on for me?"

The maid, who was standing out of Theia's line of sight, clasped her hands behind her back and shook her head, eyes pleading. Resigned, Inez removed the necklace from its resting place and draped it around Theia's throat, avoiding her carefully coifed hair, and did up the clasp.

Theia headed to the mirror to examine the results.

"It's beautiful," said Inez. "And complements your gown."

Inez had to admit that Clarisse had outdone herself, and under the most difficult of circumstances. The ball gown, of faille and satin cream silk, shimmered in the gaslight. Gold brocade and gold and silver metallic lace trimmed the bodice, the neckline, and the front of the skirt, while the back trailed a satin train. The perfect costume for the Golden Songbird's swan song, Inez thought.

Theia stroked the gems. "One hundred and forty-seven diamonds," she said. "When Graham gave it to me, he said he would always love me. That he would never leave me. I was his goddess. Perfect and pure, like my singing."

The photograph of Theia hanging in Yates's office danced before Inez's eyes. She moved toward the door, clearing her throat. "You will dazzle everyone, Theia. Your husband and the multitudes. We should leave so we are not in a rush at the opera house. Mr. Drake will be waiting."

He *was* waiting and already dressed in evening attire when Theia, Inez, and the maid arrived at the Grand.

Theia and the maid were whisked up to a room for last-minute repairs. Inez addressed Thackery, who had been waiting with Graham, and asked to see the Broadwood piano.

"We had it tuned again just today," Thackery assured her.

Inez had to admit that the squirrel-like assistant manager's attentiveness and attention to detail, not to mention his chivalry in standing up to Señor Rubio and the like, were growing on her. Finding all in order with the instrument, she went to the wings, shed her cloak, and waited. A tug at her sleeve caused her to look over, then down.

Clarisse, two fingers on Inez's lace cuff said, "Monsieur Drake bought me a seat in a box and said I could watch from there or here backstage. I am going to go to the box. I want see Madame in the dress, see how it looks from the audience."

"I'm glad you are here," said Inez. "I would like to talk with you afterward. About Yvonne."

"Ah, there is time for that tomorrow." She looked around nervously. "What I mean is, I am not certain I can tell you anything useful of Mademoiselle Marchal. Now, I should go take my seat."

Inez watched the dressmaker hurry away. *She knows something. And she is obviously hoping to put off talking with me until tomorrow. All the more reason to corner her tonight.*

Then Theia floated in, radiant on Graham's arm.

Thackery came over, beaming. "You look divine, Mrs. Drake. Everyone ready?" He looked from Theia to Inez.

They nodded.

Inez took a deep breath to banish the butterflies in her stomach.

"Let us begin!" He stepped onto the stage, giving the signal to raise the curtain.

———

For all the buildup and anticipation, Inez found it hard to recall the performance once it was done. It seemed a blur, from the moment she walked onstage, trailing in the wake of the thunderous applause that greeted Theia's entrance, to the end of the encore. She "awoke" to find Theia standing, downstage center, close to the footlights, arms raised as if to embrace or bless the audience. Flowers rained upon the stage about her feet.

The performance must have gone well, for Theia turned and bestowed a brilliant smile upon her and encouraged her to rise from the piano and step forward. Theia offered a gloved hand so they could take a bow together. Inez did, and then faded offstage to let the diva have her due and receive her final ovation.

Final.

Finale.

Fini.

How will she manage, when she awakes tomorrow morning and all the mornings after?

Graham came up beside her and said, "Excellent. You have earned every penny, Mrs. Stannert."

"Thank you." It felt like he was looming over her. She took a step away.

He added, "No need to return to the Palace Hotel. It's New Year's Eve. I'm certain you'd rather be elsewhere."

Still floating in the wake of the performance, she thought she had misheard, or misinterpreted. "But, my things—"

"I will arrange to send them to you in the morning. Your work is done, your contract complete, so we will take no more of your time." His gaze shifted, dismissing her and focusing on someone standing behind her. "Mrs. Robineau. Did you enjoy the performance?"

"Oh yes. Beautiful. Your wife, *magnifique*. Thank you for the seat."

"It was the least I could do. I understand she made many last-minute demands."

"Ah well," murmured Clarisse. "Is part of the business."

Theia beckoned for her husband to join her on the stage. Graham nodded at Inez and Clarisse, then moved toward his wife.

Inez turned back to the dressmaker, saying, "Now, we talk." But she addressed empty air.

Inez caught sight of the tiny figure slipping through a side door. She grabbed her cloak and gave chase.

The door led into a vast entrance hall, already filling with people. Finding Clarisse in the crowd would be impossible, but there was only one way out. Inez pushed her way through to the front doors with hurried apologies.

Outside, a crush of carriages blocked the street. Horses shook their manes, harnesses jingling, while drivers shouted and nudged their vehicles forward to gain a better position over their competitors. People milled about, some waiting for transportation, others taking to the sidewalks.

Clarisse was nowhere in sight.

Inez was certain the dressmaker knew something about Yvonne—where she was, where she'd gone, or where she was going. The dressmaker probably assumed she'd given Inez the slip, and wouldn't expect Inez to follow. It was New Year's Eve, after all. So, where would Clarisse go? The obvious answer was "home," behind her shop.

Inez set off. After two blocks, the sidewalks became less crowded, and Inez spotted a small figure hurrying ahead, her cloak sweeping left and then right. Inez slowed her pace to stay a half block behind, thinking it would be better to follow than confront.

Just short of the dress shop, Clarisse stopped. Inez stepped into the recessed doorway of a cutlery store. Clarisse turned in a circle, apparently checking the streets, then continued to her shop. Inez moved out of the doorway and increased her pace. A faint light shone from inside the shop, and a spark of victory coursed through her.

Clarisse, head bent, was intent on unlocking the shop door when Inez approached her, steps silent in satin slippers, well-suited for the concert hall. Clarisse pushed the door open, and Inez set a hand on her shoulder.

Clarisse gave a terrified squawk.

The door flew open, revealing Yvonne in the doorway. Theia's missing companion gasped and retreated into the shop. The light from a single lamp turned her pale hair white and painted dark shadows on her drawn features. "M-Madame Stannert?" she stuttered. "What are you doing here? What do you want?"

Inez herded Clarisse into her own shop and shut the door.

She noticed Yvonne was dressed for travel and that a reticule dangled from one arm. Two valises were packed and waiting inside the door.

Inez leaned against the closed door and crossed her arms, staring at the two women, one tall, one small.

"What I want," said Inez, "is the truth."

Chapter Forty-Two

Inez continued, "Yvonne, what happened to you? Christmas Day you just…disappeared. At least now I know where." She eyed Clarisse, who shrank under her gaze.

"I could not stay," said Yvonne faintly, then turned to Clarisse. "You are my friend. How could you betray me like this!"

Clarisse bristled. "I did not betray you, never."

Yvonne turned doubting eyes on Inez. "She did not," Inez assured her. "I asked her about you several times after your disappearance, and she never said a word."

"But you are here!"

"I followed her after she left the Grand," said Inez simply. "I suspected you two went to Mass together on Christmas. And who else would you turn to, if you were in trouble? So, now my question is, why did you leave?" Inez tried to temper intensity with gentleness. "Did it have to do with Miss Green's death? You can tell me, Yvonne. You can trust me. Please."

Clarisse poked Yvonne's sleeve. "Madame Stannert here, I think it is a sign. Talk to her. Tell her what you told me. Then you can leave with a clear conscience."

Thereafter followed a rapid-fire whispered argument between

the two in French, pitched too low and exchanged too quickly for Inez to interpret.

Whatever they said, Clarisse apparently won. Yvonne's shoulders fell, and the dressmaker said, "Come. We will all go to the back."

They moved to the rear of the store, into the workroom with its long table, dress forms, and all the accoutrements of a dressmaker's trade. Clarisse turned on the gaslights and lit a small stove. "I make tea and you talk." She pointed at a small table with two chairs.

Yvonne sank into one, Inez into the other. Inez wasted no time, figuring there might not be time to spare. "Yvonne, does this have to do with Julia Green's death? Do you know who did it? Is that why you left?"

Yvonne looked down at the table, worn and marked. "Yes," she whispered. "What happened that night, I knew. And then I made a promise, God forgive me. I could say nothing, but I could not stay and witness the evil and sin any longer."

Inez's mind raced. A promise to stay silent. A resultant guilt so strong Yvonne felt the need to flee and leave everything, *everything*, including incriminating letters and a scrapbook of memories behind. Inez could imagine only one person who commanded such power over Yvonne.

She reached out, covered Yvonne's cold hand with her own. "Theia?"

Yvonne slid her hand away from Inez's, covered her face. "Yes. Now, I have broken my promise. I will pay the price forever."

Clarisse pounced. "God does not honor a promise to sin or to hide a sin! God allows us to seek forgiveness from such promises, promises we are forced to make or make through our own stupidity or fear."

"Clarisse, you are not a priest," snapped Yvonne.

"What happened?" Inez said gently.

Yvonne shut her eyes tight. "What Julia accused her of, you heard, it was terrible."

Inez nodded, remembering how Theia had accused Julia of selling herself to advance her singing career, and how Julia had flung the accusation back in the diva's face. She now understood the words Julia had hurled at the diva, given Graham's advances and what the protégée had learned at the Melpomene.

"Then a note came for Madame. I slid it under the dressing room door. She must have read it. She came out with the beautiful cloak she always wears to performances, threw it at Julia, and said, 'Take it! Since you are the one they all want and I am done, it is yours!' She said she could not stand being there another minute with Julia. She took your overcoat for herself."

Well, that explains that, Inez thought. "It must have been difficult for you to hear and see all that," said Inez, trying to be sympathetic.

Yvonne's face fell in remembered misery. "A while later, Julia decided to go out. She looked for her own cloak, but it was missing, so she took Madame's. I should have given her mine."

"And you left the room as well?"

She glanced nervously from Inez to Clarisse. "Only for a short while. I looked outside, thinking Madame might be there. But I did not stay long. And then, Madame came back. She was shaking. She grabbed my arm, so tight it hurt. She said over and over, 'You never left my side. Say it! Swear it on the Bible!' So I did."

Clarisse gave her a cup of tea and put another one in front of Inez.

Inez said, "Go on."

Yvonne lifted the cup to her lips, then put it back down. "Madame's beautiful silk shoes were wet, soaked through. I offered to get her dry stockings and boots from the trunk, but she said no, do not open it." She stopped. "She would not allow me to look inside."

Inez nodded grimly. "Julia's missing cloak?"

"I cannot say," Yvonne whispered.

Inez sipped her tea. It was tepid, the water not having enough time to boil. "And then Mr. Drake appeared."

"And you and Julia were gone. Someone came to the door, saying that a woman had fallen over the railing to the rocks below, was certainly dead. And then I knew." Yvonne clutched the cross at her neck and closed her eyes. "By not saying anything, I am also responsible for her death."

"You didn't kill her," said Clarisse. "Don't take Madame's guilt upon yourself. She brought it on herself. And remember the dress."

"The what?" said Inez, confused.

"The ruined dress." Clarisse prodded Yvonne with a finger. "The missing gloves."

Concern rose in Inez's throat. "Are you talking about the dress that was destroyed?"

"I do not know," said Yvonne. "But, the gloves *are* missing. And, the dress was...."

She looked at Clarisse, who threw up her hands. "Why do you hesitate now? Such a little thing. You saw it. And I did too when I came to take the pieces away later." She turned to Inez. "The ruined dress, it buttoned up the back. Very tiny buttons, very tight fastenings."

"And?" Inez could not imagine where this was going.

Yvonne said, almost in a whisper, "The morning all the destruction was found, and Mr. de Bruijn came to see, Theia told him she undressed herself and put the dress on a chair. I heard her say it. But I looked at the dress when Mr. de Bruijn asked me to lay it on the floor and..." She stopped.

Clarisse sighed. "The front of the dress was ripped. The bodice, destroyed. I could not save any lace from it at all. But the back, it was *still* buttoned."

The light dawned. "You are saying Theia killed her pet, and since she couldn't undress herself..."

"Who would she call to help her undress, if not Yvonne?" said Clarisse. "And she did not call for Yvonne."

Inez rose. "I have to get back to the hotel. Find that trunk, find Mr. de Bruijn. She cannot get away with this."

Yvonne stood as well. "She had the trunk taken into her bedchamber. If you want to open it, you will need this." Yvonne opened her reticule and pulled out a ring of keys. She handed it to Inez, pointing out one. "The extra keys to her luggage. That one is for the trunk. I did not know what to do with them all. I thought of throwing them away, but..."

Inez pocketed the keys. "Does Graham suspect any of this? They had a dreadful row at the Melpomene last night."

Yvonne stood as well. "He is taking everything away from her. And I convinced her he would give her the world." Her face crumpled. "She loved another, but he had nothing. Mr. Drake had it all. He could give us," she corrected herself hastily, "give *her* a life that was secure, safe. For when you have nothing, what is love? You cannot eat it. It cannot shelter you."

"The Melpomene, before Graham. What happened there?"

Yvonne shook her head. "It was long ago. We never speak of it."

"If Graham found out about it, what do you think he would do?"

Yvonne's pale complexion went paler and she clutched Inez's hand. "Save her!"

This is what things have come to—I am being asked to save a murderess.

Inez disentangled herself from Yvonne's grip. "I must go. You are leaving too?"

"On the next ferry, after midnight. I will try to start another life, somewhere else."

Inez thought of the first time she had seen Theia: her pet bird Aria chained to her wrist, held tight with the bracelet woven from John Teague's hair. Yvonne following in her every step. The haunted look in de Bruijn's eyes when the subject of the Melpomene and Theia came up and his refusal to speak of it.

Aria was not the only one Theia had chained to herself.

Inez wondered if Yvonne would ever truly be able to start a new life or if she would forever be haunted by the old. She could not wish Yvonne well; after all, she had known but did not say. But still. Inez gave Yvonne's hand a final squeeze. "May you find peace."

Clarisse tugged Inez away from Yvonne and toward the front of the store. She whispered, "I hope you find what you need and they take Madame away and punish her as she deserves!"

"You do?" Inez was confounded by her animosity.

As she unlocked the door, Clarisse said, "She killed her own protégée, the one she called a daughter. She has destroyed how many lives, Yvonne's too. I knew Yvonne from the days of Melpomene. Madame took her and used her faith and loyalty to twist and destroy her. The Golden Songbird does not care about anyone but herself. When she says 'Do not tell anyone!' that is when one should speak. Do not let her twist you too, Madame Stannert."

"Scant chance of that," said Inez, pulling up her hood to cover her hair from the mist.

"And, it is curious. When I was making the last alterations to her gown, she said to me, 'Do not tell anyone' and I did not understand why." She leaned out the open door, frowning. "Why would Madame insist I keep quiet about the pocket she wanted sewn into her dress?"

Chapter Forty-Three

Inez wasted no time returning to the Palace Hotel. New Year's Eve inched ever closer to midnight, with no empty hacks in sight. She raced back on foot, dodging clumps of late-night strollers taking the air and preparing to welcome the end of an old year and the start of a new. As she did, she wondered if she might be too late.

Although, what did "too late" mean, under the circumstances?

Too late to break into Theia's room, upend her trunk, and look for any other evidence that she had murdered Julia?

Too late to keep Graham Drake from doing whatever he might be tempted to do to his wife, assuming he knew some or all of her secrets?

Too late to keep Theia from doing something rash with the gun that Inez was certain lay concealed in a hidden pocket of her elegant ball gown?

Merrymakers crowded the entrance and reception areas of the Palace Hotel. A long line waited for the rising rooms, but Inez wasn't waiting for anything. She dashed up the stairs, holding her skirts a little higher than proper to keep from tripping. At least she didn't have to deal with the inconvenience of a skirt train. She remembered Theia *did* have a train and that she and Graham had some kind of celebratory, farewell "do" at the Grand Opera House after the event. With luck, they wouldn't be back until after midnight and would have to wait for the elevators with everyone else. Inez hoped to be long gone from the suite by then.

She squeezed past those going up and down the staircase, glad she'd kept the keys to Yvonne's rooms. Once inside the dark music room, Inez lit a hand lamp. With the skin on the back of her neck prickling, she hurried toward the door that led to Theia's quarters.

She breathed a silent prayer to whatever god was keeping watch over her when she found the key to Theia's private rooms in its place, hanging behind the drape covering the interconnecting door. That key went into the pocket of her cloak with the others. She kept the dress pocket free of everything but her revolver.

De Bruijn's advice floated up into her consciousness and she discarded it. *Scream first, be damned.* If anyone dared to threaten her, or if it looked like someone was about to get shot or maimed, she would pull the gun first and *then* scream.

Once inside Theia's private parlor, Inez eased the door half shut and tugged the drape back over to hide the fact it was not completely closed. Once she entered Theia's bedchamber, she wanted to be sure she could hear if someone entered the music room. If that happened, she figured she would exit Theia's rooms into the hallway. If she heard someone coming directly into Theia's rooms, trapping her in the bedchamber, she could hide under a bed.

Again.

In one of her best dresses.

She hoped it wouldn't come to that.

Inez held the lamp up and looked around the parlor. The two oxblood vases stood sentry on either side of the fireplace. Ladies' chairs, a draped table, two étagères crowded with bric-a-brac and small statuettes.

She proceeded into the bedroom. Aware that the lamplight could give her away and give her less time to hide or escape, Inez ripped open the curtains covering the large bay window. She extinguished her lamp and surveyed the room. The moon shed light enough to fling shadows about, presenting everything in the starkest of contrasts: black and white, hardly a gray in sight.

Just like Theia. Black, or white. All or nothing.

Though determined to do this, she felt like an interloper, even a betrayer. *If this is how it is for me after such a short time, how must Yvonne have felt, staying years and years before finally tearing herself away.*

Midnight was closing in, the year 1881 nearly at an end. The revelry outside the window grew louder, and Inez thought she heard the boom of fireworks and the bang of guns.

She went straight to the ottoman by the wall, throwing the pillows and lace coverlet aside to reveal the trunk, its lock facing the wall. She dragged it about and pulled out the keys Yvonne had given her.

Which one is it?

She could not recall.

Inez feverishly began trying one key after another. *How many trunks did Theia bring with her? Thirty? Forty?* She stopped and muttered, "Pull yourself together." *With this many trunks and keys, they must have a system.*

She shoved the trunk so the moonlight fell full on the lock and studied the hasp. The decorative metal cover had a number scratched into it: 19. Inez examined the keys and her heart leapt to find each also had a number. It took but a moment to find key 19, fit it to the lock, and spring the hasp. Inez grabbed the metal plate and, using it as a handle, pulled up the lid. She reached into the shadowed interior, almost expecting a snake or some other guardian of secrets to bite her. The first thing she drew out was Theia's dressing gown—the pinks and silvers of the embroidery bleached dead-white and colorless by the moonlight, the silk slippery in her fingers. She reached in again. Paper crackled at her touch, a small hard object next to it.

Inez's breath caught. She withdrew both and turned to the wash of pale light to verify what they were.

Julia's pocket diary for 1881 and her signed contract with the Grand Opera House.

Anger and sorrow tore inside her, fighting for dominance. "So, Theia, it was you in Julia's room that night," she whispered. "You got what you wanted and then erased all trace of her."

Guilt gone, Inez returned to the trunk. This time, her exploring fingers touched what she had hoped to find. Soft wool, worn, warm. She pulled out the long, slow length of Julia's cloak. The wrap Julia had "lost" at the Cliff House. The mantle, a vibrant crimson in sunlight, was black as the grave in Inez's hands.

"Theia, why?" Inez murmured. The prima donna had had everything. Wealth. Health. Beauty. Now, her life would be little better than ashes.

She would have to find de Bruijn. Tell him what she found.

Inez hastily repacked the trunk with the tell-tale items, shoved it against the wall, and replaced the coverlet and the cushions. She had barely set foot in Theia's private parlor on her way to traversing the suite to Yvonne's rooms when she heard the door to the music room open.

Graham's voice came through loud and clear, "You wanted me to send Mrs. Stannert away, and you wanted to be back before midnight, and so we are. The matter facing us now, Theia, is, how we proceed from here."

Light glowed and grew around the edges of the heavy curtain covering the open door leading to the music room. Inez backed up a step, weighing her options. Retreat to the bedroom? No, she would be trapped there. Best to exit into the hallway now, while she had the chance. She bumbled past the fireplace, heading toward the hallway door. The muted hiss of ceramic scraping stone warned her of impending disaster. She whirled around to see an oxblood vase full of artificial flowers begin its tumble to the hearth. She grabbed the lip of the vase, preventing a crash.

Artful buds, blooms, and greenery slithered out and scattered. She righted the vase, only to hear something slither and slide inside, with a metallic sibilance. She plunged her hand in and pulled out—

A pair of elegant beaded gloves. They looked very much like the ones Theia was wearing when Inez had first met her. The ones that Yvonne claimed had disappeared.

No longer listening to the voices in the music room, Inez shook out the gloves to be sure they were the ones she remembered. Three small feathers drifted to the floor. They appeared white in the dim light leaching from the other room, but Inez would have bet her last dollar they were yellow. The kid palms were stained, smeared with a dried dark substance.

Inez became aware of Graham and Theia's voices in the next room, increasing in intensity, a symphony of accusations flying back and forth.

Outside the floor-to-ceiling bay window, fireworks flickered, shattering the cool moonlight. Inez, gripping the gloves, hesitated. She knew she should replace the gloves, clean up the mess, and leave. But was there time? Suppose Theia, Graham, or both came in and found her there?

"The charade is over, Theia."

"What do you mean?"

His voice was cold, hers colder still.

Graham continued, "Now I know how low you stooped before we married. I know what you are. No longer will I cater to your every whim. From now on, you will do exactly as I say."

"Oh, I don't think so." Theia's tone shifted, iron added to the ice. "From now on, I will do exactly as I *wish*."

The crackle and flash of fireworks outside disappeared beneath the bang of a gun.

Throwing aside caution, Inez abandoned her stance by the fireplace. Gloves in one hand, pocket revolver in the other, she rushed the drape and shoved it aside.

The brilliant gaslight in the music room dazzled her eyes. Squinting, Inez saw Graham, face down on the carpet, blood from his head beginning to soak the rug deep red. And Theia, kneeling beside him, trying to force a gun into his limp hand.

Chapter Forty-Four

Horror cascaded over Inez. "My god. Theia, what have you done?"

Theia looked up. Under the bright gaslights, her eyes gleamed amber, wild as a cornered animal's.

Inez's blood ran cold.

Theia struggled to her feet, the gun dangling from her hand, pointing at her husband.

Inez stepped forward, trying to see if Graham was breathing. She kept her own revolver raised, pointed to the side, ready to aim at Theia if necessary.

Theia's free hand went to her mouth. A muffled sob escaped. "He took his own life. I tried to take the gun away from him, before he used it, but I was too late."

Suddenly, she seemed to realize that her audience of one had not been choreographed into the scene. "Inez, what are you doing here?" Her eyes narrowed as she regarded Inez's hand. "Are those my gloves?"

Inez held them out, the dark stains clear in the overhead gaslights, one lone yellow feather still caught in the beading. "I found where you hid them," said Inez. From the corner of her vision, she thought she saw Graham's fingers twitch.

All that blood. Could he still be alive?

She inched sideways, hoping to distract the diva from him. The surest way to do that, she reasoned, was to keep Theia off balance. Push her with words, put *her* on the defensive for once.

Inez added an edge of accusation to her voice. "You killed your pet, didn't you? I know you and Graham had a violent argument that evening. I imagine you wanted to strangle him, but you turned your rage on that poor little creature instead."

"I would never. Aria was a gift from Graham," she said defensively.

"All the more reason. And what about Julia? Was her sin against you so grievous you had to kill her?"

Theia sneered. "She thought she could *sing*. She was but a shadow of the Golden Songbird. She thought to replace me. On the stage and in my bed." Revulsion darkened her visage. "She *betrayed* me!"

The loathing in her face vanished, replaced by a melancholia bright as moonlight and twice as false. "She broke his heart, you know. Now, he can join her. I shall mourn him, remember him as he was when he first loved me. When my mourning is done I shall return to singing and John—"

She stopped and bit her lip.

John Teague. Was that what all this is about?

Clarity dawned for Inez. Regaining John Teague's affection wasn't the goal, at least not the ultimate one. Theia wanted him back in her orbit, certainly, but there was something more she craved and longed for. Something she had to possess at any and all costs: to be center stage in life. Forever.

The muzzle of Theia's gun rose fractionally, now pointing at the rug between the diva and Inez. "Don't tell anyone!" she whispered.

The very words Clarisse warned me about. Inez took another step toward Graham. "Theia, put down the gun. Don't make this worse."

Theia backed toward the hallway door. "We can say that

Graham came after you, and you shot him in self-defense. Or that he attacked me, and you saved my life. They will believe us! How could they not? I'll call for Wolter. He knows Graham's temper. He will understand and—"

"Theia, stop!"

She didn't stop. Her small gun inched up again, aiming at Inez's feet.

Now able to see Theia's weapon clearly, Inez blinked. *My god, she bought a gun just like mine.*

Theia had her back against the hall door. The sounds of midnight festivity rang through the windows and the walls as celebrants and passersby shouted out the old year and cheered in the new.

Inez raised her weapon as well and held her breath, wondering if Theia would really pull the trigger. Inez deemed herself the better shot, but she wasn't certain she could shoot Theia in cold blood. More to the point, could Theia shoot *her*?

It might not take long, Inez thought grimly, for the diva to realize that two dead bodies on the carpet, with only one person left alive to explain the circumstances, might be the best solution to her messy situation.

Theia opened the hallway door at her back, gun now leveled at Inez's waist. The roar of revelry poured into the room. Theia's hand was now visibly shaking. It would take very little pressure on the trigger...

"Theia, stop!" Inez said again, with as much authority as she could muster.

Theia stepped into the hallway and began screaming for help.

Gambling that the singer would not shoot, now that she was screaming, Inez hurried to Graham's side. His head was a bloody mess. He didn't seem to be moving. She couldn't tell if he was alive or dead. She reached for his wrist.

Two porters and a night watchman poured in through the doorway.

Theia shouted at Inez, "Get away from my husband!" The force of her words struck Inez like a physical blow.

Inez hastily stood and backed away.

Theia turned to the Palace staff, who were agape at the scene, and cried, "She shot him! This woman, Inez Stannert, killed my husband!"

Chapter Forty-Five

JANUARY 1

"Don't let her go!" Inez shouted back. "*She's* the one who pulled the trigger."

However, Theia's hands were now empty, the gun, vanished.

Inez lowered her Smoot. "She has a pocket revolver. Check the right-hand side of—"

De Bruijn and the night manager Adams appeared, pushing aside the flabbergasted Palace staff. "Good God!" exclaimed Adams.

Seeing de Bruijn, Inez exhaled in relief.

Theia wailed, "Wolter!" and threw herself at him, and his arm went around her. To keep her from falling? To reassure her that he was there, to take care of her?

Inez suddenly felt very alone.

Adams hurried to Graham Drake and took his wrist. He turned to the night watchman. "Get the house physician! This man is still alive."

Inez added, "No thanks to his wife, who tried to kill him and blame his death on me."

Theia blanched, then pointed dramatically at Inez. "We trusted Mrs. Stannert and look how she repays us! She shot my husband!"

Inez countered, "Mrs. Drake's accusation is ridiculous, falla-cious, and a fabrication. I did not shoot anyone."

Adams held out his hand to Inez. "Madam, please, your pistol."

Inez watched de Bruijn, tracking his reaction. The initial shock on his face at Theia's accusation had been followed by dismay. Inez's assertion of innocence had only seemed to transform his dismay into doubt. His eyes narrowed. He appeared to be weigh-ing her word against Theia's.

Stung, Inez turned to the diva. "Mrs. Drake," she said coldly, "I'll wager you have never held or shot a gun before now. Oh! Pardon, I misspoke. I believe you used the firearm now hiding in your pocket to shoot out Luis Rubio's window at the Grand four nights ago."

Theia's chin rose. Her face turned ugly in anger. "You lie! You are the one who threatened to kill Señor Rubio. Not I."

Inez surrendered her gun to Adams, grip first. He took it from her.

"You are the one lying," Inez continued. "You usually do it so well, I'm surprised that you are so unconvincing now." She looked at de Bruijn and then at Adams. "I ask you to consider, who benefits from Mr. Drake's death? Not I."

A man with a dressing gown thrown over his trousers pushed his way inside. "Out, all of you," he said tersely. Carrying the black bag of a physician, he hurried to Graham's side.

Gripping Inez's arm tightly, Adams steered her out into the hall.

Face-to-face with Theia, Inez said, "What of your plans now?" She turned her attention to de Bruijn. "Theia directed Clarisse to sew a pocket into this dress. She is right-handed, so check underneath the draperies." Inez waved a finger at the gold folds of material embellishing the sides of the skirt. "On the right side seam. Just below the waist."

De Bruijn started to comply.

Theia seized his hand. "You believe her over me?" She gazed at him imploringly.

His gaze flicked to Inez. "I believe in evidence," he said, extracting himself from Theia's grasp. Evading her attempt to stop him, he removed the gun from her pocket.

"It's the same model as mine," said Inez. "Now, for the evidence." She turned to Adams. "Would you check the number of rounds in my revolver and tell us what you find?"

Adams rotated the cylinder. He looked up at Inez and then de Bruijn. "All there."

Inez turned to de Bruijn. "Now, Mrs. Drake's revolver."

Theia grabbed de Bruijn's arm. "I might have shot at her when it happened. I truly can't recall. It was so terrifying, seeing her standing there, waiting for us, and shooting Graham like that. If I did, I was only protecting myself! I think she wanted to kill me too! It's only because I screamed and had my own gun that she didn't dare."

While she talked—pleaded—de Bruijn glanced at the night watchman. The detective stepped away from Theia as the watchman advanced, saying, "Ma'am, please step back."

De Bruijn spun the cylinder and announced, "Two fired cartridges."

"The gunpowder scent should still be there," Inez said.

He passed the muzzle beneath his nose and looked at her.

She raised her eyebrows.

He nodded, and his expression said it all. She saw that he believed her, but it had been the evidence, not his trust in her, that had convinced him. It was not what she had hoped for, but it would have to do.

For now.

Chapter Forty-Six

LATER IN JANUARY

Some days after "the incident," Inez was summoned back to the Palace Hotel, at Graham Drake's request. It was a request in word only, given that Drake had sent his messenger Toby *and* a hired hack to fetch her.

When she stepped into the music room, Inez's first thought was she had entered the wrong suite. All traces of Theia had been swept away. Her displays of fashionable attire, the feminine touches throughout, the extra armoire and her multitude of trunks—all of it, gone. The original hotel furniture was back in place. The only object left from before was the Broadwood piano. Graham Drake sat in one of the chairs arranged by the fireplace. His valet stood at his elbow, looking prepared to catch him if he should keel over.

One side of Graham's head and face was bandaged. Inez wondered if he had lost an eye. If so, she reasoned, he had emerged from his brush with death a very "Lucky Duck" indeed.

He said, "Forgive me for not standing," and indicated a chair facing his on the other side of the hearth. As she approached, he added, "I understand I have you to thank for saving my life." His voice wavered, sounding hoarse.

She sat. "I am glad to see you. I had not heard as to"—she didn't want to say *whether you survived being shot in the head*, so she finished with—"your health."

He gave her a tight, polite smile that was essentially no smile at all. "We shall arrange for the return of your piano, plus pay whatever balance is owed for its use. I look forward to revisiting your store in the future. Your Chinaman has excellent taste in Oriental antiquities. I intend to add more of his selections to my collection."

She waved a hand, as much to acknowledge his words as to brush the small talk aside. "What has happened to your wife?"

There had been no notice in the newspapers. No word from de Bruijn, who had left early New Year's Day on another assignment. And now, with the parlor room cleared of Theia's possessions, it was as if she had been erased.

Graham turned his head and nodded stiffly to Charles. The valet moved a discreet distance away.

Graham returned his attention to Inez. "My wife is very ill. She has been examined by two physicians, and they concur. She is where she can do no more harm. She is being treated."

"But, she *killed* Miss Green. She is a murderess."

"The police say Miss Green took her own life. The evidence supports their conclusions."

She could not believe what she was hearing and wanted to retort that the *lack* of evidence had allowed them to take the easy way out. But even so. "She tried to kill *you!*"

He touched the bandage, then, as if realizing what he was doing, lowered his hand to his trousered leg. That hand clenched into a fist. "Evidence of her obvious mental imbalance. From the moment we arrived in the city, she became even more difficult to control, more quarrelsome, more willful—more inclined to perceive insult and injury. And now, I understand why, given her past history in San Francisco, which she kept from me, by the way. I only heard the whole of it from Yates. Coming back here unhinged her."

He shifted in his chair.

Suddenly on the alert, Charles looked over from where he stood by the bay window. When Graham made no other sign, the valet returned to his examination of the view.

"She was obsessed with Julia," Graham continued. "Obsessed with the idea that I was unfaithful to her. Which I never was."

That statement, pure and simple, stated as fact, convinced Inez beyond any other he had uttered that he was lying to her.

"Her fantasies and obsessions encouraged unhealthy brooding and led to her downward spiral. She saw betrayal around every corner."

Inez could not deny that. Theia had seen herself as the victim in every scene. *But that does not make her mad.*

He continued, "You were witness to the end result, but you did not see her decline, which was underway before you met."

Something stirred inside Inez. Shapes, hidden until now, shifted and rose out of darkness.

"You did this." She didn't even bother to frame it as a question. "This is the outcome you wanted. You wanted her declared mad. You wanted her out of the way. Theia wanted to sing, to continue being who she was and had always been. You did not. When she refused to bend, when she fought you, she became a…liability."

"Mrs. Stannert, my wife's health and well-being is my business, not yours. She is where she will be well taken care of and out of harm's way."

"Where?" Inez knew she was stepping far beyond the limits of the conversation Graham had probably plotted out for their meeting, but she would not retreat. "Where has Theia been committed?"

The moments ticked past. His eye did not waver.

He finally said, "I find your little store a charming place. An asset to the community. I am certain you would like it to remain so in the future. In that regard, I could be your ally." Left unspoken were the words "or your enemy."

She gaped at the wealthy publisher. *Is he threatening me?* Her mouth snapped shut, and she found it difficult to breathe.

His stony-eyed gaze pinned her to the chair. "I understand you encouraged my wife to buy the gun she had in her possession. Why, I wonder. Did you have a target for her in mind?"

"I had nothing in mind," said Inez, pressing her back into the tufted cushion behind her. "Mrs. Drake inquired about my revolver, so I gave her the particulars. I did not encourage her to buy one. In fact, she told me she was going to ask you to purchase a firearm for her."

Graham glanced toward the bay window. "Again, I look forward to visiting your store, once I recover." She followed his gaze. Standing next to the pulled-back drapes was the blood-red vase he had bought for Theia the first time he had been to her store— the vase that had hidden her gloves. "As I said, I am impressed with your store's selection. I know a number of investors who are looking for purveyors of fine Oriental objects of high quality. I will recommend your business to them." He turned to his valet. "Charles, please show Mrs. Stannert out."

———

After this unsatisfactory non-discussion, Inez couldn't wait to corner de Bruijn. Her chance came the next morning.

She received word from her Palace Hotel "contact" that the investigator had returned. As soon as she heard, she left her store and stormed into his office, catching him in his shirtsleeves and looking travel-worn.

She berated him without mercy.

The first words she spoke were not the ones she intended, but out they came. "You believed *her* over me. How *could* you?"

"I apologize," said de Bruijn. "Once I saw her revolver, I knew I was in error. I should have trusted that, under the circumstances, you were speaking the truth."

"Yes, you should have," said Inez, not entirely mollified.

He added, "You were correct all along about my emotions clouding my observations."

She relented a little more, but was not willing to forgive him entirely. Not yet.

With him behaving so charmingly apologetic, Inez sensed she had the advantage. She pressed forward.

"So, Mr. de Bruijn. Did you have your talk with Mr. Yates? Are you going to tell me what happened at the Melpomene those years past?" She sat in the leather chair across from his desk. "Because I am not leaving until you do."

He capitulated and told her.

Once he had finished, she felt satisfied, or at least vindicated. "If you had confided in me earlier, much of this could have been avoided."

"Perhaps." He rubbed the back of his neck.

She continued, "And do you know what Graham has done to her?" She described her conversation with Graham Drake, finishing with, "We should do something! This is all so unfair."

"And what," de Bruijn said with that damning calm of his, "would you have me do at this stage? Report Mrs. Drake to the police for the attempted murder of her husband? Her husband will clearly refuse to testify against her. Your word against his. Do you want to proceed down that road? The Palace Hotel staff will not wish to go against Mr. Drake's decision."

"But Theia killed Miss Green! She pushed her over the rail at the Cliff House."

"Did she confess this to you?"

Inez thought of her conversation in the music room with Theia, while Graham lay senseless between them, bleeding into the carpet. "Not in so many words."

"Your proof, then?"

"Yvonne knew. She was in the waiting room and saw Theia afterwards. Heard what she said."

"Is Yvonne prepared to explain all this to the police?"

Inez looked away. "She left the city for parts unknown, as you are probably aware."

"Do you have anything else we can take to the authorities?"

"I found Julia's cloak in the trunk Theia had at the Cliff House." Even as she said it, she knew what he would say to that: *And what does that prove?* Answer: It proves only that Julia's cloak ended up in the trunk, and we cannot prove who put it there or why or even when. Next question: *Where is the trunk?* Answer: Probably gone.

But de Bruijn didn't say anything. He just spread his empty hands wide on the desktop, looking immeasurably tired.

Inez sighed. "Theia fooled everyone, didn't she? Graham had his own reasons for encouraging her extreme behavior, assuming he did so. Yvonne did not want to believe what her eyes and heart told her. It took Julia's death for Yvonne to see Theia had reached the point where she would not allow anyone to stand in her way. And what did Yvonne do, once she knew? She ran. She was afraid of Theia. Probably also afraid of Graham."

Inez shook her head in disgust. Partly at Yvonne, partly at herself, and partly at de Bruijn. "We should have paid more attention as to who was doing all the finger-pointing. Who played the victim, over and over, in each scenario."

Inez looked down at her hands in her lap. Her fingers twitched, moving through the opening notes for "Ave Maria."

"Theia chose the song, set the meter of the music, and we all danced to her tune. The more fool we."

"We did what we could, under the circumstances," de Bruijn said. He stood and walked around the desk. She stood as well, thinking they were done.

Instead he said, "The performances at the Melpomene and the Grand were the first times I have heard you play."

Inez thought about it. "I suppose that would be the case."

"From the stage, you could not see the faces of the audience, so I suppose it is up to me to tell you." He took her by the shoulders.

"You have a gift, Mrs. Stannert. To ease the daily burdens of others through music, to provide an escape, if only for a while."

He released her. She could still feel the press of his fingertips on the back of her shoulders as he said, "Beyond that, you ease the burdens of the women who come to you for aid and financial assistance. We all try to make the world right, however we can. Sometimes, the grand gestures of justice elude us, and we must be content with working in the shadows, bringing about justice in smaller ways."

He escorted her toward the door.

She trailed alongside him. "I suppose your words are meant to console me, Mr. de Bruijn. Thank you. Speaking of justice, what of the hotel porter who was unfairly fired, Jacob Freeman? Did he get his small piece of justice?"

De Bruijn opened the door. "He has a new job at the Baldwin Hotel. And I am hiring him for certain tasks in my own line of work." He gave her a small smile. "Working in the shadows, as it were. We shall meet again, Mrs. Stannert. And soon."

———

The carriage stopped in front of the Napa State Asylum for the Insane, and Inez brushed the travel dust from the front of her overcoat. John Teague stepped out of the carriage and offered Inez his hand. "I hope we are not making a mistake," he said under his breath.

Inez suspected he had been mulling this over since they'd left San Francisco.

"Are you losing courage now?" she asked. "You can wait for me, if you prefer."

He shook his head. "I did not think he would bury her alive like this," muttered Teague. "She is his wife, for God's sake."

When she'd devised a covert plan for seeing Theia one last time, she had pondered who to choose as a confederate. At first, she considered de Bruijn. But he was a man who kept his secrets so close that not even the most skillful picker of locks could prevail, and she was leery as to whether he had truly told her everything about his past connection to Theia. So instead, she approached John Teague, who wore his heart on his sleeve.

Now, with their objective just up the steps and through the archway, Teague was vacillating.

Giving him a moment to compose himself, Inez dug around in her purse for the sealed letter that would guarantee their entrance. Envelope in hand, she turned to him. "I meant to say earlier, I was impressed that you managed to acquire several sheets of Graham's business letterhead. How did you accomplish that? Certainly you did not simply waltz into the newspaper building and ask for it. And the missive you composed was magnificent. Truly. No one would suspect it was manufactured out of whole cloth. And typed so neatly. You could have been a professional typewriter!"

That brought out a small smile beneath his neatly trimmed mustache and beard. "I still have connections and sympathizers at the *Times*. As for the letter itself, Graham and I were friends. Once. I knew him well. Or thought I did." He slid her a glance. "But even I couldn't replicate his signature. It looks the genuine article to me."

Standing one step above him, she winked. "I had several contracts signed by him. A little practice beforehand was required, I admit. The flourish on the D in Drake is distinctive."

"You have the makings of an excellent forger, Mrs. Stannert." She smiled. "Shall we?"

He stepped up and squinted at the words carved in the arch ahead. "In Temperance learn thou to live," he murmured. "I cannot imagine Theia ever living temperately. With her, it was all or nothing. Pure passion in the moment."

She took his arm; they walked under the arch to the door and knocked.

The door was opened by a gentleman in a proper suit and tie.

Inez had almost expected the door to be opened by an attendant of the insane, all in white and looking a bit crazed himself. She dropped Teague's arm and presented the letter. "We are here to visit Mrs. Carrington Drake. We are her cousins."

He seemed to hesitate. "We have permission from her husband to visit. Please, see for yourself." Inez flapped the letter at him until he took it. She extracted a handkerchief from her purse, murmuring, "Such a sad state of affairs. We would have come sooner, but we live at some distance."

Teague addressed her solicitously. "Calm yourself. Our cousin is in excellent hands. This asylum is one of the finest public institutions of its type."

The greeter, having scanned the letter, said, "Please, wait here inside. I shall find Mrs. Drake's doctor." He let them into a large entryway and marched away down a long hall dotted with windows that painted rectangles of sunlight on the polished wood floor.

A long, curving staircase to the left led up into a mysterious beyond. Voices, but no words, floated down from the floors above.

Inez took Teague's arm again in reassurance. A door slam echoed. Inez saw two figures—the squarely-built attendant and another, taller man—marching their way. Inez felt Teague's arm tense beneath her fingers. "Steady, cousin," she murmured.

Once they came closer, Inez saw that the taller gentleman, dressed in a very proper suit and wearing no-nonsense spectacles, had her letter in one hand and a welcoming smile on his long-boned face. The attendant went up the stairs while the gentleman introduced himself as Dr. Gardner. Gardner added, "How kind of you to come visit Mrs. Drake. Your cousin? Yes! I believe I see the resemblance around the eyes. Please, this way. An attendant has gone to fetch the lady herself. She is resting, as all our patients do this time of day."

He led them past the staircase into one of the wings of the building, saying, "We are a modern institution, with a bakery, kitchen, gasworks, laundry, mending room, infirmaries. Each patient room is well-ventilated and illuminated by a window."

"What of Theia herself and her condition?" asked Inez. "Is she improving?"

Dr. Gardner raised his eyebrows. "Did not Mr. Drake explain to you?"

Inez adopted a sorrowful expression. "He did not wish to talk about it. I believe it pains him. He said it was best if we asked you."

Dr. Gardner nodded, sympathetic. "A common response. It is very difficult for most to reflect or speak of loved ones who are not 'with us,' so to speak." He stopped by a door, and said, "The mind is a delicate and complicated mechanism. When we consider how the insane were handled mere decades ago, we must be thankful that these unfortunates are now treated with sympathy, with comfortable accommodations, nourishing food, and reliable medical care."

Teague broke in. "What, exactly, are her treatments? Does she take medications?"

"We administer paraldehyde regularly. It helps to calm manic patients. Mrs. Drake was," the physician hesitated, "difficult, at first. But medications, hydrotherapy, a firm hand, and an invaried routine have helped. She is now quite content." He opened the door. "I understand she was a famous singer. No wonder this is her favorite room."

The hard leather soles of their shoes clacked on the hardwood floor as they entered a long room. Chairs lined the bare walls, with a grand piano placed so the player could look through the window bars onto the gardens and orchards beyond. A sunbeam fell upon the keyboard, bathing the white and black keys with light.

Inez heard a voice outside the room say, "Mrs. Drake, you have visitors! Cousins."

Inez and Teague turned simultaneously to the door. Framed in the doorway, Theia blinked as if she had been asleep and was just awakening. Her hair, one of her vanities, was skimmed back into a plain knot. She wore a simple, wrinkled gray dress, gray stockings, gray slippers. She looked at Inez and Teague with an incurious blank stare.

Teague started toward her. The attendant said cheerily, "I'll be waiting out in the hall if you need anything. When you are done visiting, just give a call." He and the doctor left the room, closing the door behind them.

"Theia!" said Teague.

Theia turned a silent visage toward him. He grasped one of her hands. "Theia. Do you remember me? John. John Teague."

She slowly tipped her head to one side, as if pondering.

He pulled out his watch chain, unhooked the fob, and held it out to her. "You gave this to me. Back in Virginia City."

Theia looked but did not touch.

Everything about her was so still, so unlike the Theia that Inez remembered. It was unnerving, as if she had expected an exuberant rushing river only to find a still-water pond in its place.

Teague whispered, "What have they done to you?"

Unable to stand the heartbreaking scene, Inez moved to the piano, her solace in difficult times. She began to play, scales at first, changing the rhythm from one set to another, varying the tempo, nothing strenuous, just creating soft, slow music to fill the hollow room. Then, because she was with Theia and the memories of their times together on stage came rushing back, Inez segued into "Ave Maria."

Halfway through, letting the melody flow around her, Inez became aware that Theia had approached and now stood near, one white hand resting on the piano lid.

Still playing, Inez looked up. Theia's eyes, the brown-yellow irises almost swallowed by large black pupils, widened a bit. Her unfocused gaze sharpened and her lips parted. Inez, fingers moving languidly through the melody, held her breath, hoping, waiting, for the singer to awake and complete the music.

Theia released a long sigh. The awareness flickering in her face disappeared.

She wandered away from Inez, from Teague, and went to the open window. Inez finished and let the music fade and die. Birdsong wafted in through the window. A soft breeze ruffled Theia's hair and she crossed her arms, hugging herself.

Inez looked at Teague, a man bereft, still holding the fob created from the hair of his beloved, who no longer knew him.

"If your affection and this music cannot bring her back," Inez said to him, "she is gone."

Unable to gaze upon his face any longer, Inez rose from the piano bench. The sunbeam still slanted across the keys. Brilliant whites, darkest blacks.

No shades of gray.

All or nothing.

Inez gently lowered the keyboard cover, extinguishing the light.

———

The memory of Theia at the asylum haunted Inez when she least expected it. Now, for instance, as she waited for the ferry carrying Antonia and Carmella to release its passengers. A stiff breeze from the bay tugged at Inez's overcoat, and she pulled it closer, forcing herself to the present. The blast of the ferry horn was followed by a few passengers trickling down the gangplank. The trickle turned into a flood. Inez strained for a sight of her ward.

"Mrs. S!" Halfway down the plank, Antonia waved wildly. Carmella Donato, hidden under her veil, followed behind.

Inez held out her arms and the girl rushed her so fiercely she almost bowled Inez over. Inez laughed, the first spontaneous, happy laugh in a long time. "So, my dear Antonia, did you have a pleasant holiday?"

"Did I ever! We should go back sometime so you can meet

Carmella's family. Aunts, uncles, sooo many cousins. I missed you!" She hugged Inez fiercely.

"I missed you too."

Antonia turned her head and rested her cheek against Inez's cloak. "Did you have a good Christmas, Mrs. S? "

"Yes, I had a nice Christmas. Very quiet."

Antonia tipped her head up to see Inez. Inez pushed back the wild, dark hair that had escaped the girl's braids and straightened her crooked bonnet. She marveled at Antonia's browned skin. The girl had clearly spent much time outside without a hat, but Inez did not have the heart to give her even a gentle scold.

"Well, good. Because I had a *very* excellent Christmas!" Antonia clapped hands to her mouth. "Not that I didn't miss being here and all. But you should see where Carmella's relatives live. They have a farm. And an orchard. And chickens! And a huge garden! And a barn!"

Inez pictured her little hooligan running wild with a roiling, rambunctious crew of dark-haired Donatos, chasing chickens, probably throwing eggs at each other, clambering up into the rafters of the barn, and scrambling to the topmost branches of the trees.

Antonia added, "And I got something really special for Christmas." She turned to Carmella and took the basket from her. Inez heard a scrabbling inside, then a little peep or squeak. Inez closed her eyes. *Please, Lord. Not a bird.*

When Inez opened her eyes, Carmella had pulled up her veil and was gazing at her apologetically. "Antonia just so very much wanted one. I could not say no."

Antonia set the basket on the ground and opened one end, plunging her hands inside.

"A canary?" asked Inez, steeling herself.

"Better than that!" crowed Antonia, pulling out a tiny, mewling gray furball with four little paws, claws extended. "A kitten!"

Inez looked at Carmella reproachfully. *How could you?*

Carmella said quickly, "We have discussed this, Antonia and I. We have an agreement, pending your approval. The kitten will live with me, in my house. And, Antonia can come visit as often as she likes. Or as often as you allow, I should say."

"And I got to name her! You'll like this, Mrs. S., because you gave me the idea when you took me to hear that singer," said Antonia happily. "Kitty likes to sing, so she is *Mia Miss Diva*! That means 'my little singer' in Italian. Or something like that." She clutched the kitten to her breast. The little beast clung with its tiny claws like a burr to her coat. "So, is it all right? What Miss Donato said? Please say yes. Please! I'll do *any*thing if you say yes."

Inez thought about it and nodded. "I approve, with one added condition."

The delight in Antonia's face dimmed slightly.

Inez continued, "That you stay out of trouble at school."

Antonia exhaled with a whoosh. "I promise, Mrs. S. And I'm learning Italian. Carmella's teaching me! Listen. *Uno, due, tre, quattro...*"

Inez smiled. "I am glad to hear you plan to take your studies seriously from now on, Antonia. A new year, new beginnings." Theia's face appeared again in her mind's eye, then wavered and vanished. She added, "Time to let the past go."

AUTHOR'S NOTE

I had several sources of inspiration that provided the initial spark for *Mortal Music*. One of the first was the book *Bonanza Inn,* which related the stories of various nineteenth and early twentieth century singers and actresses—and their luggage—who visited San Francisco's Palace Hotel. These luminaries included opera singers Adelina Patti and Emma Nevada and actresses Sarah Bernhardt and Lilly Langtry. In 1887, Bernhardt arrived at her eight-room Palace Hotel suite, surrounded by a mountain of baggage and her pet parrot and baby tiger. Langtry arrived with thirty-two trunks and twenty-eight leather hat-boxes and valises, while Patti bested that count with thirty-six trunks and countless other bits of luggage. At some point, while I was poring over accounts of the trials, tribulations, and triumphs of these amazing performers and others, the fictional Theia Carrington Drake took form in my imagination. Theia tapped my shoulder and said, "Since you find them so fascinating, why don't you tell *my* story?"

But *Mortal Music* is also the story of lives beyond the stage: The dressmakers who struggled as the fashion world turned to ready-mades. The businesswomen who found their credit ruined through no fault of their own. The African-American staff of the Palace Hotel, who enjoyed some of the more lucrative positions to be had at that time, only to be dismissed and replaced in the mid-1880s. The fascinating history of the Comstock Lode and its silver rush, the wheeling and dealing that ensued (not all on the up-and-up), and the fortunes made, lost, and, in some cases, remade.

Now, a brief word on what and whom I borrowed from the real world of nineteenth century San Francisco in weaving my fiction. The Palace Hotel, the Grand Opera House, the Cliff House, and Chinatown all existed, as did Adolph Sutro, Palace manager Warren Leland, Grand Opera House owner Fred Bert, and Cliff House proprietor Captain Junius Foster. The places and people are real, but I did take liberties in fashioning my fictional universe. The newsman John Teague is based upon the real journalist Arthur McEwen, who plied his trade on and off in William Randolph Hearst's the *San Francisco Examiner*.

Two online resources proved helpful in orienting me in 1881 San Francisco: the David Rumsey Map Collection and OldSF. The latter site (oldsf.org) ties the modern-day San Francisco city map to historical images from the San Francisco Public Library's San Francisco Historical Photography Collection.

If you are curious to learn more about some of the places, people, and events that inspired and informed me, here are some references I found useful in my research that you may enjoy perusing.

ON OPERA, THE STAGE, AND THEIR WOMEN:

The American Opera Singer, by Peer G. Davis (1997)
The San Francisco Stage: A History, by Edmond M. Gagey
(1950)
*Women in the American Theatre: Actresses and Audiences 1790–
1870,* by Faye E. Dudden (1994)

COMSTOCK-RELATED READINGS:

The History of the Comstock Lode, 1850–1920, by Grant H.
Smith (1943)
"Heady Times at the Comstock Silver Mines" in *Silver Fever:
The Comstock Lode to the Carson City Mint,* edited by
Robert R. Van Ryzin (2009. Only available on CD)

SAN FRANCISCO PLACES, FACES, AND TIMES:

Adolph Sutro: A Biography, by Robert E. Stewart, Jr., and Mary
F. Stewart (1964)
*Gaudy Century: The Story of San Francisco's Hundred Years of
Robust Journalism,* by John Bruce (1948)
Genthe's Photographs of San Francisco's Old Chinatown, with
photographs by Arnold Genthe, and selection and text by
John Kuo Wei Tchen (1984)
Bonanza Inn America's First Luxury Hotel, by Oscar Lewis and
Carroll D. Hall (1939)
The San Francisco Cliff House, by Mary Germain Hountalas
with Sharon Silva (2009)
*Pioneer Urbanites: A Social and Cultural History of Black San
Francisco,* by Douglas Henry Daniels (1990)
*Making San Francisco American: Cultural Frontiers in the Urban
West, 1846–1906,* by Barbara Berglund (2007)

Capital Intentions: Female Proprietors in San Francisco, 1850–1920, by Edith Sparks (2006)

Lights and Shades in San Francisco, by Benjamin E. Lloyd (1876, available online at https://archive.org.)

"Life in an Insane Asylum," by Charles Coyle, in *The Overland Monthly*, January–June 1893. (Available online at https://archive.org. This article is a detailed look at the Napa State Insane Asylum in the late nineteenth century. The information proved invaluable for crafting the conclusion of *Mortal Music*.)

ABOUT THE AUTHOR

Ann Parker is the author of the award-winning Silver Rush historical mystery series set in 1880s Leadville, Colorado, and San Francisco, California, featuring saloon owner turned music store owner Inez Stannert. A science writer by day, Ann lives in the San Francisco Bay Area and is a member of Mystery Writers of America and Women Writing the West. Visit her online at annparker.net.

Photo by Ian McConachie